Briannon
W9-AUE-395

AVENGED

ALSO BY AMY TINTERA

Ruined
Allied

Reboot
Rebel

AVENGED

AMY TINTERA

HarperTeen is an imprint of HarperCollins Publishers.

Avenged

Copyright © 2017 by Amy Tintera
All rights reserved. Printed in the United States of America.
No part of this book may be used or reproduced in any manner whatsoever without written permission except in the case of brief quotations embodied in critical articles and reviews. For information address HarperCollins Children's Books, a division of HarperCollins Publishers, 195 Broadway, New York, NY 10007.

www.epicreads.com

ISBN 978-0-06-239664-8

Typography by Torborg Davern
18 19 20 21 22 PC/LSCH 10 9 8 7 6 5 4 3 2 1
❖
First paperback edition, 2018

ONE

THE REMAINS OF Em's home sat at the bottom of the hill. The Ruina castle was nothing but a pile of stone and dirt, weeds snaking in between the rubble. One wall remained intact, and Em liked to think it was her mother who had made sure of that. Even in death, her mother had made one last stand.

Olivia sucked in a breath as she reached the top of the hill. "I thought there would be more left."

Em took her sister's hand. Olivia was taken prisoner before their home was demolished and most of the Ruined exterminated. It was her first time seeing the castle like this.

Olivia squeezed Em's hand too tightly. "Don't worry, Em. We'll make them pay."

Olivia kept saying things like that. *Don't worry, Em.* She still worried. *Don't cry, Em. They will fear us soon enough.* She'd said that to Em immediately after killing the Lera queen. Em didn't tell her sister that she was certain everyone already feared them.

"I thought they might have cleared it away," Aren said as he stopped beside Em. He was haggard, his handsome face tight with exhaustion. The Olso warriors had been able to spare a couple of horses, but most of the Ruined made the journey on foot, and they all desperately needed a day or ten to rest.

"At least now we can sift through it and see if anything is left," Olivia said.

"I looked a year ago," Em said. "All I found was your necklace."

"*Your* necklace," Olivia corrected. "I told you I want you to have it."

Em smiled, dropping Olivia's hand and grasping the *O* pendant.

Olivia pointed to the castle. "Are we setting up camp here? We could put the hunters' heads on spikes nearby, as a warning to others."

Em swallowed down a wave of disgust and tried not to let it show on her face. Olivia and Aren had left a trail of dead bodies behind them as they traveled from Lera to Ruina over the past week. Em had convinced them to leave King Casimir and his cousin, Jovita, alive at Fort Victorra, but she hadn't bothered arguing for the hunters' lives. There was no point. Perhaps they deserved to die, after exterminating thousands of Ruined.

That's what she kept telling herself, anyway.

"They know," Em said. "I don't think there's any need."

"Besides, I don't want to smell dead-hunter head while I sleep," Aren said.

"It's your decision where we set up camp," Em said.

"Why is it my decision?" Olivia asked.

"Because you're the queen."

"They voted to abolish the monarchy after I was taken," Olivia said. "And their elected leader is dead. So, technically, I'm nothing."

"They thought you were dead," Em said. "I'm sure they consider you their queen again."

Olivia shrugged. "Let's have a meeting in a few days, when most of the Ruined have found their way back. For now, I say we build a camp right here. Let the Lerans and the hunters know we're not scared of them anymore."

"We're not scared anymore?" Aren asked quietly. A new Ruined mark had appeared on his left hand recently, a white swirl against his dark skin, and he rubbed at it absently.

"Cas promised to leave us alone," Em said, not for the first time.

Aren and Olivia exchanged a look. Em had insisted they'd be safe, that the war against the Ruined was over. Cas had said he wouldn't continue the attacks on the Ruined now that he was king. Em believed he would keep his word.

Olivia and Aren were not convinced.

An icy wind blew Em's coat open. She shoved her hands into the pockets and pulled it tight around her body. She'd taken the coat and the clothes she was wearing from a Ruined killed at the battle of Fort Victorra. She'd needed something other than the blue dress she'd worn to cross the Lera jungle, but the clothes still made her squirm when she thought about it too hard.

Em turned at the sound of laughter and saw a group of about a hundred Ruined emerging from the trees. They were exhausted from the battle at Fort Victorra, and dirty from days of walking, but smiles lit up their faces as they took in the remains of the Ruina castle.

"We'll set up here," Olivia confirmed with a nod.

"It's more brown here than I remembered," Aren said to no one in particular.

Em had to agree. She and Aren had spent weeks in lush, green Lera, next to the ocean with sparkling clean beaches. Ruina did not look good in comparison. The grass was brown and dead, the sparse trees bare. Past the castle was a giant patch of empty dirt where a cluster of shops used to be. They weren't much to look at when they were standing anyway.

She stared at the pile of debris that used to be her home. Maybe she should have suggested a different location. How long was this going to be her view? How long would she have to sleep on the ground while staring at the spot where her bedroom used to be?

The room took shape in her head—the bed with piles of pillows, the full-length mirror on the wall where she used to stand and desperately search for Ruined marks when she was younger.

The worn green chair in the corner where she curled up to read.

She expected tears to come, but a hollow feeling settled at the bottom of her stomach instead. The girl who had lived in that room was gone, and maybe she was relieved that the room was gone as well. They all needed a fresh start. They could rebuild Ruina to be even better than it was before. *Safer* than it was before. Em hadn't slept without a weapon within her grasp in a year. If there was one thing she needed—one thing all the Ruined needed—it was to find a way to feel safe again.

"I'll check on the wagon," Em said. She jogged down the hill. The wagon they'd stolen from the Lera soldiers was slowly making its way through the trees, pulled by two tired horses.

They'd mostly piled supplies for tents and extra water in the open-air wagon, but a few children and sick Ruined were inside as well. A young Ruined man named Jacobo walked alongside the horses. Mariana walked on the other side, her black braids moving as she nodded at Em. Both Mariana and Jacobo had Ruined marks on their dark-brown skin, the white lines curling up their necks and even across a cheek, in Jacobo's case.

"It's—" Em was about to say "clear," when a flash of movement caught her eye. The bush to her right rustled.

She drew her sword, catching Jacobo's eyes and nodding to the bush as she stepped toward it. He walked to the wagon, gesturing for the three children inside to come closer to him. Mariana froze.

Em carefully stepped over a log. Someone sniffed.

She parted the leaves of a bush with her blade. Two men were crouched on the ground. Their clothes were dirty, and one man had so many patches on his coat it was an array of different colors. He had a dagger clenched in his fist, but the other didn't have a weapon. Neither had any blue pins. They weren't hunters.

"Who are you?" she asked.

"We're just trying to get across to Vallos," the man with the dagger said. He stood slowly. His legs shook beneath him. He was staring straight at her chest.

"That's not what I asked. Who are you?"

"We're Vallos laborers working in the Ruina mines," he said to her chest. "Are you . . . are you Emelina Flores?" He said her name in a hushed, almost reverent, tone.

She frowned in reply, unsure how he knew that.

"The circle of vengeance. I've heard about it."

"The what?"

"Your necklace. The circle represents vengeance. 'What goes around comes around,' as they say."

Her lips twitched. Did everyone really think that was what her necklace symbolized?

The circle of vengeance. How fitting. Olivia would love it.

The man with the dagger held the weapon in front of him, but it shook in his grasp. The other had his arms pressed to his chest, fear oozing out of his every pore. She'd earned a reputation, it seemed.

"Go," she said, jerking her head. "Don't come back."

They both spun around and sprinted away from her. Everyone

ran from her now. People whispered her name, as that man had. They said it with fear.

It was what she had always wanted.

It did not feel as good as she had expected.

TWO

CAS'S MOTHER WAS buried behind Fort Victorra, in a shady spot where flowers would probably bloom in the spring.

Cas never went there. He'd watched the soldiers bury her the day after Em and Olivia disappeared, and he'd never been back.

Instead, he came to where she died.

It had rained two days ago and washed all the blood away. There was nothing left but dirt and grass and trees. The trees had been full of red and orange leaves a few days ago, but now the branches were mostly empty, the leaves smashed beneath his feet. The ugly trees seemed more appropriate, given what had happened here.

He could still see it. Em almost dying in his arms. Olivia killing his mother and rescuing her sister.

"You don't deserve to be here," a voice behind him said.

For a moment, he worried the voice was in his head. He'd been thinking the same thing. But he turned and found his cousin standing a few paces away. Jovita had her hands on her hips, ice in her eyes as she glared at him. Her dark hair blew in the wind, and an angry red scar cut down her right cheek. Em had given her that scar. She looked a little like his father. They had the same olive skin and wide mouth.

He turned away.

"It's not safe, anyway," Jovita said. Her tone was more scornful than concerned.

"The Ruined are gone. The warriors are gone."

"And whose fault is that?" Jovita stepped beside him, tapping her chin like she was thinking. "Oh, that's right. It's your fault. For freeing Olivia Flores and letting Emelina waltz right out of here."

It *was* his fault. He'd freed Olivia, and she'd killed his mother. Right after his mother almost killed Em.

He couldn't muster up any anger for Olivia. He was mostly just sad.

"I want the necklace," Jovita said, holding her hand out. "The one the queen gave you, with Weakling in it."

"I buried it with her," he said.

Her jaw clenched. "That was stupid, Cas. That necklace could have protected me from the Ruined."

Cas shrugged. The Weakling herb hurt most Ruined, but it barely seemed to slow Olivia down. He doubted the necklace would have offered much protection.

"If she'd kept that necklace instead of giving it to you, she might still be alive," Jovita spat. "And you just—"

"Two more advisers arrived during the night," he interupted. "I'm meeting with them in an hour if you want to join."

"No." Jovita turned away and started walking.

"Why? Because you already met with them behind my back?"

Jovita stopped. She looked over her shoulder, arching an eyebrow. "If you know, then it's not really behind your back, is it?" She stomped away. He watched her go, an uneasy feeling swirling in his gut.

A guard emerged from the trees as she left. It was Galo, lurking near Cas as usual. The captain of his guard rarely let Cas out of his sight these days, even when Cas would prefer to be left alone. The price of being king. Today, Galo's boyfriend and fellow guard, Mateo, was with him. Mateo stood a few paces away, his back to them as he surveyed the area for possible threats.

Cas stuffed his hands in his pockets, rounding his shoulders against the cold wind as he walked back to the fortress. Galo fell into step beside him, Mateo trailing behind them.

"Everything all right?" the guard asked quietly.

"Probably not."

Galo appeared concerned, but Cas didn't elaborate. The castle and most of his kingdom was in the hands of Olso. His cousin hated him. His parents were dead. Em was gone, and he would likely never see her again.

There wasn't much left to say.

"We confirmed the governor of the southern province died in the attack on the castle," Galo said. "But his daughter didn't, and she's here. Violet Montero. She found me this morning and asked to speak with you."

"She's here? When did she arrive?"

"Same time as you, apparently. She was lumped in with the staff and no one knew at first. She's been ill."

"Is she better?"

"Yes."

The fortress loomed in front of them, and Cas stepped over a pile of bricks into the front yard. Portions of the wall had been blown out when the Ruined and warriors attacked, and it was still damaged. It would be quite a while before it was fully repaired. Beyond the wall was Fort Victorra, a square, mostly windowless pile of bricks that Cas had come to hate.

"She's probably in the breakfast room now, if you wanted to see her," Galo said. "I can get her."

"That's fine, I'll go look. Will you confirm with the two advisers who arrived last night that we're meeting in an hour?"

"Of course." Galo rushed off.

Cas should have chosen a personal adviser by now. Galo was the captain of his guard, not his errand boy, and he felt guilty making him do both jobs.

But Fort Victorra wasn't like the Lera castle. There wasn't enough staff, and Cas had to do many things himself. There was no longer a whole crew of people to wait on him hand and foot and announce visitors.

A soldier held open the front doors of the fortress as he approached, and he murmured a thank-you and stepped inside.

He blinked as his eyes adjusted to the dark. Lanterns lined the wall as he left the entryway and walked into the large foyer, but they did little to cheer up the place.

The first few days after the attack had been quiet in the fortress, but soon people from all over Lera began to arrive, after the Olso warriors took the castle and the northern cities. Now the small building was bursting at the seams, libraries and common areas turned into sleeping quarters. Several people walked down the stairway to his left, and they froze at the bottom when they spotted him. He pretended not to notice.

He walked through the foyer and into the small room off the kitchen. Many of the guests gathered in the room every morning, so it had been dubbed "the breakfast room." Several round tables were scattered about, men and women seated at them. They didn't have a lot of food, but there were some beans and fish on the tables.

Heads turned as he walked in, voices quieting. He realized he had no idea what this Violet girl looked like.

"I need to speak with Violet?" It came out as a question. He hadn't learned to speak the way his father did, like every sentence was a command.

A slight young woman in a plain black dress stood. Her dark

hair was pulled back in a bun, accenting her high cheekbones and large, dark eyes. She appeared tired, but she smiled at Cas. She looked vaguely familiar.

"Here, Your Majesty." Despite her short stature, her voice easily carried across the room. She walked to him.

The wagon. He'd been put in a wagon with the staff the night his father died and the castle was taken. That was how he knew her. She'd helped him escape.

"I know you. Splinters in odd places," he said, repeating the words she'd said to him as she helped him slip out a crack in the wagon.

She let out an embarrassed laugh. "That was me, Your Majesty."

Everyone in the room was staring at them, and he spun on his heel, gesturing for her to follow him.

There was no place indoors he felt comfortable speaking privately, so he led her outside, to the back of the fortress. The building was still missing a portion of the rear wall since a Ruined had destroyed it, and he walked far enough away that they couldn't be overheard. To his left, a few staff members were tending to the garden, but they were out of earshot.

"I heard you were sick," he said as he stopped and turned to Violet.

"Yes. The conditions in the wagon were . . ."

"Terrible," he said, a wave of guilt crashing over him. He'd managed to save the staff he abandoned in the wagon, but it took several days. He couldn't imagine being stuck in that hot, stuffy wagon for so long. He didn't know how many had died, but it was too many.

"I never got a chance to thank you," she said. "For saving us. We know Jovita wanted you to leave us, and we all appreciate what you did."

"Of course. I couldn't just abandon you."

"Yes, you could have." She held his gaze as she spoke. "I haven't introduced myself properly. Violet Montero. My father was the governor of the southern province."

"I heard. Why didn't you identify yourself in the wagon?"

"It didn't seem all that important. What would you have done with that information?"

She had a point. He could barely think straight in the wagon. His father had just died and he'd still been reeling about Em. Violet could have told him she'd suddenly sprouted three extra heads and he probably would have simply shrugged.

"There are people here who know me," she said. "If you'd like to confirm."

"I would. Can't blame me, can you?" After Emelina pretended to be the princess of Vallos and his fiancée, he'd likely never take anyone's identity at their word ever again.

"No, I can't."

"Why didn't we meet in the castle?" he asked.

"I'd just arrived when the attack happened. I was going to come to the wedding, but my grandmother was ill and I was taking care of her."

"I'm sorry about your father," he said.

"Yours too."

"Is your mother still alive?" His breath hitched in his throat, and he focused on a spot past her shoulder.

"No. She died a few years ago."

"Are you the eldest child?"

"The only."

"Then you've inherited the southern province." He meant for the words to sound congratulatory, but they came out weary instead. He wondered if she was as thrilled to inherit the southern province as he was to inherit the throne.

"I have. I heard you were going to meet with advisers soon, and I thought I should be included."

"You should. The south is the only province that hasn't been taken over by Olso."

"It is." She said it with pride.

A powerful wind swept over them. Violet pulled her arms against her chest as her dress flapped in the cold breeze. She didn't shiver, even though she must have been freezing.

"Have you spoken with Jovita yet?" he asked carefully.

"No, Your Majesty."

"You can call me Cas." He didn't let anyone but Galo and Jovita call him Cas, but he knew how important this girl was. He needed her as an ally. As a friend. He glanced at the fortress and took a step closer to her. "Will you tell me if Jovita tries to speak with you? About anything?"

Violet drew her eyebrows together. "Is something wrong?"

"No. My cousin isn't very fond of me at the moment. I'd like to know I have you on my side if needed."

"I'm already on your side, Your—Cas."

At least someone was. "Thank you, Violet."

THREE

OLIVIA LIFTED HER head to the sky and took in a long breath. The sun had just come up, but it was hidden behind dark clouds. A chilly wind blew her dark hair across her face. After a year locked in a Lera dungeon, every breath of fresh air was a gift.

She plopped down in the middle of the rubble that used to be her home. She hadn't believed that the castle was completely gone. Olivia had thought there would be walls still standing, chests of her mother's clothes to sift through. But the fire had burned everything. The humans' fear had destroyed everything, precisely as her mother said it would.

She nudged a blackened piece of wood aside to reveal a white eye and a nose peeking out at her. The statue of Boda. She grabbed it to find only half of her head was left. Olivia must have been sitting in the remains of the library. The statue of the ancestor had stood in the corner since Wenda Flores became queen.

Olivia closed her eyes, the image of her mother taking shape in her mind. Her long dark hair was often loose, flying behind her as she zipped around the castle. She wore lavish dresses even when there was no occasion, and Olivia would always associate the sound of skirts swishing with her mother.

She tossed the statue head aside. Her mother's favorite ancestor had done nothing to save her, in the end. If anyone was going to save the Ruined, it was going to be Olivia.

"Liv."

Olivia turned to see Em walking to her. Olivia could sense humans and Ruined around her, even at great distances. But not Em. Em wasn't human or Ruined. She was the only person in the world who could sneak up on Olivia.

In Olivia's mind, she still saw the Em she'd known the first fifteen years of her life. The Em who was sarcastic and often surly, bitter about her uselessness and annoyed at having to watch Olivia practice her magic.

Or maybe she was scared, not bitter. In the past, Olivia would often look over at her sister to find Em turned away, wincing at the screams of a man Olivia was torturing. Olivia would sometimes pretend not to be able to remove a head simply because she didn't want to see the horrified expression on her sister's face.

Fear was no longer an option for Em. The year she'd spent away from Olivia had made her ruthless and dangerous. She had the same olive skin and dark hair, but the sadness in her eyes was new. Olivia thought she had it bad in the dungeon. She wasn't even fully able to grasp what Em had been through the past year.

Despite the horrors she'd endured, Em had taken down Lera, organized the Ruined, and saved Olivia. And they called Em the useless one. Olivia's mouth tasted bitter suddenly.

"About fifty more Ruined just arrived," Em said as she sat down next to Olivia. "They said they had no trouble getting out of Olso. Apparently the Olso king invited them to stay, but didn't try to detain them when they declined."

"Attempting to keep them against their will would have been deeply stupid," Olivia said.

"I expect we'll be seeing some warriors soon."

"You think so?"

"They wanted us to go to Olso to meet their king. I can't imagine they've decided to let us go."

Olivia snorted. "*Let us?* We don't need them to *let us* do anything."

"We don't want to make enemies of the warriors," Em said. "We're not strong enough to stand on our own yet."

Olivia took in a long breath, batting down the rage that swelled in her chest. Em was right, as much as she hated to admit it.

"I'll have to negotiate with the warriors, won't I?" Olivia asked.

"Probably."

"What if I kill them instead?" She grinned. "Take a strong position right out of the gate."

"I can't tell if you're kidding."

Olivia tilted her hand back and forth. "Kind of." Not at all, actually. The only thing that lessened her rage was to rip someone to shreds. She could still feel the Lera queen's heart in her hand. The pulse against her palm. The queen had deserved it. She'd been there during several of the experiments they'd run on Olivia. Ripping the queen's heart out of her chest had been kind, actually.

"I really suggest you don't kill them," Em said.

"Fine." She'd find someone else to kill. There were plenty of Lera hunters running around Ruina, attempting to get out now that they were the ones being hunted. She would close her fingers around each of their hearts soon.

"We need to find more permanent shelter," Em said. "I'd like to take a group out to the coal miners' lodgings. They should be abandoned by now, and we can use them until the castle is rebuilt."

Olivia remembered the coal miners' lodgings. They were small and pitiful, in need of updating years ago.

"Is that really our best option?" Olivia asked.

Em nudged a piece of rubble with her shoe. "Unfortunately."

Olivia thought of the fortress, with its sturdy walls and enough rooms to house a small army. Casimir was comfortable, while they sat in the mess that used to be their home. The Lerans had always been comfortable, since they took Lera from the Ruined and cast them out.

"The cabins aren't much, but I think we'll be able to house

all the Ruined there," Em said.

"You still want to take care of them?" Olivia asked.

"What do you mean?"

"The Ruined turned their backs on you. Everyone, except for Aren, chose to follow someone else. Someone who is now dead."

Sadness flickered across Em's face at the mention of Damian. Olivia had no sympathy for their dead friend, even if he had helped Em. He'd grown up with Em and Olivia only to betray them when they needed help the most. He deserved to be beheaded by the Lera king.

"They were scared," Em said. "And I proved that they were wrong to reject me."

"You sure did. And I did nothing but sit in a cell and plot a million escape attempts. Every one of which failed."

"It's not your fault that you were taken. I only took the lead because you were gone."

"You took the lead even after it had been ripped from you. You put together a plan that took down the most powerful of the four kingdoms. You pulled off a highly risky plot to kill the Vallos princess and marry the Lera prince in her place. You rescued everyone, even after they rejected you. I don't know if I would have done the same." Olivia might have let everyone die just to prove them wrong.

"You would have," Em said, ever the optimist.

"The point is, I didn't. And I've never been interested in all of the political stuff that goes along with the throne. The meetings, the discussions, the compromises. I dreaded having my husband chosen for me, and you went out and married our mortal enemy."

Em looked at the ground at the mention of Cas. She had barely spoken of the prince—now king—since leaving Lera, but Olivia had seen how they interacted with each other. It seemed Em had developed feelings for that awful boy.

"Did you actually have sex with him?" Olivia asked, trying to keep the horror out of her voice.

"No. He could tell I was terrified and he didn't push the issue."

"Huh. Strange."

"He's not like his father, Liv. He was kind to me."

"Well, at least you didn't have to sleep with him." She shuddered.

"You'll have a say in your marriage," Em said. "Especially with the way things are now. I'm sure anyone you pick will be suitable."

"You should be the one marrying for political alliances. You're clearly good at it."

"But you're the queen."

"Why do I have to be the only one? Where is the law that says I have to rule alone?"

"There is actually a law," Em said with a laugh. "Ruina law states that the eldest inherits the throne, unless the eldest is born useless. Then it goes to the next heir."

"You've proved that you're not useless. You have other powers, like our mother said."

"The Ruined will never allow someone useless to rule them."

"What if we ruled together?"

Em's eyebrows shot up. "What?"

"There are some parts of being queen that I'll be very good at. Commanding armies. Training Ruined. The dresses." She grinned when Em chuckled. "I'm a fighter. You're a politician. You can actually sit in a meeting with warriors without ripping their heads off."

"What are you suggesting?"

"A diarchy. We rule Ruina together, as queens."

"A diarchy." Em's mouth formed an O, and Olivia smiled. She knew her sister would be grateful for the opportunity to lead the Ruined. Perhaps she was even better suited for the position than Olivia, but she couldn't bring herself to give up the throne entirely. Em had made great strides to restore the Ruined to their former glory, but she was still tied up in her ludicrous feelings for Casimir. Olivia needed to guide Em and their people. Olivia needed to prove herself, after being locked away for a year.

"We'll make decisions together," Olivia said. "We'll each have certain responsibilities. We'll have certain veto powers." Olivia gently punched Em's shoulder. "Come on. You know you want to lead the Ruined. You know you should be queen."

"B-but they've already rejected me once," Em stuttered. "They won't accept me as their queen."

"We will *make* them accept you."

"Maybe we should discuss it with a few people, ask—"

"We do not ask." Olivia sat up straighter. She was a little shorter than Em, though not by much. "We *take.* We will take the throne, we will take responsibility, and we will crush anyone who defies us. Got it?"

Em let out a small laugh. "Really? Crush anyone who defies us?"

"Fine. I'll crush them. I'm good at that part." In truth, Olivia knew she needed to take a strong stance with the Ruined. They weren't going to respect a queen who'd been kidnapped and then rescued by her useless sister. Olivia had to demand, not request.

"Are you sure?" Em asked.

"Absolutely. Don't make me do this by myself. The Ruined need to be united right now. I think it will make a powerful statement if we start by coming together to lead."

Em blinked back tears. "I love you, Liv."

"I know. You married Casimir for me. I figure you must *really* love me." Olivia hopped up, extending her hand to Em. "Come on. Let's go introduce the Ruined to Queen Emelina."

FOUR

CAS DESCENDED THE steps of the fortress, turning his head at the sound of laughter coming from the rear part of the building. He walked down the hallway, Galo trailing behind him.

"Put some muscle into it!" a woman yelled.

"I am!" another female voice replied.

Cas stopped at the entrance of the kitchen to see the cook, Blanca, pushing a young girl aside with her hips. She pressed her palms into the pile of dough on the counter.

"Like this," she said. "Massage it like you're mad at it." Blanca stepped back, catching sight of Cas standing in the doorway. She straightened and wiped her hands on her apron. "Your Majesty." The young girl whirled around and squeaked out a greeting.

"Good morning," Cas said. "How are things going?"

"Very well. Have you been happy with the food?"

"Of course." He tried to give her a reassuring smile. Blanca had been an assistant chef in the castle, but the head chef was still missing. Probably dead. He pointed to the ball of dough. "I didn't know we had flour."

"It came in yesterday. One of the arrivals from Gallego City brought everything he had from his bakery so it wouldn't go bad."

He heard footsteps behind him and turned to see Daniela walking toward them, a basket of vegetables in her arms. Her wrinkled face brightened when she spotted him.

"Nice to see you, Your Majesty," she said, bowing her head. She'd been in the wagon with him, like many of the staff members at the fortress, and Cas seemed to have earned their undying loyalty as a result.

"Can I get you anything?" Blanca asked.

"No, thank you." He was headed to a meeting with Jovita and the advisers, and his stomach was too knotted to even think about food. He said good-bye and turned away. The laughter didn't pick up again as he left. Laughter always stopped when he entered a room these days.

He walked back up to the second floor of the fortress and into a large empty room. His father had always been the last to arrive at meetings; Cas had decided to do the opposite.

The staff had removed the couches and chairs and made one long table in the middle of the room from several smaller tables.

There were no windows, so several lanterns hung on the walls, and two sat on the tables. It was nothing compared to the Ocean Room at home, where the meetings were held in the Lera castle. If Cas closed his eyes, he could still see the sun sparkling off the ocean from those windows.

He sank into the chair at the head of the table. Galo lingered in the doorway.

"Sit," Cas said. He used his foot to push out the chair next to him. "Here."

Galo looked from the seat to Cas. "Are you sure?" Cas's father would never have let a guard sit at the table during an adviser meeting. That made Cas only more determined to have Galo next to him.

"Just sit down."

The guard obeyed and pulled out the chair next to him. Cas cracked his knuckles nervously as he waited. It was still unbelievable that everyone took orders from *him*.

A few minutes later, Colonel Dimas and General Amaro walked in and murmured their greetings. General Amaro avoided Cas's gaze as she sat in the seat farthest away from him.

The two advisers he'd met with yesterday entered, their heads bent together in conversation. Cas knew the older one, Julieta, fairly well. She was about the same age as his mother, and she'd lived in Royal City. He'd met the other, Danna, a few times, but she lived in the eastern province and only visited the castle a few times a year. They'd been friendly yesterday, offering condolences for his parents, but today they seemed tense. Julieta flashed Cas a smile that was obviously forced.

Violet stepped into the room, her face brightening when she spotted Cas. He gestured for her to take the seat next to Galo and she quickly scurried over.

The governor of the southern province has a daughter. She was our second choice, after Mary. She's lovely. Much prettier than Emelina.

His father's voice echoed in his head as he stole a glance at Violet. His father hadn't been wrong. Violet was striking, with her long black hair, intense dark eyes, and full lips, but the comparison to Em was inapt. Em might not have been the prettiest girl in the room, but everyone stared at her anyway. It was like she held a secret they all wanted to know.

Cas willed the image of Em out of his head. He needed to focus.

The governor of the northern province walked in, followed by a few important leaders from the western province. Cas knew he needed to start giving out official adviser titles to people since so many had died, but he hadn't had the time. He was still focused on making it through each day without breaking down into hysterical sobs.

Jovita entered last. Her dark hair was loose around her shoulders, and she wore a blue dress. Where had she gotten a dress? He'd rarely seen her wear one in the castle, much less in a fortress with limited supplies and clothing.

She took the other empty seat next to Cas. "How are you, Casimir?"

"Fine," he said, unable to hide his suspicion at the friendly greeting. "You?"

"I'm well, thank you. I noticed you left the fortress again this morning to visit the scene of the queen's death."

Every pair of eyes in the room turned to Cas. He resisted the urge to squirm beneath their stares.

"You go there often," Jovita said.

"Yes," he replied. "It gives me a chance to think."

"I understand that you're grieving, but now is the time for action, not thinking. How do you expect to get anything done if you spend most of the day wandering around aimlessly?"

"I don't spend *most* of the day there. But it appears you spend most of your day tracking my movements."

Annoyance flashed across Jovita's face. "I'm worried about you. And by extension, Lera. You've offered no plan, so—"

"I believe that's what this meeting is about," he said. "So if we're done talking about how I grieve for my mother, I'd like to move on."

Jovita snapped her mouth closed, her jaw twitching.

"Good." Cas faced forward, trying to avoid looking at his cousin. "The fortress is already at capacity, but we still have people arriving every day. We'll need more space soon, and I think the south is our best bet. I'd like to send a group of soldiers south to speak with the leaders of the southern province. We have the governor with us"—he gestured at Violet—"but I'd like to know how the people there are doing. None of them have joined us here."

"The Ruined were headed south after the battle," Danna said. "There may not be many people left."

"They were going south to Ruina," he said. "They didn't attack anyone."

Danna's eyebrows shot up. "What makes you so sure?"

"They weren't prepared for another battle when they left. They lost too many here."

"A Ruined is always prepared for battle," Jovita said. "The truth is, Emelina told you she wouldn't attack anyone if you gave her Olivia, and you stupidly believe her."

Cas tensed. He couldn't deny it. He assumed Lera still controlled the southern province because the Olso warriors hadn't invaded past the fortress yet. He didn't actually know for sure.

"I'd like to be part of the group that goes south," Violet said. She looked worried suddenly.

"Of course. As governor of the province you should lead the soldiers," he said.

"As governor of the southern province she should stay here, where it's safe," Jovita said. "We can't afford to lose any more leaders."

"What do you suggest, then?" he asked. "That we all hide in here until Olso attacks again?"

"No. With the hunters back, we have enough soldiers to launch an attack."

"On who, exactly?"

"The Ruined."

Cas didn't try to hide his incredulity. "You want to attack the Ruined?"

Jovita leaned forward. "Of course I want to attack the Ruined. The question is, why don't you? Emelina Flores killed the princess of Vallos. She partnered with Olso, took the castle, and started a war. We are in this mess because of her, and you just let her go. You ordered the hunters to stop killing the Ruined, even though they will take every opportunity to kill us!"

"They left! *We* are the ones who should be feared, not the Ruined. We murdered them without provocation."

"Without provocation?" Jovita reeled back. "Is that really what you think of the Ruined? That they're not dangerous?"

"Not all of them, no."

Jovita plastered a worried expression on her face. "I . . . I don't really know what to say to that, Cas."

"They've *just* attacked us," General Amaro said. "I don't know what else they'd have to do for you to consider them dangerous."

An uncomfortable silence settled into the room. Cas searched the faces of his advisers, trying to find someone who agreed with him. Galo and Violet were the only ones who didn't look angry or horrified. Heat rose up his neck.

"The Ruined are not my priority right now," Cas said. "We need to focus on maintaining our hold in the south and prepare to retake the castle. The best thing for Lera is—"

"You have no interest in what's best for Lera," Jovita said.

"All I've ever done is what's best for Lera!"

"You released Olivia Flores. She killed the queen and countless guards and soldiers. Was that really best for Lera?"

Cas's stomach churned. His mind was suddenly blank. He had no good response to that.

"I don't mean to attack you, Cas," Jovita said softly. No one else seemed to notice her voice was thick with condescension. "I think you need to take a step back and consider your mental state right now."

The room tilted, and Cas wondered for a moment if he *had* lost his mind. Surely going insane would be less painful than this?

"My mental state," he repeated.

"You're still grieving your parents. Your wife betrayed you. You were attacked in the jungle. I'm not judging you, Cas. Anyone would start to crack under those circumstances."

"He is *not* insane," Galo said fiercely.

Jovita held up a finger like she wasn't interested in Galo's opinion. "I didn't say he was. I was simply suggesting that perhaps you're not thinking clearly right now. Have you taken any time to rest? That might be just what you need."

"I'm fine," Cas said sharply.

Jovita cast a worried look across the table. The advisers were buying this charade, it seemed. None of them wanted to meet Cas's gaze.

"Why don't you take some time to think about my plan to

launch an attack on the Ruined?" Jovita said. "We can reconvene tomorrow after you've given it some thought."

Cas stood, his chair scraping the floor. "I don't need to think about it. The answer is no."

"But—"

"No," he repeated firmly. He strode out of the room, Galo following close behind. Whispered voices drifted out of the room as the door shut.

"They can't do anything without the king's approval," Galo said.

Cas ran a hand down his face. He wasn't so sure about that.

Almost two hundred faces stared up at Em. She swallowed, trying not to let her nervousness show on her face. She half expected the Ruined to start rioting.

Olivia stood beside her, in front of all of the Ruined who had made it to Ruina so far. They'd set up tents near the castle, and Olivia had called everyone out and ordered them to sit in the dirt as she announced the new leadership plans. The tents flapped in the wind behind the Ruined and a light rain had started to fall. Em wished, not for the first time, that they had a place to go with actual walls. She hated seeing them out in the cold.

"A diarchy," Olivia repeated. "We will rule together, as equals." Her eyes were alight with excitement, like she thought this announcement would be met with wild enthusiasm.

She was met with skepticism instead. A murmur went through

the crowd, and every pair of eyes landed on Em. Perhaps that was a good sign. The day they'd removed her from the throne, she'd known something was wrong. No one wanted to look at her.

But today, they all stared at her. Not everyone wore a kind expression, and she swallowed hard. Maybe she should say something. Explain that all she wanted was to make Ruina safe for them again. To build a home they could be proud of.

"We plan to rebuild Ruina into something even better," Olivia said before Em could get a word out. The crowd just blinked at her. They didn't have faith in either of them, apparently. Em wasn't sure if that made her feel better or worse.

A long silence followed Olivia's words. Pink spots appeared on her sister's cheeks. "We'll let you know more soon," she snapped. "Right now, we'd like to see Mariana, Aren, Ivanna, Davi, and Jacobo."

Ivanna and Davi were seated next to each other, two of the only older Ruined left. Ivanna nodded at them, but Em could see the skepticism on her face.

Aren stood, reaching out to squeeze Em's arm as they waited for the others to join them. Once they had all made their way through the crowd, Olivia led them to the tent she and Em shared. It was a tight squeeze, but they all managed to fit, sitting cross-legged in a small circle.

"I imagine you know why you're here," Olivia said. "Em and I are putting together a council to advise us on Ruined matters."

Between the five Ruined Olivia had called, all the Ruined

powers were represented—Aren controlled the body, Jacobo and Ivanna the elements, and Mariana and Davi the mind. Em and Olivia had come to the decision about the council easily—there weren't that many qualified Ruined left.

Ivanna pushed her gray hair behind her ear. "I appreciate that, but I think we need to talk about leadership."

Olivia cocked her head. "Do we?"

"Yes. You are aware that after you were taken, the Ruined abolished the monarchy and elected a new leader?"

"*Illegally* abolished the monarchy," Olivia corrected. "And your elected leader is dead."

Davi glared at Em. "Because she let him die."

A lump rose in Em's throat. She could have done more to save Damian. She'd tried so hard to stop the Lera king from executing him, but she could have acted faster. She'd made that clear when she told the Ruined the story. She didn't want to have any secrets from them.

"I was there too," Aren said tightly. "I had to hold Em back. If you want to blame someone, blame me."

"Yes, let's blame them," Olivia said flippantly. "The only two among you who actually got anything done. If it weren't for Em and Aren, you would all still be running for your lives. Or dead. But let's continue to talk about your leader, who got himself caught."

"He was helping us cross into Olso!" Davi said, his face turning red.

"To help Em and Aren take down Lera. His sacrifice isn't forgotten."

"Is there someone you would prefer to lead?" Em asked quietly. Olivia frowned at her.

"No," Jacobo replied, but he was smiling at Olivia.

"Well, we . . ." Ivanna cleared her throat. "There are some who would prefer an elected leader. Why wasn't Aren even given the opportunity to—"

"Decline," Aren said immediately.

"Aren, you're the most powerful one here, besides Olivia," Davi protested. "And you went to Lera at great risk to yourself."

"Because of Em's plan," Aren said. "Forget it. I won't accept." He gestured at Olivia. "Besides, I'm the *second* most powerful person here. Why wouldn't you want the first to lead you?"

"Valuing Ruined power over everything else has gotten us nowhere," Ivanna said. "Wenda Flores was powerful but had no talent for negotiation. She just killed everyone who didn't agree with her."

"That's a perfectly valid negotiation tactic," Olivia said. Em winced. Her sister was just proving Ivanna right.

"Em has a talent for negotiation," Aren said. "I think the whole point of this diarchy is that they balance each other out."

Ivanna glanced at Em, but didn't quite meet her eyes. "We've never had a useless leader before."

"And yet you just said we overvalue Ruined power," Em said. "Which is it?"

Ivanna snapped her mouth shut. Silence fell over the group.

Olivia chuckled for no apparent reason, and every head swiveled to her. "Do you think this is a debate? Just because a few of you want an elected leader doesn't mean it will happen. Our community was fractured a year ago. We're putting it back the way it should be."

Ivanna set her mouth in a hard line and said nothing. Davi began to protest.

"Besides, Aren will marry one of us," Olivia said. "Then he'll rule as well."

Em's eyebrows shot up at the casual mention of Aren marrying her or Olivia. Aren gave her a completely baffled look. Em pointed to herself and shook her head, which made him chuckle.

Cas's face flashed through her vision. She was already married. She'd married him as Princess Mary, but every moment of their relationship after that was real. She couldn't imagine marrying anyone else. Her chest hurt just thinking about it.

"Moving on," Olivia said. Em tried to pry her thoughts away from Cas, and only half succeeded. "We've picked a position for each of you. You may decline and suggest someone else for the position, if you choose. Aren, we'd like you to be director of combat. You'll handle Ruined training and weapons. Everything we need to prepare for battle. Davi, director of health. You'll be in charge of clean water and making sure everyone has clothes and is generally in good health. Ivanna, director of rebuilding. You'll manage getting the castle back up and rebuilding the city. You three will report to me."

"The other two will report to me," Em said. "Jacobo, we're

asking you to be director of nutrition. We need someone to oversee fishing and hunting and farming. And Mariana, we'd like you to be director of foreign affairs. You'll help me maintain relations with the Olso warriors."

Mariana nodded enthusiastically. She was young, near Em's age, and clearly excited to be chosen for the job.

"We're leaving tomorrow for the miner's cabins, and we'll need your help getting everyone ready. We want the five of you to be the voice of the Ruined. To relay what's happening to us, and to carry out our orders to them. Any problems with that?" Em asked. Everyone shook their head. "Good. Some of these positions are old, but some of them—like rebuilding—we're making up as we go along. We're open to ideas."

"But not new leadership," Davi grumbled.

"Oh, and that reminds me!" Olivia said. "Since we're at war, the Wartime Loyalty Amendment is in effect. All threats against the government or either queen will be considered treason and punished as such." She cocked her head, smiling widely at Davi. "Understood?"

Davi's face paled. Em clenched her hands together. She and Olivia hadn't actually talked about that. The Wartime Loyalty Amendment hadn't been in effect since their mother was a teenager. It didn't allow for the slightest disagreement with the royal leaders. It had not been popular.

"Understood," Ivanna said, her voice clipped. "Your Majesty."

"Fabulous." Olivia clapped her hands together. "I think we'll all work well together, don't you?"

Em glanced at the faces around her. Davi and Ivanna both looked like they wanted to smack someone. Mariana and Aren appeared nervous. Only Jacobo mirrored Olivia's smile.

Em had a feeling the council was already doomed to failure.

FIVE

"WHAT DO YOU think, Your Majesty?" Aren asked Em with a hint of amusement, and she smiled at him. He was more proud than amused, and he got the feeling she knew it.

"They look perfect."

Aren squinted at the line of log cabins in the distance. He'd set out on foot with Em, Olivia, and Mariana to find the coal miners' cabins that morning, and it had only taken a couple hours to reach them. Olivia and Mariana walked ahead of them.

There were about thirty cabins. Half of them were old, with patchy roofs and lopsided porches. They'd been there since Aren could remember. The rest were new, built by the Lera intruders.

"They must have had a lot of people here, working the mines," Aren said. "I didn't realize Lera had such an interest in coal."

"Olso does," Em said. "My mother said it's why they maintained such good relations with us."

"What do they use it for?"

"Good question."

"Their ships!" Mariana called, turning around to face them. She stopped, letting them catch up. "They use the coal in their ships to power them. I was in one on the way from Olso to Lera."

"Power them how?" Em asked.

"They said it's an engine that runs on steam. I'd never been on a ship that fast."

Olivia frowned over her shoulder at them. "So we probably haven't seen the last of the warriors, then."

"I'm sure we haven't," Em said.

Olivia made a face before turning back to the cabins. "These are depressing."

"Better than tents," Aren said.

"How long do you think it will take to rebuild the castle?" Olivia asked.

"Years," he said.

Olivia turned to him in horror. *"Years?"*

"That's what Ivanna said."

She shook her head. "No. I'm going to talk to her about speeding things up. The Ruined will never be taken seriously in these dinky little cabins."

Aren didn't think it mattered much where they lived. Castle, tent, cabin—it was all unsafe. The castle that had once been his home was gone, and he didn't particularly care about building a new one. His parents would never live there with him again, so it would never feel like a home.

Olivia broke into a jog, her dark ponytail bobbing. "Let's at least pick the best one for ourselves, Em!"

Em laughed. "Whichever one you want!"

"We're going to have to put a lot of Ruined in each cabin," Aren said. "Don't put me with Jacobo. He snores."

"You can be with me and Liv," Em said.

"Really? I thought that since you guys were queens now you'd get your own cabin."

"We have limited space." Em shrugged. "Besides, I'd prefer you nearby."

He bumped his shoulder against hers with a grin. "Anything for my queen."

"Anything? Because I'd like a hot bath and a huge meal with some fig tarts, please."

His stomach rumbled. They'd been surviving on nuts and seeds and the fish they'd caught in the river. Food was going to be a real problem soon. Not much grew in Ruina. "You and me both." He grabbed his canteen off his belt and took a sip. "There were some advantages to being in Lera, weren't there?"

Em nodded wordlessly. She was obviously trying to keep her expression neutral, but something dark passed over her features whenever Aren mentioned Lera or Cas.

He didn't understand Em's affection for Cas. He didn't want to understand it. She would never see him again anyway. At least, he hoped she would never see him again. He didn't want to see any Leran ever again. It was best that Cas was gone, even if it made Em sad.

The wind blew across the back of his neck, making his skin prick, and he swiped at it, rolling his eyes at the sky.

I know, I know, he said in his head.

The wind didn't let up, like it was positive he knew nothing. Like it knew he wasn't listening to his mother's words on repeat in his head: *The kindness you show others comes back around for you one day.*

The wind was right; he wasn't listening to his mother's words. He'd been kind his whole life, right up until his parents were murdered and his home burned to the ground. Action had made life better, not kindness.

He stole a look at Em's somber face again. They'd been friends since they were toddlers. They could usually talk about anything.

He opened his mouth to tell her that, but the words died in his throat. He always lost words when he needed them most.

They reached the cabins, and Olivia emerged from one in the middle. "The old ones are better," she said. "The new ones are smaller."

"We should take one of the smaller ones," Em said. "It'll just be me, you, and Aren."

Olivia blew out a breath of air. "Fine." She winked at Aren like she wasn't actually annoyed. She looked a lot like Em, with the same olive skin and dark hair, but a smaller, more fragile version. It was hilarious, considering.

A flash of movement caught his attention, and his head

snapped to the left. Two men were scrambling out of the last cabin. One was injured, dragging his left leg behind him, and his friend held on to his arm. They walked away from the mines, to the sparse trees to the north.

"Seems we have some stragglers," Olivia said.

"Leave them," Em said. "They can barely walk."

Olivia set her lips in a hard line. "Did they let us go when we could barely walk?" She gestured at Aren. "Did they let him go after burning half his skin off?"

Aren tucked his hands behind him, suddenly acutely aware of his wrecked flesh. He didn't actually mind the scars that covered much of his upper body—they were a reminder that he'd survived the raid on the Ruina castle, despite the Lera king's best efforts—but he didn't particularly want to be held up as an example of how bad things could get.

He shrugged when Olivia looked at him expectantly. Honestly, he hadn't planned to chase down those miners. The chances of them making it alive to Vallos on foot were slim at best.

"I guess not," Em said quietly.

"Let's go have a chat with them," Olivia said, turning to Aren. "Are you in?"

He met her gaze. Her eyes were alight with excitement. Maybe because she was still rejoicing in her freedom. Maybe because she was delighted at the idea of hunting and killing. He wasn't sure he cared which one it was.

"Of course."

Olivia jumped and looped her arm through his. "Em, are you

and Mariana good to go back and let the rest of the Ruined know we can move in? Aren and I will start cleaning cabins after we take care of those two."

"All right." Em looked at Aren. "Be careful?" It came out as a question, and Aren wasn't entirely sure why. He nodded.

Olivia tugged on his arm, leading him in the direction of the two men.

"Honestly, they should have left already," Olivia said as they walked. "If they hung around this long they're clearly too stupid to live anyway." She giggled.

He figured the men hadn't left because they were too weak to travel, but he didn't bother pointing that out. Olivia was right. The hunters never cared if a Ruined was slow or weak or injured. They killed indiscriminately.

Aren ducked under a tree branch and the two men came into view. They were moving even slower than before, and the injured one glanced over his shoulder. His eyes widened as they met Aren's. The man quickly turned away, ducking his head like he thought that would save him. Like if he didn't strike first, Aren wouldn't attack.

"I'm glad we have this opportunity. I want to show you something." Olivia cleared her throat, lifting her chin to call to the men. "Excuse me?"

The men turned slowly. Aren could pinpoint the moment they found the Ruined marks curling up Olivia's neck. His own Ruined marks had mostly disappeared beneath his scars, but a few new ones stood out against his dark skin. Fear seized the mens' faces so intensely he could almost feel their heartbeats speed up.

Maybe he *could* feel it. His Ruined power had changed and shifted since spending so much time around humans. Sometimes it was like he could feel their fear, their pain, the relief when he let them go. Ruining the body required him to focus not only on the other person's body, but also his own, and it was almost like they were one when his magic bubbled up.

"We're . . . we're leaving," the younger man sputtered.

"You." Olivia pointed at the older man. "You seem tired. Why don't you sit down?"

The man wiped a shaky hand across his forehead and didn't follow the order.

"Sit," Olivia repeated. The man's legs flew out from under him and he crashed to the dirt with a yelp. Olivia pointed to the younger man. "You. Just stand there for me."

The sinking feeling in the pit of Aren's stomach deepened. He could still leave. Olivia could do this on her own.

"I'm going to teach you how to ruin the body without exhausting your own," she said.

His attention snapped back to her. "I didn't think that was possible."

"I can do it. I don't think all Ruined are capable of it, but I bet you are."

A spark of hope filtered in through his uneasiness. The exhaustion that followed any use of his magic was his biggest weakness. It made it impossible to use his power in some situations.

"Focus on his arm. Don't do anything yet." She gestured at the younger man.

Panic flitted across the man's face and he whirled around, preparing to make a run for it.

"Nope." Olivia pointed at him again and the man's body jerked back toward them. He was rooted to the ground. She put a hand on Aren's back. "Go ahead."

He focused on the man's arm, his own arm tingling. He couldn't exactly *see* the bones, but he knew where they all were. He could snap each of them individually, if he wanted.

"You feel it here?" Olivia ran her fingers over Aren's right arm.

He shivered. "Yes."

"Separate it."

He cocked his head. "How?"

"Don't let yourself be a part of it. This is about him, not you. You're stronger than him. He can't control you. Don't let him. Repeat it in your head."

You don't control me. You don't control me. He repeated it over and over.

"Don't make a move until you've separated yourself from it. Remove your emotions. He doesn't deserve any of your emotions."

Something snapped inside of him with those last words from Olivia. Of course this man didn't deserve his emotions. Not his compassion. Not his sadness. Not even his anger.

Aren's body went cold, the tingling sensation disappearing

from his arm. The world around him went quiet.

Everything was numb. Everything he'd been feeling for the past year—gone.

That was so much better.

He never wanted any of it to come back. He wanted to hang on to this feeling forever.

"That's it." He could hear the smile in Olivia's voice. "Do it."

She didn't have to ask twice. He shattered the man's arm. A scream echoed through the forest.

Aren didn't feel different. He was usually weak and uneasy after doing that. But there was no exhaustion. In fact, he felt *better.*

"Again," Olivia said. "Whatever you want."

Aren lifted the man clean off the ground, tossing his body a few feet away. The older man scrambled up and Aren made him stumble over his own feet. The man grunted as he smacked face-first into the ground.

"You going to take care of that?" Olivia asked, pointing to where the young man was trying to run away.

Aren had snapped necks before, but this one was so easy he almost didn't realize it was done. He barely gestured at the man. Then the man was on ground, his neck twisted and his body limp.

"Feel like you could do a hundred more?" Olivia asked.

"Yes," he breathed.

She waved her hand at the older man. He wasn't sure what

she'd done, but blood splattered out of the man's chest and hit Aren's cheek.

Olivia grinned, rubbing her thumb over the splatter. She wiped the blood on her pants, then put both hands on his cheeks. "Good?"

He curled his fingers around her arms, locking his gaze on hers. "Yes. So good. Thank you."

"You are very welcome." She bounced on the balls of her feet. "I knew you could do it."

He blinked, still in a daze. The numbness had started to wear off, and something else was invading his chest. He suddenly wished he'd run away earlier. He wished he hadn't listened to her, hadn't killed that man.

Olivia looked so happy. She still had a wide smile on her face, like she couldn't see his sudden discomfort. He didn't think he'd been hiding it.

Perhaps she just didn't care.

He tried to pull away from her, but Olivia rose up on her toes and leaned her forehead against his. "You are I are going to make a great team, Aren."

SIX

CAS DIDN'T GO to the site of his mother's death after Jovita brought it up. He spent a few days locked in the castle, attending pointless meetings where everyone just yelled at one another.

But mostly they yelled at him for refusing to attack the Ruined.

He retreated to his room after the most recent meeting, which had ended with Jovita angrily stomping out. Danna and General Amaro had followed her.

Galo and Violet accompanied him into his room, closing the door quietly behind them. His room wasn't much—two lanterns on the wall, a small bed, a desk, and a wooden chair in the corner. Violet sat in the chair. Galo began pacing.

"If Jovita implies you're insane one more time, I won't be responsible for my actions," Galo said.

Cas sank down on the bed with a heavy sigh. "If she says it enough times, everyone will start to believe it." They already believed it. He could see it in the eyes of the advisers, in some of the soldiers. He didn't know what to do about it. Insisting he hadn't lost his mind would only make matters worse. Only crazy people had to defend their sanity.

He let out a short laugh and Galo gave him an exasperated look.

"Laughing at nothing will not help your case," the guard said.

"No one with any sense thinks you've gone mad," Violet said with a roll of her eyes. Cas had seen that eye roll many times in just a few days. She didn't hide her disdain for Jovita well. He liked that about her.

"Then I think there were quite a few people without any sense in that meeting," Cas said.

"No kidding," she muttered. "You need to put an end to this talk."

"How?"

"Throw Jovita out of the meetings. Remove some of the advisers from their positions. Just because they served your father doesn't mean they'll be loyal to you. Clearly."

"We're at war," Cas said. "I'm not sure it's the time to throw Lera leadership into upheaval."

"Too late. We're upheaved. And you're not going to get anywhere by being nice to all of them," she said.

Galo looked from Cas to Violet, obviously impressed.

"Let me talk to some of the advisers. Julieta and Danna aren't convinced that—" She stopped suddenly as a rumbling sound echoed through the fortress. It was low at first, and then slowly grew louder. Yells accompanied the noise.

Cas jumped to his feet and flew out the door, Galo and Violet close behind. The sound was coming from outside the fortress. He jogged down the stairs and pulled open the front door. The gray sky was overcast, the sun completely obscured.

A crowd was gathered around Jovita, who stood on top of a box not far from the front door of the fortress. The people were all stomping their feet in unison, a chant beginning to rise up from the crowd.

"Kill the Ruined! Kill the Ruined!"

"Louder!" Jovita yelled. She looked over her shoulder at Cas. "Your king is present!"

"KILL THE RUINED! KILL THE RUINED!"

Cas marched to Jovita. He grabbed her wrist and tugged her off the box.

"What are you doing?" he hissed.

"I'm showing you what everyone wants." She yanked her arm free. "As king, you're supposed to follow the wishes of your people. Not do whatever you please."

He looked at the crowd again. All the hunters were there, as were many of the soldiers. But most of the king's guard hadn't joined, and plenty of soldiers stood on the outskirts, worry etched across their features.

"This is what you want, not the people," he said.

She swept her arm out to the crowd. "What do you call this?"

"I won't discuss this again. We're not attacking the Ruined." He turned to address the crowd. "Disperse—"

"Kill the Ruined!" Jovita yelled, stepping in front of him. She nodded to General Amaro. The general moved forward, a grim look on her face.

Hands closed around Cas's arms. He twisted around to see two large soldiers behind him. He tried to pull free. They held tighter. He heard Violet gasp.

Jovita turned to face him again. "I'm sorry, Cas. We can't have a mad king while we're at war. You need time to rest and recover, and if you won't do it willingly, I'll force you to."

Cas looked from Jovita to General Amaro. "Not wanting to attack the Ruined doesn't make me *mad*."

"You won't listen to reason," General Amaro said. "Your father took a strong position with the Ruined, and now is not the time to change that policy."

"We're in this mess because of my father! Both my parents died because of their hatred of the Ruined."

"Your father died because of Emelina, and your mother died because of you," Jovita said.

Her words cut him completely in half, and for a moment he

wondered why he was still standing when half of his body was crumpled on the ground.

"Just take some time to rest, and think," Jovita said, her voice softer. "I can lead in your place until you're feeling better. I don't mind."

Cas let out a hollow laugh. "I'm sure you don't."

The edges of Jovita's lips twitched, but she managed to hold back a smile. "Please take King Casimir to his room. Lock him in for his own protection."

The soldiers pulled Cas backward. He twisted in their grasp, trying to break free.

"Please don't make a scene, Your Majesty," one of the soldiers murmured.

It was too late. Everyone in the area was staring at them. Some of the hunters smirked.

Galo made a move like he was going to lunge, but Mateo pulled him back just in time. He whispered something in Galo's ear that made his face fall.

Cas's shoulders slumped. There were too many on Jovita's side. There was no point in resisting.

Jovita stepped up on the box again. "My soldiers have reported seeing numerous Ruined on their way to Ruina. Our first order of business is to take out as many as we can. We need to stamp out the alliance between the Ruined and the warriors."

The crowd cheered as the soldiers dragged Cas up the steps of the fortress.

"I'm only sending half of you," Jovita continued, "because we need plenty of people here to protect the fortress. Those with the most pins will go. You will kill *all* Ruined, no questions asked."

More cheers rose up as Cas entered the fortress. They grew quieter as the door closed behind him.

"KILL THE RUINED!"

SEVEN

OLIVIA STEPPED OUT of her room and walked quietly past Em's bed. Her sister was still asleep, curled up under the blankets.

Sunlight had just started to stream in through the windows and into the dusty living room. It was a small, pitiful cabin. The couch had probably been there for three generations. The kitchen table sat only two people, and a good kick would have killed the thing for good. She let out an annoyed sigh as she pulled the front door open.

Aren was waiting for her just off the porch. He had a sword at his hip, but she hadn't bothered with a weapon. She never needed one.

He nodded at her as she approached. The area around the

cabins was mostly deserted, except for Ivanna, who was on her knees in a patch of brown grass not far away. Her hands were pressed to the ground, her eyes closed and her lips moving in silent prayer.

"Let's go," Olivia said as she began walking. She'd cleared a few hunters away yesterday, but she'd yet to check the area south of them.

Ivanna opened her eyes and looked from Aren to Olivia as they passed her. "Where are you going?"

"Hunting," Olivia said.

Disapproval flitted across Ivanna's features, but she said nothing. Olivia glanced at her over her shoulder as they walked away. "Ungrateful," she muttered.

"What?" Aren asked.

"She's ungrateful. We're keeping everyone safe and she just keeps complaining."

"She didn't say anything."

"I can see it in her eyes."

"Ivanna doesn't think we should go out looking for trouble."

"What, we should wait for it to come to us? Because that worked out so well for us before?"

Aren held up his hands in surrender. "I'm not saying I agree."

She picked up her pace in an effort to leave the anger behind, but it followed her as they headed south. The Ruined didn't respect her because she hadn't done anything great yet. She was just an inept heir to a great queen, living in a pathetic little cabin. She couldn't even give her people a good home, or enough food to eat. No wonder Ivanna looked at her with such disdain.

Aren shot his arm out, stopping Olivia in her tracks. He pointed straight ahead.

The trees around them were sparse and mostly bare, and she easily spotted the five men walking in their direction. Their clothes were wet and sticking to their bodies.

"Hunters," Aren said quietly.

"How can you tell?"

"The blue pins."

Olivia squinted. Every man had several blue pins on his jacket.

"Hunters deserve to die." It almost sounded as if Aren was trying to convince himself. Or her. She certainly didn't need any convincing.

"We're going to walk to Vallos?" a young red-haired man whined. He shivered.

"Unless you have a better idea," a man with a thick beard said. "You can go fish the remains of the boat out of the ocean, if you want."

The red-haired man grumbled something Olivia couldn't understand. Her magic twitched in her body, begging to be released.

"Do you have a preference?" Olivia whispered.

"No," Aren replied.

"I want the one with the beard," she said loudly. He reminded her of the Lera king.

The hunters' heads all snapped to her in unison.

One had a bow and arrow, and he darted around a tree as he aimed at her. She laughed. His head made a thudding sound as it hit the ground.

Aren had the others, so she strode to the man with a beard. She wanted him on the ground, and he was there in half a second. She sat down on his legs.

"Five pins, huh?" She yanked one off his jacket. "I heard about these from my sister. Killed fifty Ruined and you're proud of it?"

He frantically shook his head.

"I've probably killed that many people too, but you don't see me bragging about it." She cocked her head. "Although that was bragging just then, wasn't it?" She yanked his jacket open and slammed the pin down on his chest, through his shirt, and into his flesh. He howled.

"Oh, come on. That didn't hurt that much. You should have seen the size of the needles your king put in me." She pulled another pin off his jacket and shoved it into his chest, across from the other one. She did the other three as well. When she was done, he was whimpering, tears streaming down his cheeks.

"Aren, hand me the rest of the pins. He has so many spots to put them." She patted the hunter's stomach.

There was no reply. She turned to find Aren leaning against a tree, blinking. He looked like he'd been hit over the head.

"Aren!" she yelled.

His eyes shifted to hers and cleared.

"Give me their pins." She pointed to the dead hunters.

"Am I . . ." He scrunched up his face. "Am I supposed to feel like this?"

"Like what?"

"Dazed. Is it from detaching?"

"Yes. It gets better with time."

He slowly stood, brushing dirt from his pants. He turned away from her.

"Aren! Pins!"

"Just kill him," he said without turning around. The hunter began blubbering.

Olivia let out a long, exaggerated sigh. It was too bad her mother was gone. She appreciated torture more than anyone. Understood the value in it.

She climbed off the hunter. He whimpered and tried to slither away, feet scrambling across the dirt. She snapped his neck. "I was going to make a smiley face on his chest out of pins," she complained.

Aren paused and glanced over his shoulder at her. Fear flashed across his face. The second most powerful Ruined, the boy who had killed more hunters than anyone she knew, was scared of her. Perhaps this was how she earned the loyalty of the Ruined and saved them all: fear.

She smiled.

Em opened her eyes and immediately rolled over to check the bed across from her. Empty. Olivia's bed had been empty every morning for a week, since they moved into the cabins.

Em pushed off the covers and stood, walking to the small window next to her bed. Outside, a few Ruined were building a fire in the pit not far from the cabins. The sun had just come up, and they were the only ones out and about. The area in front of the cabins was mostly dirt and brown grass. It was gray again, and for a moment she thought of Lera. The blue skies and sparkling ocean. The cheese bread and colorful clothing.

She let the image of Cas take shape in her mind, smiling as he held out the cheese bread to her. If he was here, she might crawl under the covers with him and stay there all day. Ruina's gray weather wouldn't be so bad if she could spend the day in bed with him.

She pulled on her clothes and walked out of her room, the image of Cas lingering in her mind. Across the hallway, Aren's door was ajar, his bed empty.

The front door opened, bringing laughter with it. Em stepped out of the hallway to see Olivia and Aren walking inside. Olivia's cheeks were pink from the early morning chill, and she waved enthusiastically at her sister.

"What were you guys doing?" Em asked, unable to keep the suspicion from her voice. Olivia only looked that happy when she was killing someone.

"We rode south a bit, to explore the area," Aren said. He

shrugged out of his coat without meeting Em's gaze.

"It's a good thing we did. One of the Lera ships had a problem and had to come back. A bunch of hunters were on board," Olivia said.

Em was afraid to ask.

"They're dead now," Aren said.

She nodded. That was probably for the best. They weren't safe with hunters nearby.

Still, the delighted look on Olivia's face made her uncomfortable.

Aren walked to the kitchen, his strides quick and easy. "You're not exhausted from using your magic?" Em asked.

"I taught him how to use his Ruined magic without involving his own body," Olivia said. "We're teaching some of the other Ruined too. Not everyone can do it, but the most powerful ones can."

Aren poured water from the pitcher into a cup. "We'll be much safer if we can use our powers without exhausting our bodies. The best ones—"

A yell from outside cut off his words. Em grabbed her sword from the corner and flew through the front door. Ruined ran out of their cabins, their attention all in the same place: about twenty horses headed their way from the north, riders perched on each of them. A red-and-white flag flew from the front horse. Olso warriors.

"Stay behind me," Olivia said to Em as she took off running.

"Don't attack," Em called as she followed her sister. "They're our allies!"

The horses halted, dust blowing up around them. Olivia skidded to a stop, putting one arm out like she was protecting Em. The Ruined marks on her neck shifted as she swallowed. She clearly didn't believe the warriors were their allies.

There were nineteen horses total, each with a rider dressed in black. Arms were lifted in surrender. The warrior with the flag jumped off her horse and started toward them, her arms also raised. Em squinted, taking a step forward.

"It's Iria," Aren said from behind Em.

Em slid her sword into her belt and started toward Iria. Olivia grabbed her arm.

"It's all right." Em gently shook her arm free. "It's just Iria."

Olivia didn't appear convinced, but she didn't protest as Em walked away.

Iria lowered her arms as she approached Em, one side of her mouth curving up. "Emelina."

"Iria." She stopped in front of the warrior. Iria looked haggard, her black wavy hair pulled back in a messy bun. Dark circles marred the skin under her eyes. She must have barely made it home to Olso from Lera before turning around and riding south to Ruina.

"Forgive the unannounced arrival," Iria said. "We didn't know how else to approach you."

"As long as you keep your weapons lowered, we'll be fine."

"We're not here to fight," Iria said. "We've come to speak with your queen." She looked past Em at Olivia.

"You're talking to one of them."

Iria blinked. "What?"

Em lifted her shoulders, a smile spreading across her face. It was still a smile of disbelief. "Olivia and I rule Ruina together, as equals. I'm one of their queens."

Iria's expression mirrored Em's own incredulity. "Oh. Wow."

"Yeah."

"Would Olivia like to come over?" Iria asked. "I'll introduce you both to him, then."

"To who?"

Iria turned without responding. She walked to one of the warriors on horseback and extended her hand to him. He didn't take it as he jumped off the horse.

Em looked over her shoulder and gestured for her sister to join her. Olivia's frown deepened, but she stepped forward and stood next to Em.

The man who'd dismounted his horse strode toward them. He was very tall, towering over Iria, and she practically had to jog to keep up with his long strides. His black pants were dusty and the dark circles under his eyes matched Iria's, but his face was open and friendly.

"This is Emelina and Olivia Flores, queens of the Ruined," Iria said. "I'd like to introduce you to August Santana, prince of Olso."

Em's regarded him suspiciously. What was the youngest

prince of Olso doing in Ruina?

"Queens?" A grin spread across August's face. "How unusual. I like it." He bowed his head, tapping his fist to his chest once. It was the traditional way to greet a Ruined royal, and Em stood there stupidly for a moment, flabbergasted by the show of respect.

She found her senses and quickly interlaced her fingers, putting them beneath her chin and bowing deeply. Her mother had instructed her on the proper way to greet the Olso royal family, and she said a quick thanks to past Em for paying attention. Olivia stood there rigidly.

"It's nice to meet you too?" Em said, unable to keep the question out of her voice.

August seemed pleased by her confusion. His skin was lighter than hers, his hair golden. He was broad and muscular, probably almost twice her size, and normally she'd keep a hand close to her sword when facing such a man. But his expression was so relaxed, so friendly, that she didn't think it necessary.

That made her want to reach for her sword even more. They were standing close enough that she could grab her blade and have it in his chest in less than five seconds.

She resisted the urge and returned his smile. "This is unexpected."

He chuckled. "When you refused the king's invitation to come to Olso, my brother thought it best to come to you."

"We were eager to go home," she said.

"I understand. I've come to talk about our alliance. Are you open to that discussion?"

"Of course."

August looked at Olivia, like he expected her to say something as well. She remained silent.

August cleared his throat. "Is it all right if we set up camp over there?"

"That's fine." Em turned, gesturing for Mariana to join them. "Mariana is our director of foreign affairs. She'll help you get settled."

Mariana nodded and greeted August.

"Can you please give one of the cabins to Prince August?" Em asked her.

"There's no need," August said. "I'll be perfectly comfortable in my tent."

"I insist," Em said. "It's not much, but it will be more comfortable than the ground."

"Thank you, then," August said. He smiled broadly at Em. "I look forward to speaking with you more."

He turned and walked back to the other warriors.

"They're here because they want something, Em," Olivia said quietly.

Of course they wanted something. Her deal with King Lucio was supposed to be over after Olso invaded Lera, but she wasn't naive enough to believe that would actually happen. They wanted access to the mines or Ruined help or something worse. Something she wasn't prepared to give.

"I know."

EIGHT

CAS HEARD THE door open, but he didn't bother turning to look. He knew it was the soldier who delivered meals twice daily. Five days had passed since Jovita locked him in his room, and no one but that soldier had entered since.

The door shut, the click of the lock echoing in the silence. He rolled over in bed and pulled the blankets up to his chin. The breakfast tray sat on the floor near the door. He stared at it for a few moments, debating whether it was too much effort to get up.

The first day, he'd pounded on the door. Yelled for someone to let him out. Tried desperately to remove the doorknob. Nothing worked.

The second day he asked to talk to Jovita. She never came.

The third day, he gave up.

He sat up with a sigh, his stomach clenching in protest. On top of everything else, it seemed he was sick. Perhaps it was a fatal illness. That would make things much easier for Jovita.

He laughed weakly to himself as he shuffled across the room. There was a piece of meat and bread, and a small bowl of soup. He slid down onto the floor and grabbed the soup. It was sweet and thick, and his favorite part of every meal.

The soup warmed his belly, and he didn't feel much like eating the meat and bread when he finished. He climbed back into bed. He fixed his thoughts on Em, hoping that would bring dreams of her. Sometimes he imagined he'd run away with her, and left this horrible country that used to be home behind. Maybe he'd be in Ruina. Waking up beside her. Helping her prepare breakfast. Crawling back in bed with her and ignoring the world for as long as possible. His eyes drifted closed.

"Cas."

The sound of his name jerked Cas awake. He rolled over to see Galo standing at the door, the dinner tray in his hand. He thought he'd drifted off only seconds ago, but hours must have passed if dinner had arrived. He forced himself to a sitting position. Relief coursed through his body as he looked at his friend.

"I was worried you were dead. Or sent away," Cas said.

Galo studied him. "You look terrible." He pointed to the breakfast tray, where the meat and bread sat next to the empty soup bowl. "Why aren't you eating?"

"I ate some. I haven't been feeling well."

Galo put the dinner tray on the dresser and strode to Cas. He pressed his hand to Cas's forehead. "You don't have a fever."

"Perhaps it's just my misery, then." He laughed. Galo didn't.

"I'm sorry," Galo said. "I would have come earlier, but Jovita wouldn't let anyone near your room. She's gone now and—"

"Gone where?" he interrupted.

"Ruina," Galo said quietly.

"No." The word escaped from his mouth a bit strangled.

"Word has it the Ruined have set up camp near the mines. Jovita's taken an army to attack them."

"Are the warriors with the Ruined?"

"We don't know."

"Have the Ruined attacked since leaving here?"

"Not once."

"She'll give them a reason to."

A voice drifted in from the hallway, and Galo cast a look back at the door. "I shouldn't stay long. Mateo is on watch so I managed to sneak in. I wanted to let you know that I'm working on a plan to get you out of here."

Cas flopped down on his back. "Don't bother."

"Cas—"

"Where would I go?" He let out a hollow laugh. "North, to my home? The warriors have taken it and want to kill me. South, to Vallos? Where I assume those who are loyal to Jovita have fled?" A quick glance at Galo confirmed he was correct. "West, to Ruina? I'm sure the Ruined would love to have me, considering my father tried to murder them."

"We can find a place," Galo said. "Not everyone is loyal to Jovita. We just need to unite them and form a plan."

"There's no point. There's no kingdom left for me to rule, anyway."

"Of course there is! Almost the entire guard and the staff are ready to revolt. The only people who think you're not fit to lead are the idiots marching to Ruina right now. I've been talking to Violet, and she says the south would stand with you."

Cas shrugged. Stand with him to do what?

Maybe Lera deserved to go down in flames. *It's all built on the backs of the people you murdered*, Em had said to him once. She wasn't wrong. Perhaps Lera was a bloody, sinking ship, and it was time for him to abandon it.

"Let's look on the bright side," Cas said. "At least Jovita didn't murder me."

"How is that a bright side?"

"I thought it was a plus."

Galo started pacing, almost running into the desk chair. "We have enough people to overthrow them. We can—"

"No we can't," Cas interrupted. "Jovita has all the hunters and a good number of the soldiers on her side."

Galo gave him a pained look, because he knew it was true.

"If we fight, she'll win, and probably put you all to death for treason."

"Then what are we going to do?" Galo threw his hands up. "You're going to let her take the throne?"

"Maybe she wants it more."

"You're going to let Jovita take your kingdom away from you. Let her murder the Ruined and keep you locked up like an animal."

"Looks like it."

Galo grunted and grabbed the dinner tray from the dresser. He tossed it on the bedside table. A few beans bounced out of a bowl.

"At least eat something. You look like death. And you won't be able to fight without your strength."

"Good. Fighting's exhausting."

"I'll try to come back tomorrow. If you haven't eaten I'll force-feed you." Galo slammed the door behind him.

NINE

AREN WATCHED FROM the porch steps of his cabin as two warriors set up a tent nearby. The wind was strong, and they were having trouble keeping it in place as they hammered the posts into the ground. He could have offered to help, or enlisted an elemental Ruined to redirect the gusts, but he wasn't feeling particularly charitable today. Or any day, really.

"Young man, the ancestors did not bestow such a gift on you for you to keep it to yourself." His mother's voice rang clear in his ears. He was almost positive she'd never said that exact thing to him. It didn't matter. His mother's voice was always in his head, even when he didn't want it there.

"My gift won't help build a tent," he muttered out loud. He could imagine the disapproving look he'd get for that statement.

"What was that?"

Aren jumped. Iria stood in front of him. He swore that girl didn't touch the ground when she walked. She was always sneaking up on him.

"What? Nothing," he said quickly. "Hi, Iria."

She smiled. "Hi, Aren." She looked exhausted, a consequence of a brutal schedule they'd set for themselves to get to Ruina as quickly as possible. Still, she was pretty in a way that a couple of dark circles and dirty clothes couldn't hide.

"I'm glad to see you made it," she said, lowering down onto the step next to him. Her shoulder brushed his. "I searched for you and Em after the battle at Fort Victorra."

"We took off right away. Didn't want to risk retaliation for Olivia killing the queen." That wasn't entirely true. There was no chance of retaliation, not after Olivia killed the Lera queen. He hadn't seen Olivia do it—he'd been injured, lying on the ground nearby—but he'd heard Cas's panicked breathing and the strangled cries. The noise had sounded so much like Aren's cries the night his parents had died that he'd put his hands to ears in an effort to drown it out. It hadn't worked.

"You know I wouldn't have come on this trip if the warriors were up to anything bad, right?" Iria asked. Her expression was serious, and she was trying to meet his eyes. He resisted.

"I know. I can't imagine you kept me alive in the jungle just to come out here and kill me."

Something flickered across her face when he mentioned the jungle. His heart was suddenly thumping in his chest, and he rubbed a hand over the back of his neck, trying to ignore it.

"This is a nice home you've set up here," she said after an awkward silence. He just shrugged. It wasn't a home, and it certainly wasn't nice.

"We brought food," Iria continued. "Did Em tell you? Lots of beans. And some dried meat."

"I heard. Thank you." He stood, then wished he hadn't. He missed the warmth of her next to him. "Tell me if you have any trouble. Steer clear of the Ruined. Especially Olivia."

Iria got to her feet. "How is Olivia?"

"She's adjusting. She's angry, of course. She was in captivity for a year and got out to discover that ninety percent of the Ruined had been murdered. She's rarely in a charitable mood."

"I understand."

She couldn't possibly understand, but Aren didn't point that out. "You're safe here," he said instead, though he could never guarantee that.

Iria smiled at him. She crinkled her nose a little when she smiled, drawing attention to the freckles there. "Thanks, Aren."

He quickly turned away and stepped into the cabin. Olivia stood next to the window, holding back the curtain as she peeked outside.

"I know that girl," Olivia said. "She used to come to the castle when I was younger."

"Iria. She was with us in Lera."

"Right. Em mentioned that." Olivia watched as Iria walked away. "You trust them? The warriors?"

"Of course not." He paused. "I trust Iria."

She lifted an eyebrow. It was not an approving eyebrow.

"Mostly," he quickly added. "It's . . . in the jungle, when the warriors took me, she offered to let me go."

"She did what?"

I'll take that blindfold off. Iria's words from a few weeks ago rang in his ears. They'd been in the jungle, the night after the warriors had captured him and Em and Cas had escaped. He'd been blindfolded, his arms bound in front of him, when the soft voice whispered in his ear.

"She offered to let me go," he said, heat rising up his neck. The memory of Iria tugging the blindfold off took shape in his head, the way he'd blinked in the darkness to find her so close to him their noses were almost touching.

"And . . . what? You stayed anyway? Didn't you arrive at the fortress with the warriors?"

"I didn't take her up on the offer," he said. "She could have been charged with treason. She assured me the warriors weren't going to kill me, so I stayed. It was better to keep tabs on them."

"I guess," Olivia said skeptically.

Aren turned away, afraid she'd see emotions splashed across his face. The memory of that night burned so bright in his mind it was hard to keep his expression neutral.

You idiot, he'd said after she'd pulled the blindfold off, a trace of humor in his voice. *I could kill you.*

You're not going to kill me. She'd said it with such confidence that he was almost insulted. He still remembered the quiet laugh that had followed, like that was the most ridiculous thing she'd ever heard. He'd never met a human who wasn't scared of him.

He'd declined her offer, and she'd put the blindfold back on and settled down next to him. He'd woken the next morning to his head on her shoulder and the other warriors making fun of him for it. She'd discreetly squeezed his hand and disappeared from his side.

"Her first loyalty is to the warriors," Olivia said firmly. "Always will be."

Aren nodded. There was no use arguing with Olivia. There was no use trying to explain that a warrior had really had good intentions. That Iria had offered to commit treason for him.

Maybe he was stupid. Or overly optimistic. Or distracted by the way her nose crinkled when she smiled.

But Aren was almost certain Iria's loyalty rested with him, not with her fellow warriors.

TEN

LAUGHTER AND MUSIC filled the air, and Em paused on the porch of her cabin and looked for the source of the noise. The warriors had built a large fire in front of their tents. A man sat on a rock with a guitar, a crowd surrounding him.

Em glanced at the cabins around her. A few Ruined were on their porches, watching, but no one joined the warriors.

Em pulled open the front door and poked her head inside her cabin. Aren and Olivia sat at the kitchen table.

"I'm going over to say hi to the warriors. You want to come?"

Aren stood right away, but Olivia shook her head.

Em hopped off the porch and walked to the fire pit, Aren trailing behind her. Iria stood near the guitar player, watching a group of warriors dancing. She lifted a hand when she spotted

Em and Aren. She walked to them, her gaze lingering on Aren for a few moments.

Iria stuck her hand out to Em. "Prince August was looking for you. But dance with me first."

"Dance with you?"

"Come on," Iria said. "It's tradition."

"It is?"

"Well, we danced together in Lera, so I say it is." Iria grabbed her arm and pulled her to the makeshift dance floor. Iria lifted one arm, spinning Em around.

"You always have to lead," Em said, her lips twitching.

"Well, I'm a better dancer than you."

Em would have argued, if it weren't true. A burst of laughter came from behind her, and she looked over her shoulder to see Aren talking to a warrior she didn't know.

Em turned back to Iria. "Aren told me what happened in the jungle. Thank you."

"Don't mention it." Iria met Em's eyes. "Seriously. To anyone."

"Of course. I know what a risk it was for you. But I appreciate it."

Iria nodded, her attention over Em's shoulder.

"Your Majesty," a deep voice said.

Em turned to find August standing next to them. She stepped away from Iria.

He wore fresh clothes, his black pants and gray tunic only

slightly rumpled. He'd left his coat behind, and she took a quick survey of his body. No weapons that she could see. His clothes were rather formfitting, so the only possibility was a knife in his boot.

"May I have a moment with you and your sister?" he asked.

"Sure. She was in our cabin, last I saw."

August swept his arm out, indicating for Em to lead the way. She cast a quick smile at Iria before heading to the cabin with August.

The living area was empty when she stepped inside, so she left August alone and walked down the hallway to her and Olivia's room. The door was open and her sister was perched on the edge of the bed, frowning at a map in her hands.

"Did you bring a human inside?" she asked, without looking at Em.

"Prince August. He wants to talk to us."

Olivia folded the map and tossed it on the desk. "Do I have to be there?"

"He specifically asked to speak with us both."

"The entire point of this diarchy is that you have to deal with all the boring stuff."

"I thought the entire point of the diarchy was that you thought I would be a good leader," Em said, kicking her sister's leg.

Olivia kicked her back. "That too, I guess."

"At least just listen to what he has to say."

Olivia let out a long sigh as she rose from the bed. "Fine."

"And don't be hasty. We'll listen, then discuss after he leaves," Em whispered.

"Fiiiiine," Olivia said, pushing Em toward the door as she dragged out the word.

They walked back into the living area to find August still standing near the door. He nodded at Olivia.

"Thank you for agreeing to see me, Your Majesties," he said.

"You can call me Em," she said.

"You can call me Your Majesty," Olivia said.

Em winced, worried August might have been insulted. Instead, his lips curved like he was trying to hold back a laugh. Em dug an elbow into her sister's ribs.

"You can call me Olivia," she grumbled.

"Wonderful. You can call me August. Everyone does."

"Do you want something to drink? All we have is water." Em gestured to the jug on the table.

"No, thank you. I'm fine."

"Please, sit," Em said.

The living room consisted of a sofa and three chairs, two of which were in questionable condition. August took a seat in the ragged gray one, the furniture creaking as he settled into it. Em sat down on the couch next to Olivia, across from him.

"I have to admit, after seeing this place, I'm surprised you declined my brother's invitation to visit us in Olso. He would have put you up in the castle."

"We like Ruina," Olivia said. Em caught the hitch in her sister's voice. Neither of them liked Ruina all that much, especially after seeing Lera, but it was the only home they had.

"I'm sure you do, but we would have been happy to have you while your castle is being rebuilt."

"It's best if we all stay together right now," Em said. "The Ruined need leadership here, not queens off gallivanting in Olso."

"Gallivanting," August repeated with a chuckle. "Fair enough."

"Did you come here to try to convince us to go to Olso with you? If so, you're wasting your time." Olivia waved at the door. "You might as well just go back."

"No," he said. "My brother asked me to pass along that it's an open invitation, and we hope that you'll visit soon. But I understand why now isn't a good time."

"*You* understand," Olivia said, leaning forward in her chair. "But let's be honest. Your brother is the king. You have two older brothers in line for the throne ahead of you. Why did they send the least-important heir?"

"I like to think I'm a bit more important than some of my cousins."

"Do you have any real power?" Olivia asked. "If we make deals with you, will they be honored by the king? Or are you wasting our time?"

Annoyance flickered across August's face. "I'm authorized to make certain deals." He said it with the bitterness of being the least-important heir. Em bit back a laugh. Olivia looked pleased to have upset him.

He twisted his face back into a smile. It was fake this time.

"There are things I can't do, but I'll let you know if they come up. I was sent here with a specific purpose."

"And what is that?" Em asked.

"My brother wants to solidify the alliance between Olso and Ruina."

"Solidify how?" Olivia asked.

"He sent me to marry the Ruined queen."

Silence descended on the cabin. Em went numb.

"Of course, we only expected there to be one, but since there are two . . ." One side of his mouth lifted.

Marry? *Marry?* Cas's face floated across her vision.

Olivia snorted. "You can count me out."

"Olivia!" Em exclaimed.

"What?" Olivia said. "I'm not doing it."

"You'll note that I didn't ask to marry *you*." August sniffed.

"Thank goodness." Olivia turned to Em. "Sounds like he prefers you."

Em gripped the arms of her chair and eyed the door. Would it be strange if she bolted out of the room?

She couldn't marry August. Sure, he was cute, but his smile often seemed forced and she knew nothing about him. She still half expected him to do something horrible.

It was easier to marry Cas, even though she'd hated him at the time. At least she'd felt in control of the situation. This was unexpected and there was no way for her to get her footing.

"Are you open to the discussion?" August asked.

No. She hadn't even considered her next marriage. As queen, it was a given that the union would be more about politics than love, but she'd thought it was a ways off.

Cas.

The name burned a hole through her heart. She tried to ignore it. Her feelings for Cas didn't matter. It would never be him, no matter how much she wanted it.

"I know this is sudden," August said when she didn't respond. "But it could be beneficial to the Ruined as well as Olso. You need food and clothes and protection. We can provide that."

"We don't need you to provide anything," Olivia snapped. "Certainly not protection. We'll be back on our feet soon enough. I'll make sure of it."

August was clearly skeptical, but he didn't respond to that. He looked at Em, waiting for her reply.

Em could shut August down right now. Tell him to pack up and leave. Olivia would be delighted.

But Olivia was wrong. The Ruined did need Olso's help. The warriors could provide protection and supplies that Em couldn't. They could help rebuild the castle. Was marriage really such a terrible trade for the opportunity to rebuild Ruina that much faster? To provide the Ruined with a better level of security?

"Do you understand what you'd be getting into?" Em asked slowly. "A human hasn't married a Ruined for . . . centuries."

"I know."

"Our children would be Ruined. I'm useless, but that doesn't mean my children will be. They could be very powerful, like Olivia." She sucked in a breath. "Wait. You've considered that."

"Of course."

"With Ruined in the royal family, you'd never have any challengers to the throne. No successful ones, anyway."

"Exactly." He leaned forward, resting his elbows on his knees. "And with Ruined in the Olso royal family, you'd also never have to worry about us turning against you. Your blood would be our blood."

"And you would live here," she said. "In Ruina."

"Of course. Our children would be expected to spend half their time in Olso, though."

Talking about children sent blasts of terror shooting down her spine, and she let out an almost hysterical laugh.

She wanted to tell him no. She wanted to tell him she couldn't get through one minute without thinking about Cas, and she didn't want another man intruding on her brain.

Of course, maybe it was ridiculous to think he would ever take up any space in her brain. It was just an alliance marriage. She didn't need to have any feelings for him. It might even be preferable that way.

"I don't need an answer right away. Perhaps you could discuss it with your advisers and—"

August's words were cut off by a scream from outside.

Em jumped to her feet, panic seizing her chest.

She darted to the corner and grabbed her sword. Olivia was already out the door, and Em ran out behind her, August tailing them.

Aren shot out from the darkness and skidded to a stop in

front of them. "Lera soldiers," he gasped out. "At least a hundred. They're attacking now."

Behind Aren, Em could see horses and flaming torches coming over the hill. A streak of fire soared through the night and a tent burst into flames. Ruined ran out of their cabins, hastily throwing on jackets and shoes. The warriors were gathered around the flaming tent, trying to put out the fire.

"I knew it!" Olivia screamed. She took off, leaving Em in her dust. She threw a glance over her shoulder. "Aren! Ruined! With me!"

Aren ran after her. Ruined followed them, flames illuminating their faces as they sprinted toward the approaching army. Jacobo stopped and turned to face the fire. He reached his hand out and the flames snaked through the grass, past Em, and to the Lera soldiers. Two men went up in flames.

Em pressed a shaky hand to her mouth. Why were Lera soldiers attacking? Was Cas with them? Was he angry enough about his mother's death to turn against her?

She didn't have time to worry about it.

She turned to August. "Are you hiding, or are you helping?"

"Helping," he said immediately.

She pointed to the warriors behind him. "Tell them to get behind the Ruined. Every one of them needs to be wearing their red jackets if they don't want to accidentally lose their heads. Including you."

He nodded and turned to shout orders to the warriors. He faced her again and opened his mouth, but his eyes widened as he caught sight of something behind her. He grabbed Em around the waist and pulled her out of the way just in time for a flaming arrow to soar past her head. It landed on the cabin's porch. Em sucked in a breath and threw August a grateful look.

She extracted herself from his grasp and stomped out the arrow. "Come on," she said, grabbing his arm and running to the warriors.

In seconds, the warriors were in red and had their weapons drawn. A wall of Ruined stood at the top of the hill, Olivia and Aren at the center. Ivanna stood next to them, her hair blowing in the powerful wind she had created to fan the flames.

Several soldiers raced up the hill, shooting past the Ruined. Jacobo whirled around, fury burned across his features. He pointed at the flames and they slowly moved across the grass before sputtering out. His knees buckled beneath him.

Em raced to the soldiers, yelling for the warriors to follow her. Screams echoed through the night, and she suspected they weren't those of the Ruined. She knew the screams of a man getting his body twisted by Olivia.

At least ten men charged toward them, the pins on their chest glinting. Em gripped her sword a little tighter. Hunters. She'd killed plenty of them.

Iria and the other warriors pushed themselves in front of Em and August. Metal clinked as swords met. A warrior screamed as a hunter drove his sword into her gut.

Em didn't see Cas.

She shouldn't have been looking for Cas. She had more

important things to consider at the moment. Like not dying.

A soldier pushed past Iria and lunged at Em, using both hands to draw his sword back as he prepared to strike. She raised her boot and kicked him firmly in the stomach. He grunted and stumbled backward. Iria caught his shoulder and thrust her blade into his back.

Beside her, August grunted as he ducked a swinging sword. Em put a hand on his back, keeping him down as she jammed her sword into the soldier's stomach.

"Thank you," August said breathlessly as he straightened.

Em whirled around, blade raised, but there was nothing but red around her. Everyone in blue was dead in the dirt. A warrior extracted his sword from a Lera soldier, scrunching his face at the blood smeared across the blade.

Em turned to the hill, to where about twenty Ruined still stood side by side. There were no more soldiers getting through.

A few of the Ruined slumped to the ground, breathing heavily from their magic use. Jacobo was flat on his back, arms spread wide, a crazed smile on his face.

"Send more next time!" he yelled. "That was too easy!"

Relief washed over Em. They hadn't lost any Ruined, as far as she could tell. She strode forward, to where Aren and Olivia stood shoulder to shoulder, focused on the scene in front of them. She reached the top of the hill and followed their gaze. August stopped beside her.

The bodies of Lera soldiers littered the bottom of the hill. No, *parts* of soldiers. Pieces of them were strewn everywhere. Torches were discarded on the ground, burning through the grass. Abandoned swords glinted in the flames. Bile rose in her throat as she scanned the mess for Cas. There was no way to tell.

The remaining soldiers were running away, sprinting as fast as they could to the sparse trees. Olivia directed her magic at one. His head separated from his body.

August turned away. He closed his eyes and sucked in a deep breath.

Em looked back at Olivia and Aren. "I need one—" Her voice came out too quiet, and she cleared her throat. "Olivia, Aren, I need one alive. I have questions."

"That one," Aren said, pointing to a man almost to the trees. Olivia nodded and the man came to a sudden stop. He flailed his arms, but his feet remained rooted to the ground.

"Thank you," Em said. She started down the hill.

"I'm coming too," Olivia said.

"Ir-Iria, go with them." August had to choke out the words, like he was about to vomit. Em turned to find he still had his back to them. Iria sheathed her sword as she walked to Em, raising her eyebrows as if asking Em if it was all right. Em nodded.

"Are you sure you don't want to come, Your Highness?" Olivia asked sweetly. No one had ever said "Your Highness" with such contempt.

August took a step away from them without turning back. "I'm going to go check on my warriors."

Olivia snickered and strode past Em. She laughed as she bounced over a severed arm.

Iria let out a long breath as she fell into step beside Em. "Is Aren all right?"

Em glanced back at Aren, surprised by the question. His face was blank and his eyes didn't seem to be focusing. He didn't look weak, like using his magic had been a big effort. In fact, he didn't look like anything. It was as if everything about Aren had been sucked away and there was nothing left but an empty shell.

"Em!" Olivia called. She was already standing by the Lera soldier, waving for Em to hurry.

Aren blinked at Em.

Iria chewed on her lip as she watched him. She appeared worried. Should Em have been worried about Aren?

Em turned away, focusing on the soldier in front of her. He shook as Em approached him, a bead of sweat running down the side of his face.

"Why are you here?" she asked.

The man pressed his lips together and looked at Olivia nervously.

"If you tell me why you're here, I'll let you go. You can go back and tell them what became of your friends. If you don't talk, I'll let Olivia remove all of your limbs."

"Slowly." Olivia grinned. "Honestly, I'm hoping you don't talk."

"We—we were ordered to attack the Ruined camp," the soldier said.

"By who?"

"Jovita."

"Why is Jovita giving orders? Did something happen to Casimir?" Em demanded.

"He . . ." The soldier stared hard at Em, like he was desperately trying to avoid Olivia's wild gaze. "He went mad after the death of his parents and what you did to him. Jovita is filling in for him."

Em reeled back. Cas didn't go mad. Not the boy who had the presence of mind to escape the Lera castle unscathed. Not the boy who had managed to slip out of the warriors' wagon and make his way to the jungle alone. She didn't believe that he'd broken after surviving all that.

"And who told you that? Jovita?"

"And the advisers." The soldier sounded defensive suddenly.

"And where is your supposedly mad king now?"

"Jovita locked him up for his own protection."

Em pressed her hands to her forehead. With Jovita in charge, the Ruined were no longer safe. The pact she'd made with Cas meant nothing.

She looked over her shoulder at the bodies. "Is she out there? Did Jovita come with you?"

"She helped us into Ruina, but then she turned back. She's returned to Lera by now."

"How brave," Olivia said dryly.

"Is Cas at the fortress?" Em asked.

The soldier hesitated, licking his lips.

"You probably need both legs to run, right?" Olivia said,

pointing at them. "So you wouldn't like it if I ripped one off right now?"

"Yes," the soldier said quickly. "He's at the fortress."

"Good." Em gestured at her sister, and Olivia stepped closer. Em leaned in, whispering in her ear. "Kill him. Quickly."

Olivia whirled around, waving her finger in a circle. The soldier's neck snapped. His body crumpled to the ground. Iria jumped.

Olivia gave Em an approving expression. "I thought you were going to let him go."

"I was, but I couldn't let Jovita know he'd told me all that. She'd expect our next move."

"What's that?"

Em hooked her sword to her belt. "I'm going to find Jovita. And kill her."

ELEVEN

AREN COULD SENSE humans still in the area.

He could feel their heartbeats pulsing through his body. There was one down the hill who wasn't quite dead yet, and his slow, unsteady heartbeat was like a drum thumping in the night.

Em, Olivia, and Iria were walking back his way, deep in conversation. Couldn't Olivia hear that heartbeat?

"We've already been to the fortress," Iria was saying. "You can't storm back in without a plan."

"We'll make a plan," Olivia said.

"We're not going straight to the fortress," Em said. "We invade Vallos. The warriors have conquered the land north of the fortress. We'll take the south, and Jovita will be trapped. We'll force her out."

Olivia jumped excitedly. "Perfect. When do we leave?"

"You need reinforcements," Iria said. "Let August send word to Olso that we need more warriors."

Aren blinked at the dead bodies in front of them. Did they need more warriors? He and Olivia had killed all these people, with minimal help from the other Ruined.

"We would appreciate that," Em said. "But I won't wait for them to get here. They can meet us in Vallos."

"I'm not sure that's the best . . ." Iria's words faded away as Aren started down the hill. Someone called his name. He ignored them.

He almost tripped over something, and a swell of panic rose in his body when he realized it was a head.

A torch on the ground was still lit, casting a glow over the carnage in the immediate area. He should turn back. He didn't want to see.

But the *thump-thump* wouldn't stop calling to him. It was louder than the voices calling to him, louder than the strong heartbeats of the warriors.

He stopped next to the man. Aren stared into his face because he couldn't force himself to look at his mangled body.

Had he injured this one? He didn't know. It had been too dark to see their faces. There were too many of them.

The man moaned. Aren wasn't sure he was exactly conscious. Maybe. Maybe he was in pain.

The numbness left his body in a rush. He wanted it back as soon as it was gone. The boulder that had settled into his chest was almost too much to bear. Tears pricked his eyes.

Why was he crying? He didn't cry for Lera soldiers who had just attacked him.

Solia, take his soul into your care and forgive him any—

The prayer crossed his mind unbidden, and he cut it off before he could finish. He didn't pray for humans. He should have cursed his soul, not asked the ancestors to care for it.

He couldn't bring himself to do it.

He snapped the man's neck. The force of using his magic echoed through his body, and his shoulders slumped forward. It was the only kill tonight that had taken anything out of him. Olivia's instruction was perfect.

Something touched his shoulder, and he whirled around, grabbing the offending hand. He was breathing hard—*why?*—and Iria jumped, trying to pull her hand away. He didn't let go.

He could see her fear. He was usually perfectly happy to terrify people, but he didn't like it from her. This girl who had risked her life to join him in the Lera castle, who had helped him in the jungle, she shouldn't have been scared of him.

She pulled at her hand again and he released her. "Are you all right?" she asked.

"I was making sure everyone was dead." His voice sounded calmer than he felt. "No surprises."

She nodded, but her eyebrows crinkled together as she studied him. She could tell something was wrong. He quickly turned away.

"Aren! Come on!" Olivia yelled from behind him.

"I'll be there in a minute!" he called without turning around. He stepped over a body.

A hand wrapped around his arm, pulling him to a stop. "I'm pretty sure they're all dead, Aren. Come on." Iria's voice was soft, gentle, and he glanced over his shoulder at her. The flash of fear he'd seen was gone, replaced by something else. Understanding, maybe. Did she understand? He hadn't said anything.

"I'm sorry you had to do this," she said. Her fingers slid down to his hand and he jerked away. She pulled her arms into her chest, and he was tempted to grab her hand again and tell her he didn't mind, he just hadn't been expecting it.

"Do Ruined say a prayer after killing in battle?" she asked.

"Some do. I don't really pray anymore."

He forgot sometimes that she'd known his mother, the castle priest. She'd known the younger, happier Aren who prayed and believed his life would be happy.

The smell of blood around him was suddenly too much. He turned on his heel, grabbing Iria's hand and pulling her with him, away from the bodies. He dropped her hand as they reached the top of the hill, where Em and Olivia were standing with the Ruined council. Olivia frowned at him, and he quickly walked away from Iria and joined their circle. Mariana and Davi were leaning against each other in exhaustion, and Jacobo was on the ground, his hands pressed into the grass. Elemental Ruined claimed that connecting with the land after using their powers restored them. Only Ivanna appeared unruffled from the battle.

"It's a good idea," Ivanna was saying to Em. "We can't sit here and wait to be attacked anymore. If the warriors go with us, we shouldn't have a problem invading a smaller Vallos town."

"We don't need the warriors," Olivia snapped.

"Yes, we do," Ivanna said. "Emelina is right. She killed the Vallos princess; their people may very well attack us after we invade. And she's smart to consider a marriage alliance with August. We—"

"I'm sorry, what?" Aren asked.

"I was telling them about a conversation I just had with August," Em said. "August was sent here to marry the Ruined queen. It could be a smart move for us."

Aren winced, and Em lifted one shoulder, like she'd resigned herself to the idea. First the prince of Lera, now the prince of Olso. Aren didn't envy Em's suitors.

"We're not *seriously* considering this," Olivia said. "Ruined do not partner with humans."

"Things are different now. We can't keep isolating ourselves," Davi said.

"And what will partnering with them get us? More of this?" Olivia swept her arm in the direction of the Lera soldiers.

"The warriors helped us, Liv," Em said quietly.

Olivia shot her a furious look. "This time."

No one responded to that. Olivia turned away. "Don't come crying to me when they try to murder us in our sleep," she muttered as she left.

"I'll convince her," Em said as soon as Olivia was out of earshot.

"Can we trust you to take charge of this?" Ivanna asked.

Em nodded. "Of course. Prepare the Ruined to leave first thing tomorrow. I'll make sure the warriors are on board. I'm sure it will require a tentative yes to August's proposal."

"And you're fine with that?" Mariana asked.

Em hesitated for half a second, short enough that no one but Aren would notice. "Yes."

"Good," Ivanna said approvingly. "We'll follow your lead, then."

TWELVE

"I MEANT IT about force-feeding you."

Cas didn't have the energy to roll over and face Galo. He pulled his knees closer to his chest and sank deeper into his mattress. His bad shoulder was stiff from days in bed, and he winced as he shifted.

The room had been dark, but light filled the space as Galo lit the lantern. Cas squinted in the sudden brightness.

Footsteps sounded against the wooden floor, and Galo was in front of him suddenly. His anger melted into concern. He pressed the backs of his fingers to Cas's forehead.

"You're burning up," Galo said.

"I'm cold."

Galo disappeared from the room. He returned a few moments

later with two women in tow. Cas squinted up at them. Violet and Daniela.

"Is Jovita back yet?" Cas mumbled. His head was full of cotton. "What happened?"

"She's back; the soldiers are not. She only went to the border." Galo pushed Cas's shoulder, making him roll over on his back. He placed a cool rag on Cas's forehead.

Daniela unbuttoned his shirt, and he frowned down at her hands. "I'm going to rub some medicine on you, Your Majesty. It should make you feel better."

"Is anyone else sick?" Galo asked.

Daniela shook her head as she slathered a cool ointment on Cas's chest. "Not that I've heard."

Galo looked from Cas to the half-eaten breakfast tray next to the bed.

"I ate some," Cas murmured. "Are you happy now?"

Galo didn't respond as he strode over to the tray. "Who makes his meals?"

"Blanca," Violet said. "The chef."

"Go get her for me."

Violet ran out of the room and came back only moments later. Blanca was with her. Both of them looked worried.

Blanca rushed over to his dinner tray and Galo followed her. They began whispering.

"I didn't prepare that soup," Blanca said, her voice rising a little.

"The soup is the best part," Cas said, his eyes fluttering shut.

He wondered who prepared the soup. Maybe they should take over in the kitchen.

"Who takes the tray to him?" Galo's voice was tight.

"There's a soldier. He shows up to the kitchen at every mealtime. George."

"Mateo!" Galo yelled. His boots pounded against the wood. He said something Cas couldn't hear.

"Have you had that soup often, Your Majesty?" Violet asked.

"A few times recently," he mumbled.

A flurry of movement happened around him, and he hoped they were all leaving. He needed some sleep.

"Cas!" Galo's voice startled him from his sleep. He was on the floor. When had he moved onto the floor?

"Open his mouth," someone said.

He was propped up against someone, and fingers roughly opened his mouth. Violet stuck something down his throat and he gagged, trying to push away from her.

"Stay still." It was Galo behind him, keeping both of Cas's arms at his side.

He obeyed, simply because he was too weak to fight. He blinked a few times, trying to focus on the room around him. They were putting a tube down his throat.

Strange. He didn't want a tube down his throat.

His stomach lurched suddenly. He thrashed against Galo as the contents of his stomach exited through the tube. The guard held him steady like it was nothing. Where had his strength gone?

The tube disappeared after several long moments. He

swallowed. His throat burned.

"Drink," Violet said, tilting his chin up. Cool water hit his lips. He winced as it went down.

Several pairs of hands lifted him off the floor and deposited him on the bed.

"Find out what that soldier gave Cas and then toss him out of the fortress," Galo said fiercely. "Let the Ruined and the warriors have him."

"It's doubtful he acted alone," Violet said quietly. "He may have had orders . . ."

"From Jovita," Galo finished. "I don't care. Toss him out. Tell Mateo to get horses and a wagon ready. We're getting him out of here."

There was a flurry of movement around Cas, and he curled up on the bed and let his head sink into the pillow.

Then, suddenly, he was out of his room. How did he get out of his room?

He jerked his head up, surprised to find that he was on his feet. Sort of. Arms on either side of him were holding him up.

"What are you doing?" he mumbled. Someone shushed him.

He squinted at the figure next to him, the one who had a tight arm around his waist. Galo. He swung his head to his other side. Mateo. Violet was in front of them, peering around the corner.

"Go," she whispered.

The guards nudged him forward, and he attempted to walk. It didn't work.

They were at the stairs, the fortress quiet and deserted around them. Odd. He wondered where everyone had gone.

Galo and Mateo pulled him down the stairs. Daniela waited at the bottom, holding a door open for them.

"All clear," she whispered. She squeezed Cas's arm as he passed.

They were in the kitchen, then outside. It was night. Wind whipped across his face, and he looked down at his clothes. Someone had put him in a thick guard's jacket. That was thoughtful.

"Where are the horses, Mateo?" Galo asked.

"Straight ahead. We're almost there."

"Hey!" The yell made Galo and Mateo both tense. Footsteps ran toward them.

Violet had a sword. Cas hadn't noticed it, but it was in her hand, and she lunged at a man in a guard uniform. Mateo disappeared from Cas's side and Galo gripped him tighter.

Violet's sword nicked the man's arm and he staggered backward. Mateo punched him across the jaw.

Mateo darted back to Cas's side. "Hurry."

They began running, Cas's feet dragging on the ground. He wanted to run, but he was too weak. He was barely able to stay upright.

What happened to him?

Memories of soup and a tube being shoved down his throat flooded his thoughts. Had someone poisoned him?

They stopped suddenly, and Galo and Mateo heaved him into a wagon. He knew this wagon. He didn't like this wagon.

"It's all right." Violet had him under the arms, pulling him farther in. Mateo and Galo had disappeared.

In the distance, he heard yelling. He squinted, but the back of the wagon was closed. They lurched forward suddenly.

"Here." Violet put something soft under his head. "Don't worry, you're going to be fine."

His eyelids drooped against his will. "Did Jovita poison me?" he mumbled.

"We think so. We think she ordered a guard to do it."

She hated him that much? They were the only family either of them had left, and she despised him enough to murder him?

"You'll be safe now," Violet said, brushing his hair back. "I promise."

That was not a promise she could keep, but his eyes fluttered shut and he drifted off anyway.

THIRTEEN

EM ORDERED THE bodies of the Lera soldiers burned. Smoke still hung in the air as the Ruined and warriors packed their belongings and headed east to Vallos.

August asked her to wait. He sent a warrior back to Olso immediately, and he claimed warrior reinforcements would be there in less than two weeks.

She couldn't wait two weeks. She refused to sit around and wait for Jovita to attack them again. Protecting the remaining Ruined was more important than rebuilding Ruina.

The miner cabins weren't far from the Vallos border, but since they didn't have enough horses for everyone, most had to go on foot. It took two days to reach the border. The journey wasn't the same as when Em and Aren had made it months before.

Back then, they were almost killed by hunters three times as they neared Vallos.

There were no hunters now. A line of rocks marked the Vallos border, and there was no one to guard it. Vallos had always been the easiest country to cross into, but it was laughable this time.

Olivia and Aren led the pack, both of them perched on top of horses. Just over the Vallos border was a small town called Sacred Rock, which Em had decided was the most logical choice to settle down and figure out their next move. It was sparsely populated, accessible by only two main roads, and close enough to the fortress to easily launch an attack.

Sacred Rock was only a few hours by horse from Fort Victorra. A few hours from Cas. She could have turned her horse north and reached him by nightfall.

The air grew a little warmer as they rode, the land around them greener. The soil in Vallos was much more fertile than in Ruina, and Em spotted long rows of crops in the distance.

"Em," August said, pulling her out of her thoughts.

She turned to him. He hadn't said much on the journey from Ruina, and she wondered if he was angry that she'd refused to wait for warrior reinforcements.

"I'm sorry you had to leave your home again," he said.

She frowned, confused. "What?"

"You'd just gotten home and you had to leave again because of all of this." He waved his hand back at the Ruined and warriors trailing behind them. "I'm sorry about that. I know you were happy to be home."

"Oh. Uh, thanks."

He let out an embarrassed laugh. "That wasn't very good, was it? I've been trying to think up ways to strike up conversation with you."

"It could have been worse, I guess."

He grinned, showing off straight white teeth. "Thank you. I feel so much better."

Her lips twitched, but she resisted smiling at him. She still hadn't decided if she was glad for the opportunity to permanently align herself with Olso, or if she deeply resented possibly marrying this man.

"Can I say something else?" he asked.

"Why not."

"I'm glad that you're one of the queens." His voice was low, only for her. "I was sent thinking Olivia had taken the throne again. And I don't mean this as an insult to Olivia. I'm just really glad you're here too."

"Why? Because I don't have powers? You don't have to worry about me taking off your head while you sleep?"

His shoulders shook with laughter. "That is not what I meant."

"Sure it wasn't."

"It wasn't! I was being nice! We were having a moment!"

"We were not having a moment."

He let out a exaggerated sigh. "Fine. *I* was having a moment, then. I was trying to say that I like you. I'm intrigued by you. I respect you. It has nothing to do with powers."

"Would you stop? I already told you I'd think about marrying you."

August held one hand up in surrender. "See if I tell you how much I like you again."

"What a loss," she said dryly. She eyed him suspiciously. "You barely know me. You don't like me."

"I like what I've seen so far."

"What you've seen so far is a marriage alliance that will make you more than 'the least-important heir,' as my sister so delicately put it."

He shrugged. "Of course. That doesn't mean I can't like you as well."

Olivia pulled her horse to a stop, looking over her shoulder at Em. She pointed ahead of them.

The western road led straight into the heart of the town, and Em's stomach clenched as she followed her sister's finger to the sign announcing they were about to enter Sacred Rock. She'd never invaded a town before.

Olivia turned her horse so she was facing the crowd. "Ruined, team one! We're going in! All other teams follow behind! Orders are to kill."

"Liv," Em said quietly. "If some of them run, let them go."

Olivia paused for a moment in thought. "If you want. I don't see the fun in that."

A swell of laughter rose from the Ruined. This didn't seem like the time to be laughing.

Olivia kicked her heels into her horse and took off. Dust flew into the air as several Ruined followed. Team one was the most powerful Ruined, those who could take out half the town before the rest of them even got there.

Screams ripped through the air as the Ruined charged down the dirt road. Em urged her horse forward, August suddenly at her side.

She rounded a corner, the center of town coming into view. Two- and three-story buildings dotted either side of the street. There were only about fifteen or twenty buildings total, with a few homes in the surrounding area. The main road was dusty and brown, but all around was lush green grass and fenced-in areas that were probably community gardens.

Townspeople began streaming out of their homes and shops onto the road. A few of them caught sight of the Ruined and immediately turned and bolted in the opposite direction. Olivia watched them go. She glanced over her shoulder at Em, lifting one eyebrow like "are you satisfied?" Em nodded in approval.

"Everybody leaves!" Olivia yelled, dismounting her horse. She decapitated a man rushing at her with a flick of her hand. "You leave, or you die. Your choice." She pointed up to where a few people watched from the windows. "You hide, you die." The faces quickly disappeared. People ran out of the building a moment later.

Two women ran north, straight into a wall of warriors. Iria shook her head, pointing the other direction.

"Everyone goes south!" Olivia yelled. "There are two roads out of town. You take the south one, or you die!"

Em jerked her head to the woods to the east. "I'm going to check out that area."

"I'll join you," August said.

Em kicked her horse, dodging panicking townspeople in the streets. She tried not to think about where they would go. She'd been kicked out of her home before, sent out into the night shivering with no food or hope.

It was better than death, at least.

They rode to the east edge of town, where the trees stretched out around a thin path. Em knew the path well. She'd taken it herself. It was the most discreet way to travel in the area.

"Em," August said under his breath.

She followed his gaze to find a wagon not far ahead. The horses were unmanned. She leaned to the side to see a man hunched over a wheel stuck in the mud. His jacket was Lera blue.

She slid off her horse, pulling her sword from her hip. August did the same.

She carefully stepped over a log, her boots silent as they hit the ground.

"I think if we dig it out on this side—" Another guard, a young man with dark curly hair, appeared around the wagon, coming to a sudden stop when he spotted Em. "Galo," he whispered, put his hand on Galo's shoulder.

The guard on the ground jumped to his feet, his sword drawn. Em's gasped. It was Cas's best friend.

"Emelina?" Galo said in utter disbelief.

"You know them?" August asked.

She nodded, searching the area past the wagon. Was Cas nearby?

"What are you doing here?" Galo asked. "Was that commotion you?"

The wagon behind him had several pieces of wood pried away to allow air in, and Em caught movement. She stepped forward, pointing her sword to it. "What's in there?" She didn't wait for a response. She strode forward and flung the doors open.

A sword was pointed directly at her chest.

Em took a tiny step back, surveying the young woman in front of her. The sword shook, her dark eyes shining like she was about to cry. Not the most intimidating woman Em had ever met.

"Emelina?" she asked in a shaking voice. "As in Emelina Flores?"

"It's fine, Violet," Galo said from behind Em. "She won't hurt him."

Violet's forehead creased in confusion, but she slowly lowered the blade.

Em's heart had taken up residence in her throat. *She won't hurt him*, Galo had said. Who was "him"?

Violet stepped aside and Em let out a choked gasp. Cas.

He was curled up on the floor of the wagon, his head on a bundle of blankets. He was shivering, his face pale.

"What's wrong with him?" Em jumped into the wagon, falling to her knees beside him. She grasped his hand. It was too warm.

"He was poisoned," Galo said. "We think Jovita did it."

Em fought back the urge to scream in frustration. She should have killed that girl when she had the chance. She should have let Olivia rip Jovita's limbs from her body.

"We think she gave him a few doses before we realized," Galo continued. "We got him out of there are soon as we could."

"What kind of poison?" she asked. "Do you know?"

"Deadrose. That's what the guard claimed after we beat it out of him, anyway."

"That would make sense," she said, pressing her hand to his forehead. "He goes in and out of consciousness?"

"Yes," Galo said.

"My mother was poisoned with Deadrose once. Did you pump his stomach?"

"Yes. But we think he ingested some over a few days."

She swallowed down a wave of panic. That wasn't good. Deadrose worked slowly, but it worked well.

"We need to flush it out of his system." She grabbed his shoulders. "Galo, get his legs. We need to find a bed for him to rest."

"We can't stop here. Jovita will realize he's gone and—"

Em cut off Galo with a sharp look. "If you don't let him rest and flush out the poison, he'll die."

Galo snapped his mouth shut. He climbed into the wagon to grab Cas. "Mateo?" he called.

"I'm coming." The other guard climbed into the wagon to help.

"You." Em pointed at the young woman. "What was your name?"

"Violet."

"Do you know the Wild Hess herb, Violet?"

"Its leaves are kind of pink, right?"

"Yes. Find as much as you can and grind it up into a powder. Then bring it to me."

Violet hesitated, looking at Galo for confirmation. He nodded.

She lifted Cas's shoulders and Galo and Mateo grabbed his legs. They eased him out of the wagon.

"Um, Em? Is this who I think it is?" August asked. She'd completely forgotten he was there. She took a quick glance over her shoulder to make sure warriors hadn't followed August. He was still alone. If he made a move to kill Cas, she and Galo and Mateo could easily stop him.

"Yes," she said.

"And you're going to save him?" he asked incredulously. Em shot him a look so full of venom he immediately stepped back and raised his hands in surrender.

She swallowed and tried to put a more polite expression on her face. The Ruined still needed August and his warriors. But she couldn't just let Cas die. Especially not when it meant Jovita inheriting the throne and sending more soldiers to attack them.

"Who is that?" Galo asked as they began walking.

"You don't want to know."

"I think we *really* want to know," Mateo said.

"August. Youngest prince of Olso."

Galo and Mateo exchanged a look but said nothing.

"Em," Cas mumbled, his eyelids fluttering.

"I think he's coming around," Em said hopefully. She walked a little faster.

Galo shook his head. "He says your name in his sleep all the time."

The words were like a knife through her chest, and she curled her fingers around Cas's shoulders a little tighter. She probably said his name in her sleep too. He was there, in her dreams, all the time.

Em ignored the curious stares as they hauled Cas to one of the homes beyond the center of town. She kicked the door open and took a quick look around. It was a small home, with a sitting area to her left, a dining room to the right, and a kitchen behind her. Stairs led up to what must have been the bedrooms.

"I'm going to go make sure everyone has cleared out." She carefully lowered Cas onto the couch. "One of you find some clean water. Lots of it."

Mateo ran out of the house, passing Violet on the way. August stood on the street, staring at them with a flabbergasted expression. She shut the door.

"Don't let anyone but Mateo in. Lock the door when he's back." Galo and Violet nodded.

She sprinted up the stairs. She found two bedrooms, and picked the larger of the two. The bed was unmade, the sheets and comforter tangled at the end of the mattress.

There were fresh linens in a chest and she quickly replaced the old ones. She called down to Galo and Violet to bring Cas up.

They appeared a few moments later and carefully lowered

Cas onto the bed. She climbed onto the mattress behind him, lifting his shoulders to peel off his jacket. He moaned in protest.

"It's all right," she whispered in his ear. She pulled the blankets up to cover him, easing him back so he was lying against her chest. She wrapped her arms around him, pressing her cheek to his hair. "You'll be fine."

FOURTEEN

SOMETHING HAD DIED in Cas's mouth. And it had pounded on his head a few times before taking leave.

He swallowed, moaning as he shifted against something warm and solid. He was leaning against someone.

"Here," a voice said. A cup appeared in front of him. "Drink."

He frowned at the cup suspiciously.

"It's just water."

The voice sounded like Em's. Was he dreaming again? Her voice kept floating in and out of his dreams. It was so vivid he'd swear she was next to him.

He took the cup with a shaky hand and tipped some water into his mouth. Someone took the cup away when he was finished.

He turned, tilting his head up to see whose body he was snuggled up against.

Em.

He reeled back, blinking several times. He was definitely still dreaming. Or he'd died. Was this what waited for him after death? Waking up in Em's arms?

She smiled. "Hi."

"What are you . . ." His voice sounded strange.

"Galo and your friends were bringing you through Vallos to get you away from Jovita. Happened to run into me."

"What are you doing in Vallos?" He was still half sure he was hallucinating.

"Retaliating. It's a long story."

A wave of dizziness crashed over him and he let his head sink into her chest.

"Am I dying?" he mumbled.

She ran her fingers through his hair. "Absolutely not. I gave you something to help neutralize the poison. It was a rough day, but you're doing much better."

"How long have I been here?"

"Since this morning. The sun just set."

"Are Galo and Mateo all right? And Violet?"

"They're fine." She had one arm around his waist, and he found her hand, lacing their fingers together and pulling her arm in tighter.

"I can't believe you're here," he mumbled. "You're here and I'm too sick to enjoy it. And I smell."

Her chest shook with laughter. "You smell wonderful."

"No I don't."

"No, you don't." Her lips brushed across his forehead. "But I don't care. And I don't smell so great myself. I've been traveling for days. So we're even."

"How considerate," Cas said. His body wanted to whisk him back to sleep, but he forced his eyes open. He didn't want to leave Em yet. "Jovita poisoned me."

"I heard." Her voice had turned to ice.

"My cousin tried to kill me. She convinced everyone I was insane and pretty much took the throne. Now that I'm gone she's probably officially taken it."

"She'll pay for it."

"What kind of king lets his cousin steal the throne right out from under him?"

"The kind who would never dream of doing that to his cousin."

"The weak kind."

"Her reign will be short," Em said.

His eyelids fluttered shut again. He tried to open them and only half succeeded.

"Sleep," Em said in his ear. "You need the rest. I'll still be here when you wake up."

He squeezed her hand tighter. He let his head sink into her chest and gave in to sleep.

Aren tapped his fingers on the table, his gaze fixed firmly on Galo. The guard caught him staring for the hundredth time and made an annoyed sound.

"Would you stop staring?"

"Can't help it," Aren said. "I don't trust you."

"The feeling's mutual."

"Em ordered that none of you were to be harmed. We'll obey."

Galo and Mateo didn't seem convinced.

"So." Aren leaned forward, propping his chin up on his hand. "Did Cas make you the captain of his guard?"

"Yes," Galo said.

"Not doing such a great job there, friend. He's been stabbed, captured, and poisoned recently. I think he might want to consider a change of staff."

Galo's jaw twitched. "Whose fault is that?"

Aren pointed a finger at himself, pretending to be baffled. "Me?"

"I knew there was something weird about you from the moment you stepped foot in the castle."

"Yet you never figured it out," Aren said smugly. Galo looked like he was considering the best way to murder him.

Across the room, Violet stirred on the couch. She rubbed a hand across her eyes and sat up, blinking at the dark windows. "Was I asleep a long time?"

"A couple of hours," Galo said.

"Is Emelina still up there with him?"

"Yes," Aren said.

"She's been up there all day. Should I offer to take over again?"

"Don't bother," Aren said. "She's not leaving his side."

Violet stood and walked to them, sliding into the chair next to Galo. She was trying not to stare at the burns on Aren's arms and failing. Aren knew the expression well. He placed his palms flat on the table so she could get a good look.

"She actually cares for him?" Violet asked, her tone full of surprise.

"She's not up there saving his life because she hates him," Aren said dryly.

"Yes, she cares about him," Galo said. "And the feeling's mutual."

"He's more forgiving than I would be," Mateo muttered.

Aren glared at him. "And she's more forgiving than I would be."

"What does Cas have to be sorry for?" Mateo asked.

"Sitting back and letting his people murder us? His father killing her mother? Kidnapping her sister and experimenting on her for a year?"

"Cas did none of that himself," Violet said.

"Staying silent in the face of horrible atrocities is just as bad as actually committing them," Aren said.

"I don't know if I agree with that," Mateo said.

Aren opened his mouth to shoot out a reply, but Galo got there first. "Cas would agree with you," he said to Aren.

"Really."

"Yes." He didn't elaborate.

"Have you checked on him recently?" Violet asked after a brief silence. "Is he doing all right?"

"I went up not long ago. Em said he woke up for a few minutes and was actually lucid."

"Good." Violet pushed her chair back. "Can I sleep on that sofa tonight?" She looked at Aren.

"Do you mean will I rip off a few of your limbs while you sleep? Probably not. Give it a shot and see what happens."

"Aren." Violet said his name almost wearily. He hadn't realized she'd learned it. "I'm exhausted and I've spent the last few days taking care of our sick king and sneaking him out of a heavily guarded fortress. Can I sleep on that couch or not?"

He recognized her exhaustion. The kind that came with being on the run and losing everything.

"You can sleep there," he said quietly.

"Thanks." She shuffled back to it and plopped down.

Aren motioned to the stairs. "You guys go up and take the second bedroom. I'll be down here all night. No one's getting to Cas with Em around."

He'd thought the guards would put up a fight, but Galo stood and extended his hand to Mateo. "Feel free to wake me if Cas needs anything," he said.

"I will."

Their footsteps disappeared upstairs, followed by the quiet sound of a door closing. Aren sat back in his chair, running a hand down his face.

"She's your queen now? Emelina?" Violet asked. She was stretched out on the couch, her face turned to him. She'd tucked her hands beneath her face.

"She's one of them," he said.

Aren watched as Violet curled her legs into her chest. He'd started a fire, but the room was still chilly.

He let out a long sigh as he got to his feet. He grabbed a blanket off a chair and tossed it over her. She stirred, pulling it up to her chin.

"Thank you."

"Sure. I was . . . uh, I was being a jerk earlier. I wouldn't actually hurt you."

"I appreciate that."

He turned to find Iria standing in front of the open door, an odd expression on her face. She tilted her head, looking from Violet to Aren.

"No warriors," he said, striding to the door. "Sorry. Em was clear. No warriors in the house."

"I came to see if you needed anything."

"We're fine."

She lifted her chin to look into his eyes. She always did that. She stared into his eyes with such intensity it made the hairs on the back of his neck stand straight up.

He wished she would stop. It was easy to ignore how pretty Iria was when she was across the room or surrounded by warriors. But when she stood in front of him and stared at him like that he lost control of his senses.

He rubbed the back of his neck and turned his attention

to the floor. "Is there something else?" The question came out harsher than he'd intended.

She took a step back. "Sorry. No. I'll see you tomorrow."

He shut the door behind her, turning at the sound of Violet's laughter. "What?"

"You really are a jerk." She rolled over so she was facing away from him. "Some girls like that, I guess."

FIFTEEN

EM OPENED HER eyes to find Cas smiling at her.

She drew in a quick breath, bracing her hand against the mattress as she sat up. Sunlight streamed in through the window, and voices drifted in from downstairs.

"How are you feeling?" she asked.

"Terrible." He smiled as he said it. "But better."

She pressed her hand to his forehead. No fever. It had broken late last night, and he had fallen into a deep sleep. She'd dozed off with her palm against his chest, to make sure it didn't stop moving.

Cas caught her hand as she pulled it away and brushed his lips across it. He tucked it close to his body. "Where am I?"

"Vallos. Half a day's ride south of the fortress. A small town called Sacred Rock."

"Why are you in Vallos? What happened to going back to Ruina?"

She tucked her legs beneath her and told him what Jovita had done. How they'd begun building a new life in Ruina when she attacked. She told him about August, and the warriors outside.

She left out the part about August wanting to marry her.

"I'm sorry, Em," he said softly when she was finished. "I tried to stop her. I tried to convince people that the Ruined would leave us alone if we stopped killing them."

"I know. And we were. I'd ordered everyone to stay in Ruina."

He cocked his head. "*You* ordered?"

"Oh. Yes. I'm, um, the queen, actually. One of them. Olivia suggested forming a diarchy."

Cas's lips slowly turned up. "Very impressive, Your Majesty."

She nudged his leg with her foot. "Stop it."

"Yes, Your Majesty." He laughed when she wrinkled her nose at him. "You can call me 'Former Majesty.' Has a nice ring to it, doesn't it?"

Em's smile faded. "You're still the king, Cas. You just need to show Jovita you can't be beaten."

"What do you think the warriors outside would have to say about that?"

She had no reply, because he was absolutely right. The warriors had no interest in returning Lera to Cas. Just persuading the warriors not to kill him had taken some doing.

"I think I'd like a bath," Cas said. "Is that possible?"

"Sure." She slid off the bed. "I doubt you're strong enough to do it yourself, though."

He lifted an eyebrow. "Was that an offer to help?"

Her face warmed. "That was an offer to get Galo."

He sat up slowly, bracing his hands against the mattress. "Yes. Please. I will definitely need the help."

"I'll get him." She walked to the door.

"Em."

She turned. Cas's face had grown serious.

"Am I safe here?" he asked. "Should we be worried about the Vallos army attacking? I can't imagine they've forgiven you for killing their princess."

"We should definitely be worried about the Vallos army attacking. But I have Ruined and warriors on watch. This is probably the safest place for you right now."

"Thank you, Em."

"Of course."

"Come back later?"

"Absolutely." She pulled the door open and walked into the hallway. The voices downstairs stopped as she descended, all heads turning to her. Aren sat at the kitchen table alone. Mateo, Galo, and Violet were in the living area.

Galo jumped to his feet. "Is he all right?"

"Much better. He wants a bath. Can you go, Galo?"

"Of course," he said. "Mateo, can you get us some water?"

The guard nodded, grabbing a bucket from the kitchen

before hurrying out of the house. Galo jogged up the stairs.

Em looked at Violet. The girl was about the same age as her, perhaps a couple years older. She'd gathered her dark hair into a loose bun, soft tendrils framing her pretty face.

"Violet, right? Are you guard or staff?"

Violet stood, crossing the room to stand in front of Em. "Neither. I'm the governor of the southern province of Lera. Recently."

"Recently as in after the warriors attacked the castle?"

"Yes." Tears filled her eyes and she quickly blinked them away.

"You and Cas knew each other before?"

"No. We met for the first time in the wagon. The one the warriors put us in—"

"I know the one," Em interrupted. "What's your opinion on the Ruined, Violet?"

The girl jerked her head at Aren. "Well, we've established he's a jerk."

Em let out a short, startled laugh. She tried to hide it by clearing her throat. Aren rolled his eyes, but his lips twitched.

"And you organized the raid on the Lera castle that killed my father," Violet continued, returning her gaze to Em. "So I'm not inclined to like either of the Ruined in this room."

The house went silent as Violet stared at Em.

"I'm sorry about that," Em said quietly. Wariness colored Violet's features. "But I meant your opinion on the Ruined as a whole."

"I judge the Ruined like I judge everyone else. Case-by-case basis."

Em almost smiled. It didn't matter if this girl didn't like her, as long as she didn't harbor hate for the Ruined. She was Cas's biggest ally, his best hope of regaining his throne. The southern province of Lera was the largest, and as far as Em knew, the warriors hadn't taken it yet.

"This house will be for the four of you," Em said. "No one but you, Cas, Galo, and Mateo may come in unless you say it's all right. I've ordered that none of you are to be harmed. If you feel like someone is disobeying that order, come see me directly."

"Fine," Violet said.

"I will also order everyone not to speak a word about your presence. You'll be safe here, for the time being." Em walked to the front door and gestured at Aren. "Let's go." She stepped outside. Aren followed her, pulling the door closed behind them.

"Do we leave it unguarded?" he asked.

"For now. I'll be back in the evening." She scanned the area. The road in front of them led directly into the center of town, and warriors and Ruined walked by, laughter floating into the air.

"Olivia got the two of you an apartment next to the courthouse. I found a small place above the bakery," Aren said. "And Olivia wants to talk to you."

"I'll bet she does." Em rubbed her thumb across her necklace. "I need to talk to August first."

"That should be interesting," Aren said with a snort. He stepped off the porch.

"Aren."

He turned back to her, squinting in the sunlight.

"Do I have your support here? Letting them stay?"

"I guarded them all night, didn't I?"

"That's not what I meant. I know you'll do what I ask. I want to know if you think it's a stupid decision. If you'll back me up with the Ruined."

"Of course I'll back you up with the Ruined," he said. "I don't think it's a stupid decision. I think the reasoning behind it is stupid."

She looked at him curiously.

"You're letting Cas stay because you care about him. Because you're trying to hold on to a relationship that doesn't have a chance of working out. You'll have to let him go eventually, Em."

He was right, but she couldn't help the relief she felt at seeing Cas again. Like maybe these few days she'd get with him were a gift.

"But if it were me, I would keep them too," Aren continued. "You have the king of Lera in there, and the governor of the largest province. I certainly wouldn't let them go on their merry way. But that's not why you're letting them stay." He rubbed his fingers across his forehead. "I'm exhausted. I'm going to find a place to sleep."

"Thank you, Aren."

"Explain it like that, all right? The way I did? Don't bring your feelings into it."

"I won't."

"Try to get rid of those feelings, Em. You may care about him, but he's nothing compared to you. You're our queen and our savior. You'll be the best leader the Ruined have ever known. He's just a boy."

Aren's words reverberated through her body. They were spoken calmly, kindly, but they still threw her off balance. She couldn't come up with a response.

He didn't wait for one. He turned on his heel and walked away.

He didn't need for her to tell him he was right.

SIXTEEN

OLIVIA TOOK IN a long breath through her nose. It did nothing to quiet the rage bubbling in her chest.

She watched as Em left the house at the edge of town with Aren. Olivia could burst into that house and kill everyone in less than ten seconds. No more Casimir. Problem solved.

Olivia curled her fingers around the hip of the statue of Boda. Statues of the ancestors were all over this town, but none as big as the three in front of the courthouse. They were much taller than her, with ridiculous expressions on their faces that were probably supposed to be peaceful. They just looked tired, in Olivia's opinion.

She scowled at the statues and took a step to the side. All these statues had done nothing to protect anyone. The people of Sacred Rock had still been run out of their homes. They should have spent their money on weapons.

Down the street, Aren walked away from Em. Despite his sour expression, he'd spent the night guarding those Lerans because Em told him to. If there were sides, Aren was definitely on Em's.

Were there sides?

She had not given Em the opportunity to be a queen just for her to take care of Lerans. The Ruined were never going to respect their queens if they made such stupid, weak decisions.

Em headed her way, slowing when she met Olivia's eyes. Her anger was on full display, it seemed.

"It's temporary," Em said quickly as she stopped in front of Olivia. "He—"

"Inside," Olivia snapped. Ruined and warriors wandered all around them, carrying items they'd looted from shops. She wasn't having this conversation in front of an audience.

Em followed her into the apartment next to the courthouse. It was two stories, with two bedrooms upstairs and a kitchen and living area downstairs. There were bigger houses farther out, but Olivia liked the location of this one.

She slammed the door behind them and Em jumped.

"Casimir can *not* stay," Olivia said.

"Jovita poisoned him. He's not a threat. He's too weak to even walk on his own."

"Casimir is never a threat to me," Olivia scoffed. "I'm not worried about that. I'm wondering why we're nursing the king of Lera back to health."

"He promised to leave us alone. If he's king, we won't have to worry about being attacked anymore. It's in our best interests to put him back on the throne."

Olivia let out a hollow laugh. "Em, are you listening to yourself? You went to Lera to completely eliminate the Gallegos royal line. Now you want to let them continue like normal?"

"He's not like his father. He—"

"I don't care!" Olivia yelled. "I don't care if he hated his father! He is still one of the people who declared war on us. He murdered our parents. Our people. Maybe he didn't hold the sword, but he still bears part of the blame."

"I know he does," Em said quietly.

"So, what? You've just forgiven him?"

Em pressed her lips together, tears brimming in her eyes. "Yes."

Olivia blinked. The answer seemed obvious, but it was still shocking to hear out loud.

"I was angry for so long," Em said. "I thought that destroying Lera would make me feel better, but it didn't. The only thing that made me feel better was forgiving Cas."

"He doesn't deserve forgiveness. None of them do. And to offer it up is *weak*." She spat out the last word.

"I don't agree," Em said.

Olivia whirled around. She threw open the front door.

"Liv, you won't . . ." Em's voice trailed off.

"What?" Olivia shot her sister a venomous look over her shoulder. "Go kill them all right now?"

"Please don't."

She was tempted. It would certainly put a positive spin on the day. But Em's eyes were wide, pleading, and Olivia wasn't entirely sure her sister would ever forgive her for murdering Cas. That boy had made her blind.

"I won't hurt them," Olivia said. "If only because I want to say 'I told you so' when that boy betrays you."

She stomped out of the apartment, pulling the door shut so hard the building shook. A few Ruined turned and looked at her worriedly. Good. She should have had the fight with Em outside after all. Let the Ruined know that Olivia was not the weak one.

Across the street, Davi emerged from a bakery with a loaf of bread in his hand. He took a big bite and smiled. They had food, at least. And shelter. It was Em's idea, but without Olivia leading the Ruined they never could have taken the town.

She took a step back, looking up at the apartment that was her temporary home. It still wasn't good enough. Sacred Rock was a tiny town in *Vallos*, of all places. The worst of the four kingdoms, by almost every standard. It was better than the cabins, but it still wasn't enough. Not for the Ruined. Not for their queen.

She whirled around and strode into the town square. There was only one thing to do with this anger.

"Aren!" she yelled. "Aren!"

He came running. "What's wrong?"

"Nothing. I'm going hunting. You coming?"

"Hunting like . . ." His voice trailed off.

She didn't bother answering. He knew she wasn't hunting animals.

She stalked down the road, ignoring the curious stares from her fellow Ruined. The barn was up ahead to her left, and she breezed past Jacobo, who was leading a warrior's horse inside.

Aren jogged to catch up with her. "Did something happen? Why do we need to go hunting?"

"We shouldn't fool ourselves into thinking it's safe here. We need to check the surrounding area." Maybe that was true, but it wasn't why she wanted to go. If she couldn't pull Cas's spine out through his throat, then at least she could find someone else to kill.

"You're right," Aren said. "I'll come."

They took two horses from the barn. Olivia urged hers forward as they headed out of town, her hair blowing behind her.

She took the south road, the one she'd told the residents of Sacred Rock to take yesterday. There wasn't anyone just outside of town, unfortunately. She let the horse slow down as she scanned the area. Aren rode up beside her.

"Why did you stay with them last night?" she asked.

"Because Em asked me to."

"You could have said no."

"I guess I could have. I don't know. There's no use talking to Em where Cas is concerned. She never would have sent him away in that condition, so I didn't even try to fight her on it."

"It's stupid," Olivia spat. "We need to find someone else for her to obsess over."

"Well, August is giving it a go."

"She is not marrying a human." She glanced at Aren. "What about you? Any interest?"

"In Em? No. She's just a friend."

"So? Friends fall in love all the time."

"Maybe so, but that's not going to happen for me and Em."

Olivia ran a hand across her forehead. "Fine. I guess you'll be marrying me, then."

"What?"

"There aren't that many young Ruined men left," she said. "I told you before that you'd probably be marrying one of us."

"I know, but . . ." He looked nervous suddenly. "There's Jacobo. And Paulo!"

"Neither of them is as powerful as you."

He seemed at a loss for words. He must have known that was true.

"What? You don't want to be king?" she asked.

"No, it's not that, it's . . ." He swallowed, avoiding her eyes.

"I'm not marrying for love, Aren. I'm not my sister. I like you well enough, but I'm more concerned with your powers and your ability to lead the Ruined."

"You like me well enough, huh?" Aren said with a short laugh. "Terribly romantic, Liv."

She frowned at him. Romance was not the point. Aren was inarguably handsome, with those dimples and intense dark eyes, but she never cared much about looks. He was the best choice as her husband, regardless of his physical appearance.

"My marriage isn't a priority, so don't worry about it right now. It'll probably be a few years," she said.

Aren nodded wordlessly, his smile fading.

A flash of movement caught her attention, and she tugged her horse to a stop. Up ahead, on the right side of the road, someone had constructed a makeshift camp. Two poorly built tents sat in the dirt. They would fall over at the slightest gust of wind.

"There," she said, pointing.

Aren squinted. "I only see ten or so. They're probably just resting on the way to the next town."

"So?"

"I'm not—" He cut himself off, staring down at the reins in his hands.

"What?"

"I don't think we should hunt down people who are minding their own business. It feels too much like what the hunters did to us."

"Exactly. It's what they did to us. They deserve it."

"They're not hunters, Liv. They're people who left when we ordered them to. We're already worried the Vallos army might make an attempt to retake Sacred Rock."

"The Vallos army," Olivia scoffed. "When has the Vallos army been successful at anything?"

"We still shouldn't bait them. We might lose more Ruined if they attack."

"Please. They're no match for us. I can protect the Ruined."

She kicked her horse into motion. "You're weak, Aren!" she yelled over her shoulder.

He didn't follow her. She thought he might change his mind, but when she looked over her shoulder, he was frozen on top of his horse.

There were twelve humans total. A young boy spotted the Ruined marks on her neck and began screaming, and the rest of the group followed suit. She could have killed everyone quickly and stopped the noise, but she didn't.

She took her time. Her mother would have been proud.

When she turned around, Aren was gone. She could see him in the distance, riding back to the town. Not only had he refused to kill the humans, he'd run away when she did it. Pathetic.

She left one man alive, so he could tell his friends about her. She left him in the dust as she rode away.

Aren was nowhere to be seen when she returned to the barn. She guided the horse into her stall and gave her an approving pat. At least the horse could be relied on to do her job.

The eleven kills were still vibrating through her body as she walked through the center of town. If Em wasn't useless, she'd understand why forgiveness wasn't the best option. Rage was what had finally unleashed Olivia's full power. She was ten times the Ruined she'd been before Lera invaded. Every moment in that cell, surrounded by Weakling, had made her a better Ruined. Even the herb that was supposed to hurt her had made her stronger.

What was so wonderful about Casimir anyway? He was cute, sure, but Em had never been the type to swoon over handsome boys. If she had, she would have made a play for Aren years ago.

She looked down the road, to Casimir's house. One of the guards stood on the front porch, his hands on his hips. She saw the spark of fear when he spotted her. Good.

She stared him down as she walked to the house. The guard backed into the door, shielding it with his body. She stopped at the bottom of the steps.

"I want to talk to Casimir."

The guard pounded his hand on the door. "Galo!"

The door swung open to reveal another guard. Galo's eyes widened slightly as they rested on her.

"I want to talk to Casimir," she repeated.

Galo shook his head. "No."

"Are you the boss of him? Go ask him, at least."

"He's resting."

Olivia let out an annoyed sigh. She stepped back, cupping her hands around her mouth and tilting her chin up. "Casimir! It's Olivia! I want to come up and talk to you!" She paused, thinking for a moment. "I promise not to pull your beating heart out of your chest, if you're worried!"

"Hey," Galo said sharply.

Olivia dropped her hands from her mouth. "What?"

Galo glared at her. A girl appeared behind him and said something Olivia couldn't hear.

"What?" Galo said. "Seriously?"

The girl nodded.

Galo ran his hands down his face and returned his attention to Olivia. "He said you can come in."

"Wonderful." She skipped up the steps and through the open door. The girl quickly moved aside.

"I'm coming with you," Galo said. "No arguments."

"You couldn't protect him from me if you wanted to," she said, taking the steps two at a time. "But if it makes you feel better."

"If you hurt him, I swear I will—"

"Relax," she interrupted. "Em asked me not to, so I won't."

"It's there," Galo said through clenched teeth. He pointed to the door on the right.

She pushed it open without knocking. Casimir sat on the edge of the bed, his bare feet on the floor. He looked worse than the last time she'd seen him, which was really saying something, considering she'd murdered his mother at their last meeting.

She crossed her arms over her chest, fixing her gaze on him as she leaned against the wall. Galo hovered at the doorway, his fingers twitching around his sword.

"Hello," Casimir said hesitantly.

She put a finger to her lips. "Shhh. Be quiet for a minute."

Cas cast a nervous glance at Galo, but he nodded once and kept his mouth shut.

She stared at him. She didn't know what she was searching for, but she needed a moment to find whatever it was her sister saw in this boy.

Even sick, he was quite handsome. His dark hair was thick and slightly wavy. His eyes were more blue than green, but there was enough of a hint of the latter to make them mesmerizing. He had a nicely defined jaw and smooth skin that had recently been shaved.

He looked like his father. The eyes were different, but King Salomir was stamped so plainly into his features that it was hard for her to look at him without curling her lip.

"What do you think Em sees in you?" she asked, finally breaking the silence.

"What?"

"Why does she like you?"

"Umm . . ." He thought about it for a moment. "She told me once that I was kind. And thoughtful. And reasonable."

"Reasonable?" Olivia repeated incredulously. "Seriously?"

"Yes."

"How romantic."

"My father could not be reasoned with, so I consider it a compliment."

Olivia scowled.

"I'm sorry for what he did to you," Cas said. "For killing your mother. For taking you captive. For everything. I'm sorry I stood by as it happened."

"You can't be serious, Cas. You actually expect me to buy that apology?"

"What—what do you mean?"

"You're only apologizing to me so you can tell Em you did it.

So you can feel better about yourself." She took a step closer to him and heard Galo suck in a sharp breath. "I killed your mother. You hate me."

"No." He lifted his shoulders. "No. I know I should, but I don't."

She snorted. "Right."

"I'm not going to lie, it's hard to look at you. I don't think I'll ever look at you without seeing . . ." He swallowed hard. "But I understand your anger."

"You understand *nothing*."

"I don't expect you to forgive me. But I am sorry. And I want to do better."

"So, what? You forgive me? There's so much forgiveness flying around here today I can barely keep track."

"I thought it would be insulting for me to offer you my forgiveness," he said. "But if you want it, you certainly have it."

"I do not want it, and you should not be offering it." She leaned down so she was face-to-face with him. "Do you really think Em forgives you? Even if she says she does, she doesn't. There is no forgiveness for what you've done."

Cas held her gaze, but his throat moved as he swallowed. Fear radiated off of him. What she wouldn't give to snap a few of his bones.

"You know that saying, 'What goes around comes around'? It came around hard for you, didn't it? You've lost your kingdom and your parents and your health," she said.

"That hadn't escaped my attention," he said quietly.

"Good. And don't fool yourself into think you've forgiven me either. I ripped your mother's heart out and I'm not sorry. I'd do it again."

"They had it coming," Cas said, though not really to her. He appeared to be speaking more to himself than anyone.

"What?" she asked, startled. Perhaps she'd overestimated his love for his mother.

"Em said that to me once. Said she wasn't the least bit sorry about the people she'd killed. *They had it coming.*" He laughed softly. "I was sort of horrified and impressed at the same time."

Olivia took a step back, trying not to let her surprise show on her face. She'd been so obsessed with trying to figure out why Em liked Cas that she hadn't stopped to think why he liked her. There were a million things to love about Em, but the expression on his face when he talked about her was unexpected.

"Maybe it's not that I forgive you," he said. "But I don't have the strength to care. I lost everything, and I can't get it back by hating you."

"I don't feel sorry for you," she snapped. "And you haven't lost everything. You have my sister, who is bizarrely determined to return your kingdom to you. A kingdom you don't even *deserve*."

Cas turned his gaze to the ground. "You're right," he said softly. "I do still have Em."

"That's enough," Galo said. He reached out like he was going to touch her. "Let's go."

She stepped away from his grasp and glared at him. "I'm

going. I'm done here anyway." She shot a glare over her shoulder as she walked to the door, but Cas wasn't looking at her. His head was bent down to the floor. The image lingered in her mind as she ran down the stairs and out of the house.

SEVENTEEN

BY SUNSET, CAS was able to stand on his own again. He ignored Galo's protests and hobbled slowly downstairs. He was lightheaded when he reached the bottom, and he grabbed the guard's arm for a moment to steady himself.

The living room was bathed in orange light, and Violet was curled up on the couch, a book in her lap. A large bookshelf was next to the couch, and Cas wondered for the first time who this house belonged to. Would they ever get their books back?

Violet smiled at Cas. "You look good."

"I do not."

"Well, you don't look like you're about to die. It's an improvement."

"Thanks," he said with weak laugh. He let go of Galo and

shuffled toward the door. "I'm going to go sit on the porch for a while."

"That's not a good idea," Galo said.

"Em said we're allowed to be on the porch. I won't step off it. I need some fresh air." He felt cramped and awkward in a stranger's house, and he wanted to see at least a little of the town.

And he was hoping to see Em. He hated that he couldn't run out and find her. He had to wait for her to come to him, and he was worried she wouldn't. She had things to do—a kingdom to run, people to protect, wars to fight. He couldn't even help, and it made him feel pathetic.

"I'll be fine," he said as Galo tried to follow him to the door. "You can stare at me creepily through the windows, if it makes you feel better."

Galo grumbled something Cas couldn't understand, but he ignored his friend. Cas might not be the king much longer. He should get used to protecting himself.

He pulled open the door, a cool blast of air hitting his face. He took in a deep breath as he stepped out. He'd opened his window upstairs, but it had done little to ease the claustrophobia.

He slid to the ground and leaned against the wall, stretching his legs out in front of him. The house was on the edge of town, so he couldn't see much besides the outline of a few buildings. He could hear laughter coming from that direction.

Was Em over there? She hadn't come to see him after Olivia left, which made him think she didn't know her sister had visited. Or maybe she did know. Maybe she'd sent Olivia in the hopes that the two of them could actually get along. If so, that plan had failed spectacularly.

A tall figure appeared at the end of the road, moving away from the town, and hope bloomed in Cas's chest. The figure drew closer. It was a man. Aren.

Cas leaned against the house with a sigh. "Hi, Aren," he said.

Aren's head snapped to him. "Cas? Should you be out here?"

"We're allowed to be on the porch."

Aren walked closer, stopping at the bottom of the steps. "I know, but someone could still wander by and remove your head."

"I'll take my chances. Besides, Olivia didn't take my head off earlier when she was in my room, so I think I'm safe."

"Olivia was in your room?" Aren's tone was incredulous.

"Yes. She came and stared at me for a while. Then we talked. It was odd."

"Huh." Aren frowned at the dirt. "Huh."

"Have you seen Em?"

"Yeah, she's with some of the warriors. Hashing out a plan to—" He stopped suddenly, clearing his throat. "I'm sure she'll come and see you when she can."

Of course she would. Olivia was right. He did still have Em. He'd spent so much time thinking about what he'd lost that he'd forgotten about the most important person. Em stood by him, even when it didn't make any sense.

"You're making things harder for her, you know," Aren said. "Olivia's furious that you're here. The warriors want you dead, and most of the Ruined do too."

"I know. But where am I going to go? My kingdom is gone, my cousin is trying to take my throne, and my parents are dead. The only family I have left tried to murder me." He closed his eyes. Em's face appeared immediately, her lips turned up in a half smile. "Em decided not to murder me after she got to know me. That must count for something, right?"

Aren made a strange choking sound, and Cas opened his eyes to see him trying to suppress a laugh. He failed.

"I guess so," Aren said. "That sounds like her kind of logic, actually."

"We have a lot more in common these days."

"I guess you do," Aren said quietly.

"Besides, I think even if I left we'd find our way back to each other," Cas said. He lifted his head to look at the stars. "I've been thinking someone else might have a hand in that."

"What do you mean?"

"What were the odds of us finding each other in the jungle on the way to the fortress? It's a big jungle, but we still found each other. And now, in Vallos. If that wheel hadn't gotten stuck in the mud, Galo said we would have missed you all entirely. We'd be deep into Vallos by now." Cas straightened his legs, letting them fall in front of him. "My parents weren't believers, but it makes me think the ancestors really are out there, watching out for us."

"I don't know. . . ." Aren trailed off, shaking his head. "Things just happen sometimes. Coincidences."

"Maybe 'coincidence' is another word for fate." Cas smiled. "Just watch. If we get separated again, I bet we find each other."

"Ugh, gross. Could you not get that dopey look on your face, please?"

"What look?" Cas asked with a laugh.

Aren waved his hand in a circle. "This love look or whatever. I don't need to see that."

Cas had never said the word *love* to Em, but it didn't feel wrong in this moment. He grinned at Aren. "What? I can't be fond of my wife?"

"Come on. She is not your wife. You married the princess of Vallos, not Em."

He'd never married the princess of Vallos. Em might have fooled them all, but she never made much of an effort to become Mary. She was always just herself.

"You weren't seriously considering claiming your marriage is valid, were you?" Aren asked.

"Why? Would any of you listen?"

"Don't even think about it." Aren's voice went hard. "You can't hold her to—"

"Aren, relax," Cas said. "I'm not holding her to anything. We never even consummated the marriage."

Aren blinked, the anger fading from his face. "You what?"

"Oh. I assumed Em told you."

"No. Sh-she never said . . ." Aren seemed genuinely confused. "Why not?"

He hesitated and cracked a knuckle, unsure if he'd told Aren something Em didn't want him to know.

"It didn't seem like she wanted to," he said quietly.

"That was really decent of you," Aren said.

"You don't have to sound so surprised."

Aren frowned at him like he didn't like being surprised.

"Aren?" Em walked up behind Aren, her face scrunched in confusion. "What are you . . ." She spotted Cas. "Cas! You're out of bed."

"I am." He pushed his hands against the porch floor, slowly getting to his feet. He held his arms out. "Look! I can even stand by myself." A wave of dizziness crashed over him and he braced his hand against the wall. "Mostly."

She hopped up the porch steps and put an arm around his waist. He leaned into her. She was so tall. He loved how tall she was. Sturdy enough to hold him up when he needed it.

"What are you doing here?" Em asked Aren, a hint of suspicion in her voice.

"We were just talking," Cas said.

Her hair was damp, the smell of soap lingering in it, and he pressed a kiss to the side of her head.

"Ugh," Aren said. "I'm leaving."

"Bye, Aren!" Cas called as he walked away. "Thanks for the chat!"

Aren sort of waved his hand behind his back without turning around.

"What did you talk about?" Em asked.

"You." He found her hand and tugged on her fingers until she turned her body into his. He brushed his thumb over her lips and her eyelids fluttered like she approved.

He leaned forward slightly, letting his hand drift down to her neck. She closed the rest of the distance, her soft mouth covering his.

His body remembered her. Every fiber of his being lit up when she kissed him. She kept one hand on his waist but let the other tangle in his hair, and suddenly every thought he'd been considering today seemed absolutely right. He needed to stay with Em. She was his home now.

The world tilted and he broke the kiss, blinking. Em tightened the arm around his waist.

"Sorry. Being upright is still a bit of a problem." He jerked his head at the house. "Come be not upright with me?"

She glanced at the door, hesitation in her expression.

"Just sleeping. I'm not asking for anything else. I'm too weak anyway." He silently cursed that weakness. He would give anything to be able to pull Em closer and free her of some of those clothes.

"I have some things I need to tell you," she said.

"Tell me tomorrow," he said, leaning down to kiss her. He pressed his lips to hers gently, twice. "Tonight, I just want to do this."

Her lips curved up against his. "Me too," she whispered.

He took her hand, using it to keep himself steady as they walked inside and upstairs. He slid back into the bed he'd grown to hate, but it didn't seem so bad as Em kicked off her shoes and stretched out next to him.

He pulled her close to him and she buried her head in his chest. This was where he belonged. Olivia was right. He didn't deserve his kingdom. He didn't want it.

All he wanted was Em.

EIGHTEEN

EM WOKE UP to Cas's arm wrapped around her, her back against his chest. He was softly pressing his lips to the base of her neck, his breath tickling her skin.

A giggle escaped her mouth. She ducked her head, a grin spreading across her face.

"Good morning," he said, his lips grazing her neck. His fingers skimmed the bare skin of her waist, where her shirt had ridden up.

She closed her eyes as his touch sent sparks up her body. She was never leaving this bed again.

"I want to wake up with you every morning," Cas said.

"That would be nice," she breathed, imagining it for a moment. They would both be wearing less clothing and there wouldn't be the constant threat of danger hanging over their heads.

His lips disappeared from her neck and she rolled over to look at him. The color had returned to his cheeks.

"You look better," she said.

"I feel better." He rolled onto his back, blinking. "Much better, actually."

She scooted forward and lay her head on his chest. She shouldn't stay. Light was filtering in through the curtains, and she was supposed to meet with August and a few others this morning. And she had things she needed to tell Cas. Like that she was plotting to kill his only remaining family member. That she was considering a proposal from August.

Instead, she shut her eyes and listened to the beat of his heart. His fingers ran through her hair and they stayed like that for a long time, neither of them speaking. She'd spent too much of her time with Cas talking. Talking about their families or their politics or yelling about the Ruined. Maybe she needed to spend some time *not* talking to Cas.

The sun peeking through the curtains shone brighter, and she reluctantly extracted herself from his arms.

"I have to go," she said, reaching for his hand. "I'll see you later?"

He brushed his lips across her fingers. "I will be here. Given that I'm not allowed to leave, and all."

She looked at him apologetically as she climbed off the bed. "I'm sorry. You know it's for your own safety."

"I know. I wasn't complaining."

She laced up her boots and pulled her fingers through her hair. Cas sat up easily, without any of the unsteadiness she'd seen yesterday.

"How much better do you feel?" she asked, her voice soft.

"Um, a lot?"

"Like good enough that I should come back to your room tonight and . . ." She wasn't sure how she'd intended to finish that sentence.

He drew in a slow breath. He knew what she meant. "Yes."

Her cheeks warmed as she smiled. "Good. I'll see you later, then." She pulled the door open and walked out of the room, her lips still twitching as she went. Maybe she had to say good-bye to Cas soon, but she could certainly make the most of the time they had now.

She walked into town and to her apartment. Olivia was nowhere to be seen. They hadn't spoken since the fight they'd had yesterday. It was probably best to give her space until Cas and his friends left.

Em splashed some water on her face, changed her clothes, and grabbed a rolled-up map from the table. Outside, the warriors were passing out pieces of dried deer meat. She took one before heading to August's home. He'd taken up residence in a house at the far end of the main road. As far away from Cas as possible, she'd noted.

Aren stood on the porch with Iria, his hands stuffed in his pockets like he was nervous about something. He spotted Em and stepped away from Iria.

"Is Olivia already here?" she asked.

Aren shook his head. "No. The rest of the council is inside, but I haven't seen Olivia since last night."

Olivia was supposed to be in this meeting, but maybe it wasn't a surprise that she hadn't bothered to show up. She'd made it clear she had no interest in negotiating with warriors.

The front door was open, so Em walked into the house, followed by Aren and Iria. August sat on the couch in the front sitting room with a warrior named Lorena next to him. The whole Ruined council was present—Mariana, Ivanna, Davi, and Jacobo sat in chairs across from the prince. They all stood when Em entered.

August strode across the room, extending his hand to her. She hesitated before slipping her hand into his, unsure what he wanted. He raised it up and pressed his lips to her knuckles.

"Lovely to see you, Em," he said. "You disappeared for a couple days there. Busy lately?"

She quickly pulled her hand away, wishing she hadn't given it to him. The feeling of his lips lingered on her skin in an unpleasant way.

"Please, have a seat," August said.

Em sat in the chair next to Mariana, and Aren slid into the chair on her other side. Iria sat on the other side of August. The wall above their heads was discolored in the shape of a large square, and Em glanced around the room until she found a painting leaning against the wall. Its back was to her, but it must have been of one of the ancestors. The Olso royal family didn't worship the ancestors.

"Thank you for agreeing to meet this morning," Em said. She looked at Ivanna. "Any news from our lookouts?"

"Still no movement as far as we can see," Ivanna said. "If the Vallos army is organizing, we can't see them yet."

"Good." Em unrolled a map on the table in front of her. It was hastily drawn, of Vallos and southern Lera. She'd indicated the fortress north of them, and she'd drawn a star on the eastern shore.

"I think we should send a group of warriors and Ruined north to check on the status of Lera," she said. "We need to relay what's been happening here. We have the fortress surrounded to the north and south, but no real plan of action. No idea what's happening in the north. We need some strong people to travel between the two locations. If we send a group along the shore"—she pointed to the star—"here, they should be able to get north. Especially if we send a couple powerful Ruined with them. We can both write a letter for them to deliver, explaining what's happened."

"When?" August asked.

"As soon as the new batch of warriors arrive."

"It would be safer to go back through Ruina and into Olso to get to Lera," Iria said.

"Safer, but it would take weeks," Ivanna said.

"And we don't have weeks," Em said. "We need to organize as soon as possible if we're going to attack the fortress again and kill Jovita. She'll be well protected, and we can't take any risks."

"Fine," August said. "How many do you want to go?"

"I was thinking ten warriors and two or three Ruined," Em said.

"Which Ruined?" August asked.

"I don't know. I'll ask for volunteers first. I'll assign the duty if need be." Em glanced to her right. The Ruined nodded in agreement.

"I want approval of who goes," August said.

"Of course. I'll ask the same for the warriors."

"Fine. I'll make choices as soon as everyone is here." August clapped his hands together. "Now. Let's talk about the fact that you have the Lera king in a house across the street. The king my brother ordered killed."

"An order I already refused to carry out once," Em said. "What makes you think I'm going to let you kill him now?"

August closed one fist so tightly his knuckles turned white. "One could argue that your continued relationship with Lera leaders undermines your relationship with Olso."

"One could argue, or you're arguing that right now?"

"Casimir has no place here. We are at war with his country."

"It's in our best interest to make sure Jovita doesn't take the Lera throne," Em said. "We wouldn't be in this position if Jovita hadn't removed him from power."

"Oh, that's why you're harboring him?" Jacobo asked. "Not because you were kissing him on the porch last night?"

Em flushed. Silence fell over the group.

"He's proven he can't control his people," Ivanna said. "Honestly, I believed you when you said Casimir agreed not to attack us. But your agreement with him means nothing now. And we've chosen Olso as our allies, not Lera."

Em stared at the floor. Ivanna wasn't wrong. But then, neither was Em. Keeping Jovita off the Lera throne was crucial in keeping the Ruined safe.

Still, it was time for Cas to leave and make sure his claim to that throne was safe. They were right about that.

"I'll ask them to leave," Em said, her voice strained. "As soon as Cas is fully recovered. I'll give them a week."

"One day," August said. "He leaves tomorrow."

Em crossed her arms over her chest. "Five days."

"Three. I won't go any higher."

"Fine. Three. If any harm comes to him in those days, we will have a very serious problem."

"No one is going to touch him," August spat. "But you need to ask yourself if your relationship with Casimir is worth risking your alliance with the warriors. What would your people think if we all suddenly left?" His words shook, like he was barely keeping himself from yelling.

Well, Olivia would jump for joy. The more sensible Ruined, like Ivanna and Mariana, would be furious. They would know Em risked their safety for the life of one boy. A boy they hated.

She couldn't do it. Her first priority was to her people. She was their queen now, and she had to protect them, even if it meant disregarding her own wishes.

"They will leave in three days," Em said.

"Good." August's smile seemed forced. "I have nothing else, if you don't."

She stood and said a quick good-bye to the warriors. The Ruined followed her out.

"You shouldn't let Cas go at all," Jacobo said as they walked down the dirt road. "We should keep him prisoner until we don't need him anymore."

"He's not worth anything as a prisoner," Ivanna said. "Besides, there's no use destroying the potential of an alliance. We don't need it now, but you never know."

"Ruined aligning with Lera," Jacobo said with a snicker. "That'll be the day."

Ivanna shrugged. "I'm just saying that Emelina is smart to stay on good terms with them."

"Thank you," Em said, unable to keep the surprise from her voice. "Would you and Mariana start feeling out the Ruined for me? Find some who would be interested in going up north with the warriors?"

"Sure," Mariana said. Ivanna nodded, and they turned to follow Jacobo and Davi back into the center of town.

Em looked at Aren. "That was strange."

"Not really. I think you made the right call too."

"You do?"

"Yeah. You'd be doing Jovita a favor by killing Cas. Besides, he's not that . . ." Aren scrunched his face up. "He could be worse, I guess."

"Wow," Em said with a laugh. "I think that's the nicest thing I've ever heard you say about a Leran."

"Don't go spreading it around." He paused. "He told me you and he never consummated the marriage."

"He did?"

"He thought you'd already told me. Which you should have, by the way."

"Oh. Well . . ." She shrugged, avoiding his gaze.

"I was worried about that, you know. I thought you were traumatized by having to have sex with him. You could have told me you were too scared."

"I was not scared! I was . . . uncomfortable."

"I don't blame you."

She was definitely not too scared at the moment, though. She scanned the area, and found Iria walking away from the cabin. Em waved good-bye to Aren and jogged to catch up with her.

"Can I ask you a question?" Em asked as she fell into step beside her.

"I'm volunteering to join the team going north, if that's what you were thinking."

"No, but that's not a bad idea. I was actually wondering, uh, if you have any of the Juner herb. Or if you've seen a place nearby where it's growing."

Iria came to a stop, a grin spreading across her face. "Going to make use of those last three days, huh?"

Em's face flushed. "Uh, well . . ." Yes, she was. But the last thing she needed was a baby, and the Juner herb prevented pregnancy.

"There's a field of it outside of town, northeast. I saw it on our ride here."

"Do you . . . do you think you could show me? I don't actually know what it looks like."

Iria's eyebrows shot up. "Oh. Sure. We can walk. It's not far."

"Thanks."

"Your mother didn't show you?" Iria asked as they walked. "Or does it not grow in Ruina?"

"It does. I don't think it was a priority for her. I know a bunch of herbs that will kill you, though."

"Well, that's helpful too, I guess."

NINETEEN

"GOING SOMEWHERE?"

Aren jumped at the sound of the voice. Iria stood at the entrance of the barn, gathering her windblown hair into a ponytail. When he didn't reply, she pointed at the horse he'd saddled.

"I'm . . . going to check something," he said.

"To check something," she repeated, suspicion in her voice.

He swallowed down a wave of nerves. He wanted to check if Olivia had killed all those people yesterday. He'd fled like a coward when she killed the first one, and had no idea if they were all dead. Maybe she'd left some injured. Olivia knew, of course, but he couldn't bring himself to ask her. He didn't want to go anywhere near her.

A wave of panic crashed over him as Olivia's words replayed

in his head: *I guess you'll be marrying me, then.* How could he marry someone who killed without a hint of remorse? Not just without remorse, but with absolute *glee*, on occasion. What would she do when she got angry with him? He might lose a limb every time they fought.

He let out an almost hysterical laugh, and Iria looked at him with concern.

"Do you want some company?" she asked.

Yes. The word sat on the tip of his tongue. He wanted her to come. He wanted to tell someone what Olivia had done. Someone who wasn't Em. He hadn't figured out how to talk to Em about her sister yet.

"Whatever you see . . . will you keep it a secret?" he asked. "Just until we can figure out what to do."

Surprise and concern lit up Iria's face, but she nodded in agreement. He helped her saddle another horse and they rode out of the barn and through the town. He looked over his shoulder as they passed the statues of the ancestors in front of the courthouse. He didn't like those statues. Their eyes followed him wherever he went.

The sun was sinking at his left shoulder, casting an orange glow over the area, and he focused straight ahead, pretending he didn't feel the eyes of the ancestors boring into his back.

It was almost dark when he pulled the horse to a stop. The cluster of tents next to the road was still there.

Bodies littered the ground. Flies buzzed around the corpses. She'd killed them all.

Aren slid off his horse. He knew his boots hit the ground because he heard it, but his body had gone numb.

You could have stopped it. The voice in his head scream-whispered the words to him.

"What happened?" Iria gasped. She dismounted her horse and ran toward the bodies. She came to a sudden stop and pressed the back of her hand against her nose.

Aren reached for his horse. His legs wobbled beneath him. He needed something to hold him upright.

His mother was probably saying something in his head, but he couldn't hear anything but the roaring in his ears. He was partly responsible for this. He should have never followed Olivia to kill those men at the cabins in Ruina. He should have never killed with her. Look at what he'd caused.

"Aren." Iria was in front of him. He hadn't noticed her walking to him, but there she was, close enough to touch. "What happened?"

An unexpected tear fell down his cheek. He quickly wiped it away.

"Aren," Iria said softly. She reached for his hand. Her skin was soft and warm next to his, and he gratefully closed his fingers around hers.

"Olivia," he whispered.

"She killed them? Why?"

A hysterical laugh bubbled up in his throat. *Why?* Why did Olivia do anything? She hated humans.

Aren looked up at Iria. He'd thought he hated them too. He

was relieved to realize he was wrong.

"Does Em know?" Iria asked. He shook his head. "We need to tell her."

"It's already done. I didn't stop Olivia."

"The Vallos people could retaliate. They already hate Em for killing their princess. They don't need much of a push to launch an attack."

"Right." It was stupid of him not to think of that earlier. They were technically in enemy territory right now.

"Hey, Aren." Iria put both her hands on his cheeks suddenly. He blinked, every sense in his body standing at alert. "Are you all right?"

He definitely wasn't, so he didn't say anything. He stared at her instead. He could still make out her features in the dim, dying light. The freckles across the bridge of her nose. The curve of her lips. Her dark eyes.

"I'm sorry I didn't stop her," he said, because he needed to say it to someone.

"Could you have stopped her?"

"Maybe. I ran away instead."

She nodded and didn't tell him it wasn't his fault. He was glad. It would have been a lie. He liked that she didn't lie to him.

"Let's go back and tell Em." She dropped her hands from his face. "She'll know—" She turned to her horse and stopped talking abruptly. "Aren," she breathed, pointing at something. He followed her finger. In the distance, an army marched north. Headed straight for Sacred Rock.

Em stopped in front of the house, lifting her head to look up at Cas's window. It was closed, but she could see the edges of light around the curtains. The sun had set not long ago, and the chill in the air was making her even more nervous.

She knocked on the door and Galo answered. Violet and Mateo sat at the table, cards in front of them, and they said hello as she passed through.

Her footsteps were quiet as she walked up the stairs to Cas's room, but she could tell he heard her coming as soon as she opened the door. He was sitting on the edge of the bed instead of against the pillows, his feet flat on the floor. His eyes were bright and full of life again. He looked even better than he had that morning.

"Hi." She shut the door behind her. The room was lit by one lantern on the bedside table, casting a soft glow across the bed.

"Hi."

She moved closer to him until her knees brushed against his. He tilted his face up.

"The warriors want you all gone in three days," she said, because she didn't know what else to say.

He reached for her hand, lacing their fingers together. He didn't respond to that.

"And there are other things I should talk to you about," she said softly.

He put his other hand on her neck, pulling her face closer to his. "Whatever it is, I don't care."

She pressed her lips to his, softly at first. His hands circled her waist, and he parted his legs, pulling her closer to him. His fingers slipped beneath her shirt, tracing the bare skin of her back, and it didn't matter that she had something to tell him, because she'd forgotten how to talk.

She climbed into his lap, letting her knees rest on either side of him. Her lips left his for a moment, and he leaned forward to catch them again.

She'd kissed him before. She'd kissed him in this bed before, even. But this was different. This was her body on fire, her brain turned to mush. This was nothing but him and the heat of his breath on her mouth.

She found the bottom of his shirt and tugged on it until he lifted his arms. She pulled it off.

His gaze met hers briefly before he kissed her again. She would remember the way he looked at that moment forever. Eyes blazing, chin tilted up to kiss her again.

He bit down gently on her bottom lip and she practically went limp in his arms. His fingers found the buttons of her shirt and he slowly released them. His hands skimmed her bare shoulders as he pushed the shirt off. She wore nothing underneath the shirt. Her lips curved up as he took in a sharp breath.

She ran her fingers into his hair, curling them around the soft strands. His hands were against her bare skin and she suddenly decided to never put her clothes back on. She'd spent far too much time with Cas with her clothes on.

He grabbed her around the waist and pressed her into the mattress. She wrapped her legs around his hips, her fingers skimming his firm back.

His lips weren't against hers anymore, they were on her neck, then trailing lower, until sparks were shooting through her body.

His fingers fumbled with the buttons on her pants and she laughed as he sat back on her legs and tried to pull them free.

"Do you want some help there?" she asked, reaching for them.

He brushed her hand away. "No." He released the top button. "You have no idea how many times I've thought about taking your pants off. I'm doing it myself." He released the second button.

"How many times?" she asked.

He freed the last button and grabbed her pants around the waist. "A few." He dragged the pants down her legs and dropped them off the bed. "Not as many times as I relived that night I unbuttoned your dress."

"Yeah?"

He pressed his hands into the mattress on either side of her head, his hair falling into his eyes as he looked down at her. She wore only a scrap of fabric now, and her entire body lit up as he settled between her legs.

"So many times," he whispered, leaning down to kiss her.

She wrapped her arms around him, holding him as tightly as she could. If she held him tightly enough, maybe he wouldn't have to go. Maybe they could do this every night for the rest of their lives.

His fingers were curling around her thigh and pushing up to her hip when she heard the scream.

Cas went rigid, his head snapping to the window. Another scream.

Em darted off the bed, grabbing for her shirt and pants. She threw them on and ran for the door.

"Stay here," she called over her shoulder.

She didn't wait for a reply before sprinting out the door. Galo was downstairs with Mateo and Violet, and she repeated the same instructions to them.

Ruined and warriors streamed out of their homes as Em sprinted to the center of town. Aren and Iria were running from the opposite direction.

"Vallos soldiers!" Aren yelled.

Em turned, facing the direction where dark figures were approaching from the south. Horse hooves pounded the dirt. The blade of a sword caught the light of a torch.

She hadn't expected an attack from the Vallos army so soon. It was inevitable, considering they'd invaded a town and she'd killed their princess, but they weren't strong enough to take on the Ruined themselves. Why would they storm into town without backup from Lera?

"Kill them all! Every one of them!" Olivia's voice rose over the noise. She strode out of her house with Em's sword, her face

calm. She handed over Em's sword. "The warriors are waiting for orders."

Em turned to find August and his warriors gathering in the town square, dressed in red and swords already drawn. She cupped her hands around her mouth.

"Attack! No prisoners!"

TWENTY

ARENʼS CHEST SEIZED as Em called out the order. He and Iria rode as fast as they could, but the Vallos army had a head start. They barely made it back to Sacred Rock before the soldiers.

"Kill them! Kill them all!" Olivia screamed.

The Vallos soldiers were retaliating because of what Olivia had done. He couldn't blame them. They already hated the Ruined because Em killed their princess. He would have done the same.

Warriors raced past him, Em shouting orders to them. A sea of red streamed across his vision.

"Aren!" Olivia's furious voice rose over the chaos around him. He blinked. She stood several paces away, her coat billowing in the wind. "Are you going to stand there, or are you going to join me?"

Every instinct in his body told him to run. He'd never wanted to run from a fellow Ruined before.

Iria shot past his vision, calling over her shoulder to another warrior. She cast a frantic look at the advancing Vallos soldiers.

He snapped to attention. If he didn't fight, too many would die. Iria might die. He couldn't change what Olivia had done, but he could protect his friends.

He jogged to Olivia. She grabbed his hand and roughly made him turn, so he was facing the army of Vallos soldiers. Warriors scattered out of the road, leaving nothing between Aren and the approaching horses.

The Vallos soldiers were dressed in black, torches bobbing in the darkness. There were several hundred of them.

Olivia squeezed his hand. He swore he could feel her power coursing through him. He'd never felt that with any other Ruined. He didn't even know if it was possible.

Horse hooves beat against the ground. They were close enough that he could hear the yells.

"Detach," Olivia said. "I can feel the emotion coming off of you. Don't make me do this all myself."

He nodded. He cleared his mind, beating down the swell of guilt.

Two men at the front of the line toppled off their horses. Olivia had started.

"Take the left," she said.

He narrowed his eyes. He was strong. He felt nothing. He could do this.

Why couldn't he do this without blood?

Blood sprayed from the men as he tore into their chests. Olivia was so much cleaner. Why wasn't he clean?

The men on the left side began to fall, one at a time. His Ruined power sizzled in his body, sending fire through every limb.

The men were closer now. He couldn't get to all of them before they got too close.

A Vallos soldier was right in front of his face. Aren gasped, the world suddenly coming into sharp focus around him. His ability to detach slipped through his fingers.

The soldier made a fist and Aren leaned back to avoid it. It grazed his cheek. He focused on the man's neck.

Aren had meant to break his neck, but instead blood spurted from it. Everything was red. The soldier clapped his hand to it as he fell to his knees.

Aren's body felt heavy from using his magic, and he closed his eyes for a moment. He'd lost Olivia's hand and he had to work harder to detach this time.

"Aren!" Olivia's voice cut through the chaos and he opened his eyes just in time to see a soldier running straight toward him, sword drawn.

Aren tossed him aside. He forced the noise out of his head and focused only on the soldiers in front of him.

Bones broke. Heads rolled through the dirt.

He could hear Olivia laughing.

He tried to laugh. Nothing.

But there was more blood. Soldiers were running away from him. Olivia picked a few of them off.

He wiped his arm across his forehead. Everything was wet.

He looked down. Blood.

Pain seared across his flesh, and he cocked his head as he watched the new Ruined mark on the inside of his wrist split open. Weakling. They were shooting it at them.

But he couldn't even feel it. Shouldn't he have been able to feel it?

Ruined around him screamed, but he and Olivia stood their ground. The Vallos soldiers didn't have nearly as much Weakling as the fortress did, and pieces of the herb fluttered to the ground.

"Aren." Olivia pointed to something in the distance. A long line of people on foot, in wagons, on horses. The soldiers were just a distraction to allow the people to get past Sacred Rock. They were probably trying to get to Lera.

Olivia took off running. "Come on!" she yelled over her shoulder.

Aren didn't follow. Jacobo and a few other Ruined pushed past him to run after Olivia.

Screams rippled through the crowd. Bodies launched into the air and hit the ground with a thud. Olivia didn't need to use her arms to control her power, but she swung them along with the bodies like she was conducting musicians.

He turned away.

A Vallos soldier was scrambling to her knees, and she froze when Aren spotted her. A piece of dark hair fell from her bun, her heavy breath blowing it away from her bloodied face.

"Run." His words were barely a whisper and he wasn't sure if they were for her or himself. "Run."

She took off at a full sprint, dodging bodies. Ahead, a soldier held his hand out, and she grabbed it and they ran together. A warrior watched them go, raising her eyebrows at Aren. She took the bow off her back and looked at him questioningly. He shook his head.

Behind him, the screams slowly died out. The warriors around him sheathed their swords. Some of the Ruined were laughing. The few Vallos soldiers left alive were disappearing the way they came.

He blinked at the bodies around him. Last time they were dressed in blue; this time in black and yellow. No matter what kingdom they came from or what color they wore, they all ended up like this. Dead at his feet.

Em was in front of him suddenly, her forehead creased. She said something he didn't understand.

He muttered something he hoped sounded like "what?" The world was growing dark around him, his vision reduced to a tiny spot in front of him.

"I asked if you're all right," she said.

"Hmm." What a stupid question. "I told her not to."

"You told who what?"

"I told Olivia not to kill those people. They came because she killed them."

"Wait, what? Olivia killed who?"

He shook his head. He was tired of answering questions. He didn't want to be standing in front of the people he'd killed.

"Olivia!" Em yelled. She took off. "Olivia!"

Aren sidestepped a few exhausted Ruined. He wiped his hand across his face. Red. He looked down at his shirt. Red.

He wanted to run. He was telling his body to run, but it wouldn't listen. He was surprised he was even still walking. His legs seemed to be moving on their own.

He finally reached the bakery, and he started up the stairs to the little apartment above it. Was someone calling his name? It was too much effort to turn around.

He pushed open the door. He stopped over the threshold.

What was he supposed to do now? It seemed like he had come to his apartment for a reason.

"Aren."

He knew that voice.

"Aren?" Iria appeared in front of him suddenly. "What's . . ." She trailed off as she took in his appearance.

He looked down at his hands as he walked past her. Lots of blood.

"I'm sorry," he whispered.

"What?" Iria's footsteps were near.

"I'm sorry," he said again, but not to her. "I don't know if that's what you would have done, but I think . . ." He squeezed his eyes shut. "I'm sorry."

His parents didn't answer. They never did.

He looked up. Her face was drawn, like something was wrong.

Was something wrong?

He caught sight of his arms again. Blood. That's what was wrong.

He dropped to his knees, clawing at the blood. "Get it off." Why wasn't it coming off? "Get it off!"

Iria ran away from him, and for a moment he thought she was running in fear. No. She closed the front door.

He tugged at his shirt, ripping at it with such force that one of the sleeves split open.

"Here." Iria helped him pull it over his head and tossed it away. He unbuttoned his pants and leaned back, kicking them off.

"Right. Those too." Iria's voice was a little strange. "Sure."

"Get it off," he muttered, to no one in particular. He smeared the blood on one arm as he swiped at it.

Iria grabbed the bucket of water from the corner. She had a rag in her hand as she dropped to her knees in front of him.

She touched two fingers under his chin, nudging his face in her direction. She swiped the rag down one cheek and then the other. It was red when she dunked it back in the water.

He shivered as she cleaned his arms, the cold water trickling down his skin.

"Can you tell me what's wrong?" she asked.

He didn't reply. Did he have words to tell her what was wrong?

She swiped the rag down his chest, then got to her feet and deposited the bucket and rag near the door. He looked down at himself. The blood was gone.

"Hands," she said.

He didn't know why she wanted them, but he gave them to her anyway. She wrapped a bandage around his wrist, where the Weakling had hit him. Then she hauled him to his feet and guided him to the bed. That was a good idea. He curled up in a ball and there were blankets over him suddenly.

Iria knelt down next to the bed. She slipped one of her hands into his. He took in a sharp breath, the feeling of her skin against his snapping something into place in his brain. He met her gaze.

"Do you want me to go get someone?" she asked. "Em?"

"No," he said quickly. "Please don't." What would Em think of him? She would certainly judge him for being a pathetic mess after a simple battle.

"All right," she said quietly.

He pulled her hand a little closer to his chest, bending his head close to it. He didn't know why he had her hand, but he liked it.

"I didn't want to kill those people," he whispered. "My mom used to say that my power was—my power was . . ." He ducked his head into his chest, the rest of that sentence lost as his throat closed up. Tears trickled down his cheeks.

"I'm so sorry Aren," Iria whispered, putting her hand on top of his head. She held his hand a little tighter. "I'm so sorry."

TWENTY-ONE

OLIVIA SIGHED DEEPLY as she looked down at the dark spots of blood on her jacket. No wonder her mother was always going through so many clothes.

Olivia didn't sleep. She helped dispose of the bodies of the Vallos soldiers, then scouted the area for any lingering soldiers. She'd mostly been trying to avoid her sister.

Olivia pushed open the door to her apartment. Em sat at the kitchen table. The dark circles under her eyes suggested she also hadn't slept.

"Where have you been?" Em asked.

Olivia shrugged out of her coat and walked to the living room to stand in front of the fire. This apartment was better than the cabins, at least. The furniture was clean and modern, the shelves lining the walls filled with books, the artwork professional. There was a painting of every ancestor in this room, and Olivia looked over her shoulder at Boda. Her mother's favorite ancestor stared back at her from her seat in a garden.

Em looked at her expectantly, waiting for an answer to her question.

"I went to the surrounding areas to make sure there weren't more soldiers," Olivia said.

"And?"

"There were a few. I took care of them."

"Aren said the soldiers came because you killed them. What did he mean?"

Olivia scrunched up her face. "Aren's different than I remember him." She remembered a boy who barely acknowledged the warriors when they came through. Now he followed that Iria girl everywhere she went.

"He's been through a lot."

"And I haven't?" Anger seared up her body, but it came out in the form of tears. She quickly blinked them back. "I know you and Aren spent a year running for your lives, but what do you think I was doing during that time? I wasn't living a cozy life in that cell." A tear slipped down her cheek and she closed her eyes against the unwelcome images that surfaced. Being covered in Weakling. Being ordered to heal injured humans. The beatings that followed when she refused.

These were the people Em wanted to protect?

"I know," Em said softly.

Olivia opened her eyes. "Yes, I killed some of the people who fled this place."

"Unprovoked?" Em asked.

"Yes."

"Why?"

Olivia had expected Em to chastise her, not ask why. Aren wasn't the only one who had changed. Em may have wanted to protect Cas and his followers, but she was still the girl who'd killed the Vallos princess in cold blood.

"Because I don't trust them," Olivia said quietly. "Because I don't want any of my fellow Ruined to go through what I went through. I'm going to keep us safe, even if I have to kill every human to do it."

"I understand," Em said. "I know you think I don't, but I do. I've seen how dangerous they can be."

"Then why are you mad?"

"I'm not mad. I'm . . . scared."

Olivia pressed her lips together. Maybe she was scared too, but she refused to admit it. Fear was weak. She refused to be weak again.

"I'm scared I can't reason with you, Liv. I'm scared that your hatred is going to make you do something stupid that's going to get you killed." Em leaned forward, her words soft. "We need the warriors. We need to be smart. What if the Vallos army had been twice the size? What if they'd gotten past you and Aren? All of this could have ended before it started."

"But that's not the only reason, is it?" Olivia asked. "You

think it was wrong for me to kill those people."

"I do think it was wrong. But more important, I don't think it was smart. I don't think it was the action of a queen. We need to be thinking strategically. We need to plan and communicate. We won't secure the safety of the Ruined by randomly attacking small camps of people."

Olivia let out a long breath, annoyed by that logic. She couldn't argue with it. "You're right."

"Yeah?" she asked, clearly surprised.

"Yes," Olivia said with a laugh. "You're right, and you're also a hypocrite."

"How so?"

"Is keeping Cas here what a queen would do? When you know it makes me and August uncomfortable? Is that smart?"

Em dropped her eyes from Olivia's. "No," she said softly.

"Let's both be smart, then. Deal?"

Cas waited for Em all night. When she finally walked into his room after dawn, he jumped to his feet.

"Is everyone all right?" he asked. "Who was that?"

"Vallos soldiers." She leaned against the wall instead of coming to him. "Everyone is fine. We fought them back."

"Good." He wanted to go to her, to gather her into his arms, but everything about her body language said she wanted him to keep his distance.

"I need to tell you something," she said.

"All right."

"We came here to kill Jovita. It's our main mission."

He laughed. It bubbled up in his chest and burst out louder than he intended. He laughed again, almost hysterically.

"I'm serious, Cas."

"I know you are. Why else would you be here? She attacked you. You're only a few hours from the fortress." He hadn't given much thought to why Em was in Vallos. He wondered, then dismissed it. He was just happy to see her.

Em was here to respond to an attack. To kill the leader waging war on her people. She was, as usual, taking action.

"I know she's your only remaining family, but—"

"I don't care," Cas interrupted. "Kill her. Tell her I said goodbye."

Em reeled back in shock.

"You thought I'd be mad?"

"Maybe."

"She poisoned me. She locked me in a room for days. She convinced people I was insane. I don't care what you do to her."

Em nodded, turning her gaze to her shoes. "You need to leave. After we kill Jovita you can swoop in and seize power again—"

"I don't want it," he interrupted.

"What?"

"I don't want the kingdom. Let Olso have it."

"What?" she asked again with growing incredulity.

"They've already taken most of the country anyway. It's a losing battle and I'm too tired to fight it. I'd rather stay here with you."

"You can't."

"Why not? I'll renounce Lera or do whatever you want me to do. I'll send Galo, Mateo, and Violet back, if that's what they want. Let me help you. Let me fight on your side."

Em ran her hands down her face, a humorless laugh escaping her mouth. "That's the dumbest thing I've ever heard."

He blinked, surprised. "What?"

"You're going to give up? You promised me you'd make things better for the Ruined as Lera's king, and now, when you encounter even the slightest problem, you run away?"

"Slightest problem? I was declared insane, Em. My own people rejected me."

"So? You think I don't know how that feels? I didn't go off and sulk about it. I did something."

"This isn't the same. I'm ashamed of what my father did. I'm ashamed to be from Lera."

"Then make it better!"

"Why do you care?" he asked, his voice rising. "You hate Lera! I'm offering to give up everything for you, to help you—"

"I did *not* ask for that. I would never ask you to give up everything for me, and if you think I would, you don't know me very well. And clearly I don't know you that well either, because I never thought you would just give up."

"I guess not," he said bitterly. He couldn't quite meet her eyes anymore. Shame had lodged itself in his throat and refused to leave.

"Even if you have no intention of going back to Lera, you

can't stay here," she said. "It makes too many people uncomfortable. Olivia and August in particular. August has proposed a marriage alliance to me, and it's under serious consideration."

Cas's heart stopped. The room tilted sideways.

"Olso wants to make a permanent alliance with us, so he's supposed to marry me or Olivia. He prefers me."

"Oh." His voice sounded funny. While he'd been lying in bed, dreaming of staying with Em, she'd been planning a marriage to someone else. Planning an attack on the leader of another kingdom. Protecting her people.

No wonder Jovita was trying to steal the throne from him. He'd done nothing to deserve it.

"Your horses and wagon are in the barn," she said. "I think it's best you leave now. You can have a few hours to prepare." She turned to the door but paused, her hand on the knob. "It's not that I don't care about you, Cas. It's just that there are a lot of people counting on me to keep them safe, and I have to put them first."

She walked out of the room and pulled the door shut behind her. He sank down on the bed, listening to the sound of her footsteps on the stairs.

His hands shook, and he debated running after her to yell that she had no right to be mad at him. She was the reason he'd lost so much.

But he was frozen on the bed, the lump in his throat growing painfully.

"Cas?" Galo said through the door. He pushed it open, a deep frown on his face. "What's going on? Em said we need to leave."

Cas focused on his feet. "Yes. Today."

Galo closed the door and leaned against it. "What happened?"

"Olivia and August don't like us being here."

"No kidding. I'm asking why I heard yelling."

"I asked to stay with her. She didn't like that idea."

"What do you mean?" Galo asked. "How can you stay with her?"

"It's not like I have anywhere to go. Jovita has pretty much taken the throne at this point. Might as well stay with Em and join the Ruined."

Galo was silent, and Cas crossed his arms over his chest, unable to look at him. The more he said the plan aloud, the more ashamed he was of it.

Galo strode across the floor and smacked his head, knocking Cas's hair into his eyes. Cas yelped in shock.

"What the—" His words died in his throat as Galo whacked him again.

"What? You said you're nothing. I can smack a nobody around." Galo lifted his hand again and Cas scrambled off the bed and away from him.

"Would you stop?"

"No. Come here. I'm going to smack you until I knock some sense back into that brain." Galo lunged for him, and Cas ran across the bed and pressed his back against the wall.

"I get it!" he yelled, holding his arms up defensively. "I'm a total idiot."

"Yes, you are." Galo stopped a few steps in front of him. "You offered to stay with Em?"

"She said no."

"Of course she said no! I barely know the girl and I know what a terrible idea that is."

"Sure, rub it in," Cas said. "Like I don't feel bad enough right now."

"Cas," Galo said, his voice softer. "Every choice Em has made—who was it for?"

Cas looked up at the ceiling and refused to answer the question.

"It was for them," Galo said, gesturing to the front of the house. "For the Ruined. I don't doubt that she has feelings for you, but everything she does is for them."

Cas didn't respond. He had once been furious at Em for choosing the Ruined over him. She hadn't told him that the warriors were attacking and he'd lost his father and home as a result. He'd been so angry with her for making the wrong choice, for not choosing him.

But she was never going to choose him.

"August wants to marry her," he said.

"Ugh," Galo said. "That's smart. A permanent alliance between Olso and Ruina." He paused. "I'm sorry, Cas."

Cas pushed off the wall and cracked a knuckle. "Forget it.

We need to decide where we're going to go. Maybe if we go south, farther into Vallos . . ." His voice trailed off. He had no idea where to go.

"We need to go back to Lera," Galo said. "We never intended to stay in Vallos. We were going to wait until you recovered and then return to Lera and build an army in the south. You're not really going to give up, are you?"

"I don't know what I'm supposed to do! Jovita controls the army and the advisers!"

"You have Violet, which means you have the southern province, if you want it. The people in the south are going to be loyal to her. We can't let Jovita get to them first."

Maybe Em would kill Jovita sooner rather than later. He'd actually have a shot at reclaiming his throne with her gone.

Em's furious face floated through his brain, and he suddenly realized he understood the expression on her face. She was ashamed of him. She always took charge, always acted like a leader, always stood up for her people.

And what did he do? He sat in bed. He wallowed. He offered to give up everything for a girl he knew he couldn't have.

He sucked in a sharp breath as an idea occurred to him.

A leader acted. A leader took control. A leader seized opportunities.

"What?" Galo asked.

"Em's going to kill Jovita."

"Can't say I'm torn up about that."

"No. . . ." Hope swelled in Cas's chest for the first time in days. "Let's go back to the fortress."

"Why?"

"I'm going to kill Jovita first."

TWENTY-TWO

AREN OPENED HIS eyes, squinting in the orange light flooding the apartment. He scrubbed a hand down his face as his surroundings came into focus.

Iria.

The memory of last night rushed into his brain and he jerked up to a sitting position. She was sitting on the ground next to the window with her knees pulled to her chest. She turned when he moved, concern flitting across her face.

Would it be strange if he ran out the door? He could escape in less than three seconds.

He looked down. He was in his underwear.

He would look pretty ridiculous running to the door in his underwear.

More ridiculous than sitting on the floor while Iria cleaned blood off of him? Probably not.

Iria stood. "How are you feeling?"

Humiliated. Insane. Worried he might have a more tenuous grasp on reality than he'd thought.

He pulled the blankets a little farther up his waist. He'd been in less in front of a girl before, but he'd never felt this exposed.

She sat down on the edge of the bed, tucking her leg beneath her. If he reached out, he could take the hand resting on the mattress.

Had he fallen asleep holding her hand last night?

And he thought he'd reached his embarrassment limit.

She was staring at him. He hadn't answered her question.

"I'm fine," he lied. He cleared his throat. "Thank you." His glanced to where she'd been sitting by the window. "You stayed here all night?"

"It was only a few hours. Sun just came up. And I didn't think I should leave you."

He wanted to say thank you. He stared at the blankets instead.

"Do you want to tell me what happened last night?" she asked.

How could he explain what he barely understood himself? "I . . . feel strange." What an understatement.

"Strange," she repeated.

"Olivia's been teaching me how to use my powers without growing weak. How to detach so it doesn't affect me. But it's like . . . it's like it makes me detach from myself too."

"Oh."

His bloody clothes were in the corner. How many had he killed last night? He didn't even know. He used to keep track of how many hunters he killed, but now the number would be staggering.

"Maybe you're not meant to detach," Iria said. "Maybe you need to feel it."

"It makes me so weak. And people here need me to fight. I'm the strongest person besides Olivia, and everyone is counting on me."

"No one is counting on you to kill. Just because it's what Olivia wants doesn't make it right."

Her dark eyes were fixed on his, and he had the sudden urge to pull her against him and hug her. He almost wished she'd climbed into the bed with him last night. He might have put his arms around her and fallen asleep with her head tucked into his neck.

"Maybe you should talk to Em," she said after a long silence. "Tell her what's happening."

"What's Em going to do? This is my problem. It's not like Olivia is forcing me into anything." Saying those words out loud released something horrible inside of him. His hands trembled.

Olivia wasn't forcing him to do anything.

Not yet, anyway. He wouldn't put it past her to force him to marry her. He took in a shaky breath. He needed to talk to Em about that. She was the only one who could stop her sister.

"What if you got away for a while?" Iria asked. "I was thinking of joining the mission up north. You could volunteer as one of the Ruined. There's no way Olivia will come with us, and you can use the time to get your head on straight."

"I think it might be twisted permanently," he said dryly.

She put her hand on top of his head and smiled. "It looks all right to me."

He returned the smile, relief poking a tiny hole through the dread in his chest. "That's not a bad idea. I'll ask Em."

"Good." She dropped her hand.

"Uh, you'll go for sure, right? I'd feel more comfortable if you were there. You're the only warrior I actually trust," he added hastily.

Pink rose up her neck and to her cheeks. He tried to hide his grin. He was fully aware that he made plenty of girls blush, but it was different coming from Iria. He could still make her blush after seeing him at his worst?

"I'll be there," she said.

He reached for her hand almost against his will. He hadn't decided to touch her, but it was like his body had other ideas.

Her fingers curled around his, soft and warm. Relief coursed through his bones, like the mere act of holding her hand was going to cure him of everything.

"Thanks, Iria," he said quietly.

"Anytime."

He released her hand, simply because it would be weird to keep it much longer. She climbed off the bed, but her gaze lingered on him.

"Your Ruined marks are coming back," she said.

He stared at the thin white lines that intersected the scars on his chest. They didn't look the same as they used to. They were lumpy and mangled from his burned flesh.

"Yeah. I have a lot of new ones."

"Good. I didn't like that they took that away from you too."

He smiled at her and wished she hadn't gotten off the bed. His fingers twitched to reach for her again.

"Um, I should go." She turned away and strode to the door. "I'm going to try to get some sleep."

"All right." No. That wasn't what he wanted to say. He wanted to ask her to stay. He wanted to tell her it would have been fine if she slept next to him in the bed. He wanted to tell her he felt better with her here.

He said none of it. "Bye," he said as she walked out.

TWENTY-THREE

EM WAITED NEAR the wagon and horses in front of the barn, her heart in her throat. Part of her wanted to run to Cas and apologize. The other part of her wanted to smack him and tell him to stop being stupid. Had he really intended to give up everything for her?

He was headed her way with Galo, Mateo, and Violet in tow. Galo and Mateo walked past her to the wagon. Violet nodded at Em, chewing her lip like she was nervous. She climbed into the back of the wagon.

Cas stopped in front of Em. He didn't seem angry. Or happy. In fact, the blank look on his face was maybe the worst expression she'd ever seen from him.

"I shouldn't have asked to stay," he said flatly. "I'm sorry I put you in that position."

"Don't apologize. It's not that I don't want you to stay, it's—"

"Please, don't," he interrupted. "Don't explain it anymore."

She nodded, taking in a shaky breath.

"I have a proposition for you," he said.

"What's that?"

"I want to kill Jovita."

She reeled back. "What?"

"Let me kill Jovita. I can get access to her."

"How?"

"We're going back to the fortress," he said, gesturing to the wagon. "I'm going to tell Jovita I realized she was right about the Ruined."

"She tried to kill you. She may lock you away again, especially if she's suspicious of your return."

"Let me take them information. Jovita claimed I was insane because I didn't want to kill the Ruined—if I return having changed my mind, with useful information about you, she won't be able to lock me up again."

"What information do you want to take them?"

"The diarchy. Your impending marriage to August. Your plan to kill her. I'll tell them I discovered a plot to attack the fortress and kill Jovita within a month."

"And if we don't attack within a month?"

"She'll be dead by then."

Em shook her head. "It's too dangerous. Jovita has a lot of

supporters, and the information you have isn't enough."

"Then give me something. A map, a plan, something concrete I can take to Jovita. I'll say I stole it."

She shook her head. "I don't know if I have anything that . . ." She let her voice trail off, considering the various maps and plans she had locked away at home. "I wrote a letter for the Ruined and warriors to take to the soldiers at Gallego City. It basically details our position here and pledges our continued support of Olso. There's nothing too specific, but I do allude to getting rid of Lera leaders. And I put the Flores seal on it."

"Perfect. I'll say I intercepted a messenger."

Em started to turn, then reconsidered and faced Cas again. "Are you sure? You can't just walk up to Jovita and stick a knife in her gut. Her people may revolt and kill you."

"I know. Give me time. A few weeks. Let me bring some of the advisers over to my side. With Violet's help, we may be able to turn some people. At the very least, I can take control of the southern province. Then I'll figure out the best way to get rid of her."

"Or you can allow us access to the fortress and we'll do it."

"Too many people would die. If you brought Olivia in . . ." He shook his head.

"She might get carried away," Em finished.

"Yes."

"In the meantime, I can be your eyes and ears in the fortress. They'll attack you again soon, you have to know that."

"We're counting on it."

"Then let me find out when. You'll be prepared and Jovita will be humiliated a second time. It will be easy for me to convince everyone she doesn't deserve the throne. Maybe I can take it back and then order her executed for treason."

"Could you do that?" Em asked quietly.

"Yes."

She rubbed her thumb across her necklace. Having someone inside the fortress was more than she could have hoped for.

"If anyone found out you were giving information to the Ruined . . ."

"They would chop my head off," Cas finished.

"You'd have to sneak out of the fortress at least a couple times to bring me information. Could you do that?"

"I'm sure I could figure it out," he said. "And you understand that this all hinges on our agreement? That the Ruined don't attack us?"

"Of course. Once you reclaim the throne, we'll all go back to Ruina and leave you alone."

"And if you marry August?"

"What do you mean?" Her cheeks warmed.

"Will you be able to keep that promise if you marry August?"

"I have no control over the warriors, but I promise I'll never send Ruined to Lera to help. I'll make that clear if . . . if I marry him." The words stuck in her throat, and she swallowed hard. "I'll get you that letter."

She took off to her apartment. It was mercifully empty when

she stepped inside, and she let out a sigh of relief. She didn't want to explain this to Olivia.

She grabbed the letter from the desk drawer in her bedroom, turning it over to make sure the green Flores seal was still intact. It was. She turned and jogged out of the apartment.

She extended the letter to Cas as she approached him. "Don't forget to break the seal before you get back to the fortress. Otherwise you might have a hard time explaining how you know what it says."

He nodded and pulled a folded-up piece of paper out of his pocket. "I'm going to try to get away in five days. I've marked on that map where I'll be."

She unfolded the paper and looked at the rough sketch of the fortress and land in between.

"Can someone meet me in five days? I'll relay information then," he said.

"I can do it."

"If I'm not there, try to come the next day. If I don't show up either day, assume I'm dead or something went wrong."

She folded the map back up and clutched it a little too hard. "Please be careful, Cas. Jovita's not an idiot. She'll be suspicious of you."

"Of course she will. But I'm sure she'll appreciate being told she was right."

"Don't—" She cut herself off, unsure if he wanted her opinion about this.

"Don't what?"

"Don't be nice to her. Or to anyone. Go in there and threaten to execute everyone for treason."

His eyebrows shot up. "I don't think that will earn me any friends."

"You need their respect, not their friendship. Don't cower when you go back. You're their king. Remind them of it."

He held her gaze for a moment. "I will." He began to walk past her and she grabbed his wrist, pulling him to a stop.

"I don't want to marry August," she whispered. His eyes darted to hers. "I have to make smart choices, but it's not what I want. You're the only one I want."

He shook her hand off, and for a moment she thought he was going to walk away. But he turned, grabbed her around the waist, and roughly pulled her against him. She wrapped her arms around him.

He put one hand on the back of her head, holding it steady as he pressed a kiss to her cheek. "Thanks for the push."

He released her and quickly turned away.

Cas sat in the back of the wagon with Violet, their legs hanging out the open back door. Mateo hung a blue shirt as a makeshift flag on top of the wagon, and it flapped in the breeze as the horses plodded through the forest.

He ripped open the letter as they neared the fortress. Em's handwriting was messier than he'd expected, the letters loopy and running into each other. It made his chest ache. He slipped the letter into his pocket.

"I can't decide if this is brave or stupid," Violet said.

"I guess we'll find out." The sun was sinking lower in the sky, and he lifted a hand to shield his eyes. "Thanks for sticking with me."

"Don't make me regret it." She grinned and bumped her shoulder against his.

He had to force his smile. "I'll try."

"I see the fortress!" Galo called from the front of the wagon. "I think we're being watched. They're letting us get close. Do you want to go to the front or back?"

"Front," Cas replied. "Stop a good distance from the gate and we'll walk the rest of the way."

Galo obeyed, and the horses came to a stop a few minutes later. Cas offered Violet his hand as they jumped out. The gates of the fortress loomed ahead of them. The wall had been almost fully repaired while he was gone. Five guards stood in front of the gate.

"Behind me," Cas said to his friends. Galo, Mateo, and Violet lined up behind him.

One of the guards had an arrow pointed at him, and Cas lifted his hands in surrender as he walked. "I don't think you want to shoot your king!"

The guard slowly lowered his bow. "Your Majesty?"

"Nice to see you again, Jared," Galo said from behind him.

"We didn't know you'd be returning, Your Majesty," Jared said. He whispered something to the other guards. The gate opened. One quickly hurried inside.

"Why wouldn't he return?" Galo asked. Jared just swallowed.

"Should I wait here?" Cas asked, stopping a few paces from the guard.

"Um . . ." Jared looked behind him, obviously flustered. "The order was not to let anyone in without Jovita's approval. . . ."

"He's your king," Galo spat.

"It's fine," Cas said. "Best to be cautious. I'll wait here." *Jared. Loyal to Jovita.* He repeated the name several times in his head. He needed to memorize it.

His cousin burst through the gate, utter disbelief on her face. Danna and Julieta followed her. People flooded the courtyard behind them. Jovita yelled for them to go back inside, but no one moved.

Jovita let out an annoyed breath and stomped to Cas. "Cas." The scar on her cheek twitched. "I thought . . ."

"You thought perhaps I was still locked in my room? You did make it very hard for me to leave."

Silence fell over the crowd. Shock colored a few faces.

Jovita narrowed her eyes at him. "I thought you abandoned your kingdom. Considering you ran away in the middle of the night like a criminal."

"I was poisoned. I thought it best that I leave while I recovered."

Gasps rippled through the crowd.

"Are you all right, Your Majesty?" Julieta asked.

"I am, thank you. Galo took care of the guard who did it." Cas strode forward, sidestepping Jovita. "Advisers, follow me." He looked over his shoulder to see Jovita rooted in place. "Now."

The guards rushed to open the front door for him, and he walked inside and straight to the meeting room. He took the seat at the head of the table. Violet sat next to him, and the other advisers took their seats around her. Cas motioned for Galo and Mateo to stay in the room. They both hovered near him.

"The attack on the Ruined," Cas started, before Jovita had settled in her seat. "I understand it didn't go well. We lost all soldiers except one, correct?"

"That's correct," Danna said. She shot an angry look at Jovita.

"It was only our first—" Jovita began.

"Enough," Cas interrupted. "You've had plenty of time to speak. It's my turn now."

Jovita turned red, but she snapped her mouth shut.

"I've come to a few conclusions. One, sending our soldiers to attack the Ruined without proper preparation was deeply stupid. It was reckless and immature and caused us to lose soldiers when we need them most." He leveled his gaze at Jovita, but she refused to meet it. "Two, locking me up under the pretense of being insane simply because I disagreed with all of you was treasonous, a crime punishable by death in Lera."

Silence descended on the room. General Amaro's throat bobbed as she swallowed hard.

"Three, you were right about the Ruined, and because of that, I will spare your lives."

Julieta's eyebrows shot up. "What do you mean, we were right?"

"The Ruined are plotting to attack the fortress again. Emelina and Olivia have formed a diarchy and they've taken up residence in Sacred Rock. I've been there."

"You went to Sacred Rock?" Jovita sat up straighter.

"Briefly. I went to speak with Emelina about the possibility of a peace treaty between the Ruined and Lera. She was not amenable to the discussion."

Jovita snorted. "No kidding."

"However, it turns out you did accomplish one thing by attacking the Ruined." Cas turned to Jovita. "Emelina has plans to kill you. You're her highest priority."

The smug look on his cousin's face faded. "I—I guess that was to be expected."

He reached into his pocket for the letter and slid it across the table to her. "I intercepted a letter from Emelina on my way out of town. I suspect you're the leader she's talking about in it. She sent Ruined after us to kill me—she must have thought I was already taken care of."

Jovita hastily opened the letter, frowning as she read it. "It's to an Olso leader. They still have an alliance."

"They will continue to have one. Emelina is considering an offer of marriage from August, the youngest prince of Olso."

Julieta pressed her palms to her forehead. "We thought the

Ruined might reject the warriors once they were back in Ruina."

"Perhaps they would have. Then you attacked them and made their alliance even stronger." Cas looked at each adviser in turn. "This nonsense about me being insane ends now. I will admit that I was wrong about the Ruined. And you will admit that the attack on them was a mistake. From now on, we will be cautious and smart. We will form a plan to defeat the Ruined and retake the castle when it makes the most sense."

"The castle isn't a priority," Jovita said. "We still have the south, so—"

Cas slammed his hand against the table, making her jump. "It's a priority because I say it is. Argue with me again and I'll reconsider those treason charges." He stood. "That goes for all of you." He turned and walked out of the room, Galo and Mateo following him.

Cas looked over his shoulder at Galo as soon as they were out of the room. "Find all the guards who are loyal to me. Quickly. I'm going to need their protection."

TWENTY-FOUR

EM PULLED THE door to Cas's house closed behind her. It was no longer Cas's house, but she would probably always refer to it that way.

"It's clean," Em said. "They didn't leave anything behind." Mariana and Ivanna waited in the dirt at the bottom of the steps.

Mariana's eyes brightened. "Can I take it, then?"

"Sure."

Mariana scurried past Em, throwing open the door and bounding inside.

"Does she really need a whole house to herself?" Ivanna asked, with a hint of amusement.

"Might as well take advantage now. We'll probably be back in tents and the miner cabins again soon." She tried not to sigh as she said the words. As much as she hated to admit it, she didn't want to go back to Ruina. It didn't feel like home anymore.

She turned back to the center of town, Ivanna falling into step beside her. Ruined mingled outside the shops. This town was the nicest accommodations most of them had seen in more than a year, but Sacred Rock didn't feel like home either. It felt like wherever Em took the Ruined, she just put them in more danger.

"A few of the Ruined council met last night," Ivanna said quietly.

"That doesn't sound good. Who is 'a few'?"

"Me and Davi and Mariana."

Em stopped, turning to face Ivanna. "And?"

"We're concerned about Olivia. I heard the Vallos army attacked us because she provoked them."

Em didn't respond. Her silence was probably confirmation enough.

"It hasn't escaped our attention that you're the only one making smart decisions," Ivanna said.

Em looked at her in surprise. After Cas's visit, she hadn't thought the words *smart decisions* would be associated with her for quite a while.

"I won't lie to you, I didn't want you to be queen. I voted against you when Damian took over. I thought Olivia was taking pity on you when she announced the diarchy."

"Don't sugarcoat it," Em said dryly.

"I'm saying I was wrong. And I want you to know that you

can count on our support. Even if it means going against Olivia. Or removing her from the throne."

Em shifted uncomfortably. She knew what it was like to be removed from the throne. She didn't want to do that to her sister.

"I don't think that's going to be necessary. She's still upset about being captured. She just needs some time to adjust."

Ivanna seemed skeptical. "I hope so."

"You said you met with Davi and Mariana. What about Jacobo?" she asked, even though she already suspected the answer. She'd seen him following Olivia around, jumping at every order.

"I wouldn't count on his support. And I don't know about Aren, either."

"Aren's always on my side."

Ivanna didn't appear convinced, but Em was certain about Aren. He was always on her side.

"We also spoke about August," Ivanna said. "Has Aren mentioned it to you yet?"

"No. What about him?"

"I'll admit that I was excited about a marriage alliance with Olso at first, but me and the rest of the council are reconsidering."

Hope surged up her spine. "Why is that?"

"Olso owes us after abandoning us back when Lera declared war on the Ruined. I don't think a marriage should be required to secure their assistance."

"I'm not sure they'll see it that way."

Ivanna shrugged. "Then it's not a long-term alliance. They'll leave after Jovita is dead. But I don't want you to feel like you have to marry him just to make us happy. You've done enough for us."

A lump rose in Em's throat, and she blinked quickly before tears could form. "You don't think it's important to have Olso's support long-term?"

"I don't think we can count on anything long-term at this point. I'm sorry to be blunt, Emelina, but there is a possibility that August will have you killed after you have a few children."

The same thought had occurred to her. She would spend their entire marriage looking over her shoulder, sleeping with a dagger within reach.

"I'll think about it," Em said, the relief coming through in her voice.

Ivanna reached out to squeeze her arm. "Remember that you can come to me if you need anything. Even if it's just to talk things out."

"Thank you," Em said. Ivanna smiled and walked away.

Em continued slowly down the dirt path. She'd never gotten the impression the council was on Olivia's side, but she certainly never thought most of them would be firmly on *hers*.

She spotted Aren near the warrior camp, sitting in front of a large bucket with Iria. They were washing clothes.

Aren caught her watching, said something to Iria, and jogged over to Em. "I'm glad I caught you," he said. "I wanted to ask you about something."

"What's that?"

"Do you think I could volunteer to go north with the warriors?"

"What?"

"Have you already assigned Ruined to go?"

"Uh, no," she said. *Aren was going to voluntarily spend time with warriors for a week or two?*

"Then send me. Pick two weaker Ruined to go with me. I can protect the warriors."

"Why?"

He didn't meet her eyes. "I want to get away for a while."

"Get away from what?" She followed his gaze when he didn't reply. He was watching Olivia, sitting on the porch of their house.

"You know she's planning to marry me?" he asked quietly.

"I heard. How do you feel about that?"

His face was more openly haunted than she'd ever seen. He looked almost close to tears. "I can't, Em. I can't. I know I was always meant for one of you, and it's a smart political choice, but . . ." He shook his head. "Please, Em. Please don't make me."

"What? Aren, I would never make you do anything." She reached out and gently squeezed his arm. "Did you think you didn't have a choice?"

"I think Olivia assumed . . ." His voice trailed off. "And I know some of the Ruined assume it's my responsibility to lead since I'm so powerful."

"I promise it's your choice. If anyone tries to pressure you, send them my way."

He laughed and let out a shaky breath. "Thanks."

"And I think you're wrong about the Ruined wanting you to marry her. I just had a conversation with Ivanna. She's not that supportive of me marrying August. I don't think she's ready to push anyone into a marriage."

"Really? I talked to her about that a while back and she thought it was a good idea."

"She's changed her mind."

"That's a relief. I don't want that guy around forever."

"Nothing's decided yet," she said. "But there was something else."

"What?"

"Most of the council isn't happy with Olivia."

"I suspected. They don't talk to me about it because they think I'm close to Olivia."

"I thought they were mad at me about Cas, but it seems like they're more concerned with Olivia right now."

"I can't blame them."

"They might not be thrilled if they knew I was staying in contact with Cas."

His eyebrows shot up. "What?"

She quickly relayed Cas's plan to kill Jovita, and his request to meet in four days.

"Seriously?" Aren asked. "He's going to kill her for us?"

"And give us information about Lera's plans. Make her look stupid."

"Wow."

"So it's actually good that you want to go with the warriors, because I need you to protect him if you run into him. You'll get pretty close to the fortress, and Cas will be traveling south soon."

"I can try. Are you going to meet him in four days?"

"Yes."

"What does he want in return?"

"Nothing. Or nothing I hadn't already offered. A promise not to send Ruined into Lera to attack."

"He's going to try to retake the throne, right? I don't think August would approve of us helping Cas."

"I'm sure he wouldn't. I haven't told anyone about this except you," she said. "Our secret?"

Aren nodded. "Our secret."

TWENTY-FIVE

THE KITCHEN STAFF thought Cas was insane.

He'd considered many options to avoid getting poisoned again, and he'd finally settled on the one that made the most sense—he'd simply make his own food.

Galo had looked at him like he'd grown a second head and offered again to taste his food first. Cas declined that ridiculous offer. Galo pointed out that Cas didn't actually know how to cook.

Details.

"It's slimy," he said, holding up the meat from the pig Mateo had killed. He stood at the counter of the small kitchen, not far from the open window. It was one of the only rooms in the fortress with a window, and it was quickly becoming his favorite room in the building.

Blanca tried to grab it out of his hand. "Your Majesty, let me—"

He held it out of her grasp. "I'm learning how to cook pig. It's an essential skill, wouldn't you say?"

She huffed, placing her hands on her hips. Behind her, Leticia giggled.

"Season it, Your Majesty," Blanca said with a defeated sigh. She thrust a bottle into his hand.

"How much?" he asked, shaking it over the meat.

"That's good. Now turn it over and do the other side."

He did as she instructed, then heated a skillet and plopped the meat inside. "Tomorrow will you show me how to debone fish? Galo was going to take me to the river to catch some."

"You're going to catch it yourself too?" Leticia asked skeptically.

"Can't eat fish unless I catch it." He pointed to the meat. "How long is it supposed to stay in there?"

"A few more minutes," Blanca said. "And yes, I'll teach you to debone fish. Next you'll be asking Leticia how to wash your own clothes."

His brow crinkled in confusion. "Do you do more than just stick them in water with soap?"

Leticia giggled again.

"I should probably ask about that," he said. Blanca threw up her hands, grumbling something he couldn't understand.

"Were you really poisoned, Your Majesty?" Leticia asked, lowering her voice. Blanca waved a towel at her and put a finger to her lips.

"No, I don't mind," Cas said. "I was. Luckily Galo realized it in time."

"You know we would never poison you," Blanca said. "I would deliver my food to you personally, from now on."

"I know," he said gently. "But I need to learn this anyway. No need for you to go out of your way."

She gave him another baffled look, but her eyes sparkled with amusement. "Turn your meat, Your Majesty."

He did as she said. He finished cooking the meat, then cut it and placed it on plates. He'd already cut up some vegetables and distributed them. He put a small chunk of meat on a plate and pushed it toward Blanca.

"That's for you."

"I couldn't take that, Your Majesty."

"You have to tell me if it's good!"

She paused, then grabbed a knife and sliced off a piece. She lifted it to her lips and nodded as she chewed.

"Not bad."

"Thank you."

"Leticia, take those plates to the dining room for him," the cook ordered.

Leticia jumped to action, grabbing two plates. He took the other two before she could protest.

"Lead the way," he said. He watched her carefully as they

walked through the kitchen doors.

Violet, Mateo, and Galo sat at the small square table off the kitchen. It was used as the staff dining room, but Cas had asked if he and his friends could dine there tonight.

"Is it edible?" Violet asked. Her cheeks were a bit pink, probably from the glass of wine each had in front of them.

"I hope so." He put a plate down in front of her. Leticia served Galo and Mateo, then scurried out of the room before Cas could even thank her.

"Where did you find wine?" he asked as he sat down next to Violet.

"General Amaro gave it to me. Everyone is suddenly so interested in being my friend." She held up the bottle, offering some to him.

"No, thank you." He needed his head clear, always.

"Hey, this is pretty good!" Galo said, pointing to his plate.

"I'll pretend that tone isn't so surprised," Cas said. Galo grinned at him.

Cas took a bite of the meat, watching as Mateo bumped his shoulder against Galo's. They exchanged a smile. If Cas had stayed with Em, maybe he would be sitting next to her, saying things to her without words. Maybe he'd be cooking for her.

He pushed the thought out of his head. His brief fantasy of staying with Em was over, and the memory of it only caused him shame. He'd been so eager to give up on his people. On everyone in this fortress who was counting on him. On the Ruined he'd promised to protect. So many people needed him to be a strong king. He wasn't going to let them down again.

After dinner he retreated to his room and found Jovita standing in front of his door.

"Can we talk, Cas?"

"Depends. Are you going to poison me again?" He reached around her and opened the door. She followed him inside.

"I didn't poison you. If I was going to kill someone, I'd stab them in the gut. Poison is for cowards."

"Agreed," he said, holding her gaze as he sat down on the edge of the bed.

"You don't believe me?"

"Forgive me if I'm not very trusting after you tried to convince everyone I was insane."

"Forgive me if I'm still not convinced of your sanity."

"Shall I do something to prove it?"

"I was thinking—do sane people have to prove it?"

He let out a short laugh. "I suppose they don't."

She seemed annoyed he hadn't taken offense. "What are you doing, Cas? You can't really expect me to believe your opinion about the Ruined has changed so quickly."

"No. I still think what my father did was wrong. I think he and my mother would still be alive if he hadn't declared war on the Ruined. But we can't change the past. We're in this war, and we have to finish it."

"Before, you were talking like you wanted to surrender to the Ruined. Or partner with them. Be honest. You let Emelina go after she attacked the fortress."

"I let Emelina go," he said. Jovita's eyebrows shot up at the admission. "I had feelings for her."

Jovita sneered. "Your mother told me you never even consummated."

"We didn't."

"How sad." She didn't sound the least bit sad about it.

"I went to find her. I thought she . . ." He set his mouth in a hard line. "I thought she loved me."

"What gave you that idea? The fact that she killed your actual fiancée? Or was it when she refused to have sex with you?"

Cas ignored the flicker of anger in his chest. "I know I'm an idiot, Jovita. No need to rub it in."

"Sorry," she said, and almost sounded sincere.

"She was going to let Olivia kill me. She laughed at me. We barely got out of there alive."

"I could have told you that was what would happen," Jovita said. "If you'd talked to me about Emelina I could have explained that the Ruined don't love humans. Even useless ones."

Cas knew so much more about the Ruined than her. Her ignorance of them, her absolute certainty that they were nothing but evil, was her biggest weakness. It hadn't even occurred to her that he was working with Em. The thought wasn't in the realm of possibility for her.

"I think our days of talking about things is over," Cas said.

Jovita crossed her arms over her chest. "It would be better for you if we could work together."

"Better for *me*?" He laughed.

"Just because you have the title of king doesn't mean you have any power. I hope you know that. Most of the hunters and soldiers here still take orders from me."

"Really? Even after you sent a bunch of them to their deaths? How sure are you of their loyalty?"

"Sure enough."

"Fine. They can all stay with you here after I reclaim the castle. You won't be welcome there."

"You'll die if you try to retake the castle."

"That will work out just as you'd hoped."

She stomped to the door. "I didn't poison you, Cas."

"Then find out who did. I'm sure the two of you will be the best of friends."

She threw a furious look over her shoulder and slammed the door shut.

TWENTY-SIX

AREN LED THE party of warriors and Ruined out of Sacred Rock at dawn. He rode in front, Iria behind him. Clara and Santino brought up the rear. No other Ruined had volunteered for the mission, so Aren had to spend some time convincing them. Neither had very strong powers, but Olivia had forbidden any other powerful Ruined from going.

They were traveling east, to the coast of Vallos, then following it up into Lera. They passed several farms with long rows of crops just outside of Sacred Rock, but they disappeared as they neared the coast. The air grew colder, and he buttoned his coat and pulled on his gloves.

Aren had been to this area once, months ago, when he was on the run with Em. The long, overgrown grass was easy to hide in. He stepped carefully, scanning the area to make sure Vallos soldiers hadn't followed them and had the same idea.

They stopped at the base of a hill as the sun began to set. They didn't want to risk building a fire, so they ate dried meat they'd brought with them. Clara and Santino looked like they were going to eat by themselves, away from the warriors, but Aren shook his head and pointed for them to sit with the rest of the group. Dinner was eaten mostly in silence.

"Come on," Iria said after they were finished. She jumped to her feet and held her hand out to him.

He let her pull him to his feet. A few warriors were clearing sticks and rocks from the dirt and placing blankets down. "What are they doing?"

"Group sleep," she said. "We do it when it's cold. Body heat helps everyone sleep better."

"Are we included in this group sleep?" He gestured to the other Ruined.

"Unless you'd rather shiver all night." She looked at Clara. "Unless she can make it warm?"

"Not for an extended period of time. It's not a smart use of her power."

"Then come on." She walked to the sleeping area and plopped down. He hesitated.

"Are we all supposed to sleep together?" Clara asked, wrinkling her nose.

"It's up to you," Aren said. "We're welcome, apparently."

"I'm fine over here," Santino said. Clara nodded in agreement.

Aren looked back at Iria. Some of the warriors had started to sit down, but there was no one on either side of her yet. He wanted to sit next to her more than he was willing to admit.

"Your choice," he said to the Ruined, trying to sound casual. "I think it'll be warmer over there."

He walked away from them, toward Iria. He wanted to be warm. Right. That was exactly why he was doing this.

"The others don't want to?" she asked as he sat down next to her.

"No."

She reached down and grabbed the blanket at her feet, shaking the dust out. She threw it open, letting it fall over them. Aren scooted onto his back without a word.

The other warriors filed in, until there were people on either side of him and Iria. The snoring started almost immediately.

He couldn't sleep. Every time he closed his eyes they popped back open. He could sense the presence of every human around him, but one in particular. It was like Iria was emitting a signal that his body couldn't ignore. He could practically feel her heartbeat in his own chest.

The man next to Aren turned suddenly, his arm flopping onto Aren's chest. He tossed it back. A soft giggle came from beside him. Iria was on her side, grinning at him. He rolled over to face her.

"This is weird," he whispered.

"But it's warmer, right?"

"I guess."

"Ruined don't huddle for warmth?"

"Not in a big group like this." An image of Damian formed in front of him, and his voice was strained when he spoke again. "I did with Damian and Em sometimes."

"What was . . ." She trailed off, biting her lip. "Do you mind if I ask what that time was like? After the castle burned?"

The guy on the other side of Aren rolled over, nudging him. He scooted a little closer to Iria.

"It was mostly about survival," he said quietly. "At the time Damian didn't know if his parents were dead or alive—they'd been traveling—and Em and I knew ours were dead. During the day we were just trying to stay alive. But at night . . . night was bad sometimes. Night is when you have time to think."

"Did you ever consider coming north to Olso? Looking for me or other families you knew?"

"I suggested it, actually. But then the hunters came in force and no one showed up to help. We figured the warriors decided we were on our own." He didn't try to keep the bitterness from his voice.

Her dark eyes held his, full of sadness and regret. "I'm sorry, Aren. I'm so sorry. I should have fought harder. My parents should have fought harder. We should have tried to help in any way we could."

He hadn't realized he wanted an apology, but as soon as she said it, something inside him sighed in relief. "Thanks, Iria," he said softly. His hand brushed against her fingers. He didn't move. "Did you fight? You didn't tell me that."

She nodded. "We tried talking to the king and his advisers so many times. We got a group of warriors together to back us up. But we could have done more. I convinced myself it wasn't actually that bad, that you could defend yourselves."

"You're here now. Most of us really appreciate it." He paused. "*I* really appreciate it."

A small smile crossed her lips. She had pretty, full lips, and if he leaned forward a little, he could kiss her. It had been too long since he'd kissed a girl.

He quickly closed his eyes. Even if he was going to throw caution to the wind and make out with a warrior, this was certainly not the time or place. He could feel the man next to him breathing. Clara and Santino were probably watching the warriors instead of sleeping.

Iria's heartbeat slowed a little as she fell asleep. Hers was stronger than anyone's. He rolled onto his back, trying to let it lull him into sleep.

Something brushed against his arm, and he looked over to see her curled up right next him, so close her forehead tickled his skin. Her breath warmed his skin through his clothes.

He scooted a tiny bit closer to her. For warmth, he told himself.

He closed his eyes and sleep came almost immediately.

TWENTY-SEVEN

EM LIFTED HER hand to wave at the newly arrived warriors. August had requested a hundred, but only fifty arrived, with a note from the king about more joining later. Fifty was enough, for now. Aren would probably return from the north with more.

"It's a good group they sent," August said as the warriors spread out to erect more tents. "I think you'll be pleased."

Pleased wasn't the word she would have used, but she nodded anyway.

"It'll be good to have them since Aren left," August said. He obviously wanted her to gush about how wonderful his warriors were.

"It will," she said.

"Not that I mind Aren protecting my warriors during the

journey. How did you convince him?"

"I didn't. He volunteered."

"I'll have to thank him when he returns."

"Sure." Whatever Aren's reasons for going, she knew it was not to make August happy. In fact, she suspected it was more about him getting away from Olivia.

"Are you hungry? I think our dinner is ready."

She nodded, trying not to let out a huge sigh. August had killed a deer during the morning hunt, and he'd excitedly invited himself over to dinner. *Just the two of us*, he'd said. She couldn't think of a good reason to say no.

She wasn't ready to say anything at all to August yet. She desperately wanted to take the conversation with Ivanna as an excuse to decline his proposal immediately, but she feared he would take all of his warriors and leave. She wasn't sure the Ruined were strong enough to stand on their own yet.

She also wasn't sure it was smart to decline his proposal at all. Even if he did plan to dispose of her after a few years, that was a few years the Ruined could use to get back on their feet. Besides, she'd like to see him try to harm her. She'd seen him fight. He was no match for her.

Em and August walked to her apartment and found it empty except for one warrior in the kitchen. Olivia had made herself scarce, as Em had requested.

The warrior placed their plates on the table and August dismissed him. The meat and beans were better food than she'd had in weeks, and she tried not to look too enthusiastic as she ate it.

She sat back in her chair as she finished chewing the last bite. August had his head rested against his fist, a little smile on his face as he watched her. The knife she'd used to cut her meat sat on the edge of her plate. She rested one finger on the handle. She'd never been very good at knife-throwing, but August was close enough to be an easy target.

"Tell me what you want," he said.

I want you to leave? She took a sip of water. "What do you mean?"

"What do you want for the Ruined? What do you want to accomplish? What had you originally planned to do after you left Lera and rescued Olivia?"

"I planned to go back to Ruina and rebuild our life. I wanted the Ruined to be able to live in peace, without being hunted and killed."

"And after that?"

"I don't know."

"Did you have plans to marry? Do you want children?"

"I'm well aware we'll be expected to produce children," she said, her chest tightening. She wished she'd been able to finish what she started with Cas. She could still feel his hands on her, his breath on her skin.

"That's not what I asked. Do you *want* children?"

"Yes," she said. "Not immediately, but I would very much like children." Even little warrior children would be nice. A family.

Of course, August would be part of it. She tried not to wince.

"You?" she asked, only to be polite.

He shrugged. "Always expected of me, so I figured I would." He screwed up his face. "They're a bit gross when they're young, though. I think I'll like them better when they can talk and swing a sword."

He sounded like he'd be the sort of parent Em's father was. He'd been nice enough, but always seemed confused as to what to do with his children. Em could barely remember any conversations of importance with her father, because he so often avoided being alone with her and Olivia.

"Who were you going to marry if I didn't show up?" August asked suddenly.

She looked at him in confusion. "What?"

"As the eldest queen, you must have been expected to marry soon. Did you have anyone in mind?"

"No. Marriage wasn't the highest priority. We're in the middle of a war."

"I was just wondering . . ." He turned his water glass around in his hands. "You and Aren are like brother and sister. There aren't that many other eligible Ruined men. Maybe it's good I showed up." He chuckled like he was joking, but Em caught his meaning. She was supposed to be grateful he was willing to marry her.

She was feeling a strong emotion at the moment, but she was pretty sure it wasn't gratitude.

The door banged open and Olivia jumped inside, spreading her arms wide. "I'm here! Run for your lives!"

Em turned, the sight of her sister dissolving her anger. "What are you doing?"

"I'm practicing my entrances. I want to have a good one. Wait." She spread her arms again. "I'm here! Fear me."

"That was terrible," Em said. "It makes me fear you less."

"I'll work on it." Olivia pointed at August. "He looks kind of scared, though."

Em turned to August. He did seem uncomfortable now that Olivia had entered the room.

"Thank you for dinner," Em said, getting up from the table. "I'll see you tomorrow?"

August took the hint and stood. "Good night, Em. Olivia." He nodded at her as he walked out of the door.

"Did I wait too long?" Olivia asked after the door closed.

"No, good timing," Em said, flopping down on the couch. "He was starting to talk about children."

"Ew." Olivia sat down next to her. "You don't have to marry him, you know. I don't want you to."

"I know you don't. But we need the warriors."

"No we don't."

"Yes, we do. At the very least, we can't fight them *and* Lera."

"He's just using you, though."

"And I'm not doing the same to him? You think I want to marry August because I like him? I like his army."

"You don't need his army."

Em sighed. She'd never convince Olivia of this. Every time

they argued they just circled back around to the same point.

Olivia patted Em's arm. "You won't need to marry him. I promise."

"That's not really up to you."

"Don't worry, sister. I promise, you won't have to marry him."

"What do you mean?"

"I mean the Ruined will be so strong that you won't have to marry him. I suppose you still could, if you wanted, but that would be an odd choice."

"We're not strong enough right now. I know you want us to be, but—"

"I'm training some of the Ruined to use their powers without exhausting themselves. I just need a little more time. You can get rid of him soon."

"I don't want you to worry about this, Liv. Marrying him wouldn't be the worst thing. I'm being dramatic. He's not bad to look at. And he's been kind to me, I guess."

"Even if you do end up marrying him, I could get you out of it. If he turns out to be horrible, I'll just take his head off!"

"Thanks, sister," Em said with a laugh.

"Anytime." Her eyes brightened. "I've got it." She spread her arms. "I'm here! Hold on to your heads!"

"Worst one yet."

TWENTY-EIGHT

CAS EDGED OUT of his bedroom and into the hallway. The fortress was dark and quiet, a lone candle flickering at the end of the hallway.

Galo met him at the stairs and they descended them silently. A laugh came from the parlor, and they kept to the shadows. Jovita and a few hunters were in there, like they were every night.

They walked through the kitchen and into the small dining room. Violet and Mateo were already there, along with Blanca and a guard whose name Cas had forgotten.

"This is Ric," Galo said as the guard jumped to his feet.

"Your Majesty," Ric said.

"Thanks for coming," Cas said. He took a seat at the table and everyone followed, Galo sliding into the chair next to him.

"We're dividing the guard into three parts," Galo said. He nodded at Mateo and Ric. "We're going to assess each member and find out who is solidly with you, who is solidly with Jovita, and who is on the fence. We can make lists, if you'd like."

"No, it's better not to put anything in writing. Galo, why don't you spend time each day pointing out guards so I can learn their names. I'll memorize their faces."

"Sure," Galo said. "Blanca?"

"Almost all of the staff is with you," she said. "There are a few who were swayed by Jovita saying you'd lost your mind. I need some time to figure out just how loyal they are." She smiled, the creases around her eyes moving. "And most of the advisers treat me like I'm invisible. I can tell you that General Amaro is *not* happy that you were poisoned. She's barely speaking to Jovita. I think we can turn her to your side."

"Excellent," Cas said.

"Julieta's hard to read. And I'm still working on the other advisers."

"I spoke with Pedro yesterday," Violet said, referring to the governor of the western province. "He basically said he follows me, and the southern province."

"We need to make sure you maintain your hold on the southern province," Cas said. "I want us to take a trip there and meet some of the people."

"Is that safe?" Violet asked.

"The soldiers Jovita sent to check the area returned saying they found no warriors. I figured we could go after—" He cut himself off, not sure he wanted everyone to know he was meeting with Em. "Day after tomorrow," he said. Violet nodded knowingly.

"That doesn't leave us a lot of time to assess the guard," Galo said.

Cas shook his head. "You and Mateo stay here. Just Violet and I will go."

"No," Galo and Mateo said together.

"It will be a short trip," Cas said. "We're already in the southern province. And we'll attract less attention just the two of us." He turned to Violet. "If that's all right with you."

"It's no problem. May we go by my home? I'd like to see if it's still there and check on my grandmother and the staff."

"Of course." He wished he could go by his home too. He wondered if any part of the castle was still standing.

"Venturing out without even one guard right now is not going to help convince everyone you're sane," Galo said.

"Galo!" Violet exclaimed.

"What? It's true. What sane king would wander around without a guard during wartime?"

"One who wants to travel inconspicuously," Cas said. "Most people in the southern province don't know what I look like. And I can defend myself. So can Violet. I've seen her use a sword."

"I'm also solid with a bow and arrow," she said.

"Good. We'll get you one before we leave." He looked around the table. "Anything else?" Everyone shook their head. "Thank you for this. I can't tell you how much I appreciate it."

Blanca squeezed his hand as she stood, and the rest of the table followed suit.

"Galo, stay for a minute," Cas said. He waited until everyone else had left before turning to his friend. "Jovita claims she didn't poison me."

"Of course she does."

"I'm sure she's lying, but can you keep an ear out, just in case?"

Galo nodded. "I don't see who else it could be. Unless one of the advisers is making a play for the throne. . . ." His face tensed in thought. "Are you sure you want to leave her alone here? You just returned."

"It's only a few days. The southern province is more important than anything happening here."

"What are you going to do if it wasn't Jovita who poisoned you?"

"It was her," he said, but he'd had the same thought as Galo. There was a slim possibility an adviser or governor had seen an opportunity and run with it. "But if it wasn't . . . it doesn't change anything."

Aren bent down to the stream, tipping his canteen so the water flowed in. He raised it to his lips and took a sip. Beside him, Iria did the same.

They'd crossed into the southern province of Lera, and soon the air would be warmer, the trees greener. As much as he hated to admit it, he didn't mind being back in Lera. The trees were already thicker around them, a few of them still with all their leaves.

As far as he could tell, the warriors hadn't infiltrated southern Lera yet. Iria said that after they lost the battle at the fortress, most of the warriors had been ordered north, to Royal City or Gallego City. They were the two most populous areas, and it made more sense to keep a hold on them.

Aren walked back to his horse. There was no talking today, and he quietly hooked his canteen back to his bag.

He turned around. Iria was walking back from the stream. She stopped suddenly. Her face tensed.

Aren put his hand on his sword. She met his gaze, sliding her eyes to her right.

An arrow flew out of the bushes. It was headed straight for Iria.

"Attack!" he yelled, holding one arm out. He focused on Iria and her feet left the ground. She flew at him with such force that she almost knocked him over. The arrow sailed through the empty space where she used to be.

"Clara!" he yelled. She ran through his eye line, and the tree where the arrow had come from swayed left, then right. It toppled over, bringing screams with it. Three men darted out of the way, straight at Aren.

He shot all three of them back at once. He hadn't detached, hadn't used any of the training Olivia had given him. His legs should have been shaking right about now.

Instead, he could feel his power shooting through his veins. It tingled pleasantly, fueling him instead of draining him.

"Kill the Ruined!" someone yelled. A Lera hunter with several blue pins pointed at him. A warrior took off toward him.

"I've got it!" Aren called. He reached out to Iria. "May I . . ."

She looked at him in confusion, but she held her arm out. He wrapped his fingers around her wrist.

He turned back to the hunter, who was now running away from him at top speed. Aren stopped the man's feet suddenly, causing him to fall flat on his face. A warrior laughed.

Aren lifted the hunter off the ground, which usually took so much energy it made him feel sick. But he felt steady, calm, even as he snapped the man's neck.

The man hit the ground with a thud. Aren stared at him, regret filling his chest. He had to kill the hunter, otherwise he would have run back to the fortress and given them away. But sadness trickled in anyway.

He didn't mind. He liked the sadness. With this kill, at least he still felt like himself. At least he wasn't numb.

The warriors swarmed the remaining men. Aren was still holding on to Iria. He had one arm around her waist, clutching her to his side. He quickly released her.

"Thank you," she said, looking at the ground as she stepped away from him.

He wanted to touch her again as soon as she was gone. It was as if his entire body was bending toward her, begging to be close.

He looked down at his hand. It was almost like he could still feel her on his skin. Like her warmth was still radiating through his body, making him strong. He didn't feel the least bit weak, even after using his magic.

Iria had her head cocked to the side, watching him with a mixture of interest and confusion.

"What . . ." Iria let her voice trail off.

He wanted to tell her. He wanted to grab her arm again and ask her to let him experiment. But Clara and Santino and all the warriors were watching, listening.

Clara had her back pressed to a tree, something he'd seen elemental Ruined do often. Damian used to lie on the ground, arms and legs spread, saying that the dirt and the grass fueled him. He claimed he was stronger in Vallos than Ruina, because of their abundant crops and water. Ruina was too dry and desolate to fuel his Ruined magic, he said.

Aren thought they were imagining things. Elemental Ruined were always going on about being connected to nature, but he didn't think they meant it literally.

He walked away from Iria. He could almost feel her eyes following him.

"Clara," he said softly as he stopped in front of her.

"What?"

"Does leaning against that tree help you get your strength back faster?"

She nodded. "Feels like it. Some Ruined disagree. I think they're just not focusing."

"Focusing?"

"Yeah." She reached both arms back, curling her fingers

around the trunk. "You can't think of it as taking energy from the tree. You're connecting with it. You're asking it for help. When you ask, it responds."

"The tree responds."

"Hey. Don't make fun of me. You don't know. A tree is a living thing. A living thing I can command. You don't think I can communicate with it?"

"I guess you can," he murmured.

"I *definitely* can."

"Is there, like . . . a feeling?"

"Sure." She leaned her head back against the bark. "It's like I can feel the energy in my veins."

He glanced back at Iria. Was that what was happening? Could a human actually help fuel his Ruined magic?

"Why?" Clara followed his gaze. "Did something happen with that warrior?"

"I don't know."

"Aren! That's crazy."

He shushed her. "I said I don't know."

She leaned forward, lowering her voice to a whisper. "Figure it out. Do you know what that could mean for us? What Ruined like you could use humans for?"

His body tensed at the word *use.* She'd talked about communication and requests with a tree, but with a human it was *use*?

He stepped back. "I think I was imagining things. Olivia's been training me. I'm just getting stronger."

"Test it out anyway. Tell me how it goes."

"I will." He knew the words were a lie as soon as they left his mouth.

He walked back to Iria, who was standing next to her horse. Her face was open, curious, as she watched him, and he realized with a start that there was no one here he trusted more than her. Not even his fellow Ruined.

"I'll tell you later," he said under his breath as he passed her.

She mounted her horse. "Thank you saving my life, by the way."

"You already said."

"Oh. I did?" Pink tinged her cheeks, and she ducked her chin into her chest as she grabbed the saddle of her horse.

He tried to hide his amusement. Was it wrong that he liked that he flustered her?

"Duck next time," he said with a grin. "I can't constantly be saving you."

She was obviously trying not to smile. "I would have, if you hadn't decided to throw me around with your Ruined magic."

"Sure you would have."

"I would! I have very fast reflexes, you know."

He laughed, and she grinned at him, her cheeks still pink.

TWENTY-NINE

EM WAITED UNTIL Olivia was asleep to sneak out.

She put her sword and canteen on her belt and walked down the quiet, deserted street to the barn. They had Ruined and warriors on watch nearby, but she would find a way to explain later. For now, she needed to get to Cas and find out if Jovita had bought his story.

She saddled a horse and led him outside into the dark. She kicked his sides until he broke into a gallop. They slowed as the town disappeared behind them.

It wasn't far to the meeting spot—about halfway between the fortress and Sacred Rock, but her heart beat too fast the entire way. What if he wasn't there? What if Galo was there, with news of Cas's death?

The journey was mostly out in the open—no trees or hills to hide behind—and she had to admit that meeting Cas was wildly risky. There weren't any towns between Sacred Rock and the Fortress, but there were farms, and she could be easily spotted. Hopefully the farmers were asleep or had long abandoned their homes when the Ruined moved in.

She spotted a dark figure as she finally approached the meeting spot. Her heart jumped into her throat.

Two figures, actually. A shorter, slimmer person was next to the man.

She jumped off her horse and practically ran to them. It was Cas and Violet. "You're here."

"I said I would be." Cas's voice had an edge to it. She couldn't blame him, but still, it stung.

"How is everything?" she asked. "Did you make it to the fortress?"

"We made it," Cas said. "Jovita took me back. She claims she didn't poison me."

"What?"

"It's a lie. I'm sure of it."

It was too dark to read the nuances of his expression, but his tone sounded sure. The Cas she knew wouldn't be so certain. He'd question and ponder and hesitate. Perhaps he was fooling himself now, but what about in a year? Ten years? When he looked back on murdering Jovita, would he still wonder?

"Let me do it," she said quickly. "I'll kill Jovita. Find a way to lure her out and I'll take care of it."

"Why?" Cas asked.

"You know why. To spare you from killing your own family."

"She's not my family." He shrugged. "Besides, whether it's your sword or mine doesn't matter. I'll be responsible for her death."

She wished she'd told him no. She wished she'd taken him up on his offer to stay with her, despite the cost. This cold, hollow version of Cas was almost too much to take.

"I don't have any information for you yet," Cas said. "But Jovita is definitely in a holding pattern right now, so there's no need to worry about an attack." He gestured at Violet. "We're leaving from here to visit some people Violet knows in the southern province. So we should wait awhile before meeting again."

"Jovita didn't find that suspicious?"

"I told her I wanted to go home and check on my grandmother," Violet said. "It's not far."

"But, yes, she was suspicious." Cas smiled at Violet. "She knows the power Violet has over the southern province. Our friendship makes her very nervous."

Violet laughed softly, and the lump in Em's throat grew three sizes. She didn't have a right to be jealous. She was practically engaged to someone else.

Still, the knowledge that Cas and Violet were going to be traveling together, alone, made her want to curl up in the dirt and scream.

"How long until you return to the fortress?" she asked, trying to keep her voice steady.

"We figure we'll be gone about three or four nights," Cas said. "Let's plan to meet again in ten days. I'll send Galo if I can't get away."

She wanted to ask why he didn't think he'd be able to get away. She wanted to ask if he was even going to try. She wanted to ask if this was the last time she was going to see him.

"Sounds good," she said instead. Her voice betrayed the fact that nothing was good about this situation.

"Do you have any information for me?" Cas asked.

She shook her head. "We're also in a holding pattern. A group of warriors and Ruined are going north to find out the status of the warriors in Gallego City and Royal City. Aren is with them. I'll let you know what they find out."

"How far north?" Cas asked.

"Not farther than Gallego City."

"Oh."

"If I hear anything about the castle . . ."

Cas cleared his throat. "You'll tell me. I know." He stuffed his hands in his pockets. "And August? Are you officially engaged?"

Violet must have taken that as her cue to leave, because she turned and walked back to her horse.

"No," Em said quietly. "I'm still not sure it will happen. Olivia isn't crazy about the idea. And neither am I."

He stared at her but said nothing. She desperately wanted to ask about Violet, but she couldn't bring herself to betray just how jealous she was.

"I'll see you in ten days," he said. "Or Galo will."

"Try to come," she said. "Please?"

He nodded. "I will." He turned away and trudged to Violet. She waved at Em, and Em lifted her hand in reply. At least Violet stood by him. At least she seemed kind, and strong, and she was his friend. Cas had to marry someone else eventually. If it was Violet, at least Em knew he'd picked well.

It didn't make her feel any better. Tears pricked her eyes as she turned away.

She mounted her horse and rode back to Sacred Rock a little slower than she'd come. The air was cold, but she barely felt it stinging her face.

The sun was starting to come up when she approached the barn. A tall, broad figure stood in front of the doors. His hands were planted on his hips.

"Em?" he called as she drew closer. August.

"Hi," she said, trying to sound casual. She jumped off the horse and grabbed the reins. "Would you mind opening the doors?"

August pulled them open and she guided the horse inside. "Where were you?"

"Couldn't sleep."

"So you rode off in the middle of the night? They say you've been gone hours."

She led the horse into his stall and turned to face August. "I didn't go far. I was just scouting the area. I stopped for a while and sat by a stream."

"At night. By yourself."

Her heart pounded, but her voice came out smooth. "Olivia scouts this area every day. No one with any sense is nearby."

"You expect me to believe that you were just wandering around by yourself? I'm not stupid, Emelina." His voice turned angry so quickly she laid a hand on her sword.

"I never said you were, August." She strode past him out of the barn, and he followed her. She pulled the door closed behind them.

He stared at her, his jaw twitching in anger. "You're really not going to tell me what you were doing?"

"I told you. I was scouting the area. We have Ruined do it every day, as I'm sure you're aware."

"I honestly don't know what else you want from me." He let out a humorless laugh. "I bring you food and supplies and warriors and *an offer of marriage* and you still can't be bothered to even look at me twice."

"I told you I was considering your offer of marriage."

"What's there to consider?" he snapped. "The alliance is mutually beneficial. I'm sending a warrior back to Olso to say you've accepted."

"That's funny, I don't remember actually accepting."

He took a step closer to her. "You *need* me. And you should be grateful I consented to this. There are plenty of women in Olso who would fall all over themselves to marry me."

"Then why did you agree?" She crossed her arms over her chest, holding his furious gaze. "Could it be that you need me too? Perhaps more than I need you? You'd be king of the Ruined if I married you. You'll never be king of anything in Olso."

His face flushed. He had no reply to that, it seemed.

She smirked. "I can't promise you an answer until after we've taken care of Jovita. If you can't wait, then you're free to leave."

"And what will your advisers think about that?"

She looked over her shoulder at him. "I think you overestimate their affection for you, August. They'll trust my judgment."

He gave her a sour look and she smiled in return.

She was never marrying him.

THIRTY

VIOLET LED THE way through the southern province. Cas followed behind her on his horse. They didn't talk much. They rode through the night after meeting Em, and Violet said they would reach their first stop by afternoon, so they pressed on through the morning.

Their first stop was a farmhouse, where one of the captains of the southern province lived. Violet said it was likely that he was the most informed on the status of the people and land in the area.

The house was large, two stories, and looked like it hadn't been under attack yet. Farmland stretched out behind it. A long, narrow path led up to a tall iron gate in front of the house.

"We have to walk our horses up," Violet said, dismounting

her horse. "And put one hand in the air."

"Why?"

"So they know not to attack."

Cas did as he was told, one hand guiding the horse and the other straight up in the air. Through the bars of the front gate, Cas could see someone emerging from the house. The man strode across the dirt, crossing his arms over his chest as he watched them approach.

"It's me, Franco!" Violet called.

Franco ran to them and pulled the gate open with a creak. He was about the same age as Cas's father, his black hair streaked with gray. He was tall and broad, and he swept Violet clear off the ground when he embraced her.

"I'm so happy to see you, sweetheart," he said. Violet laughed as he swung her back and forth for a moment before gently putting her back down. He glanced at Cas, his brow crinkling in confusion. He looked back at Violet. "Where's your father?"

Violet shook her head, blinking several times. "He died in the attack on the castle."

"Oh no. I'm sorry, sweetheart."

"This is the rightful king of Lera, Casimir Gallegos."

Franco's eyes widened and he quickly bowed his head. "Your Majesty."

"Nice to meet you," Cas said.

Franco looked behind them in confusion. "Are your guards coming, Your Majesty?"

"It's just me and Violet."

"Please come in," he said, obviously trying to hide his surprise. He called for a young stable hand to take their horses, and led them through the gates and into the house.

His home was bright and open, with large windows that allowed plenty of light. Cas could hear running footsteps somewhere, and two small boys appeared on the stairs, full of giggles.

"Carlos, go get your sister," Franco called to them. "I want all three of you down here to meet our guest."

The taller boy disappeared, his younger brother trailing after him.

"Have a seat," Franco said, leading them to a sitting room with a beautiful view of the fields behind the house. "Are you hungry? I can have the cook whip something up for us."

"Yes, please," Violet said. They'd had only a little dried meat last night.

The two boys reappeared, a girl a couple of years younger than Cas with them.

"Violet!" the girl shrieked, running for her. She knocked Violet over onto the couch with the force of her hug.

"Nice to see you too, Paula," Violet said with a grin.

"Paula, Carlos, Bruno, I'd like you to meet the King of Lera," Franco said.

Paula let out a gasp and jumped away from Violet. She stared at Cas open-mouthed.

"Y-your Majesty," she stuttered, doing an awkward bow. The boys bowed also, Bruno's mouth hanging open when he straightened.

"You're the king?" he asked.

"Uh, well . . ." Cas chuckled. "Sort of."

"Not *sort of*," Franco said fiercely. "You *are* the king." He looked at Paula. "Will you take the boys back upstairs? I'll call you when we're ready to eat."

Paula's cheeks had turned pink, and she ducked her head and scurried out of the room with the boys.

"My wife is out visiting our neighbors," Franco said. "She should be back in the next few hours." He sat down on the couch next to Violet and briefly squeezed her hand. "She'll be so happy to see you."

"How have things been in the area?" Violet asked. "Have you been under attack at all?"

He shook his head. "Some warriors lingered after they were defeated at Fort Victorra, but we cleared them out quickly. And I haven't seen any Ruined."

Cas leaned forward, resting his forearms on his thighs. "I want to be honest with you. You know I married Emelina Flores?"

Franco nodded solemnly.

"My connection with the Ruined hasn't been severed."

"What do you mean?"

"I made a deal with Emelina. If she and the Ruined left, I would leave them alone. Jovita broke that promise, of course, and they've retaliated. They're not that far from here."

"They're not?" Franco asked nervously.

"No. I've been there," Violet said.

"The Ruined don't want Jovita in power any more than you or I do," Cas said. "I want the support of the southern province, but I'm not going to deceive you about my relationship with the Ruined."

"You think you can trust them?" Franco asked.

"I can trust Emelina. It needs to be understood that if you want me as king, it means you want someone who will stop the murders of the Ruined. I strongly oppose my father's policies regarding them. I believe that we're in this mess because of it."

"I agree," Franco said. "I was against the policy from the start. I started the petition we sent to your father."

"What petition?" Cas asked, looking at Violet. She'd told him to be honest with Franco, but she hadn't mentioned why.

"We wrote a letter to your father detailing why we were against hunting the Ruined. Most of the captains and judges in the southern province signed it. As did Violet's father."

"What did my father do?" Cas asked.

"Nothing, for several months. Then we each received a letter that said we would be removed from our posts and tried with treason if we mentioned it again."

Cas ran a hand down his face, his shame about his father overwhelming him. Had he even showed that letter to any of the advisers? Did they know they didn't have the support of the southern province? Did they have support from *any* of the provinces?

"Don't misunderstand me," Franco said. "The Ruined scare

me. My great-great-great-grandmother was enslaved by the Ruined. She kept a diary, and I still have it. The things they are capable of are terrifying."

"But those people are gone," Cas said. "The Ruined today . . . most of them want nothing to do with us. We're the monsters now, not them."

"Indeed we are," Franco said.

"Then can I count on your support?"

"You certainly can."

Franco rode with Violet to her house, and they returned with a dozen people eager to meet Cas. Neighbors trickled in all day, until Franco's house was stuffed and Cas's throat hurt from talking.

"You have our support, Your Majesty," a woman named Antonia said to him. She'd fought in his father's army. She'd been there the day they killed Wenda Flores and took Olivia. Her voice shook when she spoke about it.

"I can count on you to take the lead in assembling an army here?" he asked. "I need as many as you can spare. You can leave some behind to protect the south, but I'll need the rest."

"Of course. If you're marching north to retake the castle, I know most southerners will want to help." The lines around her eyes crinkled when she smiled.

He returned the smile and got to his feet. He waded through the crowd and pulled open the front door, sighing with relief as the chatter faded behind him.

Violet sat in one of the rocking chairs on the porch. He pulled the door closed behind him and sat in the other chair. The curtains behind them parted and Paula peeked through. She quickly disappeared when Cas waved.

"I think she likes you," Violet whispered with a giggle.

Cas leaned back in the rocking chair, propping his feet up on the railing in front of him. "She has poor taste."

"Oh, please."

"I'm a disgraced king who was recently married to a woman pretending to be someone else." He grinned. "I am rather good-looking though, aren't I?"

"Humble, too."

"At least I have one thing going for me."

"You're ridiculous." She rocked back and forth, her forehead creased in thought. "Do you want to know what your real problem is?"

"Please."

"You're in love with someone else."

"Well, yes. Obviously." His throat constricted when he thought of Em.

"I wasn't done. You're in love with someone else and you're just letting her go."

"I offered to stay with her. I don't think that's just letting her go."

"I think it is. You presented her with one option—a bad option, I might add; I'm still mad about it—and she said no, so now you're pouting."

"Tell me how you really feel, Violet."

"I will, thank you. You keep giving up when things get hard."

Anger raced down his spine. Her comment hit too close to home. "I'm here, aren't I? Not giving up."

"After trying to give up. You were going to give up being king because it got hard. Now you're going to give up Em because there are too many obstacles. You're never going to get what you want if you don't fight for it."

"You think I could have Em if I fought for her?" he asked skeptically.

"I do, yes. August wants to marry Em to align Olso with the Ruined. Why not you? Why not align Lera with the Ruined?"

"I don't think I need to list off the many reasons why that would never work. How about just the main one? Because we murdered most of them."

"And we should spend the rest of our lives trying to atone for that. It doesn't mean we can't try to find a way to make peace. I don't even like Em and I still support it."

"You don't like Em?"

"She caused the raid on the castle that killed my father." She raised an eyebrow. "Though you're in the same position, aren't you? And you managed to forgive her."

"Yes," he said quietly.

"I can't be her friend, but I understand why she did what she did. I think others can as well."

He shook his head, refusing to let in even a spark of hope.

"It's insane, Violet. I wish it were possible, but I can't see it."

"Fine," she said with a long sigh. "But I'm not marrying you."

"What?"

"I know you wanted to bring me with you to see Em to make her jealous."

"That's not the *only*—"

"Cas, please."

"It just worked out that you were with me." He paused. "But I won't lie, it crossed my mind that she would be jealous."

"She was. Was it fun torturing her?"

No. He'd seen the way she looked at Violet, the way she swallowed down words she obviously wanted to say. It had just made him feel worse.

"I'm not marrying you," Violet said. "I'm no one's second choice."

"I didn't ask!"

"I know I was under consideration to marry you before. It must have crossed your mind." She jerked her thumb at the house behind them. "I must have been asked ten times today if our relationship was more than friendly."

"I've considered it," he admitted. "You're a logical choice, of course."

"Romantic," she said dryly.

"But I'm not in a place to even think about marriage right now. I'm too . . . I don't know. Wrecked."

"I understand."

"But, uh, later, if . . ." He pressed his thumb into his pointer finger until the knuckle cracked. "Assuming I move past some things. Would you ever want to be considered again?"

"No one's second choice, Cas."

"Right."

THIRTY-ONE

AREN REACHED FOR Iria and lightly wrapped his fingers around her wrist. Her lips twitched into a smile. He'd done that exact gesture at least twenty times over the last few days. She seemed used to it.

They'd arrived in Gallego City yesterday and updated the warriors on the situation in Vallos. He'd never been to the city before, but he imagined it was more exciting when the warriors hadn't captured or driven all the Lerans out of town. The streets were empty, food rotted in abandoned carts, trash piled up outside of homes because the warriors couldn't be bothered to deal with it.

They put Aren in a room in a boarding house with Santino and Clara, and he felt strange and off balance this morning.

He'd slept next to Iria almost every night since they'd left Vallos. Something about sleeping next to her made him feel safe, even though he knew he wasn't. But he hadn't slept that well since before Lera had attacked.

When she'd approached him this morning and asked if he wanted to hunt, he'd gladly agreed. They walked a good distance from the city, into the forest, and he'd spent more time brushing his fingers to her skin than looking for animals.

He'd explained what happened when he used his magic while touching her. She'd listened quietly, and told him he was welcome to experiment. He'd thought she might be skeptical, or scared, but she'd only seemed intrigued.

Maybe he was the one who was skeptical and scared. Every time he touched her skin he felt like it was the right decision. Like he should hold on for a little longer. He let go anyway.

He'd tried grabbing a few of the other warriors, but it didn't seem to work with them. Now they all thought he was a bit odd and seemed to be keeping their distance.

Aren and Iria hadn't said a word to each other since leaving the city. He wasn't sure if it was a comfortable silence. He kept opening his mouth to say something, then changing his mind.

"How are your parents?" he blurted out suddenly. He was too loud, and if there were any animals in the immediate area, they had certainly just run away.

Iria looked at him in surprise. "They're fine."

"It occurred to me that I didn't know," he said, quieter.

"They're good. I was able to see them briefly when I got back to Olso." She glanced at him. "I didn't want to talk about them with you because . . . you know."

"Because my parents are dead," he finished for her.

"Right." She adjusted the bow on her back, avoiding his eyes.

"I thought you might marry one of the king's brothers," he said. "Your parents are pretty powerful in Olso, aren't they? You must have been under consideration."

"I was. King Lucio was promised to someone at a very young age, so it never would have been him. George prefers men. Dante is . . ." She pressed her lips together, obviously trying not to laugh.

"Dante is what?"

"Really annoying."

He laughed. "And August?"

"I know August the least of all of them. But he makes me uncomfortable."

"What do you mean?"

She stopped walking and turned to him. "He's two-faced. He acts like everyone's best friend, but he'll roll his eyes the minute your back is turned. And he's bitter about being the youngest brother. Don't let her marry him, all right? I know the alliance could be important, but it's not worth it."

"I won't. I'm not surprised, honestly. I never liked the guy much."

"You can tell Em everything I told you. I should have told her myself."

"Why didn't you?"

"If August found out I said something . . ." She trailed off.

"It would be bad," Aren finished.

"Yes. But I think it's more important for her to know."

"Thank you," he said quietly. She smiled at him.

"Do you think she's really considering marrying him?" she asked, turning and stepping around some tangled vines.

"Yes. I think she feels an obligation to do what's best for the Ruined. But, just between you and me, I doubt Olivia would ever let her do it. She doesn't want warriors around permanently."

Iria bit her lip, and he realized for the first time how strongly he disagreed with Olivia. After this was all over, was he going to never see Iria again? Were the Ruined going to isolate themselves in Ruina? His heart was heavy at the thought.

"I don't agree with Olivia," he said. "Just so you know." He'd managed to push Olivia out of his head for the past few days, but the talk of marriage brought a fresh burst of panic. "You heard she wants to marry me?" He meant for it to sound lighthearted, but his voice was strained.

Iria averted her eyes from his. "I heard."

"I'm not going to. I talked to Em before I left. It won't happen."

"Good. I mean, Olivia isn't . . ." She cleared her throat. "I meant it's good if that's what you want."

He tried not to smile. "It is."

"EMELINA FLORES!" Olivia burst through the door of their apartment and pointed an accusing finger at her sister.

Em stopped with her fork halfway to her mouth. "What?"

"You accepted August's proposal? Without telling me?"

She dropped her fork on her plate. "I did not. Who told you that?"

"Mariana. She said August sent a warrior back to Olso with the news."

Em let out an annoyed breath. "I told that idiot I wouldn't give him an answer until after we took care of Jovita."

Olivia's eyes brightened. "Idiot? Does that mean we can finally send the warriors packing?"

"I don't know. No. We need them."

Olivia slid into the seat across from her. "No, we don't. When Vallos attacked, the warriors barely needed to fight. Me and Aren can take out most of an army by ourselves. The rest of the Ruined are more than able to pick up the slack."

"Aren's not here."

"He'll be back." Olivia leaned forward, staring at Em seriously. "Be honest. You're not going to marry August. I know you love the Ruined, but you don't love us *that* much."

"No," Em admitted quietly. "I'm not going to marry him."

"Thank the ancestors." Olivia looked up at the ceiling, pressing her hands together as she silently mouthed *thank you* again.

Em's lips twitched up. "No one can know. We need to string August along for as long as we can. At least long enough for Aren and the other Ruined to return."

Olivia nodded. "Fine, but—" She stopped suddenly, her head jerking to the right. She stared at the window.

Em lifted her eyebrows in a silent question. Olivia stood

slowly and walked to the front door. She threw it open and stepped onto the street.

Em jumped out of her chair, grabbing her sword on the way out. Olivia's gaze was fixed on the kitchen window.

"I sensed a human," she said.

"Listening?" Em asked.

"Maybe." Her eyes darted over the area, and she lifted her chin before speaking again in a louder voice. "I hope the warriors know that I'll immediately remove the head of anyone I find spying."

"Come on," Em said. "It's too late to be threatening murder."

"It's never too late for murderous threats." Olivia grinned as she followed Em back inside. "But seriously, if I find someone out there, I'm killing them, no questions asked."

"I would be grateful if you'd at least let me ask a couple questions before we totally destroy our alliance with Olso."

Olivia smiled, but Em got the feeling she wouldn't heed that request. Their alliance with Olso might meet a more dramatic ending than she wanted.

She walked into the kitchen and grabbed her plate, depositing it next to the bucket on the counter. She didn't have time to worry about Olivia or spying warriors tonight. She had to meet Cas, and she needed to leave soon.

"I'm going to bed," Em lied. "Have a good night."

"You too."

She went to her room and sat down on her bed, listening to

Olivia's footsteps. After a few minutes, the door across the hall closed.

She waited about half an hour before slipping out of her room into the dark hallway. She grabbed her sword and coat and stepped outside, closing the door silently behind her.

The area around the apartment and courthouse appeared deserted, but she did a lap around the street just to be sure. Nothing. The street was empty as well, but she kept her head down as she made her way to the barn.

All the horses were accounted for in the barn, so she saddled the fastest one and rode out into the night. The journey seemed faster the second time, though her heart was in her throat again. She only half expected Cas to show up this time.

But she spotted him right away. The moon was full and bright tonight, and she could clearly see him cracking his knuckles not far up ahead. Violet was next to him.

"Hi, Em," he said as she jumped off her horse and walked to him. His face and voice were softer than last time. Some of his anger had faded.

"Hi," she said. "How was your journey?"

"Very good. We have serious support in the southern province."

"Have you been back to see Jovita yet?" she asked.

"No, we're going there next. And it's not just me that the southern province supports—they agree with my Ruined policies."

"Really."

"I found out that my father ignored their protests when he went to war with the Ruined."

"What does that mean?"

"It means that once I kill Jovita, I can guarantee your safety. Maybe more. Maybe we could even work together. Come to an agreement."

That seemed almost too much to hope for. "That would be nice, but we're not there yet. Let's talk about that after Jovita is taken care of."

"Sure," Cas said softly.

"Aren and the warriors should be headed back this way soon. Once they get here, we'll be moving north. I can get you an exact day once they're back. Let's meet again in three days."

"Is it a problem for you to get away?" Cas asked.

"It's fine," she lied.

Violet poked Cas in the ribs and walked away. Em stared after her. What did that mean? It didn't seem fair they were already communicating without words.

"How are you?" Cas asked.

"What?" Em asked, confused.

"How are you?" he repeated, with a soft laugh. "I'm just wondering how you're doing."

"Oh. Fine, I guess." Her main concern at the moment was August, but it didn't seem right to tell him about that.

"How's Olivia?"

"Better, actually. She's starting to calm down."

"Did she ever tell you she came to see me?"

"No. When?"

"A couple days after we arrived. She said she wanted to know why you liked me." He chuckled. "I don't think she figured it out."

"Nah, she did. If she hadn't, she would have told me how awful you were. I wondered why she suddenly stopped talking about you."

His eyes held hers for several seconds.

"I should go," Em said, breaking the silence. "Three days? You'll come or send Galo?"

"I'll come," he said.

She took a step back, his face disappearing into the shadows. "Bye, Cas."

"Bye, Em."

She quickly turned away, her heart pounding in her ears. It was almost worse when he was nice to her. What did being nice mean? Was he over her? Was he moving on? It was far too early to move on. He had no right.

She put a hand on the side of her horse, letting out a slow breath. She could turn around and yell at him about it, maybe. But his footsteps were growing distant, and she just listened until they disappeared.

A hand clapped over Em's mouth.

She gasped, the sound muffled against the hard grip on her mouth. She grabbed for her sword, but someone beat her to it. The handle slipped through her fingers.

"Do you think I'm an idiot?" a voice growled in her ear. August.

She twisted against him, panic shooting through her veins. He'd seen her talking to Cas. She'd just killed any hope of an alliance with Olso.

She launched her elbow backward, hitting soft flesh. August wheezed, the grip on her mouth loosening.

"Ca—" Another man darted in front of her and slapped his hand onto her mouth.

"Give it to me!" August said in a loud whisper.

A rope circled around her wrists. The man in front of her removed his hand and pulled a piece of cloth tightly around her mouth.

August leaned down so they were eye level. Even in the dark, she could see the fury on his face. "You're going to regret the day you crossed me, Emelina."

Cas mounted his horse, glancing behind him. Em had disappeared into the trees.

"It seemed like it went well." Violet said. "With Em."

"It did. She's not ready to talk about an alliance between Lera and Ruina until Jovita is gone."

"I heard that part. You know what I meant."

"I don't know. I—"

A sound echoed through the forest from behind him, cutting off his words. He looked over his shoulder.

"Did you hear that?"

"Yeah. Was it a bird?"

He jumped off his horse. "It sounded like Em."

Violet jumped off her horse as well, following him back to where they'd met Em. He squinted in the darkness. He couldn't hear the sound of her horse leaving.

A whisper echoed through the darkness. Then another.

He grabbed his sword, silently removing it from its sheath. He took another step forward, hidden behind the thick brush.

He spotted August's light hair first, catching the moonlight. He was right in front of Em, surrounded by warriors. One was tying up Em's hands.

He lunged forward, but Violet grabbed his hand, yanking him back. "Cas, look," she breathed.

He followed her pointed finger. There was a group of at least twenty warriors on foot emerging from the trees. Em was still, her eyes narrowed and clear, but he could read the fear in her stiff shoulders. His heart jumped into his throat.

"I can't leave her," he whispered.

"There are only two of us," Violet said, gripping his arm harder. "You can't help her if you're dead."

His body began to shake. He couldn't let them take Em. There was no telling what August planned to do to her.

He tossed Violet's arm off and raised his sword.

"Cas," Violet hissed. "What am I supposed to tell your people if you don't return?"

He froze. Dread trickled into his chest. He'd made promises to the people in the southern province. Galo and Mateo probably had most of the guard on his side by now. What would they all do if he died tonight?

He watched as a warrior wrapped a gag around Em's mouth. If they wanted to kill her, they would have done it. They wouldn't tie her up. He repeated it to himself as he sheathed his sword.

He stepped back, careful not to make any noise. Once he was a good distance from the warriors, he broke into a run.

"Go back to the fortress," he whispered to Violet. He practically leapt onto his horse. "Don't tell anyone but Galo and Mateo what happened."

"Where are you going?"

"To get Olivia."

THIRTY-TWO

THERE WAS A human in Olivia's home.

Her eyes sprang open and she bolted upright in bed. Moonlight filtered in from the crack in the curtains. If August was in their house, she was going to enjoy removing his head. Em could deal with it.

She placed one bare foot on the floor, then the other.

"Olivia?" a soft voice said from outside her door. Not August. But she couldn't place the voice.

"Do you want to die?" she called. The floorboards creaked as she walked across her bedroom.

"Please. It's about Em."

She swung the door open to find Cas standing before her. He

held the candle from the living room in front of him, the flame casting a glow across his panicked face.

"What about Em?"

"August took her. He had a bunch of warriors with him and he tied her up and he took her. I don't know where or . . . or . . ." The candle shook in Cas's hand, flickering light off the walls of the hallway.

She grabbed it from him and darted across the hall to Em's room. Empty.

Olivia spun around to face Cas. She stepped toward him. He stepped back.

"Why are you here? How did you see August take her?"

"We were meeting in secret," Cas said, talking quickly. "We were halfway between here and the fortress. August must have followed her. I'll show you where. If we hurry, maybe we can track them."

She ran into her room, set the candle on her dresser, and tore off her nightgown without bothering to shut the door. She grabbed the first clothes she could find and pulled them on, shoving her feet into her boots.

Cas had moved into the living room, and she grabbed him by the sleeve as she sprinted to the door.

"How did you get past the warriors and Ruined on watch?" she demanded.

"There was no one. I came straight to your house."

She whipped her head left, then right. It was quiet and gray, the first hints of morning light beginning to show in the sky.

There was no one in the streets. She should have been able to spot a warrior at the end of each road.

"Did you come alone?" she asked.

"Yes."

He must have known how incredibly risky that was. Em wasn't here to protect him. A Ruined could have killed him as soon as he set foot in Sacred Rock.

She turned away from him, lifting her chin as she screamed for the Ruined to wake up.

"Yell," she commanded Cas. He obeyed.

They came running. Mariana stopped in front of them, her mouth dropping open when she spotted Cas.

"Go with Mariana and saddle all the horses," Olivia said, shoving Cas's shoulder. "Mariana, don't let anyone kill him. I need him."

Mariana nodded, grabbing Cas by the wrist.

"But kill every warrior you see," Olivia added.

Mariana gasped, but she nodded again before taking off with Cas.

"What's going on?" Jacobo asked breathlessly as he ran to her.

"Make sure everyone is up," she said, ignoring the question. "I'll head east. You go that way."

She ran down the street, banging on doors and yelling for everyone to wake up. Everywhere she went, there were no warriors. The front door of one of their homes swung in the wind.

She returned to the center of town to see Mariana and Cas running from the stables.

"They're almost all gone," Mariana gasped. "The horses. Most of them are gone."

"I have one," Cas said. "I tied him up over there."

"I'm going with him," Olivia said to Mariana. She quickly relayed the situation to Mariana, the Ruineds' eyes growing bigger by the moment.

"Send some people south," Olivia said when she was finished. "Find as many horses as you can. I don't care how you take them. Everyone needs to be packed and ready to go by this evening. Got it?"

"Got it," Mariana said. She turned around and ran away.

Cas led Olivia to the tree where he'd tied his horse. He unwound the rope from the trunk and jumped up, offering his hand to Olivia. She took it, swinging her leg over the horse. She grabbed a handful of the coat on either side of his waist as they started moving.

The sun was shining brighter when Cas brought the horse to a stop. He pointed to a clearing.

"There," he said. "That's where they were."

The tracks in front of them were all headed west. "They're going to Olso."

"The border isn't that far. Less than two days by horse." He stood in the saddle and hopped off. "Take the horse. It'll be faster if you go by yourself."

She looked at him for a moment, trying to figure out if he was leading her into some sort of trap.

But his face was open and concerned, and he couldn't possibly be stupid enough to think he could trap her.

"Where are you going?" she asked.

"I'll walk back to the fortress. It's not that far."

It was actually a pretty long walk from here, but he must have known that.

"Fine." She slid forward, grabbing the reins.

"If you find her . . ." Cas pushed his hands through his hair. "I don't know how. Just figure out a way to let me know, all right? I need to know if she's alive."

Olivia nodded, simply because she was starting to understand there was no way to keep Em from Cas. She could tell her sister it was a bad idea until she was blue in the face. She'd never convince Em of it.

"Good luck," he said.

She kicked the side of the horse and they began moving forward. She looked over her shoulder at Cas. He was watching her leave, a deep frown on his face.

She turned away, trying to erase the concerned image from her mind. She didn't have the space inside to think about how maybe Em was right about Cas. She needed her rage right now. It was the only thing that was going to save her sister.

THIRTY-THREE

AUGUST TOOK THE gag off Em's mouth as the sun rose. He smirked as he did it, like he was challenging her to scream. They both knew there was no one around to hear her.

She'd never been to this part of Lera before. They were headed west, to Olso, and the trees were thick, the dirt road barely visible beneath the weeds. It was not an area traveled often.

Warriors surrounded her on all sides. August had cleared all the warriors out of Sacred Rock, taking horses and supplies with him, and there were far too many to even think about evading them.

But Olivia had to know something was wrong by now. She would have figured it out when Em went missing, along with

August and all the warriors. Em knew her sister. Olivia was on her way. It would not be pretty when she arrived.

"Let's go," August said. His horse was drinking from a stream, and he gestured for a warrior to bring him over.

"Do you understand what you've done?" she asked.

He settled onto his horse and gestured for a warrior to help Em up. She hated riding with him, being so close to him. She stepped away from the warrior.

"Olivia is going to kill you," she said. "Every one of you."

"That threat rings a bit empty, considering there's one of you and about a hundred of us," August said.

"You know what she can do, August. She's going to kill all of you. She's going to know you took me when I don't return and you've all disappeared."

"Yes, she will. And she's welcome to join us in the Olso castle. I'm counting on my brother to talk some sense into both of you."

Em let out a short laugh. Perhaps she'd guarded August from Olivia too well. Her sister would never let him talk any kind of sense into her. Em couldn't blame her, actually.

"What exactly are you hoping your brother will convince me of?" Em asked.

"Either you will marry me or I will simply take Ruina and rule it myself."

"You really think I'm going to marry you after this?" She held up her bound hands.

"Not into that, then?" He laughed loudly, and she rolled her eyes. "I'm not thrilled about marrying you either, Emelina. I'd rather just take Ruina. Let's hope my brother chooses that option, shall we?"

"It doesn't matter what option he chooses. Olivia will kill all of you."

"You underestimate Olso's defenses," August said. "You'll see."

The warrior waiting to help her onto the horse waved her over impatiently. She sighed loudly as he grabbed her around the waist and hoisted her up.

Regret burned in her chest. Maybe meeting with Cas had been a bad idea. She'd destroyed the alliance of the Ruined with Olso. Even if she didn't choose to marry August, she certainly didn't want them as enemies. If they invaded Ruina, she wasn't sure the Ruined could hold them off. Once again, she'd put the Ruined in more danger instead of protecting them.

Unease built in her chest as they rode through the day. They stopped to rest after the sun set, and Em barely slept, instead keeping an eye out for Olivia. She kept hoping her sister would appear. If she reached them before they made it to Olso, perhaps she'd just kill these warriors instead of burning the entire kingdom to the ground.

But deep down, Em knew Olivia couldn't possibly catch up to them that quickly. Even if she'd left Sacred Rock the moment she discovered Em was gone, the warriors were at least a half day ahead of her.

She resigned herself to her fate the next morning, as she rode on the horse with August again. She was going to the Olso castle. Olivia would most likely be close behind. Em should probably get a look at the castle quickly, because it wouldn't be long before her sister destroyed it.

The Olso border came into view late that afternoon. Under normal circumstances, the Lera side of the Olso/Lera border would have been heavily guarded by Lera soldiers. But now, there was nothing but warriors.

She leaned to the side, looking past August at the sea of red-and-white coats guarding the border. There were so many. Was the entire border this well guarded?

Something that looked like a large metal tube sat on the ground not far over the border, and she squinted at it.

"What is that?" she asked.

August chuckled. "You'll see."

She rolled her eyes. They rode past the warriors, until they reached several carriages sitting on top of two metal poles. The metal poles ran across the ground as far as she could see.

August slid off his horse and offered her his hand. She ignored it as she jumped down, her bound hands almost causing her to lose balance.

The carriages were rectangular and open-air, with one strange carriage in front. Smoke was coming out of a long tube on top, puffing up into the sky.

"You'll like this," August said, bounding ahead excitedly. "Come on!"

As if she had a choice. She trudged behind him, trying not to let her curiosity show on her face.

The carriages had wooden benches, and the warriors began to file in and sit. August plopped down in the first carriage behind the strange one and patted the seat next to him.

She sat, blowing her hair out of her face. The rest of the warriors filed in and she waited, not sure what they were all doing sitting around in a carriage with no horses.

Then, they began to move. August bounced up and down as it happened. She looked around as they began to pick up speed, baffled.

"It's a railway," he said, pointing to the smoke puffing into the sky. "It runs on steam. We've had some smaller ones near the castle for years, but this is our first intercity carriage." He clearly thought she would be impressed.

She was impressed, but she just turned away. The Ruined had mentioned something about steam engines and fast ships. No wonder the warriors always seemed to move quickly. She'd been surprised Iria was able to get to the Olso castle and back to Ruina in such a short amount of time.

"Lera's mistake," August began, his chest practically puffed out, "was thinking that eliminating the Ruined was the only way to fight them. We spent our time figuring out ways to be better than the Ruined."

She didn't see how riding along on a rail made him stronger than Olivia, but she just stared out at the mountains in the distance. She had a feeling there was a lot she didn't know about Olso.

For the first time since she'd been taken, she was worried about Olivia.

THIRTY-FOUR

"THE RUINED ARE moving! The Ruined are moving!"

Cas's head popped up at the sound of the scream echoing through the fortress. He dropped the potato in his hand and it rolled across the counter. Blanca grabbed it. "Go," she said. He ran out of the kitchen.

In the foyer, a breathless soldier stood in front of Jovita. "The Ruined. We spotted them moving north."

"Are they coming this way?" she demanded.

"It doesn't look like it. It appears as if they're passing us by."

Cas drew in a shaky breath. What did that mean? Was Olivia amassing an army to rescue Em?

It seemed more likely that Olivia hadn't found her sister, had returned for reinforcements, and they were all now headed for Olso.

"But there are no warriors with them, as far as we can see," the soldier said.

"Interesting," Jovita murmured, looking pointedly at Cas.

Cas turned to find General Amaro standing a few paces away, watching them. According to Violet, the general wasn't on Jovita's side, but she wasn't really on Cas's, either. She jerked her head, indicating he should follow her, then turned and began walking.

He trailed behind her, through the fortress and into the empty parlor. He closed the door behind them.

"Where are the Ruined going?" she asked, her voice barely above a whisper.

"Why do you think I know that?"

"You went to Sacred Rock. And you left alive."

He stared at her, unsure how much truth he could share without ending up locked in his room again.

"I've heard rumors you made deals with the captains and judges in the southern province. They say you were open about still having connections with the Ruined."

"The southern province was never in favor of the Ruined policies."

"Will you just answer my question?" General Amaro snapped. "How am I supposed to support you if you won't be honest with me?"

"Yes, I made deals with the southern province. I still have connections with the Ruined. I left Sacred Rock alive because I've promised to leave them alone. Their queen has promised to leave us alone in return."

"Their queen," General Amaro repeated. "Olivia?"

"Emelina."

She pressed a hand to her chest. "The news of their diarchy still horrifies me. Two Flores women in charge instead of one."

"Be grateful Emelina is in charge as well. Otherwise, we'd all be dead."

She regarded him skeptically. "Where are the Ruined going, then?"

"They're probably going to Olso."

"Why?"

"I can't be sure, but I believe the alliance between the Ruined and the warriors is about to break."

Her eyes widened.

"If I'm right, it will be an excellent time to head north and try to retake the castle."

"Jovita has given up the castle. She says we're staying right here until the Ruined are eliminated."

"I don't care what Jovita is doing. The south has already agreed to follow me north. As has most of the guard, and some of the soldiers."

"My soldiers only take orders from me."

"And you take orders from your king."

"We need time to form a plan to retake the north. A

strategy, more training—"

"Then you better start soon, because I'm leaving in a few days, whether you come with me or not."

She stared at him for a moment. "You're sure you can do this?"

He almost laughed. He wasn't sure of anything most days, much less his ability to command an army to retake his country. But perhaps if he pretended hard enough, the confidence would actually come.

"Yes." He said it with a little more conviction than necessary. General Amaro didn't seem to notice.

"Then I'll start preparing the soldiers."

Aren didn't want to go back to Sacred Rock. Not yet, anyway.

He glanced at Iria. She rode beside him, the other warriors and Ruined behind them. They were on their way back to Sacred Rock, and the ride from Gallego City had been uneventful so far. Aren almost wished they'd run into trouble so they could spend a few more days on the road. He knew he needed to check in with Em and Olivia, but he liked this quiet journey with Iria next to him. He didn't even mind the warriors. Em would probably be proud when he told her how well he'd gotten along with them.

Iria held her hand up suddenly, indicating for everyone to stop.

Aren snapped to attention, pulling on the reins of his horse. He slid to the ground, his boots hitting the dirt. Ahead of him, he spotted flashes of movement in the trees.

"We're warriors!" a voice yelled. A man emerged from the

trees, holding up his hands and smiling at Aren. "Hi, Aren."

"Holden," Iria said with a sigh. "You scared us. What are you doing out here?"

Several other warriors emerged from behind him, until there were eight total. They'd dismounted their horses.

"We followed the route Emelina gave you. We've cleared out of Sacred Rock," Holden said. "King August and Queen Emelina sent a group of us to find you. They didn't want you to get lost."

"Why?" Aren asked. The town was reasonably safe and in a good location. Why would Em leave?

"Attack from the Lera soldiers," Holden said. "It's half destroyed. Everyone is moving north so we can organize a response."

"Is everyone all right?" Aren asked quickly. "Were there casualties?"

"Olivia held them off pretty well," Holden said. "Rodrigo's got a note for the three Ruined from Olivia." He turned, scanning the other warriors. "Right, Rodrigo?"

A short warrior patted his pockets, then turned to his horse. "Yeah. It's here somewhere."

Aren jerked his head at Clara and Santino, indicating for them to follow him. The warriors parted as they came through, like they were afraid to get too close. Several of them scurried to Iria and the other traveling warriors.

Rodrigo dug through the pack attached to the saddle. "Hold on. I know it's in here."

Aren watched as Rodrigo searched for the letter. Had Cas

warned Em about the attack? It seemed strange that the Lera soldiers had been able to destroy so much of Sacred Rock. Maybe Cas hadn't known. Maybe—

"Aren, run!" Iria's panicked voice ripped through the air. He whirled around just in time to dodge a sword headed straight for his heart. Holden lunged forward. Aren snapped his neck. The sword fell out of the warrior's hand.

He hadn't focused to use his magic, and a wave of dizziness crashed over him. He stumbled backward, his foot hitting something.

A choked gasp escaped his mouth. Clara and Santino lay dead on the ground, blood seeping out of gaping wounds in their neck.

He looked up. Three warriors held Iria back, one of them with a hand over her mouth. The warrior flinched suddenly, pulling his hand away like she had bit him.

"Behind you!" Iria yelled.

Aren spun around to find two warriors charging at him. He threw them backward so hard the tree shook as they crashed into it.

He could run. He *needed* to run. All the remaining warriors were in a clump with Iria, and none of them were stupid enough to follow him.

Iria. She'd just betrayed her fellow warriors. There was no way they'd let her live.

He strode forward, blinking away the dizziness. The warrior had his hand on Iria's mouth again, and muffled yells he couldn't understand escaped from behind it. Her eyes were wide and she shook her head at him, obviously telling him to leave her.

The two warriors holding her arms shot through the air, and Aren didn't bother to watch where they landed. The one with a hand on Iria's mouth moved in front of her, like he was going use his body to shield her.

Aren ducked under the man's arm, using his magic to slide him a few feet away. Around Aren, warriors closed in from all sides. One was running straight for Iria's back, sword drawn.

He grabbed Iria's hand. Relief coursed through his veins and the dizziness disappeared.

He pulled her into his chest just in time to miss the blade aimed at her back.

Every warrior's feet left the ground. Aren shot them all back at once, thuds echoing through the forest as they hit the dirt.

Iria sucked in panicked breaths against his chest. He grabbed her hand firmly and broke into a run.

She didn't hesitate. She held his hand tighter and matched his strides.

They ran for several minutes, until the forest was quiet again and it was clear none of the warriors were stupid enough to follow them. Iria dropped his hand and leaned against a tree trunk, her breath coming in short, panicked gasps.

"Why did you do that?" Aren asked, also struggling to catch his breath.

"They . . . had . . . a sword," Iria gasped out.

"You could have tried to signal me discreetly!"

"You weren't looking at me."

"You betrayed them. They're going to execute you for that."

She leaned over and braced her hands against her thighs. "We don't execute people in Olso. It would be life in prison."

"Is that supposed to make me feel better?"

She let out a strangled laugh. "What did I . . ." She straightened, her eyes wide and full of tears. "I just . . ." Her breath became panicked puffs again.

Aren jumped forward and grabbed her by the arms. "Go back. Tell them Santino was messing with your mind. Tell them you realized as soon as you got away from him that he'd been confusing you the whole time."

She shook her head.

"They'll believe it if you aren't gone for long. Do you want me to hit you? I can make it look like we struggled."

She shook her head again, tears streaming down her cheeks. "I don't want to take it back. They betrayed you and—and . . ." She took in a shuddering breath. "I don't want to take it back. It was the right thing to do."

She lowered her head, sobs shaking her shoulders. He pulled her close to him, wrapping one arm around her waist and putting his other hand in her hair. She tucked her arms against his chest.

"Thank you," he said softly.

He held her for a long time, until her shoulders stopped shaking and her breathing evened out. When she pulled away from him she seemed embarrassed, wiping her cheeks and avoiding his gaze.

He wanted to tell her not to be embarrassed. He wanted to pull her back into his arms and keep her there until she wasn't sad anymore.

"I'm sorry," she said, letting out a long breath. "They told me they have Em."

He snapped to attention, all the warmth of her body against his fading. "What?"

"A warrior took me aside when Rodrigo was pretending to give you the letter. He said, 'August has Emelina. Our orders are to go back to Olso.'"

"Why would August take Em? What's he going to do with her?"

She lifted her shoulders. "I have no idea."

"Olivia wouldn't stay in Sacred Rock if she knew the warriors took Em. And if all of the warriors disappeared along with her, she's going to know what happened."

"That was deeply stupid on August's part."

"Yes, it was. Should we go to Olso? Could we get across the border?"

"No, not just the two of us. There's no way."

He rubbed his hand across the back of his neck. "Maybe we should go back to Sacred Rock. Maybe some Ruined stayed behind. Or . . ." His voice trailed off, and he looked up at the sun. They'd run south. They were close to the fortress. Dangerously close. "Cas," he said quietly.

"What?" Iria looked over her shoulder, like Cas might be standing there.

"We're not far from the fortress. He and Em were meeting secretly, sharing information. He might know what happened. And even if he doesn't . . ." *Just watch. If we get separated again, I bet we find each other.* Cas had said those words to Aren with such confidence. "Em's going to find him. Or he's going to find her." If Olivia didn't find Em first, Em would head straight for Cas. She would have nowhere else to go, if everyone had cleared out of Sacred Rock. It was the only meeting place he could think of.

"How are we going to get to him?" Iria asked.

"I have no idea."

THIRTY-FIVE

THE CARRIAGE WITH no horses stopped within view of the Olso castle. Em gaped as August dragged her toward it.

It was massive, the tallest point extending so far up into the sky she had to lift her chin to see it. Even the shorter peaks were taller than any building she'd ever seen. It was mostly white stone, with red tips at the highest points.

A moat surrounded the castle, and Em watched as a bridge lowered down, allowing them access. August nudged her in the back and she started forward.

The guards near the front entrance didn't move or even acknowledge their presence as they crossed the bridge. Their uniforms were different from the warriors'. They were still red and white, but stiffer and thicker, with big shoulder pads and tassels hanging from their chests.

The guards were in front of a large wooden door, and the one in the middle turned and grasped the handle. The doors creaked, and he stood back, staring straight ahead as they walked through.

A courtyard was beyond the gates, a door to the castle straight ahead of them. The door was open and a bulky man with short blond hair leaned against the frame, one foot crossed over the other.

"You're back," the man said. He surveyed Em. "And you've brought a prisoner."

"This is Emelina Flores. Emelina, meet my brother George."

George looked from Em to August. "Well, that's typical."

"I—"

"We sent you to marry one of the Flores sisters, and instead you bring us one as your prisoner," George interrupted. "What'd she do? Insult your hair?"

Em snorted. August glared at her.

"I had a good reason," August said through clenched teeth. "Where's Lucio?"

"On his way down. Come in." George crooked his finger at Em. She shuffled forward and he grasped her ropes, pulling at the knot.

"Don't," August said.

"Oh, come on." George released the ropes and tossed them behind her, at a warrior. "You don't need to bind her hands anymore. You're just being petty."

August stomped inside and George winked at Em.

"You're all going to die," Em said.

George threw his head back with a laugh. "You're exactly how they described."

"If you don't let me go, my sister is going to kill all of you."

"Save it, my dear. You're in Olso. King Lucio is the only one you should be pleading your case to."

George strode inside and she followed him, her eyes adjusting to the dimly lit castle. It was the exact opposite of the Lera castle. Where the Lera castle was bright and colorful, Olso's was dark and gloomy. There weren't many windows, so lanterns lined the walls, casting a glow over the white stone.

August led them down a hallway to his right. She found herself in a round, brighter entryway with two extravagant staircases that arched around and almost met at the bottom.

A man was descending the staircase on the left. He wore a deep-red tunic and black pants, his blond hair brushing his shoulders. He looked very much like August, though he was a bit shorter. This must be Lucio.

"August brought you a guest," George said. "Against her will."

Lucio stepped off the staircase and headed straight for Em without sparing a glance at his brothers. He was almost ten years older than her, but it looked more like twenty. Tiny lines appeared at the edges of his eyes as he sized her up.

"Emelina Flores," she said, since no one had bothered introducing either of them. "One of the queens of the Ruined. And yes, I was brought here against my will."

Lucio's jaw clenched. "King Lucio. Nice to finally meet you,

Emelina." He said the words like he was furious.

Then he turned and punched August in the face.

August hit the floor. "I can explain! I—"

"I sent you as a representative of Olso and you do *this*?" Lucio pointed at Em with such force that she took a tiny step back.

August sat up, bracing his hands behind him on the floor. "She betrayed us! She was communicating with Casimir behind my back!"

Lucio's gaze snapped to Em. "Is that so?"

"Yes." *No point in denying it now.*

"So you snatched her up and forced her to come here," Lucio said to his brother. "That was the best solution you could come up with."

August glowered at Lucio and said nothing.

"Come with me," Lucio said to Em. He turned and began to walk away. She followed him. Shoes squeaked against the floor, and she looked over her shoulder to see August scrambling to his feet and rushing toward them.

"Not you!" Lucio called without turning around. August stopped, fury etched across his face.

Lucio led Em through a winding hallway and opened a door on the left. He walked across the room and threw open the curtains, dust dancing in the sunlight.

The room had bare wooden floors and several crimson couches and chairs on the left side. On the right was a cabinet that had been built into the wall. It was lined with glasses and wine and bottles of brown liquid.

"Would you like a drink?" Lucio asked, striding to the bottles. He pulled one from the shelf.

"No, thank you," she said.

He took out two glasses anyway and poured some of the brown liquid into each. He handed it to her and sat down in the largest chair. "Please, sit."

She put her glass on the table and sat down on the couch. It was incredibly soft, and she sank so far in, it would take some effort to get out.

Lucio took a sip of his drink. "How did my brother get you away from the Ruined?"

"He followed me to where I was meeting Cas." She rubbed the red welts on her wrists, where the ropes had been. Lucio watched.

"Is what I heard from my warriors true, then? You've fallen in love with that Lera prince?"

She didn't respond.

Lucio leaned his head back with a moan. "That is so unfortunate."

"You have to let me go. If Olivia—"

"I had so much hope for you," Lucio interrupted. "You send word of this absolutely crazy plan to marry Casimir, and I don't mind admitting, I thought you'd be dead as soon as you stepped foot in that castle."

"Thanks for the vote of confidence," she said dryly.

"And then you do it." Lucio slapped his knee. "You do it! You marry that squirt and you get the Ruined to us and you find out where your sister is. Everything you said you were going to do, you did. And then you go and wreck it all by letting your feelings get in the way."

"My sister—"

"Your sister," Lucio repeated, raising his voice to talk over her, "definitely would not have developed any feelings. Everyone thinks her strength is in her power, but perhaps it's in keeping her emotions in check."

Em let out a humorless laugh. "You think Olivia doesn't have any emotions? You don't know her at all."

"She certainly wouldn't have fallen in love with that prince."

"She would have ripped his heart out and made a necklace out of it."

"She sounds fabulous."

Em leaned forward. "She's going to kill every one of you if you don't let me go. I guarantee you she's already on her way here."

"Oh, good! I was hoping to meet her."

"You don't understand. She won't ask questions. She will storm in here and kill everyone in her way. She's been looking for an excuse to do it, and you've given her one." Her voice edged on panic. She didn't much care what happened to Lucio and his family, but the thought of Olivia killing even more people made her stomach churn. Another massacre and she might lose the ability to reason with Olivia forever.

Lucio took a slow sip of his drink.

"Let me go. Right now," she said. "If I can get to her, I can talk some sense into her. If she sees I'm all right, I can get her to turn around before the damage is done."

"I can't do that, unfortunately," he said. "This is not how I would have done things. But you're here, and I can't just let you go. If Olivia is coming for you, we'll have a conversation when she gets here."

"Are you not listening to me? Olivia doesn't have conversations. She will kill everyone between here and the border."

"I will order my warriors to let her pass. She won't encounter any resistance in Olso."

"Oh, good. That will make it much easier for her to kill all of you."

He lifted an eyebrow at her sarcasm. "You don't have a lot of faith in Olivia, do you?"

"I have all kinds of faith in my sister. I have faith that she's not going to sit back while a foreign king takes me prisoner."

"You're not a prisoner. I'm sorry for the way August brought you here, but you're our guest now."

"If I'm your guest, then I'd like to leave."

"Perhaps 'guest' is the wrong word."

Em rolled her eyes.

"I simply meant that I'm not going to throw you in a dungeon," Lucio continued. "I'll have a room prepared for you, and you can have a bath and some new clothes. How does that sound?"

"It sounds like you're about to die."

Lucio chuckled. "You remind me of your mother. Such a hostile bunch, the Flores women."

"We have reason to be."

He drained the last of his drink and stood. "I'm sure I can get at least a few words in before Olivia rips off my head. I'm assuming she doesn't know you were meeting with Cas behind our backs?"

Em glared at the floor.

"Right. I thought so. Listen, Emelina. I'm going to be honest with you. I will have Ruina, whether I get it by marrying you to August, or by sending my warriors in to take it from you. Think about that while we wait for Olivia."

She turned away so he wouldn't see the spike of panic on her face. If Olso invaded Ruina, it would be like the Lera invasion all over again. Even if Olivia defeated the warriors, they would certainly lose more Ruined. They might lose the miners' cabins as well, and then they'd truly be left with nothing.

Lucio strode to the door, smirking at her over his shoulder. "I'll send some ladies to show you to your room. You'll feel better after you've bathed and changed."

She sat back, sinking deeper into the couch cushions. "I'll feel better when I'm not being held against my will."

He laughed, throwing the door open. "I always knew I'd like you, Emelina."

THIRTY-SIX

AREN SHIFTED ON the tree branch, his gaze fixed firmly on the fortress. He'd been up a tree with Iria for at least an hour, waiting for Lera guards or soldiers to leave.

"They may never venture beyond the walls," Iria said. She was straddling a branch on the other side of the tree, her legs dangling.

"That would be stupid. You have to send people out to scout the area, especially if you see something suspicious. They must have seen the smoke." The smoke from the fire he lit on the other side of the fortress was no longer visible in the darkness, but the lookouts must have seen it. Aren was counting on it, to draw a few guards into the forest.

"You're right," she said with a sigh, arching her back.

"I can watch by myself if you want to get down."

"I'm fine." Her dark hair was piled into a messy bun on top of her head, and a few pieces had escaped and brushed her shoulders. She pushed a strand out of her face, her eyes catching his. He was staring.

Her eyebrows lifted slightly in question, but he didn't look away. He wasn't close enough to reach out and touch her. Who had decided on this wildly stupid position in the tree?

Right. That was him.

She let out an exhalation of air that was sort of like a laugh. If they'd been closer he might have brushed her hair behind her ear and seen if it made her smile again.

He quickly looked away. He needed to focus. He was never going to get into the fortress to talk to Cas by staring at Iria.

"Do you really think Cas will know anything?" Iria asked.

"I don't know. But I'm sure Em will head back this way if she escapes August. I'm sticking near Cas until I find her."

Iria nodded, then lifted an arm to point straight ahead. "Look. They're leaving."

He straightened and followed her gaze. The fortress gates opened, and a group of about ten guards walked out.

"Perfect. Let's go." He gripped the tree branch and quickly climbed down. Iria's boots hit the ground a moment after him, and they both took off running. Aren ran as quietly as he could, ducking around tree branches and keeping Iria in the corner of his vision.

He'd chosen a route with heavy foliage, so it was unlikely

that lookouts could see them in the darkness. He stole a quick glance at the back of the fortress. He didn't hear any yelling, which was a good sign.

He slowed to a stop as they got closer to the guards and ducked behind a bush. Iria crouched down beside him.

It looked like the guards had split into two groups. Three men and two women were walking away from them, swords drawn. Aren had been hoping Galo or Mateo would be among them, but it seemed he wasn't that lucky.

"It was here," a woman said, nudging the remains of Aren's fire with her shoe.

"Can you tell which way they went?" a man asked.

"No. Certainly not in the dark. It was probably just some warriors or Ruined passing through."

"Just?" the man repeated. "I don't know about you, but that sounds bad to me."

"Let's go back," the woman said. "We'll inform the king and see what he wants us to do."

The guards turned and began walking back to the fortress. Aren closed his hand around a rock, his gaze on the guard in back, Nico. Aren had met him in the Lera castle.

He tossed the rock into the trees across from him. It landed with a soft thud. Nico whirled around. He opened his mouth to speak and Aren grasped Iria's hand, focusing his Ruined power on Nico's neck. Nico's eyes widened as he grabbed his throat. He opened his mouth wide as if he was trying to yell, but no sound escaped.

Aren ran to him as quietly as he could, carefully watching the guards in the distance. Their backs were still turned as they walked to the fortress. Nico's eyes widened in recognition.

Aren dropped Iria's hand, grabbed Nico from behind, and pulled him out of sight of the other guards. Iria grabbed Nico's wrists, yanking them behind him.

"Don't panic," Aren said quietly. The feeling of Iria's skin still lingered on his hand, his Ruined power buzzing inside him. His magical grip on Nico's throat felt almost effortless. "I'm only going to hold on until you pass out. When you wake up, we'll be gone. But I'm sorry about the clothes."

Nico's eyebrows lowered in confusion, but there was no time for explanations. His head lolled to the side a few moments later.

Aren and Iria carefully lowered him to the ground and pulled off his pants and jacket. Iria averted her eyes as Aren pushed down his pants and put on the blue ones. He shrugged out of his jacket and buttoned up the guard's jacket. He handed his clothes to Iria.

"Wait for me in the tree where we were before," he said.

"I know."

"If I'm gone too long you should just leave. It's not safe to stay here. Especially for you."

She let out a soft laugh. "I'm not leaving you, Aren." She jerked her head at the fortress. "Go."

He took off, resisting the urge to look back at her. She was probably already running to their meeting spot anyway.

He sprinted away from the guards who'd been with Nico and came up on the fortress gate from the other side. The other group of guards weren't far behind him, and he slowed a bit so it would look like he was with them.

The gates were still open, and he ducked his head into his chest as he walked through. There had to be at least a hundred guards here who knew what he looked like. He needed to find Cas, quickly.

He put a hand on his neck to cover his Ruined mark as he approached the front doors. He pulled one open, not daring to look up at the men guarding the entrance.

Inside, the fortress buzzed with noise, and he risked lifting his eyes just slightly as he crossed through the entryway. Two soldiers rushed past, pausing to glance at Aren. He quickly turned away and scratched his cheek.

"I have a report for the king from the scouting group," he said.

"He should still be in his room," the female soldier said. "Did you find anything?"

He shook his head and quickly walked past them. He had no idea where Cas's room was, which posed a problem. He couldn't ask where it was without giving himself away.

A stairway loomed in front of him, and he sidestepped an older woman and started up. The king's bedroom was probably somewhere quiet, as secluded as possible. The second floor seemed a good bet.

He stopped at the top and looked left, then right. Many of the doors were closed.

An unfamiliar woman with a basket full of clothes walked in his direction.

"The king?" he asked carefully.

She tilted her head to the doors behind her. "He's in his room."

"Thank you." He waited until she was down the steps, then cleared his throat. "Your Majesty?" he called loudly.

"Yes. Come in." Cas's voice came from the end of the hall, and Aren walked to the last door. He opened it carefully, hoping he'd gotten the room right.

Cas sat at a desk, a map rolled out in front of him. Galo sat in a chair on one side of him, Violet on the other.

Aren let out a sigh of relief and stepped into the room, closing the door behind him. Cas glanced up and did a double take, his eyes widening. He jumped out of his chair.

"Aren? How did you—what did you—why are you here? *How* are you here?"

"I grabbed one of the guards you sent out to scout. It was pretty easy, actually. You really need to work on your security." He looked pointedly at Galo, and the guard flushed.

"What do you mean, *grabbed*?" Cas asked.

"He's not dead. He'll be waking up shortly, so I have to be quick. August took Em."

"I know. I told Olivia. She went to get her."

He winced. He was glad Iria had separated from the warriors. They were all doomed.

"You came here looking for Em?" Galo asked in confusion. "You really think she'd come here?"

"I think she'll go to wherever Cas is."

"And you don't have anywhere else to go," Cas finished.

Aren nodded and quickly relayed what had happened with the warriors and other Ruined he'd been traveling with.

"Iria and I could go back to Sacred Rock," Aren said. "If the Vallos people haven't realized we left, anyway."

"Little chance of that," Cas said. "I have a better idea." He looked back at Violet. "You should take him with you when you go south."

"What?" Violet asked, clearly alarmed.

Cas turned back to Aren. "I've amassed an army there, and I'm bringing them back here. We'll be marching to Royal City."

"I have no desire to go back to Royal City," Aren said.

"You can't stay here. Sacred Rock isn't yours anymore. You can try to catch up to the Ruined, but I saw them march by a day ago. They've probably already crossed into Olso."

"I can travel faster by myself," Aren said. "I may be able to catch up to the Ruined."

"If you knew where they were," Violet said.

"I assume August took her to the castle. Olivia would think the same. Iria can tell me how to get there."

"That sounds like an excellent way to get yourself killed," Cas said.

Aren ran a hand down his face. "So, what? I'm supposed to just leave Em in Olso?"

"Olivia is already on her way. I think we can both agree that Olivia is more than capable of rescuing her sister?"

He let out an annoyed sigh. "Of course."

"Then help me. You said it yourself, Em will come find me. You protect us, and we'll protect you until you find her. Deal?"

"I don't need your protection."

"Fine. But I could really use yours. My army in the south could permanently defeat Jovita, which is exactly what Em wants. I think if Em was here, she would tell you this was a good idea." His lips twitched a little when he said the last part, like he knew how much it would annoy Aren.

"I think Em wouldn't be stupid enough to ask me to join the Lera army," he said dryly. But Cas had a point. Em did want Cas firmly on the throne, and she would probably help him if she was here. And what else was he going to do? Go hang out by the Olso border, hoping to spot Em after Olivia saved her? He had no idea when that would be, or how long it would take. He certainly wasn't going back to Ruina without her.

"I prefer to think of it as optimism," Cas said. He was smiling as if he already knew what Aren's answer would be.

Aren let out a short laugh, hardly believing the next word out of his mouth, even as he said it. "Fine. But only until I find Em."

"Deal. I need a day to get everything together. Can you wait?"

"Yes."

"Do you know the creek just south of here?"

"I do."

"Violet and a few guards will meet you there tomorrow, by

sunset." He looked at Violet for confirmation and she nodded.

Yells sounded from outside, and Aren reached for the doorknob. "Sounds like they found your guard in his underwear. I should go."

"Thank you, Aren. Don't kill anyone on the way out."

"I'll try." He pulled the door open and darted into the hallway.

"Get the guards together now!" a voice shouted.

He jogged down the stairs, his eyes on the door. People all around him were running and shouting. Someone sucked in a gasp.

"It's him!" a vaguely familiar guard pointed a shaky finger at Aren. "One of the bad Ruined!"

Aren would have laughed if he didn't have to concentrate. He tossed the guard out of his path with one quick look and sprinted to the door. Several people moved out of his way, fear etched across their faces. A woman put herself in his path, sword drawn, and he simply scooted her across the floor to the other side of the fortress.

He ran out the door and across the lawn. He could still barely feel the effects of using his magic, and he grinned as he tossed a guard away from the gate.

"Let him go!" he heard Cas yell from behind him.

He ran away from the fortress and into the woods, daring a few glances over his shoulder. They weren't following him.

He slowed when he was far enough away from the fortress to feel relatively safe, and came to a stop under the tree where he'd been earlier. He tilted his chin up to find Iria climbing down. She hit the ground lightly.

"Is everything . . ." She trailed off, cocking her head. "Why are you smiling like that? Was Em there?"

"No. They called me 'the bad one.' I thought it was funny."

"The bad one? Rude."

"You don't think I'm one of the bad ones?"

"No!"

"I think by 'bad' they mean powerful."

"Hmph." She smiled. "I guess by this expression that everything went well?"

"Yes, but I did something you might not like." He explained the plan quickly, Iria's expression turning more and more confused as he laid it out for her.

"We're joining the Lera army?"

"Temporarily. Just until I find Em."

"Uh . . ."

"You don't have to come with me if you don't want. I'll understand."

"Don't be ridiculous. I'm sticking with you."

He tried not to grin too widely. "Good." He glanced back at the fortress. "We should put some space between us and the fortress. Cas probably will have to send some people out looking for me."

Iria nodded, reaching into her bag and pulling out his clothes. She turned away as he changed. He left the guard's uniform crumpled on the ground.

"You're really not insulted when people call you bad?" Iria

asked, falling into step beside him as they began walking south.

"I'm used to it." He paused. "I, uh, would be bothered if someone I knew was scared of me. Like you."

"You know I'm not scared of you. Remember when I visited the Ruina castle a few years ago?"

"Yes. We didn't spend much time together then, did we?"

"No. Because I called you a cocky miscreant."

He let out a laugh, the memory taking shape in his head. "That's right. Wait, miscreant? You called me a miscreant?"

"I did. I don't think it fits, does it?"

"Not really. I think I would have preferred 'jerk.' Or 'cad.'" He scanned the area, but there were still no soldiers to be seen. They were probably preparing for an attack. "Why did you call me that, again?"

"I challenged you to a duel and you said sword-fighting was for peasants."

"I did?"

"Yes."

"I'm sorry. I was a cocky miscreant."

"It's all right. I actually kind of liked that about you."

"CASIMIR!" Jovita's voice rang through the fortress as she stomped across the entryway to where he stood in the doorway. "Why was there just a Ruined in here?"

"I don't know." He gestured to where Galo stood on the lawn with a few guards. "Organize a search. Bring him alive if you find him. I have questions."

"How much Weakling do we have?" Jovita asked.

"Very little," a solider replied. "We can shoot out one cannon, and it will be light."

"We should save it," Cas said. "We won't be able to get into Ruina anytime soon to get more."

"I know," Jovita snapped. She turned back to the soldier. "No Weakling for now. Everyone keep watch. I want an update every hour."

Cas brushed past her. "I'm sure my guards can give you an update after they give me one."

Jovita followed him, her footsteps so heavy he thought she must be channeling her anger into her feet. "That was *Aren*," she hissed.

"I heard."

Jovita grabbed his arm, forcing him to stop and face her. She jabbed a finger at his chest. "I know he talked to you."

"He came to my room, yes, but luckily my guards discovered something was wrong before he could harm me."

"I'm not an idiot, Cas. I know that Ruined was trying to communicate with you." She was having a hard time not yelling, and Cas could barely keep himself from grinning. Watching his cousin lose her grasp on the situation was the most fun he'd had in days.

"Aren hates me," he said. "He's made it clear a number of times. I don't know why he'd want to talk to me. I'm sure he came here to kill me."

"Cas." Jovita said his name like she was talking to a small

child. "We have to work together. If that Ruined is planning something and you don't tell me—"

"If Aren is planning something, don't you think it would be wildly stupid to waltz inside the fortress and let everyone know?"

"Then why was he here?" Jovita yelled.

He lifted his shoulders. "If we catch him, we'll ask him. But he left without killing anyone, so I think we should count ourselves lucky."

She rolled her eyes. "Please, Cas."

"In the meantime, we should order everyone to stick close to the fortress. No more scouts after this batch of guards gets back. I'm sending Violet and a few guards to check on the status of the southern province, but other than that, we're all staying put."

Jovita eyed him suspiciously. "You were just in the southern province."

"I know, but Violet wanted to go back, and it is her territory. I didn't feel right ordering her to stay here."

"You're the *king*. Learn how to order people, Cas."

"I'll work on that." He smiled at her. "I'll see you later, Jovita."

He walked away, finding Mateo standing in the entryway. Cas beckoned him over, and gestured for Violet to follow him as well. He led them into the parlor and closed the door behind them.

"Violet is leaving for Franco's tomorrow," he said to Mateo. "Will you go with her?"

"Yes," Mateo said immediately.

"You'll be meeting Aren and Iria on the way. They'll accompany you."

"Aren and Iria," Mateo repeated.

"Is the answer still yes?"

"Of course."

"We'll get you the fastest horses we can. I want everyone here and ready to march within days." He looked at Violet. "Can you do that?"

"I can do that."

THIRTY-SEVEN

OLIVIA STARED AT the line of warriors in the distance, guarding the Olso border. Did they really think that was enough to stop her?

Behind the warriors were the tallest mountains she'd ever seen. It wasn't snowing where she was, but the peaks of the mountains were white. She hoped they didn't have to cross them to get to the Olso castle.

Jacobo stood beside her, his eyes wide with excitement as he surveyed the warriors. Behind her were about two hundred Ruined, almost everyone they'd had in Sacred Rock. Most appeared more scared than excited. They didn't have anything to be scared of.

Olivia wasn't happy her sister had been kidnapped, but she

couldn't help the thrill of excitement that shot up her spine. This was her opportunity to show the Ruined she deserved to lead them. She was finally the one doing the rescuing, instead of being the weak one sitting in a cell. Once she defeated the warriors, the Ruined would never doubt her again.

Ivanna fell into step beside her. "You know what Em would do in this situation, right? She would negotiate."

"Em would negotiate because she's useless. It's her only option."

"It's not her only option, it's the one she thinks is best."

"I'm not Em."

"You're certainly not," Ivanna muttered.

Olivia whirled around. Ivanna took a step back and the rest of the Ruined stopped. Her anger must have been splashed across her features, because several of them avoided her gaze.

"If you don't want to be here, you can leave," she spat. "I'm sure Ivanna would be happy to lead you back to Sacred Rock."

"I'm here to rescue my queen," Ivanna said quietly.

"That's exactly what I'm doing! And I'd like to point out that I never wanted help from the warriors. Em wouldn't be in this mess if she'd listened to me."

Ivanna turned her eyes to the ground, but several of the Ruined nodded in agreement.

"Nothing is up for discussion anymore," Olivia said. "I am your queen, and you will do as I say without question. If you have a problem with that, you can go back to Lera and fend for yourself."

No one moved. She had to resist the urge to look smug. "Good. We are no longer friends with the warriors. *Any* of them. You will kill all of them on sight. You may take anything you like, but we'll focus on supplies after we've killed the royal family." Maybe they could even take the castle. She'd never pictured herself living in Olso, but it wasn't the worst idea. It wasn't that far from Ruina, and she wouldn't have to wait years for her own castle to be built.

She looked at the Ruined seriously. "Get behind me and pick off the warriors I miss."

She turned and strode toward the warriors. The Ruined followed her.

She glanced down the line of red-clad men and women. They didn't even have the decency to look nervous. Most of them watched the approaching Ruined with interest, like they didn't think they had a reason to be scared.

Olivia curled her fingers into a fist. She could fix that.

A warrior stepped forward as she approached. "Your Majesty. We have—"

He flew through the air, his screams fading as he shot away from them. One by one, Olivia lifted the warriors into the air and tossed them away. Faces twisted with horror. A few tried to run.

That would teach them not to be afraid of her.

She lifted the last few warriors off the ground and shot them through the air. In the distance, the bodies thudded as they hit the ground.

"That track leads to the castle," Mariana said, pointing to metal in the dirt. It disappeared in the distance. "I took the railcar the first time I was here, but it doesn't look like it's here."

Olivia blew out a frustrated breath. There were a few horses tied to a post, but she couldn't jump on one and abandon the rest of the Ruined. They needed her protection.

She started toward the tracks. "We'll go by foot."

A stern-faced woman showed Em to her room. It was impressively big, with a giant bed covered by a fluffy white blanket, a tall wardrobe, and a table along one wall. Fruit, bread, and tea sat on the table, and her stomach growled at the sight.

"Your clothes are in the wardrobe," the woman said. She stood in front of the door, arms crossed over her chest. "A girl will be in shortly with water for your bath. In the meantime, yell if you need anything." She left, pulling the door closed behind her. The click of the lock echoed across the room.

Em grabbed a piece of bread and opened the wardrobe drawer. Two pairs of pants and two red tunics hung inside. She sighed, thinking of her pretty dresses in Lera. She wondered if they were still there.

A young woman brought her bathwater and left without saying a word. The water was freezing cold, and Em bathed quickly and put on the clothes. They were soft and comfortable and had two crossed swords—the symbol of Olso—stitched onto the left side. She rolled her eyes. No doubt Lucio had thought he was hilarious.

A knock sounded at the door, and she blew out an annoyed breath.

"I'm locked in, you idiots!" she yelled.

A man chuckled, and the lock clicked. The door opened to reveal George.

"Hello. I've been appointed to give you a tour of the castle before dinner. We thought you might hate me slightly less than my brothers."

"What gives you that impression?"

"Well, I haven't kidnapped you or threatened to invade your kingdom, so I must be better than August or Lucio."

"Barely."

"Wonderful. Follow me."

She considered refusing, but she really needed to get an idea of how the castle was laid out. Maybe she could even find a sword to take August's head off.

She trudged out of the room behind George. Two warriors stood outside her door, and they stood up straighter when she appeared.

"Let's start in the east wing," George said as they walked down the stairs. "I think you'll like it."

They walked through the open room at the bottom of the stairs where Em had first come in. The castle buzzed with noise as they started down the dim hallway. Chatter and laughter followed her, and she cast a look over her shoulder to see a child dart past and disappear.

George opened a door and sunlight flooded the hallway. She

stepped inside to find a large room with art hung on almost every space of wall. There was a seating area in the middle, but from the looks of the pristine red chairs, it wasn't used often.

A tall painting immediately caught her eye. It was on the wall to her left, so big it ran floor to ceiling. The woman in the painting wore an elaborate black dress and lace gloves, her dark hair loose around her shoulders. She had one hand on her waist, and she stared out of the painting with a look that was somehow both amusement and disgust. Em knew the expression well. It was her mother.

"Why do you have a portrait of my mother?" She strode across the room to it.

"It was a gift."

"From who?"

"From Wenda Flores."

Em tried to hold back a laugh. "My mother sent you a painting of herself?"

"She was a special kind of woman, wasn't she?" George asked with a grin.

That was one way to put it. She tilted her chin up to stare at her mother's face. It was a good likeness of her, and Em expected a surge of sadness. Instead, she shifted uncomfortably and rubbed a finger across her necklace. Olivia looked very much like their mother. They were so alike, in so many ways.

"When did she send this?" she asked.

"It's been almost ten years, I think. My father loved it. He thought it was hilarious."

"Really."

"He did. He had it on display in his library for a while. He showed it to everyone."

"Nothing like an alliance with Wenda Flores to terrify guests."

George chuckled. "Exactly. But Lucio is less fond of it. He had it moved in here. He says her expression makes him uncomfortable."

"I'm sure that was her goal," Em murmured.

"Come on. Lots more to see. You can come back in here after dinner, if you'd like."

She followed him out of the room, looking over her shoulder at the painting as she left. Truth be told, her mother's expression made her a little uncomfortable as well.

George led her around the castle, to the meeting rooms and ballrooms and training rooms (there were many of those). She spotted a letter opener on a desk in one of the meeting rooms and pocketed it. She could cut open August's neck with it, if she really put some muscle into it.

The family was already seated when George took her to the dining room. A servant led her to the chair between Lucio and his wife.

"How was the tour?" Lucio asked.

"It's not nearly as nice as the Lera castle," she said with a smile. Across from her, August rolled his eyes.

"That's our castle now anyway," he said.

A staff member put a plate of food in front of her. Em picked up her knife and stabbed the chicken with more force than was necessary.

"The chicken is already dead, Em," August said. This elicited a round of laughter from his brothers and their spouses.

"I was pretending it was your face," she said to August.

George threw his head back and howled. "I like her, Auggie. It's too bad you couldn't convince her to marry you."

"I shouldn't have had to convince her of anything," August said.

Em cocked an eyebrow at him. August laid his fork down, leveling his gaze with hers.

"Uh-oh," Dante said. The second-youngest Olso prince snickered as he looked between them.

"You should have been grateful I wanted to marry you," August said.

"Yes, yes, I know. You were such a kind soul to agree to marry me, and I should fall at your feet and thank you for kidnapping me."

August's nostrils flared. "Betrayal has a price."

"You're all about to find out just how high that price is," Em said.

"And even putting aside the political benefits, it was still better for you," August said, ignoring her last comment. "You're not that pretty, and you're Ruined. There's still a chance you could develop some of those hideous marks and look even worse than you do now."

"August," Lucio said sharply. "There's no need to be rude."

"I'm never developing any Ruined marks," Em said. "But if I'd known you found them so unattractive I would have wished for them harder."

August muttered something she couldn't hear.

She leaned forward, putting her elbows on the table. "Let me ask you a question. Did you kidnap me because I betrayed you, or are you simply throwing a tantrum because I don't like you?"

His sour expression hinted that it was the latter, and she laughed as she picked up her fork again.

"So what does Casimir have that he doesn't?" George asked, amusement in his voice. August frowned at him.

Everything? She didn't know where to start. She didn't have words for Cas anymore. *Kind* and *reasonable* and *thoughtful* didn't even seem enough now. She could spend an hour explaining everything about him—his willingness to stay with her, his strength when he decided to go back to the fortress, the way his lips turned up in a smile when he woke up with her by his side, the determination in his expression when he said he was going to kill Jovita, even though she knew, deep down, he would never do it—and no one here would even begin to understand him.

Tears welled in her eyes, and she looked up from her plate, letting the table see them. Let that be the answer to George's question.

"Stop teasing our guest," Lucio said.

"Prisoner," she corrected.

George laughed and clapped Dante on the shoulder. "What

about Dante, Emelina? Do you like the look of him? I'd really like to marry you off to one of my brothers. Dinner would be so much more interesting."

"I will pass on that charming offer. You'll all be dead once Olivia arrives anyway."

Lucio's wife paused with her fork halfway to her mouth and shot her husband a worried glance. He shook his head and patted her hand.

"Besides, I think my sister was right," Em continued. "I shouldn't have considered the alliance. You did nothing to save us when the Ruined were being exterminated. You only want our help when it's convenient for you."

George had the decency to shift in discomfort, but Lucio waved his hand dismissively. "We weren't in a position to help then."

"Sure you weren't."

Lucio changed the subject, and Em took a bite of her meat and tuned them out. What would have happened if she'd listened to Olivia and sent the warriors packing? She wouldn't be trapped in the Olso castle, for one.

But she wasn't sure they would have been able to successfully invade Sacred Rock. Or maybe the Vallos soldiers might have taken the city back when they attacked. The Ruined might have simply starved to death without the warrior's supplies.

She was grateful to August for that, at least. Not that she would tell him that. His head was big enough without any help from her.

She looked up to see him watching her, and a smile spread across her face.

"What?" he asked.

"I'm just so grateful I don't have to marry you. I'm feeling really smug about how smart I am."

The table burst out laughing again.

THIRTY-EIGHT

"EM, WAKE UP!"

"Emelina! Wake up!"

"They're attacking! We have to go!" Damian's voice echoed in Em's ears as she struggled to escape from sleep's grasp. Damian. Why was Damian in her room?

She gasped, sitting straight up. August stood next to her bed, his panicked face illuminated by the lantern in his hand.

"Olivia's here," he said. "We need you to talk to her. Quickly, before she kills anyone else."

"I told you," Em said, glaring at him as she threw her blankets off.

"Would you just hurry? She won't listen to anyone."

She grabbed her pants and pulled them up her hips. August

walked to the door, leaving her in darkness as she tore her nightshirt off and pulled on the shirt and jacket Lucio had provided her. She laced up her boots and ran into the hallway to meet August.

Screams greeted her. They drifted up from below and outside. She could smell smoke.

Damian reached for her hand. "Stay with me. Don't drop my hand, no matter what."

Em took in a shaky breath and closed her eyes until the image of Damian standing in front of her dissipated.

August grabbed her wrist, roughly tugging her to the stairs. They ran down them and through the hallway, to the people standing in the smoky main entryway. Lucio and his family. Three kids were huddled together in a clump, one of them clinging to George's leg.

"Where is she?" Em asked Lucio.

"Outside. I'll come with you," Lucio said.

"That's not a good idea."

He shot her a look that clearly said he didn't care. He ran to the door, warriors appearing from all sides to accompany them. Em wondered if they actually thought they could keep their king safe.

The cold air stung her face as the doors swung open. She gasped at the scene in front of her.

Well over a hundred Ruined were making their way to the castle. The drawbridge was still up, so many were swimming across the moat, bodies of warriors floating around them. The torches lining the castle gate were lit, casting a yellow glow over the water.

A good number of Ruined were already on land, holding torches and using their magic to fan the flames already licking up the side of the castle.

Olivia stood near the edge of the moat, her clothes dripping and plastered to her body. She must have been freezing.

"Olivia!" Em screamed, running toward her.

Olivia whirled around. Her face was pale, her lips blue, but her eyes were clear and furious.

"I'm fine," Em said, grabbing her sister's hand. "Please stop."

Olivia looked Em up and down, as if confirming she was really fine. "Why?" she asked.

Em didn't have a good response to that. Not one that would convince Olivia, anyway. "Let's just go," she said, holding Olivia's hand tighter.

"Olivia." Lucio's voice was cautious as he approached them. "I'm King Lucio. I—"

"Oh, good." Olivia dropped Em's hand and narrowed her eyes at Lucio's chest. She caught the king's heart as it flew out of his chest. She tossed it over her shoulder. "I thought it was going to be harder to find him."

Em pressed a hand to her mouth. Lucio's body hit the ground with a thud. No one could say she hadn't warned him.

Panic ignited around her as the warriors realized Lucio was dead. The yells from his brothers rose above the rest of the noise, and Em wanted to press her hands to her ears.

Olivia stepped forward, making a beeline for the rest of the royal family. Em grabbed her arm.

"Don't," she pleaded. The family scattered in all directions.

Olivia shook her off with a glare. "Are you serious? They kidnapped you. They betrayed us. Just like I told you they would."

"We're not going to accomplish anything this way." Em's heart pounded in her chest, the smoke starting to burn her nostrils. She didn't want to do this again. She'd already escaped this once.

"I tried it your way," Olivia said. "I'm done trying to reason with these people. This is the only thing they understand." She raised her arm, pointing at something. Em followed her finger. George stopped in his tracks, his head separating from his body.

Then, everything exploded. One moment she was standing next to Olivia, and the next she was sprawled out on the grass near the castle. She tried to lift her head, but the world seemed to have tilted. Her ears were ringing.

Why was it so warm suddenly?

Why did her arm burn?

She blinked. Something dripped into her eyes.

Nearby, someone gasped. It was August. He was in front of her, tearing his jacket off. He launched his body on top of hers.

The world suddenly shifted back into focus. The left side of her body was on fire.

August had the fire out as soon as she realized what was happening, and he scrambled to his feet, wincing as he scanned her body. She followed his gaze to her left arm, where the jacket had burned away, along with a good portion of her flesh.

She could barely feel the pain radiating up her arm. Panic and shock reverberated through her body instead.

August was still staring at her, and she wiped her good arm across her forehead. Blood.

"I warned you," she said. The words came out sadder than she'd intended.

August's face crumpled. "I'm sorry. I'm sorry."

She jerked her head, indicating for him to run. He took off immediately, disappearing around the side of the castle.

Em stumbled to her feet, squinting in the smoke around her. What had caused that explosion?

"Em?" Olivia's panicked voice broke through the screams around her. Olivia came to a stop in front of her, her eyes wide as she surveyed her sister. She was covered in dirt but appeared mostly unharmed.

"I'll fix it." Olivia jumped in front of her, carefully lifting Em's injured arm up. She leaned over, trying to see the damage to Em's back.

Em jerked her arm away. The pain was so severe suddenly that her vision turned black. "You'll *fix* it?" Her voice sounded shrill.

"Calm down," Olivia snapped. "I'll heal you and find a Ruined to protect you until we're done."

"I wouldn't need protection if you hadn't marched in here and murdered their king!" She tried to focus on the bodies on the ground. The man dead on the ground near them had Ruined marks snaking up his arm. Em wasn't the only one who needed protection.

"He had it coming." Olivia waved her arm at something behind Em. Screams followed. Em didn't turn to look at the dead bodies.

A hysterical laugh bubbled up in her chest. "Our mother used to say that, didn't she? Everyone always had it coming. I guess she had it coming too."

"Em!" Olivia gasped.

Her arm suddenly burned so intensely it was hard to stay upright. The edges of her vision went black again. "I knew you would come. I warned them that you would destroy everything in your path. And do you want to know the worst part? Part of me hoped you wouldn't come at all." The words flowed out of her mouth almost against her will. Olivia looked like Em had slapped her. "Part of me couldn't bear the thought of you killing even more people. You killed *children* in there, Liv. Is that what a queen does?"

Olivia glared at her. "Who are you to lecture me about what a queen does? You're only queen because I *let* you—"

Another blast rocked the ground, drowning out the words. Olivia was gone again. Em was no longer standing. Grass tickled her face. She tried to roll over onto her back, but it was too much work. Darkness was closing in on her, and it was much easier to let it sweep her away.

She closed her eyes.

THIRTY-NINE

THE MAN STOPPED short as soon as he spotted Aren and screwed his face into an expression that was probably supposed to mask his fear. He failed.

"Hi, Franco," Violet said, stepping around Aren and Iria and walking closer to the house looming in front of them.

Aren touched his neck. Iria had informed him of the two new Ruined marks snaking up the side of his neck, making him far more conspicuous than he used to be. He didn't mind.

"Come on," Iria said quietly, slipping her hand into his. He let her pull him through the tall iron gate, closer to the scared man.

"Franco, this is Aren," Violet said. "And Iria. Former warrior."

Franco looked between them. "You brought me a Ruined

and an Olso warrior. You shouldn't have, Violet." One side of his mouth turned up.

"I also brought you two king's guards and a message from King Casimir," Violet said, pointing to Mateo and Ric, walking the horses through the gate behind them.

Franco turned and jerked his head toward the house. "Come on in."

Aren hesitated for a moment, unsure if he meant all of them, but Violet motioned for him and Iria to follow.

Three children crowded around the door as they approached. They all stared at Aren.

The older girl and boy stepped back, but the younger boy tilted his chin up, mouth hanging open.

"What kind are you?" he asked.

"Bruno," Franco said sharply. "Don't be rude."

"It's fine," Aren said, and found that he meant it. The boy was staring at him with interest, not fear.

"Introduce yourself first," Franco said to the boy.

"I'm Bruno," he said.

"Aren. I ruin the body."

Bruno's eyes got wider. "That's the best one!"

"Thank you. I think so too." Aren grinned.

Bruno stuck his hand out. "Make this move. You can do that, right?"

Franco chuckled, stepping between them and steering Bruno toward his brother and sister. "Why don't you kids go upstairs for a bit? I need to talk to our guests."

The children ran upstairs, Bruno twisting around to wave at Aren as he went. Aren lifted his hand before turning to face Franco.

"I wouldn't have used my powers on him without your permission," Aren said quietly.

"I appreciate that. I think it's best you don't." Franco motioned to a woman lingering by the stairs. He introduced her as his wife, Esperanza, and ushered them all into the living room.

Aren sat down next to Iria. The room was large and sunny, with brightly colored furniture, but his gaze was on the small statue of one of the ancestors on the table next to him. He could swear these statues were following him.

He scooted away from the statue. His shoulder brushed Iria's, and she fidgeted nervously as Violet outlined Cas's plan to bring an army north.

She had one hand on her thigh, tapping her fingers rapidly against her pants. Aren put his hand over hers.

"You look nervous," he said under his breath. Violet, Franco, and Esperanza were deep in conversation with Mateo and Ric about how to pull the army together, and it didn't seem like they needed input from anyone else.

"I am nervous," she whispered.

"I meant guilty. You look guilty."

"That too." She gestured at Violet and Franco. "They trust us."

"Apparently." He raised an eyebrow. "Should they?"

". . . yes?" She laughed softly. "Yes. I just—"

"Aren." Violet's voice cut off Iria's words, and they both

turned to her. "Will you go with Franco and Mateo and Ric to round up as many people as possible? We'll map out a route so you'll be back by tonight."

"What about you and Iria?"

"We'll stay here. Someone needs to stay and greet people as they arrive."

He glanced at Iria, hesitant to leave her alone.

"It's fine," she said.

"I'll take care of her," Violet said. "The first thing we're going to do is put that sword away so no one knows you're a warrior."

"Former warrior," Iria corrected quietly.

"Right. Let's not advertise it."

"Sure. I understand."

Violet stood. "Good. Are you ready, Aren?"

"Now?" he asked.

"No time to waste, unfortunately. I'll get some food together for you to take with you."

He nodded and stood, Iria following him as he walked to the front door.

"You're sure you'll be all right here?" he asked.

"I think so." She jerked her head at Violet. "She seems all right."

He stepped a little closer to her. "What were you going to say before? You said they can trust you, but there was more."

"You can trust me," she said firmly. "I didn't think about what it meant when I chose you. It makes sense that the Ruined would have turned to Lera after we betrayed you, I just didn't imagine I'd be joining the Lera army."

He swallowed, the words *when I chose you* vibrating through his body. "Do you regret it?" he asked quietly. "You can leave anytime. You know that, right?"

"I know. I told you I don't regret it."

"Ready?" Mateo asked, reaching past him to open the door. Aren nodded.

"Good luck," Iria said. Mateo and Ric walked out the door, leaving it open behind them. The sunlight streamed across Iria's face.

He took her hand again for a moment. He squeezed it because he couldn't find the right words. She smiled, and he looked over his shoulder three times as he walked away so he could memorize it.

FORTY

CAS HAD A bag packed. He'd prepared the staff and guard to leave at a moment's notice. He was constantly staring southeast, waiting for Violet to return.

The only thing he hadn't done was kill Jovita.

He'd never had the opportunity, he tried to reassure himself. He was rarely alone with her.

The reality was, he hadn't looked for an opportunity. Violet should have been back yesterday, so if he was really serious about killing Jovita, he would have already done it.

He sighed, leaning his head against the cool stone of the tower. He was at the highest point of the fortress with Galo and another guard, watching for Violet. The round tower was completely empty, nothing but a small window on one side, but it still felt cramped to Cas. He was more than ready to leave.

"She'll come," Galo said, misinterpreting Cas's sigh.

"Do you think Jovita will try to stop us?" Cas asked carefully, aware of the other guard's presence.

Galo met his eyes, sympathy flickering over his features. He didn't answer; he just stared with an expression Cas didn't understand.

"Your Majesty," the other guard said excitedly. He pointed out the window.

Cas braced his hands against the bottom of the window, leaning forward to see as far as he could. In the distance, hundreds of people rode toward the fortress on horses. More than he could count. Lera flags flew at the front and back of the group.

Cas darted out of the tower and raced down the stairs. Galo stuck with him, but the other guard took off to inform the rest of the fortress.

A soldier raced past Cas to the parlor. Jovita's voice drifted out a moment later.

"What? With Lera flags?" she asked.

"Yes. From the southeast," the soldier said.

Jovita burst out of the parlor. She stopped in her tracks when she saw Cas. "You know something about this?" she demanded.

He strode outside, footsteps scurrying after him. He glanced over his shoulder to see guards and soldiers brushing past Jovita to follow Cas.

"Open the gates!" he yelled. One of the gate guards looked

past Cas, confused, but the others immediately followed the order.

"Cas!" Jovita grabbed his shirtsleeve, forcing him to turn. "What are you doing?"

"Leaving." He shook her off. "We're riding north to take back the castle. Any of the soldiers or advisers are welcome to come with me. You are not."

She opened her mouth like she was going to argue, but her eyes caught something behind him. She paled.

Cas turned. The army was approaching the gate. Violet rode at the front, Franco beside her. A man walked in front of them, the man who had gotten Jovita's attention. Aren.

"The bad one's back!" Aren yelled, spreading his arms wide as he walked through the gate. Jovita scrambled backward. She hissed an order to a few hunters.

Aren pointed to her. "Don't make me kill you." He strode to Cas, a small smile crossing his face. Cas didn't think he'd ever seen Aren smile. Not at Cas, anyway.

"Em?" Cas asked.

He shook his head. "I haven't seen her or Olivia yet."

Cas tried to keep the panic radiating through his body off his face. What if that was the last time he saw her? What if he'd just let those warriors take her and they hurt her?

Everyone was staring at him. He didn't have time to fall apart about Em right now. He needed to believe she could take care of herself so he could focus on the task at hand. It's what she would do.

Julieta and Danna walked out of the fortress with General Amaro. The general slowed when she spotted Aren, but she nodded at Cas. Soldiers fell into step behind her.

"If any of the other advisers would like to join me, feel free," Cas said to the crowd lingering around Jovita. "If you don't come now, I promise you will never be welcome in the castle again."

Cas walked past Jovita to the gate, Aren on one side and Galo on the other. Horse hooves pounded the ground, and Mateo jumped off a horse and walked it over to Cas. He'd already attached Cas's bag to the saddle.

"Thank you," Cas said, taking the reins.

A group of hunters ran toward the staff members leaving the stables on horses, their swords drawn, and Cas pointed at them.

"Would you mind?"

"Sure." Aren grabbed Cas's wrist. "Lend me this for a minute."

Cas looked at him in confusion, but Aren was already focused on the hunters. They flew through the air, landing in a big clump at Jovita's feet.

"Hmm." Aren frowned at where his fingers were wrapped around Cas's wrist. "That's disturbing."

"What?"

Aren let go of his wrist. "Nothing. Let's get out of here. Unless . . ." He gestured at Jovita. "Do you need to take care of anything before we go?"

Cas shielded the sun from his eyes as he looked at Jovita. She seemed frozen in place, her expression more shocked than furious. He unsheathed his sword but kept it pointed at the ground as he strode toward her. She didn't have a weapon, and her eyes darted from the sword to Cas's face.

He stopped in front of her. "Did you poison me?"

"I told you I didn't."

"Are you lying?"

Her lip curled. "Why bother asking me if you're just going to assume I'm lying?" She glanced at his sword. "What? Are you going to stab me if I don't tell the truth?"

"I may stab you either way."

She leaned forward until their noses were almost touching. "Do it. If you're so sure I poisoned you, kill me in front of everyone. Prove you're as strong as your father was."

He took in a sharp breath. One side of Jovita's mouth lifted, like her words had hit exactly where she'd aimed them.

He stepped away from her and sheathed his sword. "Maybe I told Emelina I'd kill you to save you." He laughed. "I don't think I even realized that's what I was doing."

She blinked. "You did what?"

"I told her I'd kill you." He spread his arms out and shrugged. "Guess I'm not as strong as my father."

He turned away from her and walked in the direction of his army. He clapped Aren on the shoulder. "Let's go."

Em was moving. Where was she going?

Her eyes felt like they were glued together, but she managed to tear them open. Daylight. Warriors. She was in the carriage without horses again. Her head was against someone's shoulder.

She jerked up to a sitting position. Her left side screamed in protest. Her jacket had been ripped at the shoulder, and bandages covered her arm. The pain radiated through the limb, down her side, and across her back. She blinked away tears.

"You're awake!"

She squinted at the warrior next to her. He was young, and unfamiliar.

"How do you feel?" he asked. He leaned closer, squinting at her forehead. "I was worried that bump to the head was worse than we thought."

She gingerly touched her forehead to find a large lump next to her hairline. The pain from the burns almost overshadowed the throbbing in her head, but now that she was focused on it, she felt sick.

"Where are we going?"

"Lera. King August ordered us to bring you across the border."

"He what?" *King* August? She turned her head too quickly, making the world tilt sideways. "What about the Ruined? Where did they go?"

"They retreated around dawn."

"Were they . . ." Em swallowed. Was her sister even still alive? "Why did they retreat? Did they suffer loses?"

"Some. Not as many as us." The carriage came to a screeching stop, and the warrior stood, stretching his arms above his head. He looked down at her, his gaze hard. "Your sister was still alive, last I saw. She ordered the Ruined out after they'd taken heavy fire."

Olivia had left her? She'd just retreated and left Em to the warriors? Tears pricked her eyes again.

"Prince—*King*—August told me to take care of you personally. Said to patch up your wounds and deliver you over the border, unharmed."

Em blinked, bewildered. Maybe she'd hit her head harder than she thought.

"Come on. Can you walk? Never mind." The warrior leaned down, sweeping her up into his arms. She bit back a moan as the movement sent a fresh wave of pain down her body.

The warrior walked to a horse-drawn carriage near the tracks. "We're going to Gallego City. You are welcome to go all the way with us, or you can leave early. It's up to you." He stopped at the back of the carriage, gently placing her inside. "And August asked me to pass along a message."

"What message?"

"He said he's sorry for forcing you into Olso. And you're never welcome here again."

Em looked past the warrior to the mountains behind him. Even if she'd had the strength to fight him, she couldn't be bothered. Maybe Olivia was still in Olso, but Em certainly wasn't running after her again.

"I want to go to Fort Victorra," she said to the warrior.

"Fine. We'll pass by it on the way, so I can drop you."

"Why are you going to Gallego City?" she asked, but he

ignored her, turning to walk to the horses at the front of the carriage.

She scooted back, leaning her head against the wood. A few other people joined her in the carriage, and she closed her eyes so she wouldn't have to talk to them.

She slept on and off as they traveled, the carriage moving at such a fast pace she felt ill at times. The warriors took very few breaks, so she sat up straight when the carriage came to a stop.

The carriage door swung open, revealing the warrior from before. He crooked a finger at Em.

She scooted forward and planted her feet on the ground. Her legs were weak, but she managed to stand.

"This is your stop," he said.

She surveyed the lush trees around them. She had no idea where she was.

"What do you mean?" a man in the carriage asked. He crawled forward, looking between Em and the warrior. "Why are you dumping her here?"

"It's fine," Em said quietly. No one in the carriage knew who she was, it seemed.

"The path that leads to the fortress is that way," the warrior said, pointing. "It's barely an hour's walk from here."

"What?" The man grabbed the warrior's wrist. "You can't just leave—" He stopped talking as the warrior leaned down and said something in his ear. He gasped.

The man shot out of the carriage. His sword was pointed at Em's neck before she even realized he had a blade.

Her fingers instinctively went to her waist, but there was nothing there. Even if she'd had a sword, she wasn't sure she had the strength to wield it.

"The king ordered her unharmed," the warrior said. He sounded almost bored, and he made no move to stop the man. August might have ordered Em unharmed, but he probably wouldn't shed any tears if it turned out differently. And the warriors knew it.

"My family was in the castle," the man said, ignoring the warrior. His whole body shook.

She'd had nothing to do with the raid on the Olso castle. She hadn't killed his family. She'd tried to stop Olivia.

But none of that seemed to matter now. She knew that wild expression. Recognized the vengeful glint in his eye. He wasn't entirely wrong to point the sword in her direction.

"I'm sorry," she said quietly.

He made a disgusted noise and lowered the sword. He climbed back in the carriage without looking at her again.

"Go," the warrior said.

Em had nothing on her—not a canteen, or extra bandages, or food—and the warrior didn't offer anything as he swept his arm out. If the situation had been reversed, she probably wouldn't have offered anything either.

"Thank you," she said, and meant it. The carriage began moving again and disappeared into the trees.

She let out a long breath and focused straight ahead. Under normal circumstances, an hour-long walk would be a breeze. She might have jogged to speed it up.

But today her steps were heavy. She was so slow she wasn't even entirely sure she was moving at times. She had to stare at her feet to watch one in front of the other. The world blurred around her, and she almost passed out several times.

She tried to focus on something to stay awake. She thought about Aren. Was he still somewhere with the warriors, oblivious to what was happening?

She thought about Olivia. Had her sister really left her? Had she looked for Em and assumed she was dead?

You're only queen because I let *you—*

Olivia's last words to her rang in her ears. Maybe Em was relieved her sister hadn't found her. She tried to shake the emotion off, but it persisted. She knew Olivia wouldn't feel the least bit guilty about what she'd done, and Em wasn't ready to face her. She wasn't ready to admit that Olivia was a bigger problem than she'd ever anticipated. She could no longer deny the surge of fear she felt every time she thought about her sister. She was a danger to everyone in her path, including the Ruined, and Em didn't know what to do about it.

But mostly, she thought about Cas.

I'm offering to give up everything for you, to help you—

His words were on repeat in her head. Em had rejected him, and she hadn't even been nice about it. He'd offered to stay by her side forever. Why did she insist on making everything terrible? Why couldn't she have wrapped her arms around him and told him to never leave? What if she'd kicked the warriors out and let

Cas stay? They might still be in Sacred Rock.

No, they wouldn't. Olivia never would have allowed it. She would have killed him eventually, no matter how much Em begged her not to.

The thought sucked all the air out of her lungs and she had to stop for a moment. She pressed her palms to her thighs. Em was supposed to be on her sister's side, always. But for the first time, she wasn't.

The sound of horse hooves against the ground echoed through the forest, and Em stepped behind the tree. She leaned her forehead against the trunk and closed her eyes. She had to be near to the fortress. She had no idea how she would contact Cas, but maybe she'd sleep for a while before figuring it out.

She forced her eyes open and squinted at the approaching figures. They were all in black, their horses at a gallop. Two men rode in front, and she blinked as she focused on the dark-skinned one. It was Aren.

She pressed her hand to the tree, leaning forward to see the man next to him. His dark hair was still a little longer than usual, bouncing with the horse. Cas. The fortress was right behind them.

"Thank you," she mumbled as she pushed away from the tree. "Thank you."

She stumbled into the road, her good arm extended in front of her.

"Whoa!" Cas yelled. The horses all skidded to a stop, kicking up dust in between them. He squinted in the dust.

"Em?" Aren yelled.

Footsteps ran toward her. She didn't realize she still had one hand outstretched until someone took it. Cas. His other hand was on her cheek, shock coloring his features.

She meant to lean against him, but instead she was falling. She whimpered as she made contact with his body.

He wrapped an arm around her waist. He had to hold her up, but she didn't mind.

"What happened?" It was Aren's voice now. He was gingerly touching her bandages. He pulled one away from the skin and took in a sharp breath.

"Fire," Em mumbled. "Olivia killed everyone."

"Is she here?" Cas asked. Em shook her head. "Does it look bad?" he asked, quieter.

"Yes," Aren replied. "But someone did a good job dressing it. I don't think it's infected. The pain, though . . . it's bad."

"I have some herbs that will make her sleep," a familiar female voice said. Em had her face in Cas's shoulder, and she didn't have the energy to look up.

"Is that safe?" Cas asked. "What if we get attacked?"

"She can't fight like this anyway," Aren said. "We can protect her if we run into trouble."

Who was "we"? Why were Aren and Cas together? She had so many questions, but no energy to ask them.

"Is that all right with you?" Cas asked quietly. His hand was in her hair.

"Mm-hmm," she said with a nod.

"We'll do that, then. Aren, help me get her on my horse?"

Hands grabbed her around the waist, and she was suddenly in the air, then her legs were on either side of a horse. A warm body was behind her, and she sank into it.

"Thanks," Cas said. He put his hand on her chin, tilting it up. "Open your mouth. Drink this."

She did as he said, gulping down the foul-tasting liquid. The canteen disappeared.

"Are you all right?" Cas asked. "Does it hurt?"

It did hurt, but everything hurt. She leaned back, letting her head fall against his shoulder. She closed her eyes.

FORTY-ONE

OLIVIA GLARED DOWN at the warrior on the ground. She placed her boot in the center of his chest. Beside her, a few dead bodies spilled out of a wagon. A Ruined unhooked the horses so they could take them.

"I let her go," the warrior under her boot sputtered. "She wanted to go to the fortress, so I dropped her off as close as I could."

A man shouted behind her, and Olivia looked over her shoulder to see Jacobo sticking a sword in the man's chest. His head lolled to the side.

"Em wanted to go to the fortress?" she asked, focusing on the warrior under her boot. He nodded enthusiastically.

Cas. Em had run back to him at the first opportunity.

Olivia resisted the urge to scream. Nothing had gone as planned. She'd killed the entire Olso royal family, but she didn't have the castle. She'd lost about twenty Ruined in Olso—far more than she'd anticipated. Those remaining were losing faith in her. She could see it in their eyes.

And she hadn't rescued Em.

"Please—" The warrior's words died in his throat as she snapped his neck.

She planted her hands on her hips, surveying the scene around her. Over a hundred Ruined lingered. The air was chilly, the ground damp from a short burst of rain, and a few of them shivered. Most of them hadn't helped dispatch of the warriors in the wagon. They'd left that to Olivia and Jacobo.

Em's face the last time she'd seen her flickered across her vision. Her sister had been unsteady on her feet, pieces of her clothing burned away to reveal angry red flesh underneath. But she hadn't looked like she was in pain. She'd looked horrified.

All her horror was directed at Olivia. She could still feel it, like it was flaming rocks Em had hurled at her. Em had taken down an entire country to save Olivia, but when Olivia did it she was worthy of contempt?

She shook the image of Em out of her mind. Ivanna and Mariana stood apart from the other Ruined, their heads bent together as they whispered to each other and stole looks at Olivia.

"Something you'd like to share?" Olivia snapped.

Mariana stared at her for a moment. "Em wouldn't have wanted you to do that."

She was so tired of hearing about what Em wanted. Whatever Olivia did, Em wanted the opposite. Even when Olivia was rescuing her.

"Then it's a good thing Em isn't the boss of me." Olivia strode to her horse and quickly mounted it. "Let's go. She can't have gone far on foot."

She rode as fast as the horse would go. The rest of the Ruined trailed behind her and she'd have to go back for the stragglers, but she didn't slow down. The important thing was to find Em. Despite everything, she had to make sure Em wasn't dead.

Then she had to figure out what to do with the Ruined following her. She'd torn them from Sacred Rock and they couldn't go back. It was a pitiful home, but still, she knew that they'd become to grow comfortable there. Now they resented her for making them leave.

She sensed the humans before she was able to see them. A tug on the reins brought her horse to a halt. The Ruined who'd managed to keep up stopped as well.

She jumped off the horse and held out a hand, indicating for the Ruined to stay where they were. Jacobo nodded.

The sound of horse hooves and the rustling of a flag drifted through the trees, and she carefully stepped away from her horse. She walked quickly, the trees growing thicker as she approached the road. A Lera flag flashed through the leaves.

They'd left the fortress. She'd expected them to hide much longer.

Soldiers stretched out on the road in both directions in front of her, and she stood on her toes, trying to see if she recognized anyone. There were hundreds of soldiers, maybe more than she could handle alone. Annoyance flickered through her chest.

She jumped over a log and took off in the same direction as the soldiers. She needed to see who was leading this group. And kill them, maybe.

Cas. She spotted him as soon as she reached the front of the group, riding a horse with a girl tucked up against him. He had one hand on the reins and the other on her waist.

Em looked like she was asleep. *Asleep.* Surrounded by the Lera army, and her sister slept. Olivia's relief to find her sister alive was immediately swallowed by a wave of anger.

A familiar face caught her eye. Olivia gasped. Aren. He was riding not far from Cas and Em, on his own horse. No ropes bound his arms or legs. He was riding with them willingly.

Olivia darted behind a bush and sank to her knees. She clenched her fingers into fists.

Aren was *helping* them. Em had run straight from the warriors to Cas. *Traitors*, both of them.

She took a deep breath, trying to calm her racing heart. First Em and Aren wanted to partner with Olso. Now they partnered with Lera. A Ruina queen, riding with the Lera army. Olivia's mother would dig herself out of her grave and die again if she knew.

Her sister would tell her to stop and think. To be logical. Fine. She could be logical.

Cas had risked his life to tell Olivia Em had been taken. He cared about Em. There was no doubt about that.

His army rode north. There was only one reason for the king of Lera to ride north right now—to retake his castle. Considering the size of his army, he had a decent shot. If Aren was truly helping them, the odds were even better.

Em claimed that Cas would end the extermination of the Ruined. That was probably true. For his reign, anyway. He could make no guarantees about the next heir to the Lera throne. She had no confidence in future Lera kings or queens.

Was that all it took to earn her sister's loyalty? An "oops, sorry" and a promise to stop murdering people? Olivia didn't see how that was nearly enough. Nothing would be enough, but Cas could have at least offered to help them. Had he sent supplies or workers to help rebuild Ruina? Had he offered funds? Had he done anything to help them rebuild the life his people had destroyed?

No. His regret was not enough for Olivia. Regret did not give her back her mother. It didn't erase the year of torture she'd endured. No apology, no matter how sincere, was enough for her people. Accepting it would make her weak, and the Ruined would never bow to a weak queen.

And they certainly wouldn't bow to her if she took them all back to Ruina. Ruina, with its pathetic miner cabins and land where nothing would grow. She didn't want to be queen of *that.*

She curled her fingers around the grass beneath her. Lera was green. The elemental Ruined were so much happier here, surrounded by trees and plants and water. She hated to admit it, but Lera was much nicer than Ruina.

Calm washed over her, and she slowly got to her feet. She wasn't going back to Ruina. The Ruined were staying right here in Lera, where they belonged. It was the humans who had taken the other three kingdoms from them and banished them to the worst one. Her people would never doubt her again if she claimed the most powerful kingdom for them.

She walked back to where the Ruined were waiting. They looked at her expectantly.

"I found Em and Aren," she said.

"What?" Mariana blinked in surprise.

"They're with the Lera army."

"As prisoners?" Jacobo asked.

"I don't think so. We're going to follow them. I suspect they're going to Royal City, and I'd like to see how things play out."

Ivanna and Mariana looked at each other uneasily.

"If Em is with them, maybe it means they've come to an agreement," Mariana said.

"Probably. But how well did our agreement with Olso work out?"

Mariana snapped her mouth shut.

"Em and Aren are smart," Olivia said. "They could be riding with the Lera army for safety. I'm not concerned with them right now. I'm concerned with Casimir, and his desire to retake the castle."

"He can't," Jacobo said fiercely.

"No, he can't," Olivia agreed. "So we stay out of sight until we get to Royal City."

"And when we get there?" Jacobo asked.

"We keep them from reclaiming it. And we move in."

"Let's stop here," Cas said, pulling on the reins of his horse. The sun had just set, and they were in a quiet spot of Lera, between the fortress and Gallego City. There was plenty of space to set up tents between the trees, and he could see a stream not far away.

Em took in a breath as she stirred against his chest. He put a hand on her head, brushing the hair out of her face.

Aren jumped off his horse and held the reins out to Iria. "Do you mind?"

"Not at all." She dismounted her own horse and took the reins from Aren.

"I'm going to get some stuff together to change her bandages," Aren said. "Go lay her down somewhere away from everyone else."

Cas nodded. Violet appeared next to them, her arms extended to help. "Can you get down?" he asked Em.

She winced as she sat up straighter, but took Violet's waiting hand and slowly climbed off the horse. Cas jumped down and circled an arm around Em's waist.

"I'm all right," she said. "I can walk now." Her voice was still heavy but much clearer than before.

"I'm sure you can. But isn't it more fun this way?" He

tightened his arm around her waist.

She lifted her head. A sad smile crossed her face. "I found you."

"Were you looking for me?"

"Of course."

He stopped once they'd put a little distance between them and the rest of the group. He let go of her waist to pull a blanket from his pack, and spread it out on the ground. She slowly sat down on it as Aren appeared. He had his canteen and a small bag with him.

"Why don't you go wait over there?" Aren said, jerking his head behind him.

Cas glanced down at the bag. "I can do it. Do you want to just give it to me?"

"Aren. Here." Violet walked up behind them, holding out a fistful of something green. "Is this it?"

"Perfect," Aren said, putting his bag on the ground and taking the herbs. He shook his head at Cas. "Go back and get everyone settled. Assign some people to watch tonight."

"But—"

"Cas, trust me," he interrupted. "You don't want to do this."

Cas tried not to let his fear for Em show on his face.

"He's right." She looked much calmer than he felt. "I used to do this for him. You'd rather not."

"I'll come get you when I'm done," Aren said, kneeling down beside Em.

"Come on," Violet said, grabbing Cas's wrist and tugging

him away. He looked over his shoulder as he left, watching as Aren carefully pulled Em's coat off.

"She'll be fine," Violet said as they walked. "At least it's only her arm, right?"

He nodded numbly. From behind him, he heard a gasp, followed by a cry. He stopped. He wanted to run back and hold on to Em.

She cried out again. Through the trees, he could see Franco and a few other people look up at the noise.

Cas quickly walked to them, trying to keep his face neutral. "Let's go ahead and distribute the dried meat. Only half of it. And people are free to wander in the general area if they'd like to pick some fruit, but not too far."

Franco nodded, his eyes darting behind Cas. "Is she all right?"

"She'll be fine," he said, and hoped it was true. He met Franco's gaze. "You know who that is, don't you?"

"Emelina Flores."

"Yes. Is that a problem?"

"Not particularly. Sounds like the warriors have officially made enemies of the Ruined. It would be best for their leader to be on our side, don't you think?"

"Absolutely."

Franco clapped his hand on his shoulder. "Good. If you trust her, I trust her."

Cas blinked away tears. He hadn't realized how much he wanted someone to say those words to him until they came out of Franco's mouth.

He cleared his throat. "Let's set up a few people to watch. Who should we start with?"

Franco pulled a few men and women from the group, and Cas gave them their watch assignments.

"Whatever happens, you wake up Aren first," Cas instructed them. "Not me, but Aren."

"Definitely. I'm way more important than him." Aren's amused voice made Cas turn, and he found him and Em walking up behind them. Em had the blanket balled up under her good arm. Her eyes were red, and she smiled weakly at Cas.

"He's way more important than me," Cas said.

Aren rolled his eyes as he walked past Cas. "It's no fun if you agree with me."

"I didn't know you felt that way. I'm going to agree with everything you say from now on."

Aren made a sour face at Cas, but he was clearly trying not to grin. Cas turned to Em and carefully took the blanket from her. "Come on," he said.

She followed him as he walked to a spot of grass and laid the blanket down. "Aren told me how you guys ended up here together, but I'm still not sure I believe it."

"No one can resist my charms for very long." Cas offered her his hand. She waved it off and plopped down on the blanket.

"Ow." She winced.

"Well, I offered to help." He sat down next to her. She had a jacket on again, and he couldn't see her bandages. "How bad is it?"

"Not that bad. Not as bad as Aren's burns were. And it's only my arm and some of my shoulder and back."

"Olivia wouldn't heal you?"

"She tried. It was chaos." She lay down on her good side and he stretched out next to her, propping his head on his hand. "The whole royal family is dead except for August. He's taken the throne."

Cas tried not to feel bitter about that. He didn't want to wish death on even his worst enemy, but why August? Of the entire royal family, he was the only one who lived?

"He helped me out of Olso. I think he knew what a mistake he'd made."

"Really."

"But I've decided not to marry him."

Cas laughed softly. "What a surprise."

"Not a good match. I want to strangle him every time I see him, so that might put a damper on our marriage."

"I don't know. You managed to work through that with me."

"True. I did imagine choking you to death with the curtain tie-backs more than once."

Cas reached forward, brushing his hand down her cheek. "The curtain tie-backs, huh? Smart."

She caught his hand, brought it closer to her face, and brushed her lips across the backs of his fingers. "I'm sorry," she said quietly.

"We're past you wanting to murder me, Em."

"Not about that. About rejecting you when you offered to stay with me."

"Don't be. You were right."

She dropped his hand, keeping her gaze on it as it fell to the blanket. "I was?"

"It was irresponsible of me to just give up. All these people . . ." He shook his head. "They were all waiting for me. They assumed I was going to take a stand against Jovita. Imagine how disappointed they would have been if I never came back."

Em nodded. He scooted a little closer to her, nudging her chin up. He brushed his lips against hers.

"That doesn't mean I don't wish we could have stayed together." He barely pulled away from her when he said the words. When her lips turned up, he kissed her again.

"I thought you were mad at me," she said. "You seemed really angry the first time we met after you left."

"I was. I was embarrassed and confused. Being mad at you seemed like the easiest option." He brushed her hair away from her forehead, letting his fingers linger. "Violet set me straight."

"What do you mean?"

"She called me out for trying to torture you by being cold. And for bringing her with me to meet you."

Em's eyes flickered to something over his shoulder. "So, uh, you and Violet aren't . . ."

"She's no one's second choice."

"What?"

"That's what she told me. She said she would never be my second choice."

A smile twitched at Em's lips. "Have I ever mentioned how much I like Violet?"

"Yeah?" Cas asked with a laugh. "She's your new best friend?"

"I think so. She just seems really great."

Cas chuckled, rolling onto his back and holding his arms open. Em scooted forward gingerly and rested her head on his chest. He ran his hand into her hair, kissing the top of her head.

"There's never been anyone but you, Em."

FORTY-TWO

EM WOKE UP in Cas's arms. The sun was starting to rise, and the camp was quiet around her.

Cas's chest rose and fell with his breath, and she closed her eyes again. She wanted to stay here, with her cheek against his chest, for as long as possible. She snuggled closer to him, letting herself drift off again.

People began stirring as the sun rose higher in the sky. Nearby, a man cleared his throat. She opened one eye, reluctant to move.

"Cas." It was Galo's voice.

She let out a sigh and braced her good arm against the ground. Pain shot through her side as she sat up.

Cas rubbed one hand across his eyes and reached for her

with the other. He lightly closed his fingers around her wrist and looked at Galo expectantly.

"I'm sorry to wake you, but Franco and Violet need to speak with you, and we need to move soon."

Cas nodded and sat up. "Give me a few minutes."

Galo walked away, and Cas got to his feet, extending his hand to her. "How are you feeling?"

"Not too bad."

"Good." He leaned forward and pressed his lips to her forehead. "Do you need help getting ready? I can get someone for you."

"I'm fine, thanks. I could use a canteen, though, if you have one."

He reached into his bag and grabbed one, holding it out to her. "You can keep that one."

She smiled as she took it. He walked past her, brushing his hand against hers as he went. She curled her fingertips around his, holding on for an extra second.

His hand fell out of her grasp and she walked to the stream to fill the canteen and splash water on her face. When she returned, Aren was leaning against a tree, watching Cas talk to Violet and Franco. Iria stood next to him.

"You look better," Iria said to Em.

"Thanks." Em regarded Aren curiously. "What happened to the rest of the warriors you were with? Clara? Santino?"

"Clara and Santino were killed," Aren said. "I would have

been too, if it weren't for Iria." He reached out like he was going to take her hand, but seemed to think better of it. "She's going to stay with us."

With *us*? With the Ruined? Not if Olivia had anything to say about it.

"Aren, can we talk for a minute?" Em asked.

"Sure." He took a few steps away from Iria, and she turned and walked to her horse.

Em looked over her shoulder to make sure no one was nearby and leaned closer to Aren. "Are you planning on staying with Cas?"

Aren's forehead creased. "What do you mean? I'm only staying with him if you are. I assumed you wanted to find Olivia."

"I do. But . . . you didn't see her, Aren. There was no reasoning with her. She was just killing everyone."

"How is that different than usual?"

"It was."

"Are you thinking of staying with Cas permanently?"

"Of course not. Olivia needs someone to talk her down. And I won't desert the Ruined."

Aren nodded.

"I want to stay with Cas until they reach Royal City. You could be a big help in retaking the castle," she said.

"Are we sure we want to help them do that?"

"Yes, and not just for Cas. We're officially at war with Olso now. We do *not* want the warriors taking over Lera."

"Right. Enemy of my enemy is my friend, and all that."

"So let's stay with Cas long enough to see him back in the castle and make sure Jovita is out of the picture. I'm sure we'll hear news of Olivia and the rest of the Ruined by the time we reach Royal City." She glanced at Iria. "But when we find Olivia, I'm not sure she's going to take kindly to Iria."

"I'll explain how she saved me," Aren said.

"I don't know if she'll listen. You may want to talk to Iria about staying in Lera and helping Cas."

"I don't think she'll do it. She betrayed the warriors for me and the Ruined, not for Lera."

"I know. But it may be the safest choice, at least until things settle down."

Aren rubbed a hand across his neck, a pained expression crossing his face.

"You and Iria . . ." Em let her voice trail off.

"What? No. We're . . . she's . . ." He cleared his throat, lowering his eyes to the ground.

Em laughed softly. "Whatever it is, make a plan to keep her safe in Lera until we can calm Olivia down."

"She's going to hate me for abandoning her in Lera."

"You're not abandoning her. You're keeping her safe for a while."

"Not sure she's going to see it that way." He let out a long sigh. "I'll talk to her about it."

"Good. I'll discuss it with Cas later and make sure he can protect her."

Em turned and walked to where Iria was saddling her horse.

She watched Em approach with a hint of suspicion.

"Everything all right?" Iria asked hesitantly.

"Yes. Thank you for saving Aren. I know that couldn't have been an easy decision."

"Of course."

Em stepped forward, swinging her good arm around Iria's shoulders. "You annoy me far less these days."

Iria laughed. "Same."

"I'm glad we're on the same page. But don't think I'll start letting you win when we spar."

"Never."

Aren waited until they stopped for the night to approach Iria. He'd spent the day avoiding her, his guilt growing into an angry ball in the pit of his stomach.

He was going to abandon her. In Lera, of all places. She'd given up everything for him, and he was going to leave her in the country she'd been raised to hate.

He tended to his horse, then dropped his small bag on the ground next to a tree. He'd slept next to Iria last night, her shoulder brushing against his, but he wasn't stupid enough to think she'd want to sleep next to him tonight. Or any night.

He grabbed his canteen from his bag and took a long sip. Anything to delay this conversation.

The Lera soldiers were mostly settled, and Cas and Em sat around the fire with Franco and a few other southern leaders. Iria stood a few paces away. She smiled when their eyes met.

That smile almost made him want to stay with her. It would mean leaving the Ruined and joining Cas, but it didn't seem like such a bad idea when she looked at him like that.

He dropped his eyes and tossed his canteen back in his bag. He couldn't leave Em to deal with Olivia by herself. He couldn't leave the Ruined to Olivia's mercy.

He slowly walked to Iria, trying to calm his racing heart. He was more nervous than he'd been the first day in the Lera castle.

He almost reached for her hand when he stopped in front of her. It was becoming second nature, taking her hand. They both pretended it was to fuel his Ruined power, but it felt like more than that. But now didn't feel like the right time to take her hand.

"Take a walk with me?" he asked.

She nodded and followed him away from the camp, into the thick trees. It was dark, the chatter fading behind them as Aren stopped and turned to face Iria. It was hard to make out her features in the darkness. He hadn't planned that, but now he was glad for it.

"Do your powers work with Cas?" she asked before he could get a word out.

"What?"

"I saw you grabbing his wrist a few times. Does it work with him like it does with me?"

"Oh. Yeah." He wrinkled his nose. "I don't know why. He's the only one besides you."

She laughed softly. "And here I thought I was special." Her fingers brushed against his and he quickly pulled his hand back.

"Um . . ."

"What's wrong?" Iria's voice had turned serious.

He swallowed the lump in his throat. "Em and I were talking, and we think we'll need some time with Olivia before we can bring any warriors near the Ruined again."

"'Any warriors' meaning me."

"Em said Olivia was crazy in Olso. We need to talk her down or figure something out. Em asked Cas if you could stay in Lera until I can come back for you, and he said he'd be happy for you to stay in the castle and—"

"In the *Lera* castle?"

"Yes."

"I can't stay in the Lera castle."

"Cas said he would welcome you."

Iria let out a short, humorless laugh. "I'm sure he would. And he'll expect some information in return?"

"He didn't say anything about—"

"I've become worse than his mother," she interrupted. "She was the most notorious traitor in Olso, you know. We learned about her in training. How she took secrets to Lera in order to marry a king. And now I'm her!" She pressed her fingers to her temples. "No, I'm worse, because I did it during wartime."

"You don't have to give Cas any secrets," he said.

"I don't want to live in Lera. I didn't betray my fellow warriors for him, I did it for the Ruined." She didn't say *for you*, but the unsaid words hung between them.

"I know," he said quietly. "But there's nowhere else . . ." He let his voice trail off.

She pressed her lips together. "There's nowhere else for me to go."

He nodded. She turned away, blinking like she was trying not to cry.

"It will only be temporary," he said. "I'll come back and—"

"It's fine. You don't owe me anything. You didn't ask me to save you."

He grabbed her wrist, making her face him. "I'll come back, I promise. I would stay with you in Lera, but I can't abandon the Ruined right now."

"I didn't ask you to." She yanked her arm from his grasp.

"Iria, I—"

"Don't worry about it, Aren. I never expected anything from you anyway." She didn't glance at him once as she walked away.

FORTY-THREE

CAS AND THE rest of the army spent two days on the road to Gallego City. Em asked to stay with them temporarily, and he happily agreed. She alternated between riding on his horse, Aren's, and Iria's. When she was with Cas she'd wrap her arms around his waist and rest her head against his back. He almost wished the journey would never end.

They found Gallego City completely devoid of warriors. Cas had been expecting a fight. He'd worried they wouldn't even make it past Gallego City to the Royal City and the castle. He'd sent scouts up ahead and had the army in battle formation, ready to take on the warriors.

Instead, the town square was empty. A park sat in the center of Gallego City, and it was so quiet the sound of the water splashing in the fountain could be heard from a ways away. A door to one of the shops swung open in the breeze.

He dismounted his horse and walked across the street. The two-story white building housed the governor's office for the central province, but the door was locked tight. He peeked in a window. An empty desk sat in the corner of the room, the chair next to it overturned.

He walked back to his horse and looked up at Em. "I thought you said the warriors who brought you over the border were headed to Gallego City."

"They were. But they only had one carriage and could travel faster. They probably arrived yesterday."

"And left," he murmured, studying an abandoned canteen on the ground. His eyes skipped over the people around him. Many were on horses, but a large group had to walk, and he found Iria in the middle of them. He waved her over. She came slowly, her face tight like she was trying not to show her anger.

"Where would the warriors have gone?" he asked her quietly. "Why did they leave Gallego City?"

She pressed her lips together and shrugged. "I don't know. I've been with you or Aren the whole time."

"A guess?"

"I don't . . . I don't want—" She cut herself off suddenly and blinked several times. Cas realized with a start that she was about to cry. He put a hand on her arm and gently pulled her away from the crowd. She jerked her arm away but walked beside him until they were standing on the porch of the governor's building. She put her hands on her hips and turned her back to the soldiers.

"I liked it better when Em hated you," she said, roughly wiping a hand across her cheeks.

"That didn't last very long, you know. I won her over quickly."

She rolled her eyes, but a smile twitched at her lips.

"What's wrong?" he asked. "I noticed you and Aren haven't been together since they asked if you could stay in Lera. You're mad that he's leaving you?"

"Yes, but it's more than that." She nudged a rock with the toe of her shoe, staring at it as if fascinated. "I made this split-second decision to save Aren and now I'm marching to Royal City with the Lera army to fight my own people. I wasn't thinking about you or Lera when I saved him, I just didn't want him to die. I didn't think it was *right* for him to die."

"But you regret it now?" he asked uneasily. He'd trusted Aren's judgment in bringing Iria along, but it had occurred to him that having a warrior in his army was a risky decision.

"No," she said, looking up at him quickly. "Of course not. I'd do it again. It's just sinking in, what I did. I can never go back to Olso. I can never see my parents again. Not that they would want to see me. They'll disown me the minute they hear. And now I'm supposed to give the Lera king information about the warriors?"

"Not if you don't want to."

"I don't know what I want."

"My mother was a warrior, you know."

"Please don't talk about your mother with me. Being in the same category as her is making me want to scream." She winced.

"I'm sorry. I forgot for a moment that you lost her recently."

"It's fine. No one seems to have nice things to say about my parents."

She looked at him with a glimmer of sympathy.

"My mother hated Olso. She hated how only those strong enough to be warriors mattered, she hated the king, I think she even hated her own family." He lifted one shoulder. "So I can't pretend to understand how you feel. But you can stay in the castle for as long as you like, whether you want to give me information about Olso or not."

She blew out a breath. "It's really annoying when you're nice and reasonable like that."

"I'm very reasonable. Em says it's one of my best qualities." He smiled at her and started back toward his army.

"Do you have any plans to invade Olso?" she called after him.

He turned with a laugh. "Are you kidding? I don't even have my own country yet. I have no interest in invading another one."

"I'll never tell you about Olso's defenses. Or anything about warrior strategy or how we fight or anything like that."

"Understood."

"Best guess—August ordered the warriors who were here to the Lera castle or home to Olso," Iria said.

"Do you want to tell me which is more likely?"

"It depends on how bad things are in Olso. August would weigh their current defensive position in Olso against how much they want to retain their hold in Lera. King Lucio desperately wanted Lera under his control. August . . . I'm not sure. But considering he knows about your relationship with Em, he might assume you have some Ruined support. I'd say there's a good chance he ordered the warriors back to Olso, considering the losses they suffered with Olivia."

"Thank you," he said.

"Your Majesty!" a breathless voice shouted. He turned to see one of his scouts riding down the north road into the town square, her hair flying behind her. She pulled on the reins to slow as she approached him and jumped off her horse.

"Jovita," she said. "We spotted Jovita in the jungle, with all the hunters and soldiers we left at Fort Victorra."

"Headed north?" he asked.

She nodded.

He'd expected as much. He didn't think Jovita would simply sit around the fortress after he left. If he took the castle, he took the throne.

He'd hoped to stay in Gallego City for the rest of the afternoon and through the night to let everyone rest. It looked like that wasn't happening.

"We're going to have to keep moving!" he shouted. He strode back to his horse and took Em's outstretched hand. He settled down in the saddle.

He laced his fingers through Em's, doubt creeping in. "Is it more important to beat Jovita to Royal City, or to let everyone rest?"

"To beat Jovita to Royal City," she said immediately.

"They will need to be rested to fight once we get there. . . ."

"Ride through half the night today, and let people rest for three or four hours. Then ride all the next day, and stop as soon as the sun sets. Let them sleep all night so they'll be rested when we get to Royal City the next day. That's what I would do."

"Then that's what I'll do."

FORTY-FOUR

THE AIR WAS cool and salty as the Lera army approached Royal City two days later. Em took in a deep breath. She'd missed that smell.

The dirt road curved through the grass, leading to a cluster of homes. Past that, Em could see the buildings stretching up into the sky—the center of Royal City. The sun was sinking behind them, casting an orange glow across the land in front of them.

Beyond the shops was the castle. Completely intact, from the looks of it.

She was walking on foot beside Cas's horse, and she turned to smile at him. His attention was on the castle, relief splashed across his face. She glanced over her shoulder at the Lera soldiers stretched out behind her to see matching expressions on their faces.

"Your kingdom is beautiful, Cas," she said. "Have I ever told you that?"

"I don't think so. If you did, it was begrudgingly."

She laughed softly. "I mean it this time."

"Thank you." He looked down at her, their eyes meeting for a moment. "You should stay."

She smiled sadly because she knew she couldn't. But Cas just stared at her like he was serious.

"Cas, you know I can't—"

"Em," Aren interrupted. He pointed west.

She turned. The trees on the west side of the city were swaying like a storm was brewing. But around her, the air was still.

"Ruined." Her chest constricted. "Olivia."

"Why is she here?" Cas asked.

She shook her head. "I don't know. Maybe she knew I was here?" Maybe Olivia had completely destroyed Olso and had decided to move on to Lera.

Em met Aren's eyes. He was thinking the same thing.

"I'll go find her," she said.

Aren jumped off his horse. "Take my horse. I'm going to stay with Cas and Iria until they're in the castle. Is that all right?"

"Of course."

"I'll find you when it's over." Aren squeezed her arm.

Em turned to find Cas had dismounted his horse. A soldier

pulled on his horse's rein, moving to the side so they could have a modicum of privacy. It wasn't much, considering the rest of the soldiers were still moving toward the city on the road behind her.

A lump formed in her throat as she stepped closer to him. "I can probably convince Olivia to leave." She spoke softly so that only he could hear. "But I don't think I'll ever convince her to partner with humans again. It's best if we go to Ruina and not come back."

Cas's lips twitched up, which wasn't the response she'd been expecting. He stepped closer to her, sliding one hand onto her neck. His thumb stroked her jaw. "I don't think you're going to do that."

"What?"

"I know what we did to the Ruined is unforgiveable. I'll never ask for their forgiveness. But I want to find a way to make it better. I want my people to face what we did, and try to make amends."

Em shook her head. "Cas—"

"And I want you to marry me. For real this time." He leaned forward, brushing his lips against hers. "I spent so much time moping about how we couldn't be together that I forgot to fight for you. So I'm going to start. I'm going to use every bit of power I have to convince my people we need to partner with the Ruined. That you would be the best queen they ever had."

Em's breath caught in her throat, a tiny glimmer of hope shining through the doubt. "I—I don't know if . . ." She didn't know anything. She didn't know how to end that sentence.

"You know," Cas said. He was so close to her their foreheads were almost touching. "You just have to make a choice. And I have faith you're going to make the right one." He put both hands on her cheeks and kissed her. She wrapped her fingers around his wrists and kissed him back.

He pulled away and met her eyes. "I love you. I'll see you soon."

She almost reached for him as he walked to his horse. She felt like she would fall over without him holding her up.

"Cas, I . . ." She let her words trail off, but the apology was etched all over those words.

He smiled at her over his shoulder. "You'll make the right decision. I'll see you soon."

She quickly turned, blinking away tears. He had more faith in her than she deserved. She couldn't stay with him. It wasn't the right choice; it wasn't a choice at all.

Was it?

She couldn't help but think that Ruina no longer felt like home because he wasn't there.

She kept her back to him for several long moments, afraid that if she turned around, she'd see his face and run straight back to him. When she finally looked, he'd disappeared, lost in the crowd of horses and soldiers.

She reached for her horse, grasping his saddle and swinging one leg over him. There would be no choice to make if Olivia killed Cas and leveled the city.

She drove the horse forward, heading west. The trees were no longer moving, but smoke rose from the outskirts of town. Em kicked her heels into the side of the horse, urging him to go faster.

"Olivia!" She started yelling before she could see her sister or any of the Ruined. She yelled her sister's name as she passed a burning farmhouse, as she followed the trail they'd left in the dirt. She yelled Olivia's name like if she screamed it loud enough, she could actually stop all of this.

Em rounded a corner and found Olivia stopped in the middle of the dirt road. The Ruined stood in clumps around her, their faces tight with exhaustion. There were fewer than in Sacred Rock. They'd lost at least twenty, it seemed. Homes dotted either side of the road around them, but Em didn't see any people.

"Em," Olivia said, without a trace of surprise.

Em jumped off her horse and walked to her sister. She took a deep breath to steady her voice. "What are you doing here?"

"What are *you* doing here?" Olivia's tone suggested she already knew.

"The warriors dropped me in Lera. It was safer to stay with Cas until I found you." She took a step closer to her sister. "Did you follow us here?"

"Yes."

"Why didn't you show yourself sooner? I was worried."

Something like regret flashed over Olivia's face, but it was gone as soon as it came. "I wanted to see Royal City for myself."

"If you destroy the city—"

"I have no intention of destroying it. I'm going to stay."

"Stay," Em repeated slowly.

"There's nothing left for us in Ruina. I'd rather stay here. What will Cas think about that?"

Em stared at her sister. Cas would let them stay if they agreed to live peacefully. But she had a feeling that wasn't what Olivia was planning.

"Wouldn't you rather live in Lera?" Olivia asked. She took a step closer to Em, hope flitting across her face. "I know Ruina is our home, but . . ."

But it was destroyed. And it was never as nice as Lera, even before the invasion. Olivia didn't finish her sentence—perhaps she didn't want to say the words out loud—but Em knew what she meant.

"I would rather live in Lera," Em admitted quietly. "If you agree to sign a peace agreement, Cas would let us stay. I'm sure of it."

Olivia face hardened. "I'm not signing a peace agreement. Not unless it comes with the heads of the Casimir and all the advisers."

"No." The word came out harsher than she'd intended it. Em was tired of having this conversation with Olivia. She wouldn't explain again why Cas didn't deserve her rage.

"That's what I thought." Olivia whirled around, striding in the direction of the city. Most of the Ruined followed her, but a few hesitated, regarding Em worriedly.

"Stop!" Em yelled.

Olivia came to a halt, but she waited a few seconds before turning around. Her eyes flashed as she looked at Em.

"We agreed that I took care of our interactions with humans," Em said. "This counts. As your queen, I'm ordering you all to stand down."

Olivia muttered something to Jacobo. He nodded and slipped something into Olivia's hand. She kept it behind her back as she strode to Em.

"You were queen because I *let* you," Olivia spat. "You've lost that privilege now."

Em took in a sharp breath. Olivia's words hurt even more the second time.

"This land was originally ours, and I'm taking it back. Cas can get out of the way, or lose his life along with his kingdom." Olivia snapped her fingers and Jacobo and another Ruined rushed to her side. She pulled out a rope from behind her back.

Em took a step away from her sister, but it was too late. The two Ruined grabbed her by either arm, holding her in place.

"I'm sorry," Olivia said as she wrapped the rope around Em's hands. Em tried to pull them free, but the men's grips were too tight. "I've cleared this area, so you should be safe until I come back. This is for the best. Trust me."

I don't. Tears pricked Em's eyes as the words surfaced. She didn't trust Olivia. Not even a little.

The men pushed her to the ground, and Olivia wrapped a leather belt around Em's legs. She nodded as she stood.

"Good. That should hold her until we're finished." She squinted past Em. "I don't sense Aren in the area. He must have stayed with the others." She looked at Em for confirmation.

Em stared down at the ground. She'd been cocky when she told Cas she could stop Olivia. Had she really thought she could reason with her sister?

Olivia patted Em's head. "I'll be back soon. Don't worry."

Em rested her chin on her knees, refusing to meet Olivia's gaze. Her sister walked away, the Ruined following her. None of them stayed with Em.

FORTY-FIVE

CAS LOOKED OVER his shoulder, even though it had been several minutes since he'd rode away from Em and he couldn't see her anymore. Part of him could still feel her standing there, staring after him like he was insane.

She was going to make the right decision. He'd been certain of it before, but after seeing the way she looked at him, he would bet his life on it. She would come back to him soon.

He rode toward the city, weaving in between his soldiers until he was at the front of the line. Galo jogged to him on foot, looking up at Cas in concern.

"You should stay in the middle of the pack, Your Majesty."

"*Your Majesty?* We're being formal today?"

"I've decided to call you Your Majesty when we're going into battle."

"That seems arbitrary, but all right."

"I'm serious. General Amaro said it would be safer to have a few bodies in front of you."

He turned to look for General Amaro, but the soldiers were in formation farther back, behind his guards.

"I'm the one who ordered them all here to fight for me. I'm riding in front." He gave Galo a look that meant he was done discussing it.

"Fine," Galo said with a resigned sigh. "But I'm staying next to you."

"Good." Cas smiled at him before focusing straight ahead again. They were so close to the city he could hear the murmur of voices, smell the scent of meat being cooked.

They turned onto the road that led into the town square, and Cas could see people standing outside their shops and homes just ahead. Cas breathed a sigh of relief that the warriors hadn't killed all the townspeople. He knew that many of the people in Gallego City had escaped to the fortress, but he'd been worried about everyone in Royal City.

But the city looked mostly the same—a few shops were burned and being rebuilt, but other than that the road was still lined with colorful buildings, their windows advertising bread or sweets or clothing. The people in the road appeared scared but unharmed. He waved to them, which produced a few startled expressions.

He rode until he was almost in the town square, then jumped off his horse and drew his sword. A few dead bodies lay in the road, and he cast a quick glance at their uniforms. Warriors.

"That's right, you better run!" a woman was yelling, as a few warriors ran down the east road, in the direction of the ocean. Jovita. She was standing in the middle of the road with several hunters.

"Jovita," he called.

She whirled around, her lip curling. "Cas."

Several of the townspeople gasped and bowed their heads, and he realized for the first time that none of them had known who he was. He wore plain black clothes, like many of the soldiers. Only a smattering had official blue Lera uniforms.

"Everyone needs to get inside," he ordered. "Olivia Flores is here."

Jovita paled. "What? Where?"

"She's on the outskirts of town with a bunch of Ruined. She—"

"None of this would have happened if you hadn't let her go," Jovita said, her face red with fury. "If you hadn't been so—"

"Jovita, shut up!" He yelled so loudly she jumped in surprise. "I don't have time to discuss any of this with you right now." He pointed to the gawking townspeople. "All of you, inside, now. Stay there until we ring the castle bell." They quickly scurried inside, doors slamming shut down up and down the street.

"Cas," Aren said quietly. He pointed east, in the direction of the ocean. Flames lit up the night sky. The Ruined weren't far from the castle.

"Em can stop Olivia, right?" Cas asked. Aren gave him a worried look in reply.

"We're counting on Emelina Flores to save us?" Jovita strode to her horse. "We're all dead."

To his right, soldiers raced past the town and to the castle. Many of them were on foot, though a few horses galloped ahead. General Amaro led the pack, shouting orders as she charged toward the castle.

Cas ran to his horse and practically jumped onto the saddle. He kicked the side of the horse and took off, glancing over his shoulder at her. She glared at him.

He faced forward, looking at the flames again. Em could do it. He knew she could. She was stronger than Olivia, in every way that counted.

He rode to the castle, Aren and Galo running behind him. The warriors hadn't fully repaired the walls they'd destroyed in the siege, and none of the front gate remained. He spotted a piece of it lying in the grass not far away. There were several huge holes in the wall, and the soldiers marched ahead of him. They streamed into the front lawn.

Cas jumped off his horse and drew his sword. Galo ran ahead of him and ducked through one of the holes in the walls. He positioned himself in front of it as Cas climbed through. He straightened. Stopped.

He'd been expecting Olso warriors guarding the castle. Weapons. Some of the impressive technology Em had told him about.

Instead, only Cas's army was on the lawn. The front doors were open and he caught a glimpse of General Amaro as she ran inside.

Galo moved to stand at Cas's side. "Is it a trap?"

"I don't know," Cas murmured.

Shouts and footsteps sounded from the back of the castle. He turned to grab the nearest soldier. "Go to the gardens. Find out what's happening back there." The soldier nodded and left, pulling a few others with him. Iria stood a few paces away, watching, and she took off behind the soldiers.

Cas lifted his chin, taking in the sight of his home for a moment. He'd so badly wanted for it to still be standing, and he was shocked he'd gotten his wish. The castle looked the same from the outside—white stone and large windows and peaks on the top of the four towers in the corners. He stood rooted in place for a moment, staring at it. He knew that there were probably warriors inside, and he was being no help by just standing on the front lawn, but he couldn't help it.

He finally pried his gaze away. Soldiers were still running through the front door, and he followed them inside. Galo ran beside him.

There were no warriors inside, either. Soldiers rushed past him, scattering into hallways and up the stairs. Lanterns lining the wall were lit, casting a glow on the black marks snaking up the walls from the fire. The table that used to sit against the wall in the entryway was gone, a black mark in its place, and the bottom few steps of the staircase were burned. But otherwise the staircase was intact. The warriors must have put the fire out quickly.

"Your Majesty." A soldier was in front of him suddenly. "Let me take you somewhere safe."

He shook his head and sidestepped the soldier. He ran to the back of the castle and ducked into the kitchen. Plates with half-eaten food lay abandoned on the staff table. A mug of tea was still steaming.

Cas pushed open the back door and rushed outside. The warriors were all running away. They streamed across the lawn, hopping the wall and disappearing.

"They're getting in a ship!" a voice above him yelled. Cas looked up to see Franco in the tower, pointing in the direction of the ocean.

"They didn't even put up a fight?" the soldier beside Cas asked, clearly baffled.

"Olivia. They got word to run, not fight."

"Smart," a voice from behind him said. Cas turned to find Aren standing in the doorway of the kitchen with Galo.

"Will you stay here for a minute?" Cas asked Aren. "Yell if you spot any Ruined or warriors coming this way."

Aren nodded, and Cas turned and walked back into the castle. "Tell the guards to check every room of the castle," he said to Galo. "Every place someone could hide. Make sure the castle is clear."

Galo nodded and grabbed the nearest guard, repeating the order quickly. He stayed at Cas's side as he turned a corner. Cas considered going up to the tower to watch the warriors leave, to his bedroom, to Em's room, but his feet led him directly to a sitting room on the first floor. He stepped inside.

His father's blood still stained the wooden floor. The window Cas had used to escape was closed, and his father's body was gone, but other than that, it was exactly the same as he remembered it. He took in a shaky breath.

"We'll have someone clean that," Galo said quietly.

Cas didn't think that would help much. He turned on his heel and quickly walked out of the room. He kind of wished the fire had destroyed that room.

The hallways had once been brightly colored—red and orange and blue and green, different every time you turned a corner. They were mostly black now, and he trailed his fingers along a formerly green wall as he walked back to the front of the castle. He would have them painted to match the original color. So many things had to change, but he thought maybe he'd leave just this one thing the same.

He rounded a corner and stepped back into the foyer at the main entrance. Some of the staff was trickling in, and he heard a laugh from somewhere in the castle. The air was full of excitement and anticipation suddenly. Their bright faces filled Cas with hope.

Mateo ran to the front door, his eyes finding Cas. *Jovita,* he mouthed.

Cas weaved around the staff members and stepped outside. Jovita stood in front of the remains of the gate, a small group of hunters behind her. Her gaze was above his head, on the castle, but she slowly lowered it until their eyes met. She lifted an eyebrow.

"Should I call some guards to make sure she doesn't come in?" Galo asked.

Jovita took a step back, like she knew what Galo had just said. She held Cas's stare for another moment before turning and walking away. The hunters followed her. One of them grinned at Cas as he left and ran a finger across his neck.

"Did he just—" Galo darted forward and Cas grabbed his arm.

"Let them go."

"He just threatened the king."

"I have bigger things to worry about."

"You're going to have to deal with her eventually," Galo said.

"I know."

Cas stepped inside and he and Galo closed the doors. The staff members were clustered at the bottom of the stairs, looking at him excitedly, and he squeezed Daniela's arm as he passed her.

He hurried across the castle, back through the kitchen, and out the back door again. Aren was still there with a few soldiers and Franco. They were all looking at the sky. Cas followed their gaze.

"What?" he asked.

"The Ruined are close," Aren said.

Franco looked from Aren to Cas. "Do the warriors have the right idea? Should we be running?"

"We don't have anywhere else to go." Cas's voice was calm. "Have faith in Em."

He closed his eyes for a moment. *You'll make the right decision.*

FORTY-SIX

AREN HAD ALL the faith in the world in Em, but he couldn't deny that the wind whipping across his face was Ruined-made. They were close.

Screams sounded from beyond the wall. He'd seen Iria run across the gardens toward the back wall just a few minutes ago.

"Go inside," he said to Cas. "Stay there until I say it's safe."

Cas nodded and strode back inside the castle. Franco and the soldiers followed him.

Aren ran across the lawn and through the gardens, to what remained of the stone wall. Large chunks of it still stood, but parts of it had been blown away by the Olso attack. He jumped over the rubble.

The area behind the castle was nothing but open land. It was dark and mostly deserted, but he could see the backs of warriors as they scurried away from him. He followed them.

Homes and shops were to his left, but he ran in the direction of the ocean, where he could see several large ships docked. Red Olso flags flapped in the breeze.

Surely Iria wouldn't try to go back to Olso? He hadn't killed all the warriors they were with. Plenty of them knew that she'd betrayed them and taken off with Aren.

He ran up a hill and skidded to a stop. The scene in front of him was such chaos he had to blink a couple times to take it all in. Warriors ran in all directions, shouting orders at each other. Some of them scurried onto the boats, others were running off the ship, swords drawn. Olivia strode toward the dock, a group of Ruined behind her. Her coat billowed in the wind, and Aren could see the fury etched on her face, even from this distance. She left a trail of dead warriors behind her.

Em wasn't with her.

"Aim! Warriors, aim!"

Ten warriors stood their ground in the grass just in front of the docks. A long metal cylinder was perched on each of their shoulders. Another warrior was behind each of them, a small torch in each of their hands. They were all staring at the Ruined.

Aren ran as fast as he could down the hill, but a hand caught his before he could reach the bottom.

"Don't move," Iria said, pulling his hand in closer to her like she was afraid he wouldn't obey.

"What are those?" he asked, pointing to the cylinder on the warriors' shoulders.

"Hand cannons. Tell the Ruined to run."

"Run!" Aren yelled without question. "Ruined, run!"

A few chins lifted to look at him, but no one followed the order.

"Aren, move those warriors. Just—"

Fire exploded from the cannons, the ground shaking from the force of the blast. Aren jumped, instinctively throwing an arm over his face.

Ruined bodies flew through the air and landed hard in the dirt. Smoke curled up to the sky, obscuring the rest of the Ruined. Aren squinted, but he couldn't see anything. Dread rose in his chest as the screams started.

Then, all the warriors rose off the ground and launched across the dock. Their bodies landed in the water with a splash. Olivia strode through the smoke, her expression wild as she used her Ruined magic to completely clear the area of warriors. A piece of metal was lodged in her arm, blood running down her hand and dripping off her fingers, but she didn't appear to care.

The smoke began to clear, revealing bodies of dead Ruined behind her. Aren squeezed his eyes shut and turned into Iria's shoulder.

"Aren, she's going to kill everyone," Iria breathed.

He took in a shaky breath and forced his eyes open again. He dropped Iria's hand. "Hide. I'll be right back."

She nodded and jogged down the hill, crouching behind one of the beams at the edge of the dock. Aren waited until she was well hidden before yelling Olivia's name.

Olivia turned. Her entire face lit up. She spread her arms wide, like she wanted a hug. "Aren!"

He walked slowly down the hill. His hands were shaking, and he took several deep breaths. Olivia would not tolerate weakness.

He stopped in front of her, clasping his hands behind his back. "Em's fine. I found her."

"I know. We chatted."

An uneasy feeling crept up Aren's chest. "Where is she?"

"I left her somewhere safe. She's fine." She squinted at the warriors getting on the boat behind him. "You want to help me with this?"

"Just let them leave."

"No." She turned on her heel and started walking. She narrowed her eyes at something.

A group of warriors ran down the dock. Several of them ran for the boat, but one went straight for the beam where Iria was hiding. He held his hand out and yelled something. Olivia looked from him to the group of warriors almost to the boat. A man screamed as blood spurted from his chest.

"Olivia, no! Let them go!" Aren darted in front of her, blocking her view.

She glared at him and shoved her hands against his shoulders, pushing him out of the way. She focused on Iria.

Aren launched his body into Olivia's. She yelped as they hit the dirt together. He sat on her legs and used both his hands to cover her eyes.

"What are you doing?" she growled. She clawed at his wrists.

"Just listen to me for a minute. Iria helped me. She saved me."

"I don't care. I'm done listening to you and Em and all the excuses you make for them." She managed to tear one of his hands away and glared at him. His entire body tingled suddenly. His lips parted in shock.

"Are you trying to use your magic on me?"

She freed her other hand and pushed him off her. His body tingled again. A blip of fear raced up his spine.

"If you're going to act like a human, I'm going to treat you like one," she said.

The Ruined weren't able to use their magic on each other. Not normally. But Olivia wasn't normal.

But, neither was he.

His cast a glance at Iria. A few warriors were around her now, trying to coax her to the boat. Her gaze was locked on his. He could still feel the warmth of her hand in his, the way his body always leaned into her when she was near.

He snapped his attention back to Olivia. He summoned up every bit of power he had.

Her feet slid backward in the dirt. She gasped.

He stepped forward, willing her backward. It wasn't like moving a human—every little movement sucked power from him.

"Aren—" Her words were lost in a gasp as he pushed her away with all his might. She flew off the dock and landed in a heap at the base of the hill. Her head popped up. He was glad he couldn't see her expression from this distance. She might have killed him with one look.

He turned around, meaning to run, but the world tilted around him. He stumbled and almost fell.

"Aren!" Iria ran toward him. She was just a blur, but he held his hand out. She grabbed it, her other hand on his cheek. He leaned into her touch, relief flooding through him. Iria's eyes widened at something behind him.

Footsteps. He grabbed Iria's waist as he spun around. Olivia was running right to them.

He dropped to the ground, pulling Iria with him. He wrapped his arms and legs around her, trying to cover every part of her body with his. He put one hand on the back of her head and ducked it into his shoulder.

The footsteps stopped next to them.

"Please. Not her. Please, Olivia." He held Iria tighter.

Silence answered him. Iria clutched his shirt in her hands, her breath coming out in short gasps.

Olivia made a disgusted sound. "You're weak, Aren."

He could see only her shoes, and they lingered for several agonizing seconds. Finally, she turned. She stumbled a bit as she began walking like she was dizzy.

"You're weak!" she screamed again.

He pulled back and put both his hands on Iria's cheeks. "Are you all right?"

She nodded, tears spilling onto her cheeks. She took in a ragged breath.

A warrior skidded to a stop behind her and grabbed her under the arms. He yanked her to her feet.

Aren shot up, almost stumbling as the world spun around him. Two more warriors had appeared around Iria. He recognized them. They'd been there when Iria betrayed them.

A sword. There was a sword pointed at Aren's chest.

"He saved you!" Iria yelled. "He saved all of us!"

Aren blinked, meeting the warrior's gaze. Her face was dirty, her eyes red-rimmed. Her sword shook.

"I'm sorry," he said quietly. "I'm sorry about Olivia."

"Leave him," another warrior said. There were at least six around them now that Aren could see. "We need to get out of here."

The warrior lowered her sword. Iria let out a big sigh.

They were dragging Iria away. Away from him.

"No." He stumbled forward, reaching for Iria's hand. Her fingers caught his for a moment.

A warrior shoved him. "You have no right to interfere with an Olso prisoner."

"Let her come with me. Please."

"Go. Now." The warrior nudged his sword against Aren's chest.

"It's fine," Iria said.

He shook his head vigorously. She was crying, and tears welled in his own eyes. If he hadn't used all of his energy on Olivia, he could have blown every one of these warriors into the ocean.

"Just go, Aren!" she yelled.

He jumped forward, putting one hand on her neck as he leaned down so his lips brushed against her ear. A warrior grabbed his shoulder, but he used his other arm to hold on to Iria's waist.

"I'll find you. I don't care if I have to break into every prison in Olso. I'll find you. I promise."

Another hand clapped down on his shoulder, and two warriors roughly pulled him away. His butt hit the ground.

She met his eyes, a smile breaking through her tears.

FORTY-SEVEN

EM PULLED AT the ropes on her wrists until her skin was red and angry. They didn't budge.

She kicked her feet. If she could get her feet free, she could at least run. What if a Lera soldier or a warrior happened by? What did her sister expect her to do then?

The belt around her ankles held firm, and she let out a frustrated yell. Olivia had left her defenseless.

A loud boom sounded from the east, and her head popped up. She'd heard that sound before, in Olso.

She pressed her lips together, fighting back tears. Her fear for Cas and Olivia overwhelmed her for a moment, and she considered curling up into a ball and sobbing.

Footsteps pounded the dirt, and Em stiffened. She tried to yank her hands apart.

Mariana and Ivanna appeared around the corner. Mariana skidded to a stop in front of her and dropped to her knees, grabbing the ropes. She tugged at the knot.

"We got away as fast as we could," she said. "We didn't want Olivia to know we were coming back for you." She pulled Em's hands free.

Em reached for the belt around her ankles. "Are they at the castle?"

"Should be by now," Ivanna said. "But at least half the Ruined aren't interested in fighting anymore. She can't make us kill with her."

Em tossed the belt aside and jumped to her feet. "I won't tell her you helped me."

"Tell her," Mariana said fiercely. "We're not ashamed of helping our queen. We only snuck away because we didn't want to give her the opportunity to stop us."

Em blinked back tears as she shot them a grateful smile. She broke into a run.

Mariana and Ivanna's footsteps pounded behind her as she sprinted down the road. The castle loomed to her right, the windows bright yellow against the dark. She looked over her shoulder as she passed it, to the room she thought used to be hers. The lanterns had been lit in there too.

She faced forward. Yells could be heard as she got closer to the ocean. She pumped her arms, running as fast as she could.

She darted up a hill and found her sister immediately.

"Why are you all just standing there? Grab him!" Olivia voice shook, her finger pointing to a figure walking away from the harbor. Aren.

Olivia stood in front of a crowd of Ruined, half of them collapsed on the ground from exhaustion. She put her hands on her knees, her hair shielding her face as she lowered her head. Something had finally exhausted her.

Behind her, an Olso ship was pulling away from the dock. A second ship was still docked, but judging by the shouts and frantic running, it was about to depart shortly.

Olivia hadn't noticed Em yet, so she ran to Aren instead. He was headed in the direction of the remaining Olso ship, and Em grabbed his arm to stop him. His shoulder slumped forward like it was almost too much effort for him to stand.

"What happened?" she whispered.

"She tried to kill Iria. I used my powers on Olivia, Em."

"What?" The word from Em made Olivia turn.

"I figured those ropes wouldn't hold you for long," Olivia said, a hint of pride in her voice. "Not much keeps you down, does it?"

Em swallowed, glancing at the Ruined behind Olivia. A few still appeared strong, ready to fight, but many looked worried. Ivanna and Mariana stood at the top of the hill, staring at the dead Ruined in horror.

Olivia pointed at Aren. "Did he tell you what he did?"

"Yes," Em said quietly.

"A Ruined has never betrayed their own before," Olivia said. "What should we do?"

"One thing at a time," Em said. "Let's get out of here. Between the warriors and Cas's army, we can't win this. Especially not with the Ruined exhausted like this."

"I can take them myself," Olivia said. "And I still have a few who can fight."

"It's over, Olivia. Let's go home. Let's go rebuild the castle."

"It is *not*," Olivia said. She pointed at Aren. "And if he hadn't betrayed us, we could take them all easily. Isn't there a punishment written in the laws somewhere about betraying fellow Ruined? I think the punishment is death."

Em's chest tightened. She didn't remember what the punishment was, but the fact that Olivia had even mentioned executing Aren was terrifying. Em couldn't remember a Ruined ever being executed.

You just have to make a choice. And I have faith you're going to make the right one.

"We can't lose any more Ruined," Em said. "Let's go back to Ruina and—"

"We're not going back to Ruina." Olivia spread her arms wide. "I like it better here." She pointed to the castle. "Our people deserve that castle. I'm going to give it to them."

Em closed her fingers around the hilt of her sword. She hadn't even realized she was going to do it until her hand was there, twitching to remove the blade from her waist.

Four steps to get to Olivia, one second to draw her sword,

another to sink the blade into her chest. Easy.

Em swallowed down a sudden swell of horror. She would never hurt her sister.

Still, she was right. It would be easy. Her sister wasn't good with a sword. And she could never use her magic on Em, not unless Em let her. She wasn't like Aren, or the rest of the Ruined. She wasn't even like the humans. Em was the only person Olivia had no power over.

Em drew in a shaky breath and slowly released her grip on her sword. Olivia hadn't seemed to notice. She never noticed weapons. They were rarely a threat to her.

She walked slowly to her sister, turning over her words in her head. She could remind Olivia that Cas had told her about August's betrayal, that he had had been the one to release Olivia from her prison.

Olivia met her gaze and all of Em's words died in her throat. She'd forgotten that expression. She'd seen it so many times from her mother, but she'd buried it deep in the back of her memory because she'd always hated it. Or maybe she was just scared of it.

Olivia's eyes were hard, her mouth set in a hard line. Her expression was challenging, like she had already prepared a response to every single thing Em was going to say. There was no reasoning with her. She'd never change Olivia's mind. It was either join her sister or betray her.

You'll make the right decision.

"You'll lose if you attack the castle right now," Em said. Her voice was too quiet, and she had to clear her throat. "Look behind you at the Ruined and tell me you really think most of them will make it through this."

Olivia glanced behind her. She obviously tried to keep her expression neutral, but disappointment flashed across her features.

"I don't want to attack Lera like this," Em said. "Not when we'll probably lose. Let's go somewhere and get organized. Let's attack them when we know we can win."

Olivia opened her mouth, then closed it. She stared at Em like she wasn't sure what was going on.

"I'm not leaving Lera," Olivia finally said.

"Fine. We'll go somewhere nearby."

"You're telling me you're going to help me plan an attack on Lera," Olivia said skeptically.

"I already did it once."

"And you regret it. Don't try to tell me you don't."

"I regret hurting Cas. So I have a condition."

"A condition."

"I get him. I will tell you everything I know about Lera and their defenses and help you with anything you want. You can have his castle and his country and everything else. But I get to have him, alive." The lies fell out of her mouth easily. She was good at lying. Even to her sister, it seemed.

"You really think he's going to want you after you do that to him again?"

"I think you underestimate his love for me."

Olivia's face changed, her head cocking to the side as she

considered it. "All right, fine. He'll be powerless and useless at that point, anyway." Olivia let out a long sigh, glancing over at the Ruined on the ground. "I hate to admit it, but the warriors' technology surprised me. I lost more than I thought I would. We could use some time to figure out how to defend against it."

Em discreetly let out a relieved breath. Her brain was already racing, trying to figure out how to save Cas's kingdom without losing Olivia forever.

Olivia's lip curled as she looked at Aren. "What about him?"

"He didn't just protect Iria because of his feelings," Em said. "She made him more powerful, and he wanted to keep her close. How do you think he was able to use his power on you?"

Olivia gasped, and Em knew she'd just given her sister the most dangerous piece of information yet. They would probably have to take a few prisoners for Olivia to experiment with.

"He still shouldn't have used his magic on me," Olivia said.

"That's true. Let me speak to him. I understand how feelings can get in the way. I'll talk some sense into him. If we can't reason with him, we'll put him in a cell. We can't afford to lose even one more Ruined."

"Good. I like it. Best not to give up on him, since he's so powerful. I'll tell the others." Olivia spun on her heel and Em turned away, pressing a hand to her mouth to stifle a sob.

Aren stared at her wide-eyed. "Em, you're not really—"

She gave him a sharp look and he immediately stopped talking. "Yell at me. Tell me you need Iria."

Confusion flashed across Aren's face for half a second. But he quickly obeyed. "I need her!" he yelled. "Iria is one of us!"

"I'm sorry about this," Em muttered, then reeled back and slapped him across the face. "Pull yourself together!" she yelled, loud enough for everyone to hear. "She's just a girl! She's nothing compared to you! Compared to us!"

Aren worked his jaw around and nodded silently.

"I can't convince her," Em whispered. "And if we leave her I don't know what will happen."

Aren lifted his eyebrows in question, but his terrified expression suggested he had already caught on to her plan.

"The only way we can stop this is by sticking with her. If we bring Ruined to our side, she won't have enough people to attack anyone. I know several who would be on our side right away."

"Me too," Aren said. He looked at Olivia. "If this goes bad . . ."

"We're probably dead."

"The Ruined don't betray each other."

"Then we're about to be the first." She moved closer to him and grabbed his hand. "If you want to run now, I understand. Cas would welcome you."

Aren shook his head. "No way. I stick with you, always." He lifted one shoulder. "Besides, it can't be any more dangerous than infiltrating the Lera castle, right?"

Em glanced at Olivia. She was pulling a piece of metal out of her arm, wincing as blood ran down her skin.

Em took in a shaky breath. "Debatable."

She looked over her shoulder, at the Olso ships departing

the harbor. The warriors wouldn't be back anytime soon. The Ruined were on their own, for better or worse.

Her gaze shifted to the Lera castle. Cas and the Lerans also had no other kingdom left to rely on. Em might be their only ally.

She almost laughed. Emelina Flores, Lera's most important ally.

Her amusement faded as she turned to face her sister again. Olivia was staring at her and Aren. "Are we leaving? Will we have to drag you, Aren?"

"I'm coming," Aren said. He looped his arm through Em's.

"Good." Olivia crossed her arms over her chest. Em had never seen someone regard her with such intense suspicion. "Lead the way, sister. I assume you have a plan?"

Em met her sister's gaze. "You bet I do."

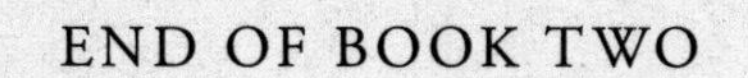
END OF BOOK TWO

ACKNOWLEDGMENTS

Writing the second book in a trilogy is never easy, but I'm lucky to have so many wonderful people supporting me and the *Ruined* series. Big thank-yous to:

My editor, Emilia Rhodes, for your continued enthusiasm for the series and for edits that are never *too* terrifying.

My agent, Emmanuelle Morgen—thanks for loving this book right away, even in its early stages.

Thank you to Gina Rizzo, publicist extraordinaire, and Alice Jerman, for working so hard on all my books.

Michelle Krys—I'm so lucky to have such a wonderful crit partner! I'm sorry I didn't take your note about Cas and Em's "blissful moment," but I'm evil.

Thank you to all the authors who joined me in doing signings for *Ruined* so I wouldn't have to be alone—Julie Murphy, Debra Driza, Roshani Chokshi, Aprilynne Pike, Amy Lukavics, Chris Howard, Amie Kaufman, Jay Kristoff, and Shannon Messenger.

All the authors who help keep me sane—Julie, Natalie, Tess, Michelle, Bethany, Shannon—you guys are the best. Thank you to Kate Johnston for telling everyone about the total lack of rape culture in the *Ruined* world. Thank you to Amie Kaufman for the wonderful blurb, because I was too late to put it in the last acknowledgments. Thank you to Maurene Goo for introducing me to Korean dramas. My writing will never be the same, and I mean that in the best way possible.

Fairy Loot—thank you for putting *Ruined* in your subscription box!

BookPeople in Austin—thank you for doing a preorder campaign for *Ruined* with me, and for being the best indie bookstore around!

Thanks to my family, especially my parents, for always supporting me and buying an obscene number of my books.

My sister, Laura, my first crit partner, thank you for reading all my books, even when they're terrible first drafts. And my continued apologies about Olivia.

And a big thank-you to all the readers. The YA community is the best community, and I'm so thrilled to be a part of it.

Read on for an Excerpt from

ALLIED

ONE

EMELINA FLORES WAS no one's hero.

Smoke filled the air. Distantly, she heard someone laugh. The sound was manically gleeful, and Em knew it was her sister, Olivia. She didn't turn around to confirm.

The flames licked up the white pillars at the front of the governor's home. It was a large, cheery two-story home, the first thing that greeted visitors to the town of Westhaven. There was no reason to destroy it.

Except that it pleased Olivia.

Em glanced over her shoulder. Olivia Flores stood a few paces away, the flames illuminating her delighted face. Her dark hair blew in the wind. Beside her, Jacobo grinned at the flames he'd created. He could also use his Ruined magic to make rain and extinguish the flames, but that wasn't how this game was played.

Behind her, about a hundred Ruined huddled together. They were all the Ruined left in the entire world. They'd had more just a few weeks ago, in Ruina, when they thought they could return to their home and live in peace. But Olivia would never find peace.

Aren stood next to Em, both of them a safe distance from the fire. He nudged her arm and nodded at something ahead. She followed his gaze.

The people of Westhaven were fleeing. Some carried bags and rode horses, but most were on foot, running away without a single belonging. Hundreds of them streamed down the street, all headed east. East was Royal City, and the castle. East was Cas—King Casimir.

It was not the first time Em and Olivia had taken over a town and driven the human inhabitants away. But it was the first time they'd done it in Lera.

Em looked at Olivia again. Her sister saw the humans, but she made no move to stop them. She caught Em's eye and made a face like, *Are you happy now?*

Em nodded like she was. She'd always been good at lying.

"There are people in that house," Aren said, pointing to where a woman's face was pressed to a window, mouth open like she was screaming. Em couldn't hear her at this distance.

"Olivia blocked the doors." And Em was no one's hero.

Em had suggested the Ruined invade Westhaven, the town

west of Royal City. It was far enough from the castle to keep Cas safe, but not so far that Em couldn't reach him if she needed. She'd studied Lera when making her plan to steal Princess Mary's identity and marry Cas, and she knew the surrounding cities well. It took only a day to reach Westhaven on foot from Royal City.

"Come on," Olivia said to Jacobo. "Let's go make sure the rest of the buildings are empty." She strode past Em and Aren.

"No more fires," Em said quietly.

Olivia paused, glancing over her shoulder. "Sorry?"

"No more fires. We need somewhere to sleep."

"Whatever you say, sister."

Jacobo turned so he was walking backward. He grinned at the fire again. "I'll put that one out in a while, before it spreads. But let's not rush."

Because if he rushed, the people inside might survive. He stared at Em like he was challenging her to bring up that point.

"Fine," Em said.

He turned around and walked with Olivia down the dirt road that curved into town. Ahead of them, the windows of homes and buildings were bright against the night sky, candles and lanterns left lit as the inhabitants fled.

The Ruined trickled after Olivia and Jacobo. Mariana bit her lip as she passed Em, obviously looking for a plan or direction. Mariana had once thought Em was inept as well as useless; now she always looked to her for guidance.

Em had nothing.

A scream drifted out of the house. The woman had disappeared from the window, perhaps giving up after realizing Olivia had tied the bigger windows shut, winding pieces of rope through the handles. Em hoped she'd gone to get a chair or something to try to break it.

"Em," Aren said softly.

"Go with the Ruined," she said, and took a step toward the house.

"Do you want help?" he asked.

"No." She wouldn't ask Aren to help with a fire. They'd both been caught in the flames that destroyed the Ruina castle—their home—but only Aren bore the scars, his dark skin covered in them from the waist up to his neck. The scars she'd acquired in the Olso castle fire were far less serious. They only covered her left arm and some of her torso.

Em glanced back at Aren as she walked toward the house. He was ignoring her order to go with the other Ruined. He stood rooted in place, watching her. Perhaps he was curious if she was actually going to save those people.

She was curious herself.

There was a door on the west side of the house, a heavy box in front of it. She pushed the box out of the way and stuck her hand in her coat. She turned her face away as she grasped the door handle with her coat-covered hand and flung it open. She quickly stepped back. Smoke poured out of the open door.

"Hey," she said, her voice barely a whisper. She cleared her throat. A quick scan of the area confirmed only Aren was nearby.

"Hey! Is there anyone in there?" she called again, louder.

A figure appeared in the smoke. It was a woman, a white cloth pressed to her mouth. She coughed as she darted out of the house. A small child trailed behind her, his mouth also covered by a rag.

The woman collapsed into Em, a mess of tears and hysteria. Em stumbled backward and the woman's hands found nothing but air. She hit her knees. She immediately turned and grabbed her son. Tears streaked down his cheeks.

"Are you all right?" she practically screamed to the boy. He coughed and nodded. She clutched him close to her chest and turned back to Em. "Thank you. Thank you . . . so . . . much." Her sobs made it hard to talk.

Em rubbed her thumb across her *O* necklace, her sister's necklace, but quickly dropped it when she realized her sister would not approve of what she was doing.

"You need to leave," she said. "Now."

The woman stood on shaky legs and scooped her son off the ground. Her cheeks were smudged with soot, and she blinked at Em through watery eyes. She was clearly trying to figure out who Em was.

"Emelina Flores," Em said.

The woman sucked in a breath. All of Lera knew who Em was. The girl who had killed the princess of Vallos and impersonated her in order to marry the prince. The girl who had partnered with the kingdom of Olso to launch an attack on Royal City and invade Lera.

"You rode with King Casimir to take back Royal City," the woman said.

Em's eyebrows shot up. She'd done that as well, just two days ago. News traveled fast.

"Go to Royal City," Em said. "Ask for an audience with the king. They'll give it to you if you tell them you have a message about me."

The woman nodded, wiping the tears from her face. She squared her shoulders, as if happy to have been given a task.

"Tell Cas—King Casimir—that we're here."

The woman nodded with more enthusiasm than was necessary. "I'll tell him you saved me."

Em wasn't going to ask for that, and she felt both embarrassed and proud as she imagined the woman relaying that to Cas.

You'll make the right decision.

He'd said those words to her just a day ago, the last time she saw him. He'd been so confident she would choose him, that she wouldn't let her sister destroy everything. She almost wished she could see his face when he discovered he was right.

He would probably be smug. And unsurprised.

"Tell him I will find a way to get a message to him, eventually," Em said.

"I can take it," the woman said eagerly.

"I don't have a plan. Maybe don't tell him that part. Or, do. I don't know."

The woman squinted, some of the confidence slipping from her expression. Em knew the feeling. She'd lied to Olivia—and to Aren, and to everyone—when she said she had a plan of what to do next. In reality, she had had no idea.

"Just tell him he's safe for now. But I need time to figure out the next step."

The woman appeared reassured. "I will."

Em pointed east. "Go."

The woman stepped forward, tears filling her eyes again as she closed her fingers around Em's arm. "Thank you so much. I'll tell everyone you saved me."

The woman turned and ran. A disbelieving laugh escaped Em's lips.

Emelina Flores, the girl who killed the princess, the girl who destroyed Lera, the girl who rode with the king to put it back together.

Emelina Flores, the hero.

No one would believe it.

TWO

"THE RUINED DO not have *horns*." Cas tried to keep the exasperation from his voice, but it crept in anyway.

The man in front of him gave him a deeply suspicious look. "I've seen paintings."

"The artist took some liberties." Cas shifted on his throne. The Great Hall was full of Lera citizens lined up to talk to him. The room was sometimes filled with tables for dining, or featured musicians at the back wall so people could dance. But today the hall was empty, tables cleared out, only a blue rug running up the center of the room that stopped at Cas's feet. His guards stood on either side of him and mingled with the people, checking baskets for weapons.

He'd insisted they take a few days for the people of Lera to bring their questions about the Ruined to him, and the guards were doing their best to keep him safe in the process. Cas thought the number of guards in the room was excessive, but just recently he'd been stabbed, shot by an arrow, and poisoned, so what did he know?

Two hours in, and he was starting to doubt this plan. Most of the people of Lera had never even seen a Ruined, and the rumors had not been kind to them. An alliance with the Ruined felt unrealistic at best.

"Are you sure?" the man asked, still skeptical about the horns. His wrinkled face was scrunched up like he'd have to rethink every idea he'd ever had. Or he thought Cas was insane. The latter was more likely, actually.

"Positive. I have met many Ruined."

The man must have known this—everyone knew Cas had married Emelina Flores, that Olivia had killed his mother, and that he'd spent time with the Ruined in Vallos after being poisoned by his own cousin—but the man still didn't seem convinced.

"Thank you for coming," Cas said. The man opened his mouth to say more, but two guards swooped in to show him to the door. The guards around him were much more stiff and serious than Galo, Cas's best friend and captain of his guard. Galo had asked for a few days off to travel north and check on his family, and Cas had agreed.

"Would you like to take a break?" Violet asked. She stood next to him, greeting people as they came in and introducing herself as the governor of the southern province. Violet put people at ease, with her pretty face and calm smile.

"No. Let's keep going. I want to at least get through everyone in the room."

She nodded and beckoned for the guards to let the next woman come forward. She bowed her head as she approached, her light hair falling over her shoulders as she did it.

"Is it true the Ruined can kill you with just one look?" she asked as she straightened.

"That is true," he said. "Some of them can. But I think it's more important that they chose not to, don't you think?"

And so it continued for an hour, the people asking questions and Cas trying his best to answer them. Some of them were outright hostile, like the woman who yelled that Cas's father and grandfather and great-grandfather would be ashamed that their descendant defended the Ruined. Considering Cas's father was dead as a direct result of his Ruined policies, he couldn't muster up much of a reaction to that.

He spent a lot of time actively trying not to think about his dead mother and father. He'd had time to slow down and really think about what had happened to them since returning to the castle. He was occasionally overwhelmed with grief, then with guilt, for missing people who had murdered so many. It was better to just not think of them at all.

Luckily most of the Lerans who had come to talk to him were kind enough not to bring up the late king and queen. Few were supportive of his ideas about the Ruined, but there were some who were just curious, and it gave Cas hope. The Ruined and

Lerans wouldn't be best friends anytime soon, but perhaps they could be in the same room without killing each other.

"There's one more," Violet said when Cas finally rose from his throne. "But I think you should take this one in private."

The guard led them out of the hall. The Grand Hall was on the second floor of the castle, which hadn't been damaged by the Olso invasion weeks before. The first floor had blackened walls and some rooms that were nearly totally destroyed. But the second floor was still bright and merry, the walls painted red and green and blue and purple—a different shade every time you turned a corner.

Cas's office was also on the second floor, an office that had technically been his father's but was rarely used. The late king had preferred to take meetings in his private library, where there were comfortable chairs and a view of the ocean. Cas liked the small office, tucked away in the west corner of the castle.

A young woman waited in front of the office door with four guards. Her clothes were dark with dirt or soot, but her face was bright like she'd just scrubbed it clean. A little boy stood next to her.

"Your Majesty," the woman said with a bow of her head. "Thank you for seeing me."

"Of course. Please come in." He opened the door to the office and swept inside. A large wooden desk was to his left, shelves of books stretching up the wall behind it. Directly before him was a tall window with four chairs and a small round table in front of it that overlooked the west entrance of the castle. As usual, a jug of water and a pot of tea were on the table, along with some breads and sweets. They were replenished several times a day, though Cas never saw the staff member do it.

He gestured for the woman and the boy to sit. The little boy scurried to the table, eyeing the pastries.

"Please, help yourself," he said. The woman nodded to the little boy. His eyes lit up, and he grabbed a tart and plunked down in one of the chairs.

The woman extended a tin to Cas as he sat. "It's cheese bread. I know it's your favorite."

"Thank you," he said with a smile, even though it would have to be thrown out. He wasn't allowed to eat anything that wasn't prepared under strict supervision of a guard, or was prepared by Cas himself, which always gave the kitchen staff a laugh.

The guard took the tin from Cas's hands. Three guards had followed them into the office, including the one hovering over his shoulder.

"What can I do for you?" Cas asked the woman.

"I've come with a message from Emelina Flores."

Cas's eyebrows shot up. "Violet," he said quietly.

"Please wait outside," Violet said to the guards.

"Your Majesty—" the hovering guard began.

"I will call if I need you," Cas said firmly. The guard obviously wanted to argue, but he quickly shuffled out of the room, taking his two friends with him. Violet looked at him questioningly, and he motioned for her to stay. She closed the door and walked across the room to join them.

Cas turned back to the woman. "Where did you see Emelina Flores?"

"Westhaven. I am—was—a maid in the governor's household. The Ruined have taken over the town."

Cas already knew this. He'd sent soldiers to follow the Ruined and they'd reported back just yesterday about the Ruined's movements.

"Emelina said you're safe for now, but she needs some time to figure out the next step. She'll get another message to you eventually."

A smile twitched at Cas's lips. He'd already assumed as much, but it was nice to hear.

"She saved me," the woman said. She gestured to her son. "Both of us. The Ruined lit the house on fire and trapped us inside, but she saved us."

"I'm not surprised," Cas said. "She's not what people say."

The woman nodded enthusiastically. "She's not. I've been telling people."

"Good. Keep doing that." He paused, cracking a knuckle. "How . . . how was she? Did she look all right?"

"She seemed well. Taller than I expected."

He chuckled. "Yes."

"I don't think the other Ruined knew what she was doing when she saved me. She waited until they left."

He nodded. There was no way Olivia knew Em had rescued this woman. Olivia was probably the one who lit the house on fire. "Do you have a place to stay?"

The woman shook her head, worry crossing her face as she glanced at the little boy still happily eating his tart.

"We have shelters set up." He turned to Violet. "Will you have someone take them to the kitchen for a meal, then to the shelter?"

"Of course, Your Majesty," Violet said.

"Thank you for bringing the message," Cas said to the woman. Violet opened the door to relay instructions to the guards.

The woman bowed to Cas again as she left. The boy trailed after her, his eyes round as he stared at Cas. His mouth was now smeared with cherry.

Violet shut the door. Cas strode across the office to his desk and flopped down in his chair. "How long until my next meeting? And what is my next meeting, by the way? Have they narrowed down candidates for my secretary? You shouldn't have to know all this."

Violet walked to his desk and sat down in one of the chairs placed in front of it. She'd been indispensable in the fortress, and had proved to be an even more powerful ally as they worked to secure Cas's power as king. "Yes, they have a couple of candidates. You'll meet with them soon. And your next meeting is in half an hour with me and the new governors. They've found Jovita."

Cas looked up quickly. "They found her? When?"

"We just received word. A few soldiers are following her, discreetly, like you asked. But she's amassed an army of hunters and former soldiers who betrayed you—a small army, but it's bigger than when she left Lera a few days ago."

"And you think this army . . . is to attack me?"

"You, and the Ruined. Perhaps not in that order. She's headed west, which is worrying us."

"Why?"

"Because there's nothing west, except the jungle. Until you get to Olso."

He took in a sharp breath. "You think she's going to make a deal with August."

"We can't be sure. She could just be planning to hide in the jungle for a while. But our messenger said she's showed no signs of stopping yet."

Anger bubbled in his veins, more intense than he had expected. Jovita had already lost to the Ruined once. She'd sent hundreds of Lera soldiers to Ruina to be slaughtered by them. She'd lost to Cas, too, when the majority of Lerans had aligned behind him. But she refused to accept defeat, even at a point when Lera was in danger of being attacked by Olivia.

"Would they be able to kill her? The soldiers who are following her?" Cas asked. The words popped out of his mouth so suddenly he was almost surprised to hear them.

Violet appeared surprised as well. "I'm sure they could, if you gave that order before she reached the Olso border."

He should have killed her himself, when he had the chance. He'd told Em that he would, then he'd hesitated until it was too late. He would have saved himself a lot of trouble by just getting rid of her.

The thought startled him, and he looked up at Violet to see

her wearing a slightly alarmed expression. His anger must have been apparent.

"We'll discuss it at the meeting," he said, dropping his eyes to his desk.

"Sure." Violet stood. "Is there anything else?"

He kept his gaze on his desk, pretending to examine a list of refugees in Royal City shelters. "Is it possible to find out—for sure—if Jovita was the one who poisoned me at the fortress?"

"We could certainly try. You don't think it was her?"

"I do, but she always denied it. I'd like to know for sure."

"I will see if anyone has information."

"Thank you." Perhaps it would be easier to order Jovita's death if he knew, definitively, that she had tried to kill him. Surely that would help ease the uncomfortable feeling in the pit of his stomach. She deserved to die. He just needed to be certain of it.